The Best
Dr. Thorndyke
Detective Stories

R. AUSTIN FREEMAN

Selected with an Introduction by

E. F. BLEILER

DOVER PUBLICATIONS, INC.
NEW YORK

The Best Dr. Thorndyke Detective Stories, first published by Dover Publications, Inc., in 1973, is a selection of detective stories written by R. Austin Freeman, with a new introduction by E. F. Bleiler written specially for the present edition.
The original source for each story in this collection is indicated in the note on sources, p. 275.

International Standard Book Number: 0-486-20388-3
Library of Congress Catalog Card Number: 72-78377

Manufactured in the United States of America
Dover Publications, Inc.
180 Varick Street
New York N.Y. 10014

Introduction to the Dover Edition

Richard Austin Freeman's career as a writer of detective and mystery fiction is one of the longest in the English language. It ranges from 1902, with a pseudonymous series about a genteel criminal to *The Unconscious Witness*, published in 1942, when he was almost 80 years old. Indicative of his power is the fact that *Mr. Polton Explains*, in some ways his best novel, was written in part in a bomb shelter in 1939, when Freeman was 77 years old.

For the first twenty-five years of his career, at least, he dominated the world of British detective fiction. Doyle's best work already lay in the past, and even after the emergence of a new generation of writers in the late 1920's and 30's, Freeman was always in the forefront of the form. Today, with Chesterton, who is remembered for other reasons, he is one of the very few Edwardian detective story writers who are still read.

R. Austin Freeman* (1862–1943) was born in London, the son of a tailor. After training as a pharmacist, he graduated as a surgeon from Middlesex Hospital Medical College, where he later taught for a time. His speciality was ear, nose and throat. After serving for a short time as house physician, since he did not have the funds to set up in practice, he joined the colonial service, and was sent to the Gold Coast as an assistant surgeon. At this time the Gold Coast (present-day Ghana) was a group of semi-independent kingdoms, still unacculturated, subject to incursions by the European colonial powers who were eager to annex them. The French had been attempting to buy the favor of the native kings, and a British expedition, including Freeman, set out to investigate. It was mostly through Freeman's intelligence and tact that the expedition was not

---

*For full biographical information the reader should consult Norman Donaldson's fine study, *In Search of Dr. Thorndyke,* Bowling Green University Popular Press, Bowling Green, Ohio, 1971.

massacred, and his future seemed assured in the colonial service. He came down with black-water fever however, and was invalided home to England, recovery years in the future. Africa, of course, often enters into his fiction, an Africa that he knew better than any other English author of his day.

On his return to England Freeman found his economic situation precarious, what with a family to support and broken health. For several years he scraped out an existence in medical side paths: as an acting physician in Holloway Prison, as an immigration examiner at the Port of London, and later, in World War I, as an induction physician. Much of these hard days, too, can be found in his work: the sure knowledge of prison life, trial procedures, the personality of the professional criminal, and the sympathy for the unestablished medical man. These days also colored his views about immigrants to Great Britain, particularly the political refugees from the Slavic world, for whom he had little sympathy.

Writing came to Freeman as a desperation move, since he was physically unable to maintain a full practice. He sold occasional pieces in the late 1890's, but his first real success came with the Romney Pringle rogue stories which were published in *Cassell's Magazine* in 1902 and 1903. These were written in collaboration with a friend, Dr. John Pitcairn.

In 1905 Freeman published his first independent novel, *The Golden Pool,* which was based on the lore he had accumulated in Africa. Recounting the adventures of a young Englishman who steals a fetish treasure, it is a colorful, thrilling story, all the more unusual in being ethnographically accurate. The white man's factory, the bush, the trade trails, village life, tribal wars, various ethnic groups are all described with vividness. Today, one can fault the novel for specious morality, but it remains a remarkable book. Before the rise of the modern African states it used to be required reading for members of the British colonial services in Africa.

With the publication of *The Red Thumb Mark* in 1907, Freeman found his metier, as a writer of serious detective stories, and from this, the first Dr. Thorndyke novel, until his last published work he remained both the leading practitioner of the so-called scientific detective story and "the philosopher turned detective." A remarkably versatile man, who was equally at home in the workshop or the studio, Freeman took pride in developing and testing (as far as was legally possible) various criminal techniques and the devices that

Dr. Thorndyke used to solve crimes. While Freeman, a very modest man, deprecated the idea that he was years ahead of applied police criminology, he was pleased at having anticipated the professionals in dust analysis, examination of blood, footprint preservation and other techniques. He was equally serious in his study of legal procedures and courtroom conduct, to the extent that his novels have been cited in British legal textbooks on evidence.

Dr. John Evelyn Thorndyke is, of course, R. Austin Freeman's finest creation, and about three-quarters of Freeman's fiction is devoted to him. This includes 11 novels and 42 short stories and nouvelles, two of which are doublets for novels. These are the stories that created Freeman's fame, and these are the stories that are still the most living mystery fiction from their period.

Freeman's other fiction is somewhat miscellaneous. Several books are concerned with mildly humorous, semipicaresque characters, persons who live astride the boundary of the law. Of these *The Exploits of Danby Croker* (1916) and *The Surprising Experiences of Mr. Shuttlebury Cobb* (1927) have a lightness of touch that renders them distinctive, although some readers find their flippancy distasteful. *The Unwilling Adventurer* (1913), a sea adventure set in the eighteenth century, has many good Stevensonian touches. *The Uttermost Farthing* (1914) has an unusual publishing history. It was originally serialized in *Pearson's Magazine* in England, but for years no British publisher would reprint it: it was too gruesome. It was first printed in the United States as a book; here its ghoulish gusto aroused no comment.

Freeman also wrote a fair amount of material other than fiction. This ranges from his excellent account of his African experiences, *Travels and Life in Ashanti and Jaman* (1898), which has some ethnographic importance, to reviews and review-articles on eugenics. *Social Decay and Regeneration* (1921), a large book on social philosophy, created a stir when it appeared with an introduction by Havelock Ellis. Dean Inge reviewed it over ten pages. Reading it today is not always pleasant, however, since many of the ideas embodied in the stories seem less palatable when expounded seriously. In brief, it anticipates H. G. Wells's new samurai. Today it is a period piece, unlike Thorndyke, who survives well.

II

Of the individual stories in this collection "The Case of Oscar Brodski," "A Case of Premeditation," and "The Echo of a Mutiny" share a historical significance. They are members of a subgenre that Freeman invented, the inverted detective story. As Freeman has recounted in his essay "The Art of the Detective Story":

> Some years ago I devised, as an experiment, an inverted detective story in two parts. The first part was a minute and detailed description of a crime, setting forth the antecedents, motives, and all attendant circumstances. The reader had seen the crime committed, knew all about the criminal, and was in possession of all the facts. It would have seemed that there was nothing left to tell, but I calculated that the reader would be so occupied with the crime that he would overlook the evidence. And so it turned out. The second part, which described the investigation of the crime, had to most readers the effect of new matter.

The second part, of course, *did* have new matter: Dr. Thorndyke. Freeman, with his customary modesty, missed the point of his achievement. The reader continues with interest because of Dr. Freeman's art, and as a result of this art "The Case of Oscar Brodski" has always been considered one of the landmarks in the history of the detective story.

"The Moabite Cipher," "The Blue Sequin," "The Mandarin's Pearl" and "The Aluminium Dagger" have been taken from *John Thorndyke's Cases,* which first appeared in 1909. The first collection of short stories about Thorndyke, it shows the remarkable ability that Freeman had for turning colorful facts into rational investigation. Donaldson, in his *In Search of Dr. Thorndyke,* describes the hours of observation and experiment which Freeman and a friend spent in gathering microscopic material and even constructing a workable dagger-gun.

"Thirty-One New Inn" is an accidental discovery, located by chance browsing through a file of early *Adventure* magazines. It is a short version of the well-known novel, *The Mystery of 31 New Inn,* as the Thorndyke enthusiast will recognize. In all probability it is the first story written about Thorndyke, around 1905, which was presumed lost. So far as is known, it was never published in Great Britain, and Freeman himself never made reference to its publication. In a radio address in the 1930's, however, he did refer to it as the story that established the personality and career of Thorndyke and his associates. In the text that has been reprinted here, it will be observed that a reference is made to the novel *The Red Thumb Mark,* which was written later, but published earlier. This is obviously an interpolation made for periodical publication, as can be determined if the text of the nouvelle is compared with that of the full novel.

III

This selection includes much of R. Austin Freeman's best work, but not all of it. A half-dozen novels and another half-dozen short stories could well have been included. But it does include special favorites, and one story that is likely to be unfamiliar to almost everyone.

As for Freeman's work as a whole, Raymond Chandler, whose essay "The Simple Art of Murder" did much toward demolishing the classical detective story, had this to say in a letter to Hamish Hamilton, the British publisher:

> This man Austin Freeman is a wonderful performer. He has no equal in his genre, and he is also a much better writer than you might think, if you were superficially inclined, because in spite of the immense leisure of his writing, he accomplishes an even suspense which is quite unexpected. . . . There is even a gaslight charm about his Victorian love affairs, and those wonderful walks across London. . . .

Most of us agree with Chandler.

E. F. BLEILER

P. E. I., 1971.

Contents

The Case of Oscar Brodski

PART I—THE MECHANISM OF CRIME

A surprising amount of nonsense has been talked about conscience. On the one hand remorse (or the "again-bite," as certain scholars of ultra-Teutonic leanings would prefer to call it); on the other hand "an easy conscience": these have been accepted as the determining factors of happiness or the reverse.

Of course there is an element of truth in the "easy conscience" view, but it begs the whole question. A particularly hardy conscience may be quite easy under the most unfavourable conditions—conditions in which the more feeble conscience might be severely afflicted with the "again-bite." And, then, it seems to be the fact that some fortunate persons have no conscience at all; a negative gift that raises them above the mental vicissitudes of the common herd of humanity.

Now, Silas Hickler was a case in point. No one, looking into his cheerful, round face, beaming with benevolence and wreathed in perpetual smiles, would have imagined him to be a criminal. Least of all, his worthy, high-church housekeeper, who was a witness to his unvarying amiability, who constantly heard him carolling light-heartedly about the house and noted his appreciative zest at meal-times.

Yet it is a fact that Silas earned his modest, though comfortable, income by the gentle art of burglary. A precarious trade and risky withal, yet not so very hazardous if pursued with judgement and moderation. And Silas was eminently a man of judgement. He worked invariably alone. He kept his own counsel. No confederate had he to turn King's Evidence at a pinch; no one he knew would bounce off in a fit of temper to Scotland Yard. Nor was he greedy and thriftless, as most criminals are. His "scoops" were few and far between, carefully planned, secretly executed, and the proceeds judiciously invested in "weekly property."

In early life Silas had been connected with the diamond industry, and he still did a little rather irregular dealing. In the trade he was suspected of transactions with I.D.B.'s, and one or two indiscreet dealers had gone so far as to whisper the ominous word " fence." But Silas smiled a benevolent smile and went his way. He knew what he knew, and his clients in Amsterdam were not inquisitive.

Such was Silas Hickler. As he strolled round his garden in the dusk of an October evening, he seemed the very type of modest, middle-class prosperity. He was dressed in the travelling suit that he wore on his little continental trips; his bag was packed and stood in readiness on the sitting-room sofa. A parcel of diamonds (purchased honestly, though without impertinent questions, at Southampton) was in the inside pocket of his waistcoat, and another more valuable parcel was stowed in a cavity in the heel of his right boot. In an hour and a half it would be time for him to set out to catch the boat train at the junction; meanwhile there was nothing to do but to stroll round the fading garden and consider how he should invest the proceeds of the impending deal. His housekeeper had gone over to Welham for the week's shopping, and would probably not be back until eleven o'clock. He was alone in the premises and just a trifle dull.

He was about to turn into the house when his ear caught the sound of footsteps on the unmade road that passed the end of the garden. He paused and listened. There was no other dwelling near, and the road led nowhere, fading away into the waste land beyond the house. Could this be a visitor? It seemed unlikely, for visitors were few at Silas Hickler's house. Meanwhile the footsteps continued to approach, ringing out with increasing loudness on the hard, stony path.

Silas strolled down to the gate, and, leaning on it, looked out with some curiosity. Presently a glow of light showed him the face of a man, apparently lighting his pipe; then a dim figure detached itself from the enveloping gloom, advanced towards him and halted opposite the garden. The stranger removed a cigarette from his mouth and, blowing out a cloud of smoke, asked—

"Can you tell me if this road will take me to Badsham Junction?"

"No," replied Hickler, "but there is a footpath farther on that leads to the station."

"Footpath!" growled the stranger. "I've had enough of footpaths. I came down from town to Catley intending to walk across to the junction. I started along the road, and then some fool directed me to a short cut, with the result that I have been blundering about in the dark for the last half-hour. My sight isn't very good, you know," he added.

"What train do you want to catch?" asked Hickler.

"Seven fifty-eight," was the reply.

"I am going to catch that train myself," said Silas, "but I shan't be starting for another hour. The station is only three-quarters of a mile from here. If you like to come in and take a rest, we can walk down together and then you'll be sure of not missing your way."

"It's very good of you," said the stranger, peering, with spectacled eyes, at the dark house, "but—I think——"

"Might as well wait here as at the station," said Silas in his genial way, holding the gate open, and the stranger, after a momentary hesitation, entered and, flinging away his cigarette, followed him to the door of the cottage.

The sitting-room was in darkness, save for the dull glow of the expiring fire, but, entering before his guest, Silas applied a match to the lamp that hung from the ceiling. As the flame leaped up, flooding the little interior with light, the two men regarded one another with mutual curiosity.

"Brodski, by Jingo!" was Hickler's silent commentary, as he looked at his guest. "Doesn't know me, evidently—wouldn't, of course, after all these years and with his bad eyesight. Take a seat, sir," he added aloud. "Will you join me in a little refreshment to while away the time?"

Brodski murmured an indistinct acceptance, and, as his host turned to open a cupboard, he deposited his hat (a hard, grey felt) on a chair in a corner, placed his bag on the edge of the table, resting his umbrella against it, and sat down in a small arm-chair.

"Have a biscuit?" said Hickler, as he placed a whisky-bottle on the table together with a couple of his best star-pattern tumblers and a siphon.

"Thanks, I think I will," said Brodski. "The railway journey and all this confounded tramping about, you know——"

"Yes," agreed Silas. "Doesn't do to start with an empty stomach. Hope you don't mind oat-cakes; I see they're the only biscuits I have."

Brodski hastened to assure him that oat-cakes were his special and peculiar fancy; and in confirmation, having mixed himself a stiff jorum, he fell to upon the biscuits with evident gusto.

Brodski was a deliberate feeder, and at present appeared to be somewhat sharp set. His measured munching being unfavourable to conversation, most of the talking fell to Silas; and, for once, that genial transgressor found the task embarrassing. The natural thing would have been to discuss his guest's destination and perhaps the object of his journey; but this was precisely what Hickler avoided doing. For he knew both, and instinct told him to keep his knowledge to himself.

Brodski was a diamond merchant of considerable reputation, and in a large way of business. He bought stones principally in the rough, and of these he was a most excellent judge. His fancy was for stones of somewhat unusual size and value, and it was well known to be his custom, when he had accumulated a sufficient stock, to carry them himself to Amsterdam and supervise the cutting of the rough stones. Of this Hickler was aware, and he had no doubt that Brodski was now starting on one of his periodical excursions; that somewhere in the recesses of his rather shabby clothing was concealed a paper packet possibly worth several thousand pounds.

Brodski sat by the table munching monotonously and talking little. Hickler sat opposite him, talking nervously and rather wildly at times, and watching his guest with a growing fascination. Precious stones, and especially diamonds, were Hickler's specialty. "Hard stuff"—silver plate—he avoided entirely; gold, excepting in the form of specie, he seldom touched; but stones, of which he could carry off a whole consignment in the heel of his boot and dispose of with absolute safety, formed the staple of his industry. And here was a man sitting opposite him with a parcel in his pocket containing the equivalent of a dozen of his most successful "scoops"; stones worth perhaps—— Here he pulled himself up short and began to talk rapidly, though without much coherence. For, even as he talked, other words, formed subconsciously, seemed to insinuate themselves into the interstices of the sentences, and to carry on a parallel train of thought.

"Gets chilly in the evenings now, doesn't it?" said Hickler.

"It does indeed," Brodski agreed, and then resumed his slow munching, breathing audibly through his nose.

"Five thousand at least," the subconscious train of thought resumed; "probably six or seven, perhaps ten." Silas fidgeted in his chair and endeavoured to concentrate his ideas on some topic of interest. He was growing disagreeably conscious of a new and unfamiliar state of mind.

"Do you take any interest in gardening?" he asked. Next to diamonds and weekly "property," his besetting weakness was fuchsias.

Brodski chuckled sourly. "Hatton Garden is the nearest approach——" He broke off suddenly, and then added, "I am a Londoner, you know."

The abrupt break in the sentence was not unnoticed by Silas, nor had he any difficulty in interpreting it. A man who carries untold wealth upon his person must needs be wary in his speech.

"Yes," he answered absently, "it's hardly a Londoner's hobby." And then, half consciously, he began a rapid calculation. Put it at five thousand pounds. What would that represent in weekly property? His last set of houses had cost two hundred and fifty pounds apiece, and he had let them at ten shillings and sixpence a week. At that rate, five thousand pounds represented twenty houses at ten and sixpence a week—say ten pounds a week—one pound eight shillings a day—five hundred and twenty pounds a year—for life. It was a competency. Added to what he already had, it was wealth. With that income he could fling the tools of his trade into the river and live out the remainder of his life in comfort and security.

He glanced furtively at his guest across the table, and then looked away quickly as he felt stirring within him an impulse the nature of which he could not mistake. This must be put an end to. Crimes against the person he had always looked upon as sheer insanity. There was, it is true, that little affair of the Weybridge policeman, but that was unforeseen and unavoidable, and it was the constable's doing after all. And there was the old housekeeper at Epsom, too, but, of course, if the old idiot would shriek in that insane fashion—well, it was an accident, very regrettable, to be sure, and no one could be more sorry for the mishap than himself. But deliberate homicide!—robbery from the person! It was the act of a stark lunatic.

Of course, if he had happened to be that sort of person, here was the opportunity of a lifetime. The immense booty, the empty house, the solitary neighbourhood, away from the main road and from other habitations; the time, the darkness—but, of course, there was the body to be thought of; that was always the difficulty. What to do with the body—— Here he caught the shriek of the up express, rounding the curve in the line that ran past the waste land at the back of the house. The sound started a new train of thought, and, as he followed it out, his eyes fixed themselves on the unconscious and taciturn Brodski, as he sat thoughtfully sipping his whisky. At length, averting his gaze with an effort, he rose suddenly from his chair and turned to look at the clock on the mantelpiece, spreading out his hands before the dying fire. A tumult of strange sensations warned him to leave the house. He shivered slightly, though he was rather hot than chilly, and, turning his head, looked at the door.

"Seems to be a confounded draught," he said, with another slight shiver; "did I shut the door properly, I wonder?" He strode across the room and, opening the door wide, looked out into the dark garden. A desire, sudden and urgent, had come over him to get out into the open air, to be on the road and have done with this madness that was knocking at the door of his brain.

"I wonder if it is worth while to start yet," he said, with a yearning glance at the murky, starless sky.

Brodski roused himself and looked round. "Is your clock right?" he asked.

Silas reluctantly admitted that it was.

"How long will it take us to walk to the station?" inquired Brodski.

"Oh, about twenty-five minutes to half-an-hour," repied Silas, unconsciously exaggerating the distance.

"Well," said Brodski, "we've got more than an hour yet, and it's more comfortable here than hanging about the station. I don't see the use of starting before we need."

"No; of course not," Silas agreed. A wave of strange emotion, half-regretful, half-triumphant, surged through his brain. For some moments he remained standing on the threshold, looking out dreamily into the night. Then he softly closed the door; and, seemingly without the exercise of his volition, the key turned noiselessly in the lock.

He returned to his chair and tried to open a conversation with the taciturn Brodski, but the words came faltering and disjointed. He felt his face growing hot, his brain full and intense, and there was a faint, high-pitched singing in his ears. He was conscious of watching his guest with a new and fearful interest, and, by sheer force of will, turned away his eyes; only to find them a moment later involuntarily returning to fix the unconscious man with yet more horrible intensity. And ever through his mind walked, like a dreadful procession, the thoughts of what that other man—the man of blood and violence—would do in these circumstances. Detail by detail the hideous synthesis fitted together the parts of the imagined crime, and arranged them in due sequence until they formed a succession of events, rational, connected and coherent.

He rose uneasily from his chair, with his eyes still riveted upon his guest. He could not sit any longer opposite that man with his hidden store of precious gems. The impulse that he recognized with fear and wonder was growing more ungovernable from moment to moment. If he stayed it would presently overpower him, and then—— He shrank with horror from the dreadful thought, but his fingers itched to handle the diamonds. For Silas was, after all, a criminal by nature and habit. He was a beast of prey. His livelihood had never been earned; it had been taken by stealth or, if necessary, by force. His instincts were predacious, and the proximity of unguarded valuables suggested to him, as a logical consequence, their abstraction or seizure. His unwillingness to let these diamonds go away beyond his reach was fast becoming overwhelming.

But he would make one more effort to escape. He would keep out of Brodski's actual presence until the moment for starting came.

"If you'll excuse me," he said, "I will go and put on a thicker pair of boots. After all this dry weather we may get a change, and damp feet are very uncomfortable when you are travelling."

"Yes; dangerous too," agreed Brodski.

Silas walked through into the adjoining kitchen, where, by the light of the little lamp that was burning there, he had seen his stout, country boots placed, cleaned and in readiness, and sat down upon a chair to make the change. He did not, of course, intend to wear the country boots, for the diamonds were concealed in those he had on. But he would make the change and then alter his mind; it would all help to pass the time. He took a deep breath. It was a relief, at any rate, to be out of that room. Perhaps, if he stayed away, the temptation would pass. Brodski would go on his way—he wished that he was going alone—and the danger would be over—at least—and the opportunity would have gone—the diamonds——

He looked up as he slowly unlaced his boot. From where he sat he could see Brodski sitting by the table with his back towards the kitchen door. He had finished eating now, and was composedly rolling a cigarette. Silas breathed heavily, and, slipping off his boot, sat for a while motionless, gazing steadily at the other man's back. Then he unlaced the other boot, still staring abstractedly at his unconscious guest, drew it off, and laid it very quietly on the floor.

Brodski calmly finished rolling his cigarette, licked the paper, put away his pouch, and, having dusted the crumbs of tobacco from his knees, began to search his pockets for a match. Suddenly, yielding to an uncontrollable impulse, Silas stood up and began stealthily to creep along the passage to the sitting-room. Not a sound came from his stockinged feet. Silently as a cat he stole forward, breathing softly with parted lips, until he stood at the threshold of the room. His face flushed duskily, his eyes, wide and staring, glittered in the lamplight, and the racing blood hummed in his ears.

Brodski struck a match—Silas noted that it was a wooden vesta—lighted his cigarette, blew out the match and flung it into the fender. Then he replaced the box in his pocket and commenced to smoke.

Slowly and without a sound Silas crept forward into the room, step by step, with catlike stealthiness, until he stood close behind Brodski's chair—so close that he had to turn his head that his breath might not stir the hair upon the other man's head. So, for half-a-minute, he stood motionless, like a symbolical statue of Murder, glaring down with horrible, glittering eyes upon the unconscious diamond merchant, while his quick breath passed without a sound through his open mouth and his fingers writhed slowly like tentacles of a giant hydra. And then, as noiselessly as ever, he backed away to the door, turned quickly and walked back into the kitchen.

He drew a deep breath. It had been a near thing. Brodski's life had hung upon a thread. For it had been so easy. Indeed, if he had happened, as he stood behind the man's chair, to have a weapon—a hammer, for instance, or even a stone——

He glanced round the kitchen and his eye lighted on a bar that had been left by the workmen who had put up the new greenhouse. It was an odd piece cut off from a square, wrought-iron stanchion, and was about a foot long and perhaps three-quarters of an inch thick. Now, if he had had that in his hand a minute ago——

He picked the bar up, balanced it in his hand and swung it round his head. A formidable weapon this: silent, too. And it fitted the plan that had passed through his brain. Bah! He had better put the thing down.

But he did not. He stepped over to the door and looked again at Brodski, sitting, as before, meditatively smoking, with his back towards the kitchen.

Suddenly a change came over Silas. His face flushed, the veins of his neck stood out and a sullen scowl settled on his face. He drew out his watch, glanced at it earnestly and replaced it. Then he strode swiftly but silently along the passage into the sitting-room.

A pace away from his victim's chair he halted and took deliberate aim. The bar swung aloft, but not without some faint rustle of movement, for Brodski looked round quickly even as the iron whistled through the air. The movement disturbed the murderer's aim, and the bar glanced off his victim's head, making only a trifling wound. Brodski sprang up with a tremulous, bleating cry, and clutched his assailant's arms with the tenacity of mortal terror.

Then began a terrible struggle, as the two men, locked in a deadly embrace, swayed to and fro and trampled backwards and forwards. The chair was overturned, an empty glass swept from the table and, with Brodski's spectacles, crushed beneath stamping feet. And thrice that dreadful, pitiful, bleating cry rang out into the night, filling Silas, despite his murderous frenzy, with terror lest some chance wayfarer should hear it. Gathering his great strength for a final effort, he forced his victim backwards onto the table and, snatching up a corner of the tablecloth, thrust it into his face and crammed it into his mouth as it opened to utter another shriek. And thus they remained for a full two minutes, almost motionless, like some dreadful group of tragic allegory. Then, when the last faint twitchings had died away, Silas relaxed his grasp and let the limp body slip softly onto the floor.

It was over. For good or for evil, the thing was done. Silas stood up, breathing heavily, and, as he wiped the sweat from his face, he looked at the clock. The hands stood at one minute to seven. The whole thing had taken a little over three minutes. He had nearly an hour in which to finish his task. The goods train that entered into his scheme came by at twenty minutes past, and it was only three hundred yards to the line. Still, he must not waste time. He was now quite composed, and only disturbed by the thought that Brodski's cries might have been heard. If no one had heard them it was all plain sailing.

He stooped, and, gently disengaging the table-cloth from the dead man's teeth, began a careful search of his pockets. He was not long finding what he sought, and, as he pinched the paper packet and felt the little hard bodies grating on one another inside, his faint regrets for what had happened were swallowed up in self-congratulations.

He now set about his task with business-like briskness and an attentive eye on the clock. A few large drops of blood had fallen on the table-cloth, and there was a small bloody smear on the carpet by the dead man's head. Silas fetched from the kitchen some water, a nail-brush and a dry cloth, and, having washed out the stains from the table-cover—not forgetting the deal table-top underneath—and cleaned away the smear from the carpet and rubbed the damp places dry, he slipped a sheet of paper under the head of the corpse to prevent further contamination. Then he set the table-cloth straight, stood the chair upright, laid the broken spectacles on the table and picked up the cigarette, which had been trodden flat in the struggle, and flung it under the grate. Then there was the broken glass, which he swept up into a dust-pan. Part of it was the remains of the shattered tumbler, and the rest the fragments of the broken spectacles. He turned it out onto a sheet of paper and looked it over carefully, picking out the larger recognizable pieces of the spectacle-glasses and putting them aside on a separate slip of paper, together with a sprinkling of the minute fragments. The remainder he shot back into the dust-pan and, having hurriedly put on his boots, carried it out to the rubbish-heap at the back of the house.

It was now time to start. Hastily cutting off a length of string from his string-box—for Silas was an orderly man and despised the oddments of string with which many people make shift—he tied it to the dead man's bag and umbrella and slung them from his shoulder. Then he folded up the paper of broken glass, and, slipping it and the spectacles into his pocket, picked up the body and threw it over his shoulder. Brodski was a small, spare man, weighing not more than nine stone; not a very formidable burden for a big, athletic man like Silas.

The night was intensely dark, and, when Silas looked out of the back gate over the waste land that stretched from his house to the railway, he could hardly see twenty yards ahead. After listening cautiously and hearing no sound, he went out, shut the gate softly behind him and set forth at a good pace, though carefully, over the broken ground. His progress was not as silent as he could have wished, for, though the scanty turf that covered the gravelly land was thick enough to deaden his footfalls, the swinging bag and umbrella made an irritating noise; indeed, his movements were more hampered by them than by the weightier burden.

The distance to the line was about three hundred yards. Ordinarily he would have walked it in from three to four minutes, but now, going cautiously with his burden and stopping now and again to listen, it took him just six minutes to reach the three-bar fence that separated the waste land from the railway. Arrived here he halted for a moment and once more listened attentively, peering into the darkness on all sides. Not a living creature was to be seen or heard in this desolate spot, but far away, the shriek of an engine's whistle warned him to hasten.

Lifting the corpse easily over the fence, he carried it a few yards farther to a point where the line curved sharply. Here he laid it face downwards, with the neck over the near rail. Drawing out his pocket-knife, he cut through the knot that fastened the umbrella to the string and also secured the bag; and when he had flung the bag and umbrella on the track beside the body, he carefully pocketed the string, excepting the little loop that had fallen to the ground when the knot was cut.

The quick snort and clanking rumble of an approaching goods train began now to be clearly audible. Rapidly, Silas drew from his pockets the battered spectacles and the packet of broken glass. The former he threw down by the dead man's head, and then, emptying the packet into his hand, sprinkled the fragments of glass around the spectacles.

He was none too soon. Already the quick, laboured puffing of the engine sounded close at hand. His impulse was to stay and watch; to witness the final catastrophe that should convert the murder into an accident or suicide. But it was hardly safe: it would be better that he should not be near lest he should not be able to get away without being seen. Hastily he climbed back over the fence and strode away across the rough fields, while the train came snorting and clattering towards the curve.

He had nearly reached his back gate when a sound from the line brought him to a sudden halt; it was a prolonged whistle accompanied by the groan of brakes and the loud clank of colliding trucks. The snorting of the engine had ceased and was replaced by the penetrating hiss of escaping steam.

The train had stopped!

For one brief moment Silas stood with bated breath and mouth agape like one petrified; then he strode forward quickly to the gate, and, letting himself in, silently slid the bolt. He was undeniably alarmed. What could have happened on the line? It was practically certain that the body had been seen; but what was happening now? and would they come to the house? He entered the kitchen, and having paused again to listen—for somebody might come and knock at the door at any moment—he walked through the sitting-room and looked round. All seemed in order there. There was the bar, though, lying where he had dropped it in the scuffle. He picked it up and held it under the lamp. There was no blood on it; only one or two hairs. Somewhat absently he wiped it with the table-cover, and then, running out through the kitchen into the back garden dropped it over the wall into a bed of nettles. Not that there was anything incriminating in the bar, but, since he had used it as a weapon, it had somehow acquired a sinister aspect to his eye.

He now felt that it would be well to start for the station at once. It was not time yet, for it was barely twenty-five minutes past seven; but he did not wish to be found in the house if any one should come. His soft hat was on the sofa with his bag, to which his umbrella was strapped. He put on the hat, caught up the bag and stepped over to the door; then he came back to turn down the lamp. And it was at this moment, when he stood with his hand raised to the burner, that his eye, travelling by chance into the dim corner of the room, lighted on Brodski's grey felt hat, reposing on the chair where the dead man had placed it when he entered the house.

Silas stood for a few moments as if petrified, with the chilly sweat of mortal fear standing in beads upon his forehead. Another instant and he would have turned the lamp down and gone on his way; and then—— He strode over to the chair, snatched up the hat and looked inside it. Yes, there was the name, "Oscar Brodski," written plainly on the lining. If he had gone away, leaving it to be discovered, he would have been lost; indeed, even now, if a search-party should come to the house, it was enough to send him to the gallows.

His limbs shook with horror at the thought, but in spite of his panic he did not lose his self-possession. Darting through into the kitchen, he grabbed up a handful of the dry brush-wood that was kept for lighting fires and carried it to the sitting-room grate where he thrust it on the extinct, but still hot, embers, and crumpling up the paper that he had placed under Brodski's head—on which paper he now noticed, for the first time, a minute bloody smear—he poked it in under the wood, and, striking a wax match, set light to it. As the wood flared up, he hacked at the hat with his pocket knife and threw the ragged strips into the blaze.

And all the while his heart was thumping and his hands a-tremble with the dread of discovery. The fragments of felt were far from inflammable, tending rather to fuse into cindery masses that smoked and smouldered than to burn away into actual ash. Moreover, to his dismay, they emitted a powerful resinous stench mixed with the odour of burning hair, so that he had to open the kitchen window (since he dared not unlock the front door) to disperse the reek. And still, as he fed the fire with small cut fragments, he strained his ears to catch, above the crackling of the wood, the sound of the dreaded footsteps, the knock on the door that should be as the summons of Fate.

The time, too, was speeding on. Twenty-one minutes to eight! In a few minutes more he must set out or he would miss the train. He dropped the dismembered hat-brim on the blazing wood and ran upstairs to open a window, since he must close that in the kitchen before he left. When he came back, the brim had already curled up into a black, clinkery mass that bubbled and hissed as the fat, pungent smoke rose from it sluggishly to the chimney.

Nineteen minutes to eight! It was time to start. He took up the poker and carefully beat the cinders into small particles, stirring them into the glowing embers of the wood and coal. There was nothing unusual in the appearance of the grate. It was his constant custom to burn letters and other discarded articles in the sitting-room fire: his housekeeper would notice nothing out of the common. Indeed, the cinders would probably be reduced to ashes before she returned. He had been careful to notice that there were no metallic fittings of any kind in the hat, which might have escaped burning.

Once more he picked up his bag, took a last look round, turned down the lamp and, unlocking the door, held it open for a few moments. Then he went out, locked the door, pocketed the key (of which his housekeeper had a duplicate) and set off at a brisk pace for the station.

He arrived in good time after all, and, having taken his ticket, strolled through onto the platform. The train was not yet signalled, but there seemed to be an unusual stir in the place. The passengers were collected in a group at one end of the platform, and were all looking in one direction down the line; and, even as he walked towards them, with a certain tremulous, nauseating curiosity, two men emerged from the darkness and ascended the slope to the platform, carrying a stretcher covered with a tarpaulin. The passengers parted to let the bearers pass, turning fascinated eyes upon the shape that showed faintly through the rough pall; and, when the stretcher had been borne into the lamp-room, they fixed their attention upon a porter who followed carrying a hand-bag and an umbrella.

Suddenly one of the passengers started forward with an exclamation. "Is that his umbrella?" he demanded.

"Yes, sir," answered the porter, stopping and holding it out for the speaker's inspection.

"My God!" ejaculated the passenger; then, turning sharply to a tall man who stood close by, he said excitedly: "That's Brodski's umbrella. I could swear to it. You remember Brodski?" The tall man nodded, and the passenger, turning once more to the porter, said: "I identify that umbrella. It belongs to a gentleman named Brodski. If you look in his hat you will see his name written in it. He always writes his name in his hat."

"We haven't found his hat yet," said the porter; "but here is the station-master coming up the line." He awaited the arrival of his superior and then announced: "This gentleman, sir, has identified the umbrella."

"Oh," said the station-master, "you recognize the umbrella, sir, do you? Then perhaps you would step into the lamp-room and see if you can identify the body."

The passenger recoiled with a look of alarm.

"Is it—is he—very much injured?" he asked tremulously.

"Well, yes," was the reply. "You see, the engine and six of the trucks went over him before they could stop the train. Took his head clean off, in fact."

"Shocking! shocking!" gasped the passenger. "I think, if you don't mind—I'd—I'd rather not. You don't think it's necessary, doctor, do you?"

"Yes, I do," replied the tall man. "Early identification may be of the first importance."

"Then I suppose I must," said the passenger.

Very reluctantly he allowed himself to be conducted by the station-master to the lamp-room, as the clang of the bell announced the approaching train. Silas Hickler followed and took his stand with the expectant crowd outside the closed door. In a few moments the passenger burst out, pale and awe-stricken, and rushed up to his tall friend. "It is!" he exclaimed breathlessly. "It's Brodski! Poor old

Brodski! Horrible! horrible! He was to have met me here and come on with me to Amsterdam."

"Had he any—merchandise about him?" the tall man asked; and Silas strained his ears to catch the reply.

"He had some stones, no doubt, but I don't know what. His clerk will know, of course. By the way, doctor, could you watch the case for me? Just to be sure it was really an accident or—you know what. We were old friends, you know, fellow townsmen, too; we were both born in Warsaw. I'd like you to give an eye to the case."

"Very well," said the other. "I will satisfy myself that—there is nothing more than appears, and let you have a report. Will that do?"

"Thank you. It's excessively good of you, doctor. Ah! here comes the train. I hope it won't inconvenience you to stay and see to this matter."

"Not in the least," replied the doctor. "We are not due at Warmington until to-morrow afternoon, and I expect we can find out all that is necessary to know and still keep our appointment."

Silas looked long and curiously at the tall, imposing man who was, as it were, taking his seat at the chessboard, to play against him for his life. A formidable antagonist he looked, with his keen, thoughtful face, so resolute and calm. As Silas stepped into his carriage he looked back at his opponent, and thinking with deep discomfort of Brodski's hat, he hoped that he had made no other oversight.

PART II—THE MECHANISM OF DETECTION

(Related by Christopher Jervis, M.D.)

The singular circumstances that attended the death of Mr. Oscar Brodski, the well-known diamond merchant of Hatton Garden, illustrated very forcibly the importance of one or two points in medico-legal practice which Thorndyke was accustomed to insist were not sufficiently appreciated. What those points were, I shall leave my friend and teacher to state at the proper place; and meanwhile, as the case is in the highest degree instructive, I shall record the incidents in the order of their occurrence.

The dusk of an October evening was closing in as Thorndyke and I, the sole occupants of a smoking compartment, found ourselves approaching the little station of Ludham; and, as the train slowed down, we peered out at the knot of country people who were waiting on the platform. Suddenly Thorndyke exclaimed in a tone of surprise: "Why, that is surely Boscovitch!" and almost at the same moment a brisk, excitable little man darted at the door of our compartment, and literally tumbled in.

"I hope I don't intrude on this learned conclave," he said, shaking hands genially, and banging his Gladstone with impulsive violence into the rack; "but I saw your faces at the window, and naturally jumped at the chance of such pleasant companionship."

"You are very flattering," said Thorndyke; "so flattering that you leave us nothing to say. But what in the name of fortune are you doing at—what's the name of the place—Ludham?"

"My brother has a little place a mile or so from here, and I have been spending a couple of days with him," Mr. Boscovitch explained. "I shall change at Badsham Junction and catch the boat train for Amsterdam. But whither are you two bound? I see you have your mysterious little green box up on the hat-rack, so I infer that you are on some romantic quest, eh? Going to unravel some dark and intricate crime?"

"No," replied Thorndyke. "We are bound for Warmington on a quite prosaic errand. I am instructed to watch the proceedings at an inquest there to-morrow on behalf of the Griffin Life Insurance Office, and we are travelling down to-night as it is rather a cross-country journey."

"But why the box of magic?" asked Boscovitch, glancing up at the hat-rack.

"I never go away from home without it," answered Thorndyke. "One never knows what may turn up; the trouble of carrying it is small when set off against the comfort of having one's appliances at hand in case of an emergency."

Boscovitch continued to stare up at the little square case covered with Willesden canvas. Presently he remarked: "I often used to wonder what you had in it when you were down at Chelmsford in connection with that bank murder—what an amazing case that was, by the way, and didn't your methods of research astonish the police!" As he still looked up wistfully at the case, Thorndyke good-naturedly lifted it down and unlocked it. As a matter of fact he was rather proud of his "portable laboratory," and certainly it was a triumph of condensation, for, small as it was—only a foot square by four inches deep—it contained a fairly complete outfit for a preliminary investigation.

"Wonderful!" exclaimed Boscovitch, when the case lay open
before him, displaying its rows of little re-agent bottles, tiny test-
tubes, diminutive spirit-lamp, dwarf microscope and assorted
instruments on the same Lilliputian scale; "it's like a doll's house—
everything looks as if it was seen through the wrong end of a telescope. But are these tiny things really efficient? That microscope
now——"

"Perfectly efficient at low and moderate magnifications," said
Thorndyke. "It looks like a toy, but it isn't one; the lenses are the
best that can be had. Of course, a full-sized instrument would be
infinitely more convenient—but I shouldn't have it with me, and
should have to make shift with a pocket-lens. And so with the rest of
the under-sized appliances; they are the alternative to no appliances."

Boscovitch pored over the case and its contents, fingering the
instruments delicately and asking questions innumerable about
their uses; indeed, his curiosity was but half appeased when, half-
an-hour later, the train began to slow down.

"By Jove!" he exclaimed, starting up and seizing his bag, "here
we are at the junction already. You change here too, don't you?"

"Yes," replied Thorndyke. "We take the branch line on to
Warmington."

As we stepped out onto the platform, we became aware that something unusual was happening or had happened. All the passengers
and most of the porters and supernumeraries were gathered at one
end of the station, and all were looking intently into the darkness
down the line.

"Anything wrong?" asked Mr. Boscovitch, addressing the station-
inspector.

"Yes, sir," the official replied; "a man has been run over by the
goods train about a mile down the line. The station-master has gone
down with a stretcher to bring him in, and I expect that is his lantern
that you see coming this way."

As we stood watching the dancing light grow momentarily brighter,
flashing fitful reflections from the burnished rails, a man came out
of the booking office and joined the group of onlookers. He attracted
my attention, as I afterwards remembered, for two reasons: in the
first place his round, jolly face was excessively pale and bore a
strained and wild expression, and, in the second, though he stared
into the darkness with eager curiosity he asked no questions.

The swinging lantern continued to approach, and then suddenly two men came into sight bearing a stretcher covered with a tarpaulin, through which the shape of a human figure was dimly discernible. They ascended the slope to the platform, and proceeded with their burden to the lamp-room, when the inquisitive gaze of the passengers was transferred to a porter who followed carrying a handbag and umbrella and to the station-master who brought up the rear with his lantern.

As the porter passed, Mr. Boscovitch started forward with sudden excitement.

"Is that his umbrella?" he asked.

"Yes, sir," answered the porter, stopping and holding it out for the speaker's inspection.

"My God!" ejaculated Boscovitch; then, turning sharply to Thorndyke, he exclaimed: "That's Brodski's umbrella. I could swear to it. You remember Brodski?"

Thorndyke nodded, and Boscovitch, turning once more to the porter, said: "I identify that umbrella. It belongs to a gentleman named Brodski. If you look in his hat, you will see his name written in it. He always writes his name in his hat."

"We haven't found his hat yet," said the porter; "but here is the station-master." He turned to his superior and announced: "This gentleman, sir, has identified the umbrella."

"Oh," said the station-master, "you recognize the umbrella, sir, do you? Then perhaps you would step into the lamp-room and see if you can identify the body."

Mr. Boscovitch recoiled with a look of alarm. "Is it—is he—very much injured?" he asked nervously.

"Well, yes," was the reply. "You see, the engine and six of the trucks went over him before they could stop the train. Took his head clean off, in fact."

"Shocking! shocking!" gasped Boscovitch. "I think—if you don't mind—I'd—I'd rather not. You don't think it necessary, doctor, do you?"

"Yes, I do," replied Thorndyke. "Early identification may be of the first importance."

"Then I suppose I must," said Boscovitch; and, with extreme reluctance, he followed the station-master to the lamp-room, as the loud ringing of the bell announced the approach of the boat train. His inspection must have been of the briefest, for, in a few moments, he burst out, pale and awe-stricken, and rushed up to Thorndyke.

"It is!" he exclaimed breathlessly. "It's Brodski! Poor old Brodski! Horrible! horrible! He was to have met me here and come on with me to Amsterdam."

"Had he any—merchandise about him?" Thorndyke asked; and as he spoke, the stranger whom I had previously noticed edged up closer as if to catch the reply.

"He had some stones, no doubt," answered Boscovitch, "but I don't know what they were. His clerk will know, of course. By the way, doctor, could you watch the case for me? Just to be sure it was really an accident or—you know what. We were old friends, you know, fellow townsmen, too; we were both born in Warsaw. I'd like you to give an eye to the case."

"Very well," said Thorndyke. "I will satisfy myself that there is nothing more than appears, and let you have a report. Will that do?"

"Thank you," said Boscovitch. "It's excessively good of you, doctor. Ah, here comes the train. I hope it won't inconvenience you to stay and see to the matter."

"Not in the least," replied Thorndyke. "We are not due at Warmington until to-morrow afternoon, and I expect we can find out all that is necessary to know and still keep our appointment."

As Thorndyke spoke, the stranger, who had kept close to us with the evident purpose of hearing what was said, bestowed on him a very curious and attentive look; and it was only when the train had actually come to rest by the platform that he hurried away to find a compartment.

No sooner had the train left the station than Thorndyke sought out the station-master and informed him of the instructions that he had received from Boscovitch. "Of course," he added, in conclusion, "we must not move in the matter until the police arrive. I suppose they have been informed?"

"Yes," replied the station-master; "I sent a message at once to the Chief Constable, and I expect him or an inspector at any moment. In fact, I think I will slip out to the approach and see if he is coming." He evidently wished to have a word in private with the police officer before committing himself to any statement.

As the official departed, Thorndyke and I began to pace the now empty platform, and my friend, as was his wont, when entering on a new inquiry, meditatively reviewed the features of the problem.

"In a case of this kind," he remarked, "we have to decide on one of three possible explanations: accident, suicide or homicide; and our decision will be determined by inferences from three sets of facts: first, the general facts of the case; second, the special data obtained by examination of the body, and, third, the special data obtained by examining the spot on which the body was found. Now the only general facts at present in our possession are that the deceased was a diamond merchant making a journey for a specific purpose and probably having on his person property of small bulk and great value. These facts are somewhat against the hypothesis of suicide and somewhat favourable to that of homicide. Facts relevant to the question of accident would be the existence or otherwise of a level crossing, a road or path leading to the line, an enclosing fence with or without a gate, and any other facts rendering probable or otherwise the accidental presence of the deceased at the spot where the body was found. As we do not possess these facts, it is desirable that we extend our knowledge."

"Why not put a few discreet questions to the porter who brought in the bag and umbrella?" I suggested. "He is at this moment in earnest conversation with the ticket collector and would, no doubt, be glad of a new listener."

"An excellent suggestion, Jervis," answered Thorndyke. "Let us see what he has to tell us." We approached the porter and found him, as I had anticipated, bursting to unburden himself of the tragic story.

"The way the thing happened, sir, was this," he said, in answer to Thorndyke's question: "There's a sharpish bend in the road just at that place, and the goods train was just rounding the curve when the driver suddenly caught sight of something lying across the rails. As the engine turned, the head-light shone on it and then he saw it was a man. He shut off steam at once, blew his whistle, and put the brakes down hard, but, as you know, sir, a goods train takes some stopping; before they could bring her up, the engine and half-a-dozen trucks had gone over the poor beggar."

"Could the driver see how the man was lying?" Thorndyke asked.

"Yes, he could see him quite plain, because the head-lights were full on him. He was lying on his face with his neck over the near rail on the down side. His head was in the four-foot and his body by the side of the track. It looked as if he had laid himself out a-purpose."

"Is there a level crossing thereabouts?" asked Thorndyke.

"No, sir. No crossing, no road, no path, no nothing," said the porter, ruthlessly sacrificing grammar to emphasis. "He must have come across the fields and climbed over the fence to get onto the permanent way. Deliberate suicide is what it looks like."

"How did you learn all this?" Thorndyke inquired.

"Why, the driver, you see, sir, when him and his mate had lifted the body off the track, went on to the next signal-box and sent in his report by telegram. The station-master told me all about it as we walked down the line."

Thorndyke thanked the man for his information, and, as we strolled back towards the lamp-room, discussed the bearing of these new facts.

"Our friend is unquestionably right in one respect," he said; "this was not an accident. The man might, if he were near-sighted, deaf or stupid, have climbed over the fence and got knocked down by the train. But his position, lying across the rails, can only be explained by one of two hypotheses: either it was, as the porter says, deliberate suicide, or else the man was already dead or insensible. We must leave it at that until we have seen the body, that is, if the police will allow us to see it. But here comes the station-master and an officer with him. Let us hear what they have to say."

The two officials had evidently made up their minds to decline any outside assistance. The divisional surgeon would make the necessary examination, and information could be obtained through the usual channels. The production of Thorndyke's card, however, somewhat altered the situation. The police inspector hummed and hawed irresolutely, with the card in his hand, but finally agreed to allow us to view the body, and we entered the lamp-room together, the station-master leading the way to turn up the gas.

The stretcher stood on the floor by one wall, its grim burden still hidden by the tarpaulin, and the hand-bag and umbrella lay on a large box, together with the battered frame of a pair of spectacles from which the glasses had fallen out.

"Were these spectacles found by the body?" Thorndyke inquired.

"Yes," replied the station-master. "They were close to the head and the glass was scattered about on the ballast."

Thorndyke made a note in his pocket-book, and then, as the inspector removed the tarpaulin, he glanced down on the corpse, lying limply on the stretcher and looking grotesquely horrible with its displaced head and distorted limbs. For fully a minute he remained silently stooping over the uncanny object, on which the inspector was now throwing the light of a large lantern; then he stood up and said quietly to me: "I think we can eliminate two out of the three hypotheses."

The inspector looked at him quickly, and was about to ask a question, when his attention was diverted by the travelling-case which Thorndyke had laid on a shelf and now opened to abstract a couple of pairs of dissecting forceps.

"We've no authority to make a *post mortem*, you know," said the inspector.

"No, of course not," said Thorndyke. "I am merely going to look into the mouth." With one pair of forceps he turned back the lip and, having scrutinized its inner surface, closely examined the teeth.

"May I trouble you for your lens, Jervis?" he said; and, as I handed him my doublet ready opened, the inspector brought the lantern close to the dead face and leaned forward eagerly. In his usual systematic fashion, Thorndyke slowly passed the lens along the whole range of sharp, uneven teeth, and then, bringing it back to the centre, examined with more minuteness the upper incisors. At length, very delicately, he picked out with his forceps some minute object from between two of the upper front teeth and held it in the focus of the lens. Anticipating his next move, I took a labelled microscope-slide from the case and handed it to him together with a dissecting needle, and, as he transferred the object to the slide and spread it out with the needle, I set up the little microscope on the shelf.

"A drop of Farrant and a cover-glass, please, Jervis," said Thorndyke.

I handed him the bottle, and, when he had let a drop of the mounting fluid fall gently on the object and put on the cover-slip, he placed the slide on the stage of the microscope and examined it attentively.

Happening to glance at the inspector, I observed on his countenance a faint grin, which he politely strove to suppress when he caught my eye.

"I was thinking, sir," he said apologetically, "that it's a bit off the track to be finding out what he had for dinner. He didn't die of unwholesome feeding."

Thorndyke looked up with a smile. "It doesn't do, inspector, to assume that anything is off the track in an inquiry of this kind. Every fact must have some significance, you know."

"I don't see any significance in the diet of a man who has had his head cut off," the inspector rejoined defiantly.

"Don't you?" said Thorndyke. "Is there no interest attaching to the last meal of a man who has met a violent death? These crumbs, for instance, that are scattered over the dead man's waistcoat. Can we learn nothing from them?"

"I don't see what you can learn," was the dogged rejoinder.

Thorndyke picked off the crumbs, one by one, with his forceps, and, having deposited them on a slide, inspected them, first with the lens and then through the microscope.

"I learn," said he, "that shortly before his death, the deceased partook of some kind of whole-meal biscuits, apparently composed partly of oatmeal."

"I call that nothing," said the inspector. "The question that we have got to settle is not what refreshments had the deceased been taking, but what was the cause of his death: did he commit suicide? was he killed by accident? or was there any foul play?"

"I beg your pardon," said Thorndyke, "the questions that remain to be settled are, who killed the deceased and with what motive? The others are already answered as far as I am concerned."

The inspector stared in sheer amazement not unmixed with incredulity.

"You haven't been long coming to a conclusion, sir," he said.

"No, it was a pretty obvious case of murder," said Thorndyke. "As to the motive, the deceased was a diamond merchant and is believed to have had a quantity of stones about his person. I should suggest that you search the body."

The inspector gave vent to an exclamation of disgust. "I see," he said. "It was just a guess on your part. The dead man was a diamond merchant and had valuable property about him; therefore he was murdered." He drew himself up, and, regarding Thorndyke with stern reproach, added: "But you must understand, sir, that this is a judicial inquiry, not a prize competition in a penny paper. And, as to searching the body, why, that is what I principally came for." He ostentatiously turned his back on us and proceeded systematically to turn out the dead man's pockets, laying the articles, as he removed them, on the box by the side of the hand-bag and umbrella.

While he was thus occupied, Thorndyke looked over the body generally, paying special attention to the soles of the boots, which, to the inspector's undissembled amusement, he very thoroughly examined with the lens.

"I should have thought, sir, that his feet were large enough to be seen with the naked eye," was his comment; "but perhaps," he added, with a sly glance at the station-master, "you're a little near-sighted."

Thorndyke chuckled good-humouredly, and, while the officer continued his search, he looked over the articles that had already been laid on the box. The purse and pocket-book he naturally left for the inspector to open, but the reading-glasses, pocket-knife and card-case and other small pocket articles were subjected to a searching scrutiny. The inspector watched him out of the corner of his eye with furtive amusement; saw him hold up the glasses to the light to estimate their refractive power, peer into the tobacco pouch, open the cigarette book and examine the watermark of the paper, and even inspect the contents of the silver match-box.

"What might you have expected to find in his tobacco pouch?" the officer asked, laying down a bunch of keys from the dead man's pocket.

"Tobacco," Thorndyke replied stolidly; "but I did not expect to find fine-cut Latakia. I don't remember ever having seen pure Latakia smoked in cigarettes."

"You do take an interest in things, sir," said the inspector, with a side glance at the stolid station-master.

"I do," Thorndyke agreed; "and I note that there are no diamonds among his collection."

"No, and we don't know that he had any about him; but there's a gold watch and chain, a diamond scarf-pin, and a purse containing"—he opened it and tipped out its contents into his hand—"twelve pounds in gold. That doesn't look much like robbery, does it? What do you say to the murder theory now?"

"My opinion is unchanged," said Thorndyke, "and I should like to examine the spot where the body was found. Has the engine been inspected?" he added, addressing the station-master.

"I telegraphed to Bradfield to have it examined," the official answered. "The report has probably come in by now. I'd better see before we start down the line."

We emerged from the lamp-room and, at the door, found the station-inspector waiting with a telegram. He handed it to the station-master, who read it aloud.

"The engine has been carefully examined by me. I find small smear of blood on near leading wheel and smaller one on next wheel following. No other marks." He glanced questioningly at Thorndyke, who nodded and remarked: "It will be interesting to see if the line tells the same tale."

The station-master looked puzzled and was apparently about to ask for an explanation; but the inspector, who had carefully pocketed the dead man's property, was impatient to start and, accordingly, when Thorndyke had repacked his case and had, at his own request, been furnished with a lantern, we set off down the permanent way, Thorndyke carrying the light and I the indispensable green case.

"I am a little in the dark about this affair," I said, when we had allowed the two officials to draw ahead out of earshot; "you came to a conclusion remarkably quickly. What was it that so immediately determined the opinion of murder as against suicide?"

"It was a small matter but very conclusive," replied Thorndyke. "You noticed a small scalp-wound above the left temple? It was a glancing wound, and might easily have been made by the engine. But—the wound had bled; and it had bled for an appreciable time. There were two streams of blood from it, and in both the blood was firmly clotted and partially dried. But the man had been decapitated; and this wound, if inflicted by the engine, must have been made after the decapitation, since it was on the side most distant from the engine as it approached. Now, a decapitated head does not bleed. Therefore, this wound was inflicted before the decapitation.

"But not only had the wound bled: the blood had trickled down in two streams at right angles to one another. First, in the order of time as shown by the appearance of the stream, it had trickled down the side of the face and dropped on the collar. The second stream ran from the wound to the back of the head. Now, you know, Jervis, there are no exceptions to the law of gravity. If the blood ran down the face towards the chin, the face must have been upright at the time; and if the blood trickled from the front to the back of the head, the head must have been horizontal and face upwards. But the man when he was seen by the engine-driver, was lying *face downwards*. The only possible inference is that when the wound was inflicted, the man was in the upright position—standing or sitting; and that subsequently, and while he was still alive, he lay on his back for a sufficiently long time for the blood to have trickled to the back of his head."

"I see. I was a duffer not to have reasoned this out for myself," I remarked contritely.

"Quick observation and rapid inference come by practice," replied Thorndyke. "But, tell me, what did you notice about the face?"

"I thought there was a strong suggestion of asphyxia."

"Undoubtedly," said Thorndyke. "It was the face of a suffocated man. You must have noticed, too, that the tongue was very distinctly swollen and that on the inside of the upper lip were deep indentations made by the teeth, as well as one or two slight wounds, obviously caused by heavy pressure on the mouth. And now observe how completely these facts and inferences agree with those from the scalp wound. If we knew that the deceased had received a blow on the head, had struggled with his assailant and been finally borne down and suffocated, we should look for precisely those signs which we have found."

"By the way, what was it that you found wedged between the teeth? I did not get a chance to look through the microscope."

"Ah!" said Thorndyke, "there we not only get confirmation, but we carry our inferences a stage further. The object was a little tuft of some textile fabric. Under the microscope I found it to consist of several different fibres, differently dyed. The bulk of it consisted of wool fibres dyed crimson, but there were also cotton fibres dyed blue and a few which looked like jute, dyed yellow. It was obviously a parti-coloured fabric and might have been part of a woman's dress, though the presence of the jute is much more suggestive of a curtain or rug of inferior quality."

"And its importance?"

"Is that, if it is not part of an article of clothing, then it must have come from an article of furniture, and furniture suggests a habitation."

"That doesn't seem very conclusive," I objected.

"It is not; but it is valuable corroboration."

"Of what?"

"Of the suggestion offered by the soles of the dead man's boots. I examined them most minutely and could find no trace of sand, gravel or earth, in spite of the fact that he must have crossed fields and rough land to reach the place where he was found. What I did find was fine tobacco ash, a charred mark as if a cigar or cigarette had been trodden on, several crumbs of biscuit, and, on a projecting brad, some coloured fibres, apparently from a carpet. The manifest suggestion is that the man was killed in a house with a carpeted floor, and carried from thence to the railway."

I was silent for some moments. Well as I knew Thorndyke, I was completely taken by surprise; a sensation, indeed, that I experienced anew every time that I accompanied him on one of his investigations. His marvellous power of co-ordinating apparently insignificant facts, of arranging them into an ordered sequence and making them tell a coherent story, was a phenomenon that I never got used to; every exhibition of it astonished me afresh.

"If your inferences are correct," I said, "the problem is practically solved. There must be abundant traces inside the house. The only question is, which house is it?"

"Quite so," replied Thorndyke; "that is the question, and a very difficult question it is. A glance at that interior would doubtless clear up the whole mystery. But how are we to get that glance? We cannot enter houses speculatively to see if they present traces of a murder. At present, our clue breaks off abruptly. The other end of it is in some unknown house, and, if we cannot join up the two ends, our problem remains unsolved. For the question is, you remember, who killed Oscar Brodski?"

"Then what do you propose to do?" I asked.

"The next stage of the inquiry is to connect some particular house with this crime. To that end, I can only gather up all available facts and consider each in all its possible bearings. If I cannot establish any such connection, then the inquiry will have failed and we shall have to make a fresh start—say, at Amsterdam, if it turns out that Brodski really had diamonds on his person, as I have no doubt he had."

Here our conversation was interrupted by our arrival at the spot where the body had been found. The station-master had halted, and he and the inspector were now examining the near rail by the light of their lanterns.

"There's remarkably little blood about," said the former. "I've seen a good many accidents of this kind and there has always been a lot of blood, both on the engine and on the road. It's very curious."

Thorndyke glanced at the rail with but slight attention: that question had ceased to interest him. But the light of his lantern flashed onto the ground at the side of the track—a loose, gravelly soil mixed with fragments of chalk—and from thence to the soles of the inspector's boots, which were displayed as he knelt by the rail.

"You observe, Jervis?" he said in a low voice, and I nodded. The inspector's boot-soles were covered with adherent particles of gravel and conspicuously marked by the chalk on which he had trodden.

"You haven't found the hat, I suppose?" Thorndyke asked, stooping to pick up a short piece of string that lay on the ground at the side of the track.

"No," replied the inspector, "but it can't be far off. You seem to have found another clue, sir," he added, with a grin, glancing at the piece of string.

"Who knows," said Thorndyke. "A short end of white twine with a green strand in it. It may tell us something later. At any rate we'll keep it," and, taking from his pocket a small tin box containing, among other things, a number of seed envelopes, he slipped the string into one of the latter and scribbled a note in pencil on the outside. The inspector watched his proceedings with an indulgent smile, and then returned to his examination of the track, in which Thorndyke now joined.

"I suppose the poor chap was near-sighted," the officer remarked, indicating the remains of the shattered spectacles; "that might account for his having strayed onto the line."

"Possibly," said Thorndyke. He had already noticed the fragments scattered over a sleeper and the adjacent ballast, and now once more produced his "collecting-box," from which he took another seed envelope. "Would you hand me a pair of forceps, Jervis," he said; "and perhaps you wouldn't mind taking a pair yourself and helping me to gather up these fragments."

As I complied, the inspector looked up curiously.

"There isn't any doubt that these spectacles belonged to the deceased, is there?" he asked. "He certainly wore spectacles, for I saw the mark on his nose."

"Still, there is no harm in verifying the fact," said Thorndyke, and he added to me in a lower tone, "Pick up every particle you can find, Jervis. It may be most important."

"I don't quite see how," I said, groping amongst the shingle by the light of the lantern in search of the tiny splinters of glass.

"Don't you?" returned Thorndyke. "Well, look at these fragments; some of them are a fair size, but many of these on the sleeper are mere grains. And consider their number. Obviously, the condition of the glass does not agree with the circumstances in which we find it. These are thick concave spectacle-lenses broken into a great number of minute fragments. Now how were they broken? Not merely by falling, evidently: such a lens, when it is dropped, breaks into a small number of large pieces. Nor were they broken by the wheel passing over them, for they would then have been reduced to fine powder, and that powder would have been visible on the rail, which it is not. The spectacle-frames, you may remember, presented the same incongruity; they were battered and damaged more than they would have been by falling, but not nearly so much as they would have been if the wheel had passed over them."

"What do you suggest, then?" I asked.

"The appearances suggest that the spectacles had been trodden on. But, if the body was carried here, the probability is that the spectacles were carried here too, and that they were then already broken; for it is more likely that they were trodden on during the struggle than that the murderer trod on them after bringing them here. Hence the importance of picking up every fragment."

"But why?" I inquired, rather foolishly, I must admit.

"Because, if, when we have picked up every fragment that we can find, there still remains missing a larger portion of the lenses than we could reasonably expect, that would tend to support our hypothesis and we might find the missing remainder elsewhere. If, on the other hand, we find as much of the lenses as we could expect to find, we must conclude that they were broken on this spot."

While we were conducting our search, the two officials were circling around with their lanterns in quest of the missing hat; and, when we had at length picked up the last fragment, and a careful search, even aided by a lens, failed to reveal any other, we could see their lanterns moving, like will-o'-the-wisps, some distance down the line.

"We may as well see what we have got before our friends come back," said Thorndyke, glancing at the twinkling lights. "Lay the case down on the grass by the fence; it will serve for a table."

I did so, and Thorndyke, taking a letter from his pocket, opened it, spread it out flat on the case, securing it with a couple of heavy stones, although the night was quite calm. Then he tipped the contents of the seed envelope out on the paper, and, carefully spreading out the pieces of glass, looked at them for some moments in silence. And, as he looked, there stole over his face a very curious expression; with sudden eagerness he began picking out the larger fragments and laying them on two visiting-cards which he had taken from his card-case. Rapidly and with wonderful deftness he fitted the pieces together, and, as the reconstituted lenses began gradually to take shape on their cards I looked on with growing excitement, for something in my colleague's manner told me that we were on the verge of a discovery.

At length the two ovals of glass lay on their respective cards, complete save for one or two small gaps; and the little heap that remained consisted of fragments so minute as to render further reconstruction impossible. Then Thorndyke leaned back and laughed softly.

"This is certainly an unlooked-for result," said he.

"What is?" I asked.

"Don't you see, my dear fellow? *There's too much glass.* We have almost completely built up the broken lenses, and the fragments that are left over are considerably more than are required to fill up the gaps."

I looked at the little heap of small fragments and saw at once that it was as he had said. There was a surplus of small pieces.

"This is very extraordinary," I said. "What do you think can be the explanation?"

"The fragments will probably tell us," he replied, "if we ask them intelligently."

He lifted the paper and the two cards carefully onto the ground, and, opening the case, took out the little microscope, to which he fitted the lowest-power objective and eye-piece—having a combined magnification of only ten diameters. Then he transferred the minute fragments of glass to a slide, and, having arranged the lantern as a microscope-lamp, commenced his examination.

"Ha!" he exclaimed presently. "The plot thickens. There is too much glass and yet too little; that is to say, there are only one or two fragments here that belong to the spectacles; not nearly enough to complete the building up of the lenses. The remainder consists of a soft, uneven, moulded glass, easily distinguished from the clear, hard optical glass. These foreign fragments are all curved, as if they had formed part of a cylinder, and are, I should say, portions of a wine-glass or tumbler." He moved the slide once or twice, and then continued: "We are in luck, Jervis. Here is a fragment with two little diverging lines etched on it, evidently the points of an eight-rayed star—and here is another with three points—the ends of three rays. This enables us to reconstruct the vessel perfectly. It was a clear, thin glass—probably a tumbler—decorated with scattered stars; I dare say you know the pattern. Sometimes there is an ornamented band in addition, but generally the stars form the only decoration. Have a look at the specimen."

I had just applied my eye to the microscope when the station-master and the inspector came up. Our appearance, seated on the ground with the microscope between us, was too much for the police officer's gravity, and he laughed long and joyously.

"You must excuse me, gentlemen," he said apologetically, "but really, you know, to an old hand, like myself, it does look a little—well—you understand—I dare say a microscope is a very interesting and amusing thing, but it doesn't get you much forrader in a case like this, does it?"

"Perhaps not," replied Thorndyke. "By the way, where did you find the hat, after all?"

"We haven't found it," the inspector replied, a little sheepishly.

"Then we must help you to continue the search," said Thorndyke. "If you will wait a few moments, we will come with you." He poured a few drops of xylol balsam on the cards to fix the reconstituted lenses to their supports and then, packing them and the microscope in the case, announced that he was ready to start.

"Is there any village or hamlet near?" he asked the station-master.

"None nearer than Corfield. That is about half-a-mile from here."

"And where is the nearest road?"

"There is a half-made road that runs past a house about three hundred yards from here. It belonged to a building estate that was never built. There is a footpath from it to the station."

"Are there any other houses near?"

"No. That is the only house for half-a-mile round, and there is no other road near here."

"Then the probability is that Brodski approached the railway from that direction, as he was found on that side of the permanent way."

The inspector agreeing with this view, we all set off slowly towards the house, piloted by the station-master and searching the ground as we went. The waste land over which we passed was covered with patches of docks and nettles, through each of which the inspector kicked his way, searching with feet and lantern for the missing hat. A walk of three hundred yards brought us to a low wall enclosing a garden, beyond which we could see a small house; and here we halted while the inspector waded into a large bed of nettles beside the wall and kicked vigorously. Suddenly there came a clinking sound mingled with objurgations, and the inspector hopped out holding one foot and soliloquizing profanely.

"I wonder what sort of a fool put a thing like that into a bed of nettles!" he exclaimed, stroking the injured foot. Thorndyke picked the object up and held it in the light of the lantern, displaying a piece of three-quarter inch rolled iron bar about a foot long. "It doesn't seem to have been there very long," he observed, examining it closely; "there is hardly any rust on it."

"It has been there long enough for me," growled the inspector, "and I'd like to bang it on the head of the blighter that put it there."

Callously indifferent to the inspector's sufferings, Thorndyke continued calmly to examine the bar. At length, resting his lantern on the wall, he produced his pocket-lens, with which he resumed his investigation, a proceeding that so exasperated the inspector that that afflicted official limped off in dudgeon, followed by the station-master, and we heard him, presently, rapping at the front door of the house.

"Give me a slide, Jervis, with a drop of Farrant on it," said Thorndyke. "There are some fibres sticking to this bar."

I prepared the slide, and, having handed it to him together with a cover-glass, a pair of forceps and a needle, set up the microscope on the wall.

"I'm sorry for the inspector," Thorndyke remarked, with his eye applied to the little instrument, "but that was a lucky kick for us. Just take a look at the specimen."

I did so, and, having moved the slide about until I had seen the whole of the object, I gave my opinion. "Red wool fibres, blue cotton fibres and some yellow, vegetable fibres that look like jute."

"Yes," said Thorndyke; "the same combination of fibres as that which we found on the dead man's teeth and probably from the same source. This bar has probably been wiped on that very curtain or rug with which poor Brodski was stifled. We will place it on the wall for future reference, and meanwhile, by hook or by crook, we must get into that house. This is much too plain a hint to be disregarded."

Hastily repacking the case, we hurried to the front of the house, where we found the two officials looking rather vaguely up the unmade road.

"There's a light in the house," said the inspector, "but there's no one at home. I have knocked a dozen times and got no answer. And I don't see what we are hanging about here for at all. The hat is probably close to where the body was found, and we shall find it in the morning."

Thorndyke made no reply, but, entering the garden, stepped up the path, and having knocked gently at the door, stooped and listened attentively at the keyhole.

"I tell you there's no one in the house, sir," said the inspector irritably; and, as Thorndyke continued to listen, he walked away muttering angrily. As soon as he was gone, Thorndyke flashed his lantern over the door, the threshold, the path and the small flower-beds; and, from one of the latter, I presently saw him stoop and pick something up.

"Here is a highly instructive object, Jervis," he said, coming out to the gate, and displaying a cigarette of which only half-an-inch had been smoked.

"How instructive?" I asked. "What do you learn from it?"

"Many things," he replied. "It has been lit and thrown away unsmoked; that indicates a sudden change of purpose. It was thrown away at the entrance to the house, almost certainly by some one entering it. That person was probably a stranger, or he would have taken it in with him. But he had not expected to enter the house, or he would not have lit it. These are the general suggestions; now as to the particular ones. The paper of the cigarette is of the kind known as the 'Zig-Zag' brand; the very conspicuous water-mark is quite easy to see. Now Brodski's cigarette book was a 'Zig-Zag' book—so called from the way in which the papers pull out. But let us see what the tobacco is like." With a pin from his coat, he hooked out from the unburned end a wisp of dark, dirty brown tobacco, which he held out for my inspection.

"Fine-cut Latakia," I pronounced, without hesitation.

"Very well," said Thorndyke. "Here is a cigarette made of an unusual tobacco similar to that in Brodski's pouch and wrapped in an unusual paper similar to those in Brodski's cigarette book. With due regard to the fourth rule of the syllogism, I suggest that this cigarette was made by Oscar Brodski. But, nevertheless, we will look for corroborative detail."

"What is that?" I asked.

'You may have noticed that Brodski's match-box contained round wooden vestas—which are also rather unusual. As he must have lighted the cigarette within a few steps of the gate, we ought to be able to find the match with which he lighted it. Let us try up the road in the direction from which he would probably have approached."

We walked very slowly up the road, searching the ground with the lantern, and we had hardly gone a dozen paces when I espied a match lying on the rough path and eagerly picked it up. It was a round wooden vesta.

Thorndyke examined it with interest and having deposited it, with the cigarette, in his "collecting-box," turned to retrace his steps. "There is now, Jervis, no reasonable doubt that Brodski was murdered in that house. We have succeeded in connecting that house with the crime, and now we have got to force an entrance and join up the other clues." We walked quickly back to the rear of the premises, where we found the inspector conversing disconsolately with the station-master.

"I think, sir," said the former, "we had better go back now; in fact, I don't see what we came here for, but—here! I say, sir, you mustn't do that!" For Thorndyke, without a word of warning, had sprung up lightly and thrown one of his long legs over the wall.

"I can't allow you to enter private premises, sir," continued the inspector; but Thorndyke quietly dropped down on the inside and turned to face the officer over the wall.

"Now, listen to me, inspector," said he. "I have good reasons for believing that the dead man, Brodski, has been in this house, in fact, I am prepared to swear an information to that effect. But time is precious; we must follow the scent while it is hot. And I am not proposing to break into the house off-hand. I merely wish to examine the dust-bin."

"The dust-bin!" gasped the inspector. "Well, you really are a most extraordinary gentleman! What do you expect to find in the dust-bin?"

"I am looking for a broken tumbler or wine-glass. It is a thin glass vessel decorated with a pattern of small, eight-pointed stars. It may be in the dust-bin or it may be inside the house."

The inspector hesitated, but Thorndyke's confident manner had evidently impressed him.

"We can soon see what is in the dust-bin," he said, "though what in creation a broken tumbler has to do with the case is more than I can understand. However, here goes." He sprang up onto the wall, and, as he dropped down into the garden, the station-master and I followed.

Thorndyke lingered a few moments by the gate examining the ground, while the two officials hurried up the path. Finding nothing of interest, however, he walked towards the house, looking keenly about him as he went; but we were hardly half-way up the path when we heard the voice of the inspector calling excitedly.

"Here you are, sir, this way," he sang out, and, as we hurried forward, we suddenly came on the two officials standing over a small rubbish-heap and looking the picture of astonishment. The glare of their lanterns illuminated the heap, and showed us the scattered fragments of a thin glass, star-pattern tumbler.

"I can't imagine how you guessed it was here, sir," said the inspector, with a new-born respect in his tone, "nor what you're going to do with it now you have found it."

"It is merely another link in the chain of evidence," said Thorndyke, taking a pair of forceps from the case and stooping over the heap. "Perhaps we shall find something else." He picked up several small fragments of glass, looked at them closely and dropped them again. Suddenly his eye caught a small splinter at the base of the heap. Seizing it with the forceps, he held it close to his eye in the strong lamplight, and, taking out his lens, examined it with minute attention. "Yes," he said at length, "this is what I was looking for. Let me have those two cards, Jervis."

I produced the two visiting-cards with the reconstructed lenses stuck to them, and, laying them on the lid of the case, threw the light of the lantern on them. Thorndyke looked at them intently for some time, and from them to the fragment that he held. Then, turning to the inspector, he said: "You saw me pick up this splinter of glass?"

"Yes, sir," replied the officer.

"And you saw where we found these spectacle-glasses and know whose they were?"

"Yes, sir. They are the dead man's spectacles, and you found them where the body had been."

"Very well," said Thorndyke; "now observe"; and, as the two officials craned forward with parted lips, he laid the little splinter in a gap in one of the lenses and then gave it a gentle push forward, when it occupied the gap perfectly, joining edge to edge with the adjacent fragments and rendering that portion of the lens complete.

"My God!" exclaimed the inspector. "How on earth did you know?"

"I must explain that later," said Thorndyke. "Meanwhile we had better have a look inside the house. I expect to find there a cigarette— or possibly a cigar—which has been trodden on, some whole-meal biscuits, possibly a wooden vesta, and perhaps even the missing hat."

At the mention of the hat, the inspector stepped eagerly to the back door, but, finding it bolted, he tried the window. This also was securely fastened and, on Thorndyke's advice, we went round to the front door.

"This door is locked too," said the inspector. "I'm afraid we shall have to break in. It's a nuisance, though."

"Have a look at the window," suggested Thorndyke.

The officer did so, struggling vainly to undo the patent catch with his pocket-knife.

"It's no go," he said, coming back to the door. "We shall have to——" He broke off with an astonished stare, for the door stood open and Thorndyke was putting something in his pocket.

"Your friend doesn't waste much time—even in picking a lock," he remarked to me, as we followed Thorndyke into the house; but his reflections were soon merged in a new surprise. Thorndyke had preceded us into a small sitting-room dimly lighted by a hanging lamp turned down low.

As we entered he turned up the light and glanced about the room. A whisky-bottle was on the table, with a siphon, a tumbler and a biscuit-box. Pointing to the latter, Thorndyke said to the inspector: "See what is in that box."

The inspector raised the lid and peeped in, the station-master peered over his shoulder, and then both stared at Thorndyke.

"How in the name of goodness did you know that there were whole-meal biscuits in the house, sir?" exclaimed the station-master.

"You'd be disappointed if I told you," replied Thorndyke. "But look at this." He pointed to the hearth, where lay a flattened, half-smoked cigarette and a round wooden vesta. The inspector gazed at these objects in silent wonder, while, as to the station-master, he continued to stare at Thorndyke with what I can only describe as superstitious awe.

"You have the dead man's property with you, I believe?" said my colleague.

"Yes," replied the inspector; "I put the things in my pocket for safety."

"Then," said Thorndyke, picking up the flattened cigarette, "let us have a look at his tobacco-pouch."

As the officer produced and opened the pouch, Thorndyke neatly cut open the cigarette with his sharp pocket-knife. "Now," said he, "what kind of tobacco is in the pouch?"

The inspector took out a pinch, looked at it and smelt it distastefully. "It's one of those stinking tobaccos," he said, "that they put in mixtures—Latakia, I think."

"And what is this?" asked Thorndyke, pointing to the open cigarette.

"Same stuff, undoubtedly," replied the inspector.

"And now let us see his cigarette papers," said Thorndyke.

The little book, or rather packet—for it consisted of separated papers—was produced from the officer's pocket and a sample paper abstracted. Thorndyke laid the half-burnt paper beside it, and the inspector, having examined the two, held them up to the light.

"There isn't much chance of mistaking that 'Zig-Zag' watermark," he said. "This cigarette was made by the deceased; there can't be the shadow of a doubt."

"One more point," said Thorndyke, laying the burnt wooden vesta on the table. "You have his match-box?"

The inspector brought forth the little silver casket, opened it and compared the wooden vestas that it contained with the burnt end. Then he shut the box with a snap.

"You've proved it up to the hilt," said he. "If we could only find the hat, we should have a complete case."

"I'm not sure that we haven't found the hat," said Thorndyke. "You notice that something besides coal has been burned in the grate."

The inspector ran eagerly to the fire-place and began, with feverish hands, to pick out the remains of the extinct fire. "The cinders are still warm," he said, "and they are certainly not all coal cinders. There has been wood burned here on top of the coal, and these little black lumps are neither coal nor wood. They may quite possibly be the remains of a burnt hat, but, lord! who can tell? You can put together the pieces of broken spectacle-glasses, but you can't build up a hat out of a few cinders." He held out a handful of little, black, spongy cinders and looked ruefully at Thorndyke, who took them from him and laid them out on a sheet of paper.

"We can't reconstitute the hat, certainly," my friend agreed, "but we may be able to ascertain the origin of these remains. They may not be cinders of a hat, after all." He lit a wax match and, taking up one of the charred fragments, applied the flame to it. The cindery mass fused at once with a crackling, seething sound, emitting a dense smoke, and instantly the air became charged with a pungent, resinous odour mingled with the smell of burning animal matter.

"Smells like varnish," the station-master remarked.

"Yes. Shellac," said Thorndyke; "so the first test gives a positive result. The next test will take more time."

He opened the green case and took from it a little flask, fitted for Marsh's arsenic test, with a safety funnel and escape tube, a small folding tripod, a spirit lamp and a disc of asbestos to serve as a sand-bath. Dropping into the flask several of the cindery masses, selected after careful inspection, he filled it up with alcohol and placed it on the disc, which he rested on the tripod. Then he lighted the spirit lamp underneath and sat down to wait for the alcohol to boil.

"There is one little point that we may as well settle," he said presently, as the bubbles began to rise in the flask. "Give me a slide with a drop of Farrant on it, Jervis."

I prepared the slide while Thorndyke, with a pair of forceps, picked out a tiny wisp from the table-cloth. "I fancy we have seen this fabric before," he remarked, as he laid the little pinch of fluff in the mounting fluid and slipped the slide onto the stage of the microscope. "Yes," he continued, looking into the eye-piece, "here are our old acquaintances, the red wool fibres, the blue cotton and the yellow jute. We must label this at once or we may confuse it with the other specimens."

"Have you any idea how the deceased met his death?" the inspector asked.

"Yes," replied Thorndyke. "I take it that the murderer enticed him into this room and gave him some refreshments. The murderer sat in the chair in which you are sitting, Brodski sat in that small arm-chair. Then I imagine the murderer attacked him with that iron bar that you found among the nettles, failed to kill him at the first stroke, struggled with him and finally suffocated him with the table-cloth. By the way, there is just one more point. You recognize this piece of string?" He took from his "collecting-box" the little end of twine that had been picked up by the line. The inspector nodded. "If you look behind you, you will see where it came from."

The officer turned sharply and his eye lighted on a string-box on the mantelpiece. He lifted it down, and Thorndyke drew out from it a length of white twine with one green strand, which he compared with the piece in his hand. "The green strand in it makes the identification fairly certain," he said. "Of course the string was used to secure the umbrella and hand-bag. He could not have carried them in his hand, encumbered as he was with the corpse. But I expect our other specimen is ready now." He lifted the flask off the tripod, and, giving it a vigorous shake, examined the contents through his lens. The alcohol had now become dark-brown in colour, and was noticeably thicker and more syrupy in consistence.

"I think we have enough here for a rough test," said he, selecting a pipette and a slide from the case. He dipped the former into the flask and, having sucked up a few drops of the alcohol from the bottom, held the pipette over the slide on which he allowed the contained fluid to drop.

Laying a cover-glass on the little pool of alcohol, he put the slide on the microscope stage and examined it attentively, while we watched him in expectant silence.

At length he looked up, and, addressing the inspector, asked: "Do you know what felt hats are made of?"

"I can't say that I do, sir," replied the officer.

"Well, the better quality hats are made of rabbits' and hares' wool —the soft under-fur, you know—cemented together with shellac. Now there is very little doubt that these cinders contain shellac, and with the microscope I find a number of small hairs of a rabbit. I have, therefore, little hesitation in saying that these cinders are the remains of a hard felt hat; and, as the hairs do not appear to be dyed, I should say it was a grey hat."

At this moment our conclave was interrupted by hurried footsteps on the garden path and, as we turned with one accord, an elderly woman burst into the room.

She stood for a moment in mute astonishment, and then, looking from one to the other, demanded: "Who are you? and what are you doing here?"

The inspector rose. "I am a police officer, madam," said he. "I can't give you any further information just now, but, if you will excuse me asking, who are you?"

"I am Mr. Hickler's housekeeper," she replied.

"And Mr. Hickler; are you expecting him home shortly?"

"No, I am not," was the curt reply. "Mr. Hickler is away from home just now. He left this evening by the boat train."

"For Amsterdam?" asked Thorndyke.

"I believe so, though I don't see what business it is of yours," the housekeeper answered.

"I thought he might, perhaps, be a diamond broker or merchant said Thorndyke. "A good many of them travel by that train."

"So he is," said the woman, "at least he has something to do with diamonds."

"Ah. Well, we must be going, Jervis," said Thorndyke, "we have finished here, and we have to find an hotel or inn. Can I have a word with you inspector?"

The officer, now entirely humble and reverent, followed us out into the garden to receive Thorndyke's parting advice.

"You had better take possession of the house at once, and get rid of the housekeeper. Nothing must be removed. Preserve those cinders and see that the rubbish-heap is not disturbed, and, above all, don't have the room swept. The station-master or I will let them know at the police station, so that they can send an officer to relieve you."

With a friendly "good-night" we went on our way, guided by the station-master; and here our connection with the case came to an end. Hickler (whose Christian name turned out to be Silas) was, it is true, arrested as he stepped ashore from the steamer, and a packet of diamonds, subsequently identified as the property of Oscar Brodski, found upon his person. But he was never brought to trial, for on the return voyage he contrived to elude his guards for an instant as the ship was approaching the English coast, and it was not until three days later, when a hand-cuffed body was cast up on the lonely shore by Orfordness, that the authorities knew the fate of Silas Hickler.

"An appropriate and dramatic end to a singular and yet typical case," said Thorndyke, as he put down the newspaper. "I hope it has enlarged your knowledge, Jervis, and enabled you to form one or two useful corollaries."

"I prefer to hear you sing the medico-legal doxology," I answered, turning upon him like the proverbial worm and grinning derisively (which the worm does not).

"I know you do," he retorted, with mock gravity, "and I lament your lack of mental initiative. However, the points that this case illustrates are these: First, the danger of delay; the vital importance of instant action before that frail and fleeting thing that we call a clue has time to evaporate. A delay of a few hours would have left us with hardly a single datum. Second, the necessity of pursuing the most trivial clue to an absolute finish, as illustrated by the spectacles. Third, the urgent need of a trained scientist to aid the police; and, last," he concluded, with a smile, "we learn never to go abroad without the invaluable green case."

A Case of Premeditation

PART I—THE ELIMINATION OF MR. PRATT

The wine merchant who should supply a consignment of *petit vin* to a customer who had ordered, and paid for, a vintage wine, would render himself subject to unambiguous comment. Nay! more; he would be liable to certain legal penalties. And yet his conduct would be morally indistinguishable from that of the railway company which, having accepted a first-class fare, inflicts upon the passenger that kind of company which he has paid to avoid. But the corporate conscience, as Herbert Spencer was wont to explain, is an altogether inferior product to that of the individual.

Such were the reflections of Mr. Rufus Pembury when, as the train was about to move out of Maidstone (West) station, a coarse and burly man (clearly a denizen of the third-class) was ushered into his compartment by the guard. He had paid the higher fare, not for the cushioned seats, but for seclusion or, at least, select companionship. The man's entry had deprived him of both, and he resented it.

But if the presence of this stranger involved a breach of contract, his conduct was a positive affront—an indignity; for, no sooner had the train started than he fixed upon Mr. Pembury a gaze of impertinent intensity, and continued thereafter to regard him with a stare as steady and unwinking as that of a Polynesian idol.

It was offensive to a degree, and highly disconcerting withal. Mr. Pembury fidgeted in his seat with increasing discomfort and rising temper. He looked into his pocket-book, read one or two letters and sorted a collection of visiting-cards. He even thought of opening his umbrella. Finally, his patience exhausted and his wrath mounting to boiling-point, he turned to the stranger with frosty remonstrance.

"I imagine, sir, that you will have no difficulty in recognizing me, should we meet again—which God forbid."

"I should recognize you among ten thousand," was the reply, so unexpected as to leave Mr. Pembury speechless.

"You see," the stranger continued impressively, "I've got the gift of faces. I never forget."

"That must be a great consolation," said Pembury.

"It's very useful to me," said the stranger, "at least, it used to be, when I was a warder at Portland—you remember me, I dare say: my name is Pratt. I was assistant-warder in your time. God-forsaken hole, Portland, and mighty glad I was when they used to send me up to town on reckernizing duty. Holloway was the house of detention then, you remember; that was before they moved to Brixton."

Pratt paused in his reminiscences, and Pembury, pale and gasping with astonishment, pulled himself together.

"I think," said he, "you must be mistaking me for some one else."

"I don't," replied Pratt. "You're Francis Dobbs, that's who you are. Slipped away from Portland one evening about twelve years ago. Clothes washed up on the Bill next day. No trace of fugitive. As neat a mizzle as ever I heard of. But there are a couple of photographs and a set of finger-prints at the Habitual Criminals Register. P'r'aps you'd like to come and see 'em?"

"Why should I go to the Habitual Criminals Register?" Pembury demanded faintly.

"Ah! Exactly. Why should you? When you are a man of means, and a little judiciously invested capital would render it unnecessary?"

Pembury looked out of the window, and for a minute or more preserved a stony silence. At length he turned suddenly to Pratt. "How much?" he asked.

"I shouldn't think a couple of hundred a year would hurt you," was the calm reply.

Pembury reflected awhile. "What makes you think I am a man of means?" he asked presently.

Pratt smiled grimly. "Bless you, Mr. Pembury," said he, " I know all about you. Why, for the last six months I have been living within half-a-mile of your house."

"The devil you have!"

"Yes. When I retired from the service, General O'Gorman engaged me as a sort of steward or caretaker of his little place at Baysford —he's very seldom there himself—and the very day after I came down, I met you and spotted you, but, naturally, I kept out of sight myself. Thought I'd find out whether you were good for anything before I spoke, so I've been keeping my ears open and I find you are good for a couple of hundred."

There was an interval of silence, and then the ex-warder resumed—

"That's what comes of having a memory for faces. Now there's Jack Ellis, on the other hand; he must have had you under his nose for a couple of years, and yet he's never twigged—he never will either," added Pratt, already regretting the confidence into which his vanity had led him.

"Who is Jack Ellis?" Pembury demanded sharply.

"Why, he's a sort of supernumerary at the Baysford Police Station; does odd jobs; rural detective, helps in the office and that sort of thing. He was in the Civil Guard at Portland, in your time, but he got his left forefinger chopped off, so they pensioned him, and, as he was a Baysford man, he got this billet. But he'll never reckernize you, don't you fear."

"Unless you direct his attention to me," suggested Pembury.

"There's no fear of that," laughed Pratt. "You can trust me to sit quiet on my own nest-egg. Besides, we're not very friendly. He came nosing round our place after the parlourmaid—him a married man, mark you! But I soon boosted him out, I can tell you; and Jack Ellis don't like me now."

"I see," said Pembury reflectively; then, after a pause, he asked: "Who is this General O'Gorman? I seem to know the name."

"I expect you do," said Pratt. "He was governor of Dartmoor when I was there—that was my last billet—and, let me tell you, if he'd been at Portland in your time, you'd never have got away."

"How is that?"

"Why, you see, the general is a great man on bloodhounds. He kept a pack at Dartmoor and, you bet, those lags knew it. There were no attempted escapes in those days. They wouldn't have had a chance."

"He has the pack still, hasn't he?" asked Pembury.

"Rather. Spends any amount of time on training 'em, too. He's always hoping there'll be a burglary or a murder in the neighbourhood so as he can try 'em, but he's never got a chance yet. P'r'aps the crooks have heard about 'em. But, to come back to our little arrangement: what do you say to a couple of hundred, paid quarterly, if you like?"

"I can't settle the matter off-hand," said Pembury. "You must give me time to think it over."

"Very well," said Pratt. "I shall be back at Baysford to-morrow evening. That will give you a clear day to think it over. Shall I look in at your place to-morrow night?"

"No," replied Pembury; "you'd better not be seen at my house, nor I at yours. If I meet you at some quiet spot, where we shan't be seen, we can settle our business without any one knowing that we have met. It won't take long, and we can't be too careful."

"That's true," agreed Pratt. "Well, I'll tell you what. There's an avenue leading up to our house; you know it, I expect. There's no lodge, and the gates are always ajar, excepting at night. Now I shall be down by the six-thirty at Baysford. Our place is a quarter of an hour from the station. Say you meet me in the avenue at a quarter to seven. How will that do?"

"That will suit me," said Pembury; "that is, if you are sure the bloodhounds won't be straying about the grounds."

"Lord bless you, no!" laughed Pratt. "D'you suppose the general lets his precious hounds stray about for any casual crook to feed with poisoned sausage? No, they're locked up safe in the kennels at the back of the house. Hallo! This'll be Swanley, I expect. I'll change into a smoker here and leave you time to turn the matter over in your mind. So long. To-morrow evening in the avenue at a quarter to seven. And, I say, Mr. Pembury, you might as well bring the first instalment with you—fifty, in small notes or gold."

"Very well," said Mr. Pembury. He spoke coldly enough, but there was a flush on his cheeks and an angry light in his eyes, which, perhaps, the ex-warder noticed; for when he had stepped out and shut the door, he thrust his head in at the window and said threateningly—

"One more word, Mr. Pembury-Dobbs: no hanky-panky, you know. I'm an old hand and pretty fly, I am. So don't you try any chickery-pokery on me. That's all." He withdrew his head and disappeared, leaving Pembury to his reflections.

The nature of those reflections, if some telepathist—transferring his attention for the moment from hidden court-yards or missing thimbles to more practical matters—could have conveyed them into the mind of Mr. Pratt, would have caused that quondam official some surprise and, perhaps a little disquiet. For long experience of the criminal, as he appears when in durance, had produced some rather misleading ideas as to his behaviour when at large. In fact, the ex-warder had considerably under-estimated the ex-convict.

Rufus Pembury, to give him his real name—for Dobbs was literally a *nom de guerre*—was a man of strong character and intelligence. So much so that, having tried the criminal career and found it not worth pursuing, he had definitely abandoned it. When the cattle-boat that picked him up off Portland Bill had landed him at an American port, he brought his entire ability and energy to bear on legitimate commercial pursuits, and with such success that, at the end of ten years, he was able to return to England with a moderate competence. Then he had taken a modest house near the little town of Baysford, where he had lived quietly on his savings for the last two years, holding aloof without much difficulty from the rather exclusive local society; and here he might have lived out the rest of his life in peace but for the unlucky chance that brought the man Pratt into the neighbourhood. With the arrival of Pratt his security was utterly destroyed.

There is something eminently unsatisfactory about a blackmailer. No arrangement with him has any permanent validity. No undertaking that he gives is binding. The thing which he has sold remains in his possession to sell over again. He pockets the price of emancipation, but retains the key of the fetters. In short, the blackmailer is a totally impossible person.

Such were the considerations that had passed through the mind of Rufus Pembury, even while Pratt was making his proposals; and those proposals he had never for an instant entertained. The ex-warder's advice to him to "turn the matter over in his mind" was unnecessary. For his mind was already made up. His decision was arrived at in the very moment when Pratt had disclosed his identity. The conclusion was self-evident. Before Pratt appeared he was living in peace and security. While Pratt remained, his liberty was precarious from moment to moment. If Pratt should disappear, his peace and security would return. Therefore Pratt must be eliminated.

It was a logical consequence.

The profound meditations, therefore, in which Pembury remained immersed for the remainder of the journey, had nothing whatever to do with the quarterly allowance; they were concerned exclusively with the elimination of ex-warder Pratt.

Now Rufus Pembury was not a ferocious man. He was not even cruel. But he was gifted with a certain magnanimous cynicism which ignored the trivialities of sentiment and regarded only the main issues. If a wasp hummed over his tea-cup, he would crush that wasp; but not with his bare hand. The wasp carried the means of aggression. That was the wasp's look-out. *His* concern was to avoid being stung.

So it was with Pratt. The man had elected, for his own profit, to threaten Pembury's liberty. Very well. He had done it at his own risk. That risk was no concern of Pembury's. *His* concern was his own safety.

When Pembury alighted at Charing Cross, he directed his steps (after having watched Pratt's departure from the station) to Buckingham Street, Strand, where he entered a quiet private hotel. He was apparently expected, for the manageress greeted him by his name as she handed him his key.

"Are you staying in town, Mr. Pembury?" she asked.

"No," was the reply. "I go back to-morrow morning, but I may be coming up again shortly. By the way, you used to have an encyclopædia in one of the rooms. Could I see it for a moment?"

"It is in the drawing-room," said the manageress. "Shall I show you?—but you know the way, don't you?"

Certainly Mr. Pembury knew the way. It was on the first floor; a pleasant old-world room looking on the quiet old street; and on a shelf, amidst a collection of novels, stood the sedate volumes of *Chambers's Encyclopædia.*

That a gentleman from the country should desire to look up the subject of "hounds" would not, to a casual observer, have been unnatural. But when from hounds the student proceeded to the article on blood, and thence to one devoted to perfumes, the observer might reasonably have felt some surprise; and this surprise might have been augmented if he had followed Mr. Pembury's subsequent proceedings, and specially if he had considered them as the actions of a man whose immediate aim was the removal of a superfluous unit of the population.

Having deposited his bag and umbrella in his room, Pembury set forth from the hotel as one with a definite purpose; and his footsteps led, in the first place, to an umbrella shop in the Strand, where he selected a thick rattan cane. There was nothing remarkable in this, perhaps; but the cane was of an uncomely thickness and the salesman protested. "I like a thick cane," said Pembury.

"Yes, sir; but for a gentleman of your height" (Pembury was a small, slightly-built man) "I would venture to suggest——"

"I like a thick cane," repeated Pembury. "Cut it down to the proper length and don't rivet the ferrule on. I'll cement it on when I get home."

His next investment would have seemed more to the purpose, though suggestive of unexpected crudity of method. It was a large Norwegian knife. But not content with this he went on forthwith to a second cutler's and purchased a second knife, the exact duplicate of the first. Now, for what purpose could he want two identically similar knives? And why not have bought them both at the same shop? It was highly mysterious.

Shopping appeared to be a positive mania with Rufus Pembury. In the course of the next half-hour he acquired a cheap hand-bag, an artist's black-japanned brush-case, a three-cornered file, a stick of elastic glue and a pair of iron crucible-tongs. Still insatiable, he repaired to an old-fashioned chemist's shop in a by-street, where he further enriched himself with a packet of absorbent cotton-wool and an ounce of permanganate of potash; and, as the chemist wrapped up these articles, with the occult and necromantic air peculiar to chemists, Pembury watched him impassively.

"I suppose you don't keep musk?" he asked carelessly.

The chemist paused in the act of heating a stick of sealing-wax, and appeared as if about to mutter an incantation. But he merely replied: "No, sir. Not the solid musk; it's so very costly. But I have the essence."

"That isn't as strong as the pure stuff, I suppose?"

"No," replied the chemist, with a cryptic smile, "not *so* strong, but strong enough. These animal perfumes are so very penetrating, you know; and so lasting. Why, I venture to say that if you were to sprinkle a table-spoonful of the essence in the middle of St. Paul's, the place would smell of it six months hence."

"You don't say so!" said Pembury. "Well, that ought to be enough for anybody. I'll take a small quantity, please, and, for goodness' sake, see that there isn't any on the outside of the bottle. The stuff isn't for myself, and I don't want to go about smelling like a civet cat."

"Naturally you don't, sir," agreed the chemist. He then produced an ounce bottle, a small glass funnel and a stoppered bottle labelled "Ess. Moschi," with which he proceeded to perform a few trifling feats of legerdemain.

"There, sir," said he, when he had finished the performance, "there is not a drop on the outside of the bottle, and, if I fit it with a rubber cork, you will be quite secure."

Pembury's dislike of musk appeared to be excessive, for, when the chemist had retired into a secret cubicle as if to hold converse with some familiar spirit (but actually to change half-a-crown), he took the brush-case from his bag, pulled off its lid, and then, with the crucible-tongs, daintily lifted the bottle off the counter, slid it softly into the brush-case, and, replacing the lid, returned the case and tongs to the bag. The other two packets he took from the counter and dropped into his pocket, and, when the presiding wizard, having miraculously transformed a single half-crown into four pennies, handed him the product, he left the shop and walked thoughtfully back towards the Strand. Suddenly a new idea seemed to strike him. He halted, considered for a few moments and then strode away northward to make the oddest of all his purchases.

The transaction took place in a shop in the Seven Dials, whose strange stock-in-trade ranged the whole zoological gamut, from water-snails to Angora cats. Pembury looked at a cage of guinea-pigs in the window and entered the shop.

"Do you happen to have a dead guinea-pig?" he asked.

"No; mine are all alive," replied the man, adding, with a sinister grin: "But they're not immortal, you know."

Pembury looked at the man distastefully. There is an appreciable difference between a guinea-pig and a blackmailer. "Any small mammal would do," he said.

"There's a dead rat in that cage, if he's any good," said the man. "Died this morning, so he's quite fresh."

"I'll take the rat," said Pembury; "he'll do quite well."

The little corpse was accordingly made into a parcel and deposited in the bag, and Pembury, having tendered a complimentary fee, made his way back to the hotel.

After a modest lunch he went forth and spent the remainder of the day transacting the business which had originally brought him to town. He dined at a restaurant and did not return to his hotel until ten o'clock, when he took his key, and tucking under his arm a parcel that he had brought in with him, retired for the night. But before undressing—and after locking his door—he did a very strange and unaccountable thing. Having pulled off the loose ferrule from his newly-purchased cane, he bored a hole in the bottom of it with the spike end of the file. Then, using the latter as a broach, he enlarged the hole until only a narrow rim of the bottom was left. He next rolled up a small ball of cotton-wool and pushed it into the ferrule; and, having smeared the end of the cane with elastic glue, he replaced the ferrule, warming it over the gas to make the glue stick.

When he had finished with the cane, he turned his attention to one of the Norwegian knives. First, he carefully removed with the file most of the bright, yellow varnish from the wooden case or handle.

Then he opened the knife, and, cutting the string of the parcel that he had brought in, took from it the dead rat which he had bought at the zoologist's. Laying the animal on a sheet of paper, he cut off its head, and, holding it up by the tail, allowed the blood that oozed from the neck to drop on the knife, spreading it over both sides of the blade and handle with his finger.

Then he laid the knife on the paper and softly opened the window. From the darkness below came the voice of a cat, apparently perfecting itself in the execution of chromatic scales; and in that direction Pembury flung the body and head of the rat, and closed the window. Finally, having washed his hands and stuffed the paper from the parcel into the fire-place, he went to bed.

But his proceedings in the morning were equally mysterious. Having breakfasted betimes, he returned to his bedroom and locked himself in. Then he tied his new cane, handle downwards, to the leg of the dressing-table. Next, with the crucible-tongs, he drew the little bottle of musk from the brush-case, and, having assured himself, by sniffing at it, that the exterior was really free from odour, he withdrew the rubber cork. Then, slowly and with infinite care, he poured a few drops—perhaps half-a-teaspoonful—of the essence on the cotton-wool that bulged through the hole in the ferrule, watching the absorbent material narrowly as it soaked up the liquid. When it was saturated he proceeded to treat the knife in the same fashion, letting fall a drop of the essence on the wooden handle—which soaked it up readily. This done, he slid up the window and looked out. Immediately below was a tiny yard in which grew, or rather survived, a couple of faded laurel bushes. The body of the rat was nowhere to be seen; it had apparently been spirited away in the night. Holding out the bottle, which he still held, he dropped it into the bushes, flinging the rubber cork after it.

His next proceeding was to take a tube of vaseline from his dressing-bag and squeeze a small quantity onto his fingers. With this he thoroughly smeared the shoulder of the brush-case and the inside of the lid, so as to ensure an air-tight joint. Having wiped his fingers, he picked the knife up with the crucible-tongs, and, dropping it into the brush-case, immediately pushed on the lid. Then he heated the tips of the tongs in the gas flame to destroy the scent, packed the tongs and brush-case in the bag, untied the cane—carefully avoiding contact with the ferrule—and, taking up the two bags, went out, holding the cane by its middle.

There was no difficulty in finding an empty compartment, for first-class passengers were few at that time in the morning. Pembury waited on the platform until the guard's whistle sounded, when he stepped into the compartment, shut the door and laid the cane on the seat with its ferrule projecting out of the off-side window, in which position it remained until the train drew up in Baysford station.

Pembury left his dressing-bag at the cloak-room, and, still grasping the cane by its middle, he sallied forth. The town of Baysford lay some half-a-mile to the east of the station; his own house was a mile along the road to the west; and half-way between his house and the station was the residence of General O'Gorman. He knew the place well. Originally a farmhouse, it stood on the edge of a great expanse of flat meadows and communicated with the road by an avenue, nearly three hundred yards long, of ancient trees. The avenue was shut off from the road by a pair of iron gates, but these were merely ornamental, for the place was unenclosed and accessible from the surrounding meadows—indeed, an indistinct footpath crossed the meadows and intersected the avenue about half-way up.

On this occasion Pembury, whose objective was the avenue, elected to approach it by the latter route; and at each stile or fence that he surmounted, he paused to survey the country. Presently the avenue arose before him, lying athwart the narrow track, and, as he entered it between two of the trees, he halted and looked about him.

He stood listening for a while. Beyond the faint rustle of leaves no sound was to be heard. Evidently there was no one about, and, as Pratt was at large, it was probable that the general was absent.

And now Pembury began to examine the adjacent trees with more than a casual interest. The two between which he had entered were respectively an elm and a great pollard oak, the latter being an immense tree whose huge, warty bole divided about seven feet from the ground into three limbs, each as large as a fair-sized tree, of which the largest swept outward in a great curve half-way across the avenue. On this patriarch Pembury bestowed especial attention,

walking completely round it and finally laying down his bag and
cane (the latter resting on the bag with the ferrule off the ground)
that he might climb up, by the aid of the warty outgrowths, to
examine the crown; and he had just stepped up into the space
between the three limbs, when the creaking of the iron gates was
followed by a quick step in the avenue. Hastily he let himself down
from the tree, and, gathering up his possessions, stood close behind
the great bole.

"Just as well not to be seen," was his reflection, as he hugged the
tree closely and waited, peering cautiously round the trunk. Soon a
streak of moving shadow heralded the stranger's approach, and he
moved round to keep the trunk between himself and the intruder. On
the footsteps came, until the stranger was abreast of the tree; and
when he had passed Pembury peeped round at the retreating figure.
It was only the postman, but then the man knew him, and he was
glad he had kept out of sight.

Apparently the oak did not meet his requirements, for he stepped
out and looked up and down the avenue. Then, beyond the elm, he
caught sight of an ancient pollard hornbeam—a strange, fantastic
tree whose trunk widened out trumpet-like above into a broad
crown, from the edge of which multitudinous branches uprose like
the limbs of some weird hamadryad.

That tree he approved at a glance, but he lingered behind the
oak until the postman, returning with brisk step and cheerful
whistle, passed down the avenue and left him once more in solitude.
Then he moved on with a resolute air to the hornbeam.

The crown of the trunk was barely six feet from the ground. He
could reach it easily, as he found on trying. Standing the cane against
the tree—ferrule downwards, this time—he took the brush-case from
the bag, pulled off the lid, and, with the crucible-tongs, lifted out
the knife and laid it on the crown of the tree, just out of sight,
leaving the tongs—also invisible—still grasping the knife. He was
about to replace the brush-case in the bag, when he appeared to
alter his mind. Sniffing at it, and finding it reeking with the sickly
perfume, he pushed the lid on again and threw the case up into the
tree, where he heard it roll down into the central hollow of the
crown. Then he closed the bag, and, taking the cane by its handle,
moved slowly away in the direction whence he had come, passing
out of the avenue between the elm and the oak.

His mode of progress was certainly peculiar. He walked with

excessive slowness, trailing the cane along the ground, and every few paces he would stop and press the ferrule firmly against the earth, so that, to any one who should have observed him, he would have appeared to be wrapped in an absorbing reverie.

Thus he moved on across the fields, not, however, returning to the high road, but crossing another stretch of fields until he merged into a narrow lane that led out into the High Street. Immediately opposite to the lane was the police station, distinguished from the adjacent cottages only by its lamp, its open door and the notices pasted up outside. Straight across the road Pembury walked, still trailing the cane, and halted at the station door to read the notices, resting his cane on the doorstep as he did so. Through the open doorway he could see a man writing at a desk. The man's back was towards him, but, presently, a movement brought his left hand into view, and Pembury noted that the forefinger was missing. This, then, was Jack Ellis, late of the Civil Guard at Portland.

Even while he was looking the man turned his head, and Pembury recognized him at once. He had frequently met him on the road between Baysford and the adjoining village of Thorpe, and always at the same time. Apparently Ellis paid a daily visit to Thorpe—perhaps to receive a report from the rural constable—and he started between three and four and returned between seven and a quarter past.

Pembury looked at his watch. It was a quarter past three. He moved away thoughtfully (holding his cane, now, by the middle), and began to walk slowly in he direction of Thorpe—westward.

For a while he was deeply meditative, and his face wore a puzzled frown. Then, suddenly, his face cleared and he strode forward at a brisker pace. Presently he passed through a gap in the hedge, and, walking in a field parallel with the road, took out his purse—a small pigskin pouch. Having frugally emptied it of its contents, excepting a few shillings, he thrust the ferrule of his cane into the small compartment ordinarily reserved for gold or notes.

And thus he continued to walk on slowly, carrying the cane by the middle and the purse jammed on the end.

At length he reached a sharp double curve in the road whence he could see back for a considerable distance; and here opposite a small opening, he sat down to wait. The hedge screened him effectually from the gaze of passers-by—though these were few enough—without interfering with his view.

A quarter of an hour passed. He began to be uneasy. Had he been mistaken? Were Ellis's visits only occasional instead of daily, as he had thought? That would be tiresome though not actually disastrous. But at this point in his reflections a figure came into view, advancing along the road with a steady swing. He recognized the figure. It was Ellis.

But there was another figure advancing from the opposite direction: a labourer, apparently. He prepared to shift his ground, but another glance showed him that the labourer would pass first. He waited. The labourer came on and, at length, passed the opening, and, as he did so, Ellis disappeared for a moment in a bend of the road. Instantly Pembury passed his cane through the opening in the hedge, shook off the purse and pushed it into the middle of the footway. Then he crept forward, behind the hedge, towards the approaching official, and again sat down to wait. On came the steady tramp of the unconscious Ellis, and, as it passed, Pembury drew aside an obstructing branch and peered out at the retreating figure. The question now was, would Ellis see the purse? It was not a very conspicuous object.

The footsteps stopped abruptly, Looking out, Pembury saw the police official stoop, pick up the purse, examine its contents and finally stow it in his trousers pocket. Pembury heaved a sigh of relief; and, as the dwindling figure passed out of sight round a curve in the road, he rose, stretched himself, and strode away briskly.

Near the gap was a group of ricks, and, as he passed them, a fresh idea suggested itself. Looking round quickly he passed to the farther side of one and, thrusting his cane deeply into it, pushed it home with a piece of stick that he picked up near the rick, until the handle was lost among the straw. The bag was now all that was left, and it was empty—for his other purchases were in the dressing-bag which, by the way, he must fetch from the station. He opened it and smelt the interior, but, though he could detect no odour, he resolved to be rid of it if possible.

As he emerged from the gap a wagon jogged slowly past. It was piled high with sacks, and the tail-board was down. Stepping into the road, he quickly overtook the wagon, and, having glanced round, laid the bag lightly on the tail-board. Then he set off for the station.

On arriving home he went straight up to his bedroom, and, ringing for his housekeeper, ordered a substantial meal. Then he took off his clothes and deposited them, even to his shirt, socks and necktie, in a trunk, wherein his summer clothing was stored with a plentiful sprinkling of naphthol to preserve it from the moth. Taking the packet of permanganate of potash from his dressing-bag, he passed into the adjoining bathroom, and, tipping the crystals into the bath, turned on the water. Soon the bath was filled with a pink solution of the salt, and into this he plunged, immersing his entire body and thoroughly soaking his hair. Then he emptied the bath and rinsed himself in clear water, and, having dried himself, returned to the bedroom and dressed himself in fresh clothing. Finally he took a hearty meal, and then lay down on the sofa to rest until it should be time to start for the rendezvous.

Half-past six found him lurking in the shadow by the station-approach, within sight of the solitary lamp. He heard the train come in, saw the stream of passengers emerge, and noted one figure detach itself from the throng and turn on to the Thorpe road. It was Pratt, as the lamplight showed him; Pratt, striding forward to the meeting-place with an air of jaunty satisfaction and an uncommonly creaky pair of boots.

Pembury followed him at a safe distance, and rather by sound than sight, until he was well past the stile at the entrance to the footpath. Evidently he was going on to the gates. Then Pembury vaulted over the stile and strode away swiftly across the dark meadows.

When he plunged into the deep gloom of the avenue, his first act was to grope his way to the hornbeam and slip his hand up onto the crown and satisfy himself that the tongs were as he had left them. Reassured by the touch of his fingers on the iron loops, he turned and walked slowly down the avenue. The duplicate knife—ready opened—was in his left inside breast-pocket, and he fingered its handle as he walked.

Presently the iron gate squeaked mournfully, and then the rhythmical creak of a pair of boots was audible, coming up the avenue. Pembury walked forward slowly until a darker smear emerged from the surrounding gloom, when he called out——

"Is that you, Pratt?"

"That's me," was the cheerful, if ungrammatical response, and, as he drew nearer, the ex-warder asked: "Have you brought the rhino, old man?"

The insolent familiarity of the man's tone was agreeable to Pembury: it strengthened his nerve and hardened his heart. "Of course," he replied; "but we must have a definite understanding, you know."

"Look here," said Pratt, "I've got no time for jaw. The general will be here presently; he's riding over from Bingfield with a friend. You hand over the dibs and we'll talk some other time."

"That is all very well," said Pembury, "but you must understand——" He paused abruptly and stood still. They were now close to the hornbeam, and, as he stood, he stared up into the dark mass of foliage.

"What's the matter?" demanded Pratt. "What are you staring at?" He, too, had halted and stood gazing intently into the darkness.

Then, in an instant, Pembury whipped out the knife and drove it, with all his strength, into the broad back of the ex-warder, below the left shoulder-blade.

With a hideous yell Pratt turned and grappled with his assailant. A powerful man and a competent wrestler, too, he was far more than a match for Pembury unarmed, and, in a moment, he had him by the throat. But Pembury clung to him tightly, and, as they trampled to and fro and round and round, he stabbed again and again with the viciousness of a scorpion, while Pratt's cries grew more gurgling and husky. Then they fell heavily to the ground, Pembury underneath. But the struggle was over. With a last bubbling groan, Pratt relaxed his hold and in a moment grew limp and inert. Pembury pushed him off and rose, trembling and breathing heavily.

But he wasted no time. There had been more noise than he had bargained for. Quickly stepping up to the hornbeam, he reached up for the tongs. His fingers slid into the looped handles; the tongs grasped the knife, and he lifted it out from its hiding-place and carried it to where the corpse lay, depositing it on the ground a few feet from the body. Then he went back to the tree and carefully pushed the tongs over into the hollow of the crown.

At this moment a woman's voice sounded shrilly from the top of the avenue.

"Is that you, Mr. Pratt?" it called.

Pembury started and then stepped back quickly, on tiptoe, to the body. For there was the duplicate knife. He must take that away at all costs.

The corpse was lying on its back. The knife was underneath it, driven in to the very haft. He had to use both hands to lift the body, and even then he had some difficulty in disengaging the weapon. And, meanwhile, the voice, repeating its question, drew nearer.

At length he succeeded in drawing out the knife and thrust it into his breast-pocket. The corpse fell back, and he stood up gasping.

"Mr. Pratt! Are you there?" The nearness of the voice startled Pembury, and, turning sharply, he saw a light twinkling between the trees. And then the gates creaked loudly and he heard the crunch of a horse's hoofs on the gravel.

He stood for an instant bewildered—utterly taken by surprise. He had not reckoned on a horse. His intended flight across the meadows towards Thorpe was now impracticable. If he were overtaken he was lost, for he knew there was blood on his clothes and his hands were wet and slippery—to say nothing of the knife in his pocket.

But his confusion lasted only for an instant. He remembered the oak tree; and, turning out of the avenue, he ran to it, and, touching it as little as he could with his bloody hands, climbed quickly up into the crown. The great horizontal limb was nearly three feet in diameter, and, as he lay out on it, gathering his coat closely round him, he was quite invisible from below.

He had hardly settled himself when the light which he had seen came into full view, revealing a woman advancing with a stable lantern in her hand. And, almost at the same moment, a streak of brighter light burst from the opposite direction. The horseman was accompanied by a man on a bicycle.

The two men came on apace, and the horseman, sighting the woman, called out: "Anything the matter, Mrs. Parton?" But, at that moment, the light of the bicycle lamp fell full on the prostrate corpse. The two men uttered a simultaneous cry of horror; the woman shrieked aloud: and then the horseman sprang from the saddle and ran forward to the body.

"Why," he exclaimed, stooping over it, "it's Pratt"; and, as the cyclist came up and the glare of his lamp shone on a great pool of blood, he added: "There's been foul play here, Hanford."

Hanford flashed his lamp around the body, lighting up the ground for several yards.

"What is that behind you, O'Gorman?" he said suddenly; "isn't it a knife?" He was moving quickly towards it when O'Gorman held up his hand.

"Don't touch it!" he exclaimed. "We'll put the hounds onto it. They'll soon track the scoundrel, whoever he is. By God! Hanford, this fellow has fairly delivered himself into our hands." He stood for a few moments looking down at the knife with something uncommonly like exultation, and then, turning quickly to his friend, said: "Look here, Hanford; you ride off to the police station as hard as you can pelt. It is only three-quarters of a mile; you'll do it in five minutes. Send or bring an officer and I'll scour the meadows meanwhile. If I haven't got the scoundrel when you come back, we'll put the hounds onto the knife and run the beggar down."

"Right," replied Hanford, and without another word he wheeled his machine about, mounted and rode away into the darkness.

"Mrs. Parton," said O'Gorman, "watch that knife. See that nobody touches it while I go and examine the meadows."

"Is Mr. Pratt dead, sir?" whimpered Mrs. Parton.

"Gad! I hadn't thought of that," said the general. "You'd better have a look at him; but mind! nobody is to touch that knife or they will confuse the scent."

He scrambled into the saddle and galloped away across the meadows in the direction of Thorpe; and, as Pembury listened to the diminuendo of the horse's hoofs, he was glad that he had not attemped to escape; for that was the direction in which he had meant to go, and he would surely have been overtaken.

As soon as the general was gone, Mrs. Parton, with many a terror-stricken glance over her shoulder, approached the corpse and held the lantern close to the dead face. Suddenly she stood up, trembling violently, for footsteps were audible coming down the avenue. A familiar voice reassured her.

"Is anything wrong, Mrs. Parton?" The question proceeded from one of the maids who had come in search of the elder woman, escorted by a young man, and the pair now came out into the circle of light.

"Good God!" ejaculated the man. "Who's that?"

"It's Mr. Pratt," replied Mrs. Parton. "He's been murdered."

The girl screamed, and then the two domestics approached on tiptoe, staring at the corpse with the fascination of horror.

"Don't touch that knife," said Mrs. Parton, for the man was about to pick it up. "The general's going to put the bloodhounds onto it."

"Is the general here, then?" asked the man; and, as he spoke, the drumming of hoofs, growing momentarily louder, answered him from the meadow.

O'Gorman reined in his horse as he perceived the group of servants gathered about the corpse. "Is he dead, Mrs. Parton?" he asked.

"I am afraid so, sir," was the reply.

"Ha! Somebody ought to go for the doctor; but not you, Bailey. I want you to get the hounds ready and wait with them at the top of the avenue until I call you."

He was off again into the Baysford meadows, and Bailey hurried away, leaving the two women staring at the body and talking in whispers.

Pembury's position was cramped and uncomfortable. He dared not move, hardly dared to breathe, for the women below him were not a dozen yards away; and it was with mingled feelings of relief and apprehension that he presently saw from his elevated station a group of lights approaching rapidly along the road from Baysford. Presently they were hidden by the trees, and then, after a brief interval, the whirr of wheels sounded on the drive and streaks of light on the tree-trunks announced the new arrivals. There were three bicycles, ridden respectively by Mr. Hanford, a police inspector and a sergeant; and, as they drew up, the general came thundering back into the avenue.

"Is Ellis with you?" he asked as he pulled up.

"No, sir," was the reply. "He hadn't come in from Thorpe when we left. He's rather late to-night."

"Have you sent for a doctor?"

"Yes, sir, I've sent for Dr. Hills," said the inspector, resting his bicycle against the oak. Pembury could smell the reek of the lamp as he crouched. "Is Pratt dead?"

"Seems to be," replied O'Gorman, "but we'd better leave that to the doctor. There's the murderer's knife. Nobody has touched it. I'm going to fetch the bloodhounds now."

"Ah! that's the thing," said the inspector. "The man can't be far away." He rubbed his hands with a satisfied air as O'Gorman cantered away up the avenue.

In less that a minute there came out from the darkness the deep baying of a hound followed by quick footsteps on the gravel. Then into the circle of light emerged three sinister shapes, loose-limbed and gaunt, and two men advancing at a shambling trot.

"Here, inspector," shouted the general, "you take one; I can't hold 'em both."

The inspector ran forward and seized one of the leashes, and the general led his hound up to the knife, as it lay on the ground. Pembury, peering cautiously round the bough, watched the great brute with almost impersonal curiosity; noted its high poll, its wrinkled forehead and melancholy face as it stooped to snuff suspiciously at the prostrate knife.

For some moments the hound stood motionless, sniffing at the knife; then it turned away and walked to and fro with its muzzle to the ground. Suddenly it lifted its head, bayed loudly, lowered its muzzle and started forward between the oak and the elm, dragging the general after it at a run.

The inspector next brought his hound to the knife, and was soon bounding away to the tug of the leash in the general's wake.

"They don't make no mistakes, they don't," said Bailey, addressing the gratified sergeant, as he brought forward the third hound, "you'll see——" But his remark was cut short by a violent jerk of the leash, and the next moment he was flying after the others, followed by Mr. Hanford.

The sergeant daintily picked the knife up by its ring, wrapped it in his handkerchief and bestowed it in his pocket. Then he ran off after the hounds.

Pembury smiled grimly. His scheme was working out admirably in spite of the unforeseen difficulties. If those confounded women would only go away, he could come down and take himself off while the course was clear. He listened to the baying of the hounds, gradually growing fainter in the increasing distance, and cursed the dilatoriness of the doctor. Confound the fellow! Didn't he realize that this was a case of life or death? These infernal doctors had no sense of responsibility.

Suddenly his ear caught the tinkle of a bicycle bell; a fresh light appeared coming up·the avenue and then a bicycle swept up swiftly to the scene of the tragedy, and a small elderly man jumped down by the side of the body. Giving his machine to Mrs. Parton, he stooped over the dead man, felt the wrist, pushed back an eyelid, held a match to the eye and then rose. "This is a shocking affair, Mrs. Parton," said he. "The poor fellow is quite dead. You had better help me to carry him to the house. If you two take the feet I will take the shoulders."

Pembury watched them raise the body and stagger away with it up the avenue. He heard their shuffling steps die away and the door of the house shut. And still he listened. From far away in the meadows came, at intervals, the baying of the hounds. Other sounds there was none. Presently the doctor would come back for his bicycle, but, for the moment, the coast was clear. Pembury rose stiffly. His hands had stuck to the tree where they had pressed against it, and they were still sticky and damp. Quickly he let himself down to the ground, listened again for a moment, and then, making a small circuit to avoid the lamplight, softly crossed the avenue and stole away across the Thorpe meadows.

The night was intensely dark, and not a soul was stirring in the meadows. He strode forward quickly, peering into the darkness and stopping now and again to listen; but no sound came to his ears, save the now faint baying of the distant hounds. Not far from his house, he remembered, was a deep ditch spanned by a wooden bridge, and towards this he now made his way; for he knew that his appearance was such as to convict him at a glance. Arrived at the ditch, he stooped to wash his hands and wrists; and, as he bent forward, the knife fell from his breast-pocket into the shallow water at the margin. He groped for it, and, having found it, drove it deep into the mud as far out as he could reach. Then he wiped his hands on some water-weed, crossed the bridge and started homewards.

He approached his house from the rear, satisfied himself that his housekeeper was in the kitchen, and, letting himself in very quietly with his key, went quickly up to his bedroom. Here he washed thoroughly —in the bath, so that he could get rid of the discoloured water— changed his clothes and packed those that he took off in a portmanteau.

By the time he had done this the gong sounded for supper. As he took his seat at the table, spruce and fresh in appearance, quietly cheerful in manner, he addressed his housekeeper. "I wasn't able to finish my business in London," he said. "I shall have to go up again to-morrow."

"Shall you come home the same day?" asked the housekeeper.

"Perhaps," was the reply, "and perhaps not. It will depend on circumstances."

He did not say what the circumstances might be, nor did the housekeeper ask. Mr. Pembury was not addicted to confidences. He was an eminently discreet man: and discreet men say little.

PART II—RIVAL SLEUTH-HOUNDS

(*Related by Christopher Jervis, M.D.*)

The half-hour that follows breakfast, when the fire has, so to speak, got into its stride, and the morning pipe throws up its clouds of incense, is, perhaps, the most agreeable in the whole day. Especially so when a sombre sky, brooding over the town, hints at streets pervaded by the chilly morning air, and hoots from protesting tugs upon the river tell of lingering mists, the legacy of the lately-vanished night.

The autumn morning was raw: the fire burned jovially. I thrust my slippered feet towards the blaze and meditated, on nothing in particular, with cat-like enjoyment. Presently a disapproving grunt from Thorndyke attracted my attention, and I looked round lazily. He was extracting, with a pair of office shears, the readable portions of the morning paper, and had paused with a small cutting between his finger and thumb.

"Bloodhounds again," said he. "We shall be hearing presently of the revival of the ordeal by fire."

"And a deuced comfortable ordeal, too, on a morning like this," I said, stroking my legs ecstatically. "What is the case?"

He was about to reply when a sharp rat-tat from the little brass knocker announced a disturber of our peace. Thorndyke stepped over to the door and admitted a police inspector in uniform, and I stood up, and, presenting my dorsal aspect to the fire, prepared to combine bodily comfort with attention to business.

"I believe I am speaking to Dr. Thorndyke," said the officer, and, as Thorndyke nodded, he went on: "My name, sir, is Fox, Inspector Fox of the Baysford Police. Perhaps you've seen the morning paper?"

Thorndyke held up the cutting, and, placing a chair by the fire, asked the inspector if he had breakfasted.

"Thank you, sir, I have," replied Inspector Fox. "I came up to town by the late train last night, so as to be here early, and stayed at an hotel. You see, from the paper, that we have had to arrest one of our own men. That's rather awkward, you know, sir."

"Very," agreed Thorndyke.

"Yes; it's bad for the force and bad for the public too. But we had to do it. There was no way out that we could see. Still, we should like the accused to have every chance, both for our sake and his own, so the chief constable thought he'd like to have your opinion on the case, and thought that, perhaps, you might be willing to act for the defence."

"Let us have the particulars," said Thorndyke, taking a writing-pad from a drawer and dropping into his arm-chair. "Begin at the beginning," he added, "and tell us all you know."

"Well," said the inspector, after a preliminary cough, "to begin with the murdered man: his name is Pratt. He was a retired prison warder, and was employed as steward by General O'Gorman, who is a retired prison governor—you may have heard of him in connection with his pack of bloodhounds. Well, Pratt came down from London yesterday evening by a train arriving at Baysford at six-thirty. He was seen by the guard, the ticket collector and the outside porter. The porter saw him leave the station at six-thirty-seven. General O'Gorman's house is about half-a-mile from the station. At five minutes to seven the general and a gentleman named Hanford and the general's housekeeper, a Mrs. Parton, found Pratt lying dead in the avenue that leads up to the house. He had apparently been stabbed, for there was a lot of blood about, and a knife—a Norwegian knife—was lying on the ground near the body. Mrs. Parton had thought she heard some one in the avenue calling out for help, and, as Pratt was just due, she came out with a lantern. She met the general and Mr. Hanford, and all three seem to have caught sight of the body at the same moment. Mr. Hanford cycled down to us, at once, with the news; we sent for a doctor, and I went back with Mr. Hanford and took a sergeant with me. We arrived at twelve minutes past seven, and then the general, who had galloped his horse over the meadows each side of the avenue without having seen anybody, fetched out his bloodhounds and led them up to the knife. All three hounds took up the scent at once—I held the leash of one of them—and they took us across the meadows without a pause or a falter, over stiles and fences, along a lane, out into the town, and then, one after the other, they crossed the road in a bee-line to the police station, bolted in at the door, which stood open, and made straight for the desk, where a supernumerary officer, named Ellis, was writing. They made a rare to-do, struggling to get at him, and it was as much as we could manage to hold them back. As for Ellis, he turned as pale as a ghost."

"Was any one else in the room?" asked Thorndyke.

"Oh, yes. There were two constables and a messenger. We led the hounds up to them, but the brutes wouldn't take any notice of them. They wanted Ellis."

"And what did you do?"

"Why, we arrested Ellis, of course. Couldn't do anything else—especially with the general there."

"What had the general to do with it?" asked Thorndyke.

"He's a J.P. and a late governor of Dartmoor, and it was his hounds that had run the man down. But we must have arrested Ellis in any case."

"Is there anything against the accused man?"

"Yes, there is. He and Pratt were on distinctly unfriendly terms. They were old comrades, for Ellis was in the Civil Guard at Portland when Pratt was warder there—he was pensioned off from the service because he got his left forefinger chopped off—but lately they had had some unpleasantness about a woman, a parlourmaid of the general's. It seems that Ellis, who is a married man, paid the girl too much attention—or Pratt thought he did—and Pratt warned Ellis off the premises. Since then they had not been on speaking terms."

"And what sort of man is Ellis?"

"A remarkably decent fellow he always seemed; quiet, steady, good-natured; I should have said he wouldn't have hurt a fly. We all liked him—better than we liked Pratt, in fact; for poor Pratt was what you'd call an old soldier—sly, you know, sir—and a bit of a sneak."

"You searched and examined Ellis, of course?"

"Yes. There was nothing suspicious about him except that he had two purses. But he says he picked up one of them—a small, pigskin pouch—on the footpath of the Thorpe road yesterday afternoon; and there's no reason to disbelieve him. At any rate, the purse was not Pratt's."

Thorndyke made a note of this on his pad, and then asked: "There were no blood-stains or marks on his clothing?"

"No. His clothing was not marked or disarranged in any way."

"Any cuts, scratches or bruises on his person?"

"None whatever," replied the inspector.

"At what time did you arrest Ellis?"

"Half-past seven exactly."

"Have you ascertained what his movements were? Had he been near the scene of the murder?"

"Yes; he had been to Thorpe and would pass the gates of the avenue on his way back. And he was later than usual in returning, though not later than he has often been before."

"And now, as to the murdered man: has the body been examined?"

"Yes; I had Dr. Hills's report before I left. There were no less than seven deep knife-wounds, all on the left side of the back.

There was a great deal of blood on the ground, and Dr. Hills thinks Pratt must have bled to death in a minute or two."

"Do the wounds correspond with the knife that was found?"

"I asked the doctor that, and he said 'Yes,' though he wasn't going to swear to any particular knife. However, that point isn't of much importance. The knife was covered with blood, and it was found close to the body."

"What has been done with it, by the way?" asked Thorndyke.

"The sergeant who was with me picked it up and rolled it in his handkerchief to carry in his pocket. I took it from him, just as it was, and locked it in a dispatch-box, handkerchief and all."

"Has the knife been recognized as Ellis's property?"

"No sir, it has not."

"Were there any recognizable footprints or marks of a struggle?" Thorndyke asked.

The inspector grinned sheepishly. "I haven't examined the spot, of course, sir," said he, "but, after the general's horse and the blood-hounds and the general on foot and me and the gardener and the sergeant and Mr. Hanford had been over it twice, going and returning, why, you see, sir——"

"Exactly, exactly," said Thorndyke. "Well, inspector, I shall be pleased to act for the defence; it seems to me that the case against Ellis is in some respects rather inconclusive."

The inspector was frankly amazed. "It certainly hadn't struck me in that light, sir," he said.

"No? Well, that is my view; and I think the best plan will be for me to come down with you and investigate matters on the spot."

The inspector assented cheerfully, and, when he had provided him with a newspaper, we withdrew to the laboratory to consult time-tables and prepare for the expedition.

"You are coming, I suppose, Jervis?" said Thorndyke.

"If I shall be of any use," I replied.

"Of course you will," said he. "Two heads are better than one, and, by the look of things, I should say that ours will be the only ones with any sense in them. We will take the research case, of course, and we may as well have a camera with us. I see there is a train from Charing Cross in twenty minutes."

For the first half-hour of the journey Thorndyke sat in his corner, alternately conning over his notes and gazing with thoughtful eyes out of the window. I could see that the case pleased him, and was careful not to break in upon his train of thought. Presently, however, he put away his notes and began to fill his pipe with a more companionable air, and then the inspector, who had been wriggling with impatience, opened fire.

"So you think, sir, that you see a way out for Ellis?"

"I think there is a case for the defence," replied Thorndyke. "In fact, I call the evidence against him rather flimsy."

The inspector gasped. "But the knife, sir? What about the knife?"

"Well," said Thorndyke, "what about the knife? Whose knife was it? You don't know. It was covered with blood. Whose blood? You don't know. Let us assume, for the sake of argument, that it was the murderer's knife. Then the blood on it was Pratt's blood. But if it was Pratt's blood, when the hounds had smelt it they should have led you to Pratt's body, for blood gives a very strong scent. But they did not. They ignored the body. The inference seems to be that the blood on the knife was not Pratt's blood."

The inspector took off his cap and gently scratched the back of his head. "You're perfectly right, sir," he said. "I'd never thought of that. None of us had."

"Then," pursued Thorndyke, "let us assume that the knife was Pratt's. If so, it would seem to have been used in self-defence. But this was a Norwegian knife, a clumsy tool—not a weapon at all—which takes an appreciable time to open and requires the use of two free hands. Now, had Pratt both hands free? Certainly not after the attack had commenced. There were seven wounds, all on the left side of the back; which indicates that he held the murderer locked in his arms and that the murderer's arms were around him. Also, incidentally, that the murderer is right-handed. But, still, let us assume that the knife was Pratt's. Then the blood on it was that of the murderer. Then the murderer must have been wounded. But Ellis was not wounded. Then Ellis is not the murderer. The knife doesn't help us at all."

The inspector puffed out his cheeks and blew softly. "This is getting out of my depth," he said. "Still, sir, you can't get over the bloodhounds. They tell us distinctly that the knife is Ellis's knife and I don't see any answer to that."

"There is no answer because there has been no statement. The bloodhounds have told you nothing. You have drawn certain inferences from their actions, but those inferences may be totally wrong and they are certainly not evidence."

"You don't seem to have much opinion of bloodhounds," the inspector remarked.

"As agents for the detection of crime," replied Thorndyke, "I regard them as useless. You cannot put a bloodhound in the witness-box. You can get no intelligible statement from it. If it possesses any knowledge, it has no means of communicating it. The fact is," he continued, "that the entire system of using bloodhounds for criminal detection is based on a fallacy. In the American plantations these animals were used with great success for tracking runaway slaves. But the slave was a known individual. All that was required was to ascertain his whereabouts. That is not the problem that is presented in the detection of a crime. The detective is not concerned in establishing the whereabouts of a known individual, but in discovering the identity of an unknown individual. And for this purpose bloodhounds are useless. They may discover such identity, but they cannot communicate their knowledge. If the criminal is unknown they cannot identify him: if he is known, the police have no need of the bloodhound.

"To return to our present case," Thorndyke resumed, after a pause; "we have employed certain agents—the hounds—with whom we are not *en rapport,* as the spiritualists would say; and we have no 'medium'. The hound possesses a special sense—the olfactory—which in man is quite rudimentary. He thinks, so to speak, in terms of smell, and his thoughts are untranslatable to beings in whom the sense of smell is undeveloped. We have presented to the hound a knife, and he discovers in it certain odorous properties; he discovers similar or related odorous properties in a tract of land and a human individual—Ellis. We cannot verify his discoveries or ascertain their nature. What remains? All that we can say is that there appears to exist some odorous relation between the knife and the man Ellis. But until we can ascertain the nature of that relation, we cannot estimate its evidential value or bearing. All the other 'evidence' is the product of your imagination and that of the general. There is, at present, no case against Ellis."

"He must have been pretty close to the place when the murder happened," said the inspector.

"So, probably, were many other people," answered Thorndyke; "but had he time to wash and change? Because he would have needed it."

"I suppose he would," the inspector agreed dubiously.

"Undoubtedly. There were seven wounds which would have taken some time to inflict. Now we can't suppose that Pratt stood passively while the other man stabbed him—indeed, as I have said, the position of the wounds shows that he did not. There was a struggle. The two men were locked together. One of the murderer's hands was against Pratt's back; probably both hands were, one clasping and the other stabbing. There must have been blood on one hand and probably on both. But you say there was no blood on Ellis, and there doesn't seem to have been time or opportunity for him to wash."

"Well, it's a mysterious affair," said the inspector; "but I don't see how you are going to get over the bloodhounds."

Thorndyke shrugged his shoulders impatiently. "The bloodhounds are an obsession," he said. "The whole problem really centres around the knife. The questions are, whose knife was it? and what was the connection between it and Ellis? There is a problem, Jervis," he continued, turning to me, "that I submit for your consideration. Some of the possible solutions are exceedingly curious."

As we set out from Baysford station, Thorndyke looked at his watch and noted the time. "You will take us the way that Pratt went," he said.

"As to that," said the inspector, "he may have gone by the road or by the footpath; but there's very little difference in the distance."

Turning away from Baysford, we walked along the road westward, towards the village of Thorpe, and presently passed on our right a stile at the entrance to a footpath.

"That path," said the inspector, "crosses the avenue about halfway up. But we'd better keep to the road." A quarter of a mile further on we came to a pair of rusty iron gates one of which stood open, and, entering, we found ourselves in a broad drive bordered by two rows of trees, between the trunks of which a long stretch of pasture meadows could be seen on either hand. It was a fine avenue, and, late in the year as it was, the yellowing foliage clustered thickly overhead.

When we had walked about a hundred and fifty yards from the gates, the inspector halted.

"This is the place," he said; and Thorndyke again noted the time.

"Nine minutes exactly," said he. "Then Pratt arrived here about fourteen minutes to seven, and his body was found at five minutes to seven—nine minutes after his arrival. The murderer couldn't have been far away then."

"No, it was a pretty fresh scent," replied the inspector. "You'd like to see the body first, I think you said, sir?"

"Yes; and the knife, if you please."

"I shall have to send down to the station for that. It's locked up in the office."

He entered the house, and, having dispatched a messenger to the police station, came out and conducted us to the outbuilding where the corpse had been deposited. Thorndyke made a rapid examination of the wounds and the holes in the clothing, neither of which presented anything particularly suggestive. The weapon used had evidently been a thick-backed, single-edged knife similar to the one described, and the discolouration around the wounds indicated that the weapon had a definite shoulder like that of a Norwegian knife, and that it had been driven in with savage violence.

"Do you find anything that throws any light on the case?" the inspector asked, when the examination was concluded.

"That is impossible to say until we have seen the knife," replied Thorndyke; "but while we are waiting for it, we may as well go and look at the scene of the tragedy. These are Pratt's boots, I think?" He lifted a pair of stout laced boots from the table and turned them up to inspect the soles.

"Yes, those are his boots," replied Fox, "and pretty easy they'd have been to track, if the case had been the other way about. Those Blakey's protectors are as good as a trademark."

"We'll take them, at any rate," said Thorndyke; and, the inspector having taken the boots from him, we went out and retraced our steps down the avenue.

The place where the murder had occurred was easily identified by a large dark stain on the gravel at one side of the drive, half-way between two trees—an ancient pollard hornbeam and an elm. Next to the elm was a pollard oak with a squat, warty bole about seven feet high, and three enormous limbs, of which one slanted half-way across the avenue; and between these two trees the ground was covered with the tracks of men and hounds superimposed upon the hoof-prints of a horse.

"Where was the knife found?" Thorndyke asked.

The inspector indicated a spot near the middle of the drive, almost opposite the hornbeam and Thorndyke, picking up a large stone, laid it on the spot. Then he surveyed the scene thoughtfully, looking up and down the drive and at the trees that bordered it, and, finally, walked slowly to the space between the elm and the oak, scanning the ground as he went. "There is no dearth of footprints," he remarked grimly, as he looked down at the trampled earth.

"No, but the question is, whose are they?" said the inspector.

"Yes, that is the question," agreed Thorndyke; "and we will begin the solution by identifying those of Pratt."

"I don't see how that will help us," said the inspector. "We know he was here."

Thorndyke looked at him in surprise, and I must confess that the foolish remark astonished me too, accustomed as I was to the quick-witted officers from Scotland Yard.

"The hue and cry procession," remarked Thorndyke, "seems to have passed out between the elm and the oak; elsewhere the ground seems pretty clear." He walked round the elm, still looking earnestly at the ground, and presently continued: "Now here, in the soft earth bordering the turf, are the prints of a pair of smallish feet wearing pointed boots; a rather short man, evidently, by the size of foot and length of stride, and he doesn't seem to have belonged to the procession. But I don't see any of Pratt's; he doesn't seem to have come off the hard gravel." He continued to walk slowly towards the hornbeam with his eyes fixed on the ground. Suddenly he halted and stooped with an eager look at the earth; and, as Fox and I approached, he stood up and pointed. "Pratt's footprints—faint and fragmentary, but unmistakable. And now, inspector, you see their importance. They furnish the time factor in respect of the other footprints. Look at this one and then look at that." He pointed from one to another of the faint impressions of the dead man's foot.

"You mean that there are signs of a struggle?" said Fox.

"I mean more than that," replied Thorndyke. "Here is one of Pratt's footprints treading into the print of a small, pointed foot; and there at the edge of the gravel is another of Pratt's nearly obliterated by the tread of a pointed foot. Obviously the first pointed footprint was made before Pratt's, and the second one after his; and the necessary inference is that the owner of the pointed foot was here at the same time as Pratt."

"Then he must have been the murderer!" exclaimed Fox.

"Presumably," answered Thorndyke; "but let us see whither he went. You notice, in the first place, that the man stood close to this tree"—he indicated the hornbeam—"and that he went towards the elm. Let us follow him. He passes the elm, you see, and you will observe that these tracks form a regular series leading from the hornbeam and not mixed up with the marks of the struggle. They were, therefore, probably made after the murder had been perpetrated. You will also notice that they pass along the backs of the trees—outside the avenue, that is; what does that suggest to you?"

"It suggests to me," I said, when the inspector had shaken his head hopelessly, "that there was possibly some one in the avenue when the man was stealing off."

"Precisely," said Thorndyke. "The body was found not more than nine minutes after Pratt arrived here. But the murder must have taken some time. Then the housekeeper thought she heard some one calling and came out with a lantern, and, at the same time, the general and Mr. Hanford came up the drive. The suggestion is that the man sneaked along outside the trees to avoid being seen. However, let us follow the tracks. They pass the elm and they pass on behind the next tree; but wait! There is something odd here." He passed behind the great pollard oak and looked down at the soft earth by its roots. "Here is a pair of impressions much deeper than the rest, and they are not a part of the track since their toes point towards the tree. What do you make of that?" Without waiting for an answer he began closely to scan the bole of the tree and especially a large, warty protuberance about three feet from the ground. On the bark above this was a vertical mark, as if something had scraped down the tree, and from the wart itself a dead twig had been newly broken off and lay upon the ground. Pointing to these marks Thorndyke set his foot on the protuberance, and, springing up, brought his eye above the level of the crown, whence the great boughs branched off.

"Ah!" he exclaimed. "Here is something much more definite." With the aid of another projection, he scrambled up into the crown of the tree, and, having glanced quickly round, beckoned to us. I stepped up on the projecting lump and, as my eyes rose above the crown, I perceived the brown, shiny impression of a hand on the edge. Climbing into the crown, I was quickly followed by the inspector, and we both stood up by Thorndyke between the three boughs. From where we stood we looked on the upper side of the great limb that swept out across the avenue; and there on its lichen-covered surface, we saw the imprints in reddish-brown of a pair of open hands.

"You notice," said Thorndyke, leaning out upon the bough, "that he is a short man; I cannot conveniently place my hands so low. You also note that he has both forefingers intact, and so is certainly not Ellis."

"If you mean to say, sir, that these marks were made by the murderer," said Fox, "I say it's impossible. Why, that would mean that he was here looking down at us when we were searching for him with the hounds. The presence of the hounds proves that this man could not have been the murderer."

"On the contrary," said Thorndyke, "the presence of this man with bloody hands confirms the other evidence, which all indicates that the hounds were never on the murderer's trail at all. Come now, inspector, I put it to you: Here is a murdered man; the murderer has almost certainly blood upon his hands; and here is a man with bloody hands, lurking in a tree within a few feet of the corpse and within a few minutes of its discovery (as is shown by the footprints); what are the reasonable probabilities?"

"But you are forgetting the bloodhounds, sir, and the murderer's knife," urged the inspector.

"Tut, tut, man!" exclaimed Thorndyke; "those bloodhounds are a positive obsession. But I see a sergeant coming up the drive, with the knife, I hope. Perhaps that will solve the riddle for us."

The sergeant, who carried a small dispatch-box, halted opposite the tree in some surprise while we descended, when he came forward with a military salute and handed the box to the inspector, who forthwith unlocked it, and, opening the lid, displayed an object wrapped in a pocket-handkerchief.

"There is the knife, sir," said he, "just as I received it. The handkerchief is the sergeant's."

Thorndyke unrolled the handerchief and took from it a large-sized Norwegian knife, which he looked at critically and then handed to me. While I was inspecting the blade, he shook out the handkerchief and, having looked it over on both sides, turned to the sergeant.

"At what time did you pick up this knife?" he asked.

"About seven-fifteen, sir; directly after the hounds had started. I was careful to pick it up by the ring, and I wrapped it in the handkerchief at once."

"Seven-fifteen," said Thorndyke. "Less than half-an-hour after the murder. That is very singular. Do you observe the state of this handkerchief? There is not a mark on it. Not a trace of any bloodstain;

which proves that when the knife was picked up, the blood on it was already dry. But things dry slowly, if they dry at all, in the saturated air of an autumn evening. The appearances seem to suggest that the blood on the knife was dry when it was thrown down. By the way, sergeant, what do you scent your handkerchief with?"

"Scent, sir!" exclaimed the astonished officer in indignant accents; "me scent my handkerchief! No, sir, certainly not. Never used scent in my life, sir."

Thorndyke held out the handkerchief, and the sergeant sniffed at it incredulously. "It certainly does seem to smell of scent," he admitted, "but it must be the knife." The same idea having occurred to me, I applied the handle of the knife to my nose and instantly detected the sickly-sweet odour of musk.

"The question is," said the inspector, when the two articles had been tested by us all, "was it the knife that scented the handkerchief or the handkerchief that scented the knife?"

"You heard what the sergeant said," replied Thorndyke. "There was no scent on the handkerchief when the knife was wrapped in it. Do you know, inspector, this scent seems to me to offer a very curious suggestion. Consider the facts of the case: the distinct trail leading straight to Ellis, who is, nevertheless, found to be without a scratch or a spot of blood; the inconsistencies in the case that I pointed out in the train, and now this knife, apparently dropped with dried blood on it and scented with musk. To me it suggests a carefully-planned, coolly-premeditated crime. The murderer knew about the general's bloodhounds and made use of them as a blind. He planted this knife, smeared with blood and tainted with musk, to furnish a scent. No doubt some object, also scented with musk, would be drawn over the ground to give the trail. It is only a suggestion, of course, but it is worth considering."

"But, sir," the inspector objected eagerly, "if the murderer had handled the knife, it would have scented him too."

"Exactly; so, as we are assuming that the man is not a fool, we may assume that he did not handle it. He will have left it here in readiness, hidden in some place whence he could knock it down, say, with a stick, without touching it."

"Perhaps in this very tree, sir," suggested the sergeant pointing to the oak.

"No," said Thorndyke, "he would hardly have hidden in the

tree where the knife had been. The hounds might have scented the place instead of following the trail at once. The most likely hiding-place for the knife is the one nearest that spot where it was found." He walked over to the stone that marked the spot, and, looking round, continued: "You see, that hornbeam is much the nearest, and its flat crown would be very convenient for the purpose—easily reached even by a short man, as he appears to be. Let us see if there are any traces of it. Perhaps you will give me a 'back up,' sergeant, as we haven't a ladder."

The sergeant assented with a faint grin, and, stooping beside the tree in an attitude suggesting the game of leap-frog, placed his hands firmly on his knees. Grasping a stout branch, Thorndyke swung himself up on the sergeant's broad back, whence he looked down into the crown of the tree. Then, parting the branches, he stepped onto the ledge and disappeared into the central hollow.

When he re-appeared he held in his hands two very singular objects; a pair of iron crucible-tongs and an artist's brush-case of black-japanned tin. The former article he handed down to me, but the brush-case he held carefully by its wire handle as he dropped to the ground.

"The significance of these things is, I think, obvious," he said. "The tongs were used to handle the knife with and the case to carry it in, so that it should not scent his clothes or bag. It was very carefully planned."

"If that is so," said the inspector, "the inside of the case ought to smell of musk."

"No doubt," said Thorndyke; "but before we open it, there is a rather important matter to be attended to. Will you give me the Vitogen powder, Jervis?"

I opened the canvas-covered "research case" and took from it an object like a diminutive pepper-caster—an iodoform dredger in fact —and handed it to him. Grasping the brush-case by its wire handle, he sprinkled the pale yellow powder from the dredger freely all round the pull-off lid, tapping the top with his knuckles to make the fine particles spread. Then he blew off the superfluous powder, and the two police officers gave a simultaneous gasp of joy; for now, on the black background, there stood out plainly a number of finger-prints, so clear and distinct that the ridge-pattern could be made out with perfect ease.

"These will probably be his right hand," said Thorndyke. "Now for the left." He treated the body of the case in the same way, and, when he had blown off the powder, the entire surface was spotted with yellow, oval impressions. "Now, Jervis," said he, "if you will put on a glove and pull off the lid, we can test the inside."

There was no difficulty in getting the lid off, for the shoulder of the case had been smeared with vaseline—apparently to produce an airtight joint—and, as it separated with a hollow sound, a faint, musky odour exhaled from its interior.

"The remainder of the inquiry," said Thorndyke, when I had pushed the lid on again, "will be best conducted at the police station, where, also, we can photograph these finger-prints."

"The shortest way will be across the meadows," said Fox; "the way the hounds went."

By this route we accordingly travelled, Thorndyke carrying the brush-case tenderly by its handle.

"I don't quite see where Ellis comes in in this job," said the inspector, as we walked along, "if the fellow had a grudge against Pratt. They weren't chums."

"I think I do," said Thorndyke. "You say that both men were prison officers at Portland at the same time. Now doesn't it seem likely that this is the work of some old convict who had been identified—and perhaps blackmailed—by Pratt, and possibly by Ellis too? That is where the value of the finger-prints comes in. If he is an old 'lag' his prints will be at Scotland Yard. Otherwise they are not of much value as a clue."

"That's true, sir," said the inspector. "I suppose you want to see Ellis."

"I want to see that purse that you spoke of, first," replied Thorndyke. "That is probably the other end of the clue."

As soon as we arrived at the station, the inspector unlocked a safe and brought out a parcel. "These are Ellis's things," said he, as he unfastened it, "and that is the purse."

He handed Thorndyke a small pigskin pouch, which my colleague opened, and, having smelt the inside, passed to me. The odour of musk was plainly perceptible, especially in the small compartment at the back.

"It has probably tainted the other contents of the parcel," said Thorndyke, sniffing at each article in turn, "but my sense of smell is not keen enough to detect any scent. They all seem odourless to me, whereas the purse smells quite distinctly. Shall we have Ellis in now?"

The sergeant took a key from a locked drawer and departed for the cells, whence he presently re-appeared accompanied by the prisoner—a stout, burly man, in the last stage of dejection.

"Come, cheer up, Ellis," said the inspector. "Here's Dr. Thorndyke come down to help us and he wants to ask you one or two questions."

Ellis looked piteously at Thorndyke, and exclaimed: "I know nothing whatever about this affair, sir, I swear to God I don't."

"I never supposed you did," said Thorndyke. "But there are one or two things that I want you to tell me. To begin with, that purse: where did you find it?"

"On the Thorpe road, sir. It was lying in the middle of the footway."

"Had any one else passed the spot lately? Did you meet or pass any one?"

"Yes, sir, I met a labourer about a minute before I saw the purse. I can't imagine why he didn't see it."

"Probably because it wasn't there," said Thorndyke. "Is there a hedge there?"

"Yes, sir; a hedge on a low bank."

"Ha! Well, now, tell me: is there any one about here whom you knew when you and Pratt were together at Portland? Any old lag— to put it bluntly—whom you and Pratt have been putting the screw on."

"No, sir, I swear there isn't. But I wouldn't answer for Pratt. He had a rare memory for faces."

Thorndyke reflected. "Were there any escapes from Portland in your time?" he asked.

"Only one—a man named Dobbs. He made off to the sea in a sudden fog and he was supposed to be drowned. His clothes washed up on the Bill, but not his body. At any rate, he was never heard of again."

"Thank you, Ellis. Do you mind my taking your finger-prints?"

"Certainly not, sir," was the almost eager reply; and the office inking-pad being requisitioned, a rough set of finger-prints was produced; and when Thorndyke had compared them with those on the brush-case and found no resemblance, Ellis returned to his cell in quite buoyant spirits.

Having made several photographs of the strange finger-prints, we returned to town that evening, taking the negatives with us; and while we waited for our train, Thorndyke gave a few parting injunctions to the inspector. "Remember," he said, "that the man must have washed his hands before he could appear in public. Search the banks of every pond, ditch and stream in the neighbourhood for footprints like those in the avenue; and, if you find any, search the bottom of the water thoroughly, for he is quite likely to have dropped the knife into the mud."

The photographs, which we handed in at Scotland Yard that same night, enabled the experts to identify the finger-prints as those of Francis Dobbs, an escaped convict. The two photographs—profile and full-face—which were attached to his record, were sent down to Baysford with a description of the man, and were, in due course, identified with a somewhat mysterious individual, who passed by the name of Rufus Pembury and who had lived in the neighbourhood as a private gentleman for some two years. But Rufus Pembury was not to be found either at his genteel house or elsewhere. All that was known was, that on the day after the murder, he had converted his entire "personalty" into "bearer securities," and then vanished from mortal ken. Nor has he ever been heard of to this day.

"And, between ourselves," said Thorndyke, when we were discussing the case some time after, "he deserved to escape. It was clearly a case of blackmail, and to kill a blackmailer—when you have no other defence against him—is hardly murder. As to Ellis, he could never have been convicted, and Dobbs, or Pembury, must have known it. But he would have been committed to the Assizes, and that would have given time for all traces to disappear. No, Dobbs was a man of courage, ingenuity and resource; and, above all, he knocked the bottom out of the great bloodhound superstition."

The Echo of a Mutiny

PART I—DEATH ON THE GIRDLER

Popular belief ascribes to infants and the lower animals certain occult powers of divining character denied to the reasoning faculties of the human adult; and is apt to accept their judgment as finally overriding the pronouncements of mere experience.

Whether this belief rests upon any foundation other than the universal love of paradox it is unnecessary to inquire. It is very generally entertained, especially by ladies of a certain social status; and by Mrs. Thomas Solly it was loyally maintained as an article of faith.

"Yes," she moralized, "it's surprisin' how they know, the little children and the dumb animals. But they do. There's no deceivin' *them*. They can tell the gold from the dross in a moment, they can, and they reads the human heart like a book. Wonderful, I call it. I suppose it's instinct."

Having delivered herself of this priceless gem of philosophic thought, she thrust her arms elbow-deep into the foaming wash-tub and glanced admiringly at her lodger as he sat in the doorway, supporting on one knee an obese infant of eighteen months and on the other a fine tabby cat.

James Brown was an elderly seafaring man, small and slight in build and in manner suave, insinuating and perhaps a trifle sly. But he had all the sailor's love of children and animals, and the sailor's knack of making himself acceptable to them, for, as he sat with an empty pipe wobbling in the grasp of his toothless gums, the baby beamed with humid smiles, and the cat, rolled into a fluffy ball and purring like a stocking-loom, worked its fingers ecstatically as if it were trying on a new pair of gloves.

"It must be mortal lonely out at the lighthouse," Mrs. Solly resumed. "Only three men and never a neighbour to speak to; and, Lord! what a muddle they must be in with no woman to look after them and keep 'em tidy. But you won't be overworked, Mr. Brown, in these long days; daylight till past nine o'clock. I don't know what you'll do to pass the time."

"Oh, I shall find plenty to do, I expect," said Brown, "what with cleanin' the lamps and glasses and paintin' up the ironwork. And that reminds me," he added, looking round at the clock, "that time's getting on. High water at half-past ten, and here it's gone eight o'clock."

Mrs. Solly, acting on the hint, began rapidly to fish out the washed garments and wring them out into the form of short ropes. Then, having dried her hands on her apron, she relieved Brown of the protesting baby.

"Your room will be ready for you, Mr. Brown," said she, "when your turn comes for a spell ashore; and main glad me and Tom will be to see you back."

"Thank you, Mrs. Solly, ma'am," answered Brown, tenderly placing the cat on the floor; "you won't be more glad than what I will." He shook hands warmly with his landlady, kissed the baby, chucked the cat under the chin, and, picking up his little chest by its becket, swung in onto his shoulder and strode out of the cottage.

His way lay across the marshes, and, like the ships in the offing, he shaped his course by the twin towers of Reculver that stood up grotesquely on the rim of the land; and as he trod the springy turf, Tom Solly's fleecy charges looked up at him with vacant stares and valedictory bleatings. Once, at a dyke-gate, he paused to look back at the fair Kentish landscape: at the grey tower of St. Nicholas-at-Wade peeping above the trees and the faraway mill at Sarre, whirling slowly in the summer breeze; and, above all, at the solitary cottage where, for a brief spell in his stormy life, he had known the homely joys of domesticity and peace. Well, that was over for the present, and the lighthouse loomed ahead. With a half-sigh he passed through the gate and walked on towards Reculver.

Outside the whitewashed cottages with their official black chimneys a petty-officer of the coast-guard was adjusting the halyards of the flagstaff. He looked round as Brown approached, and hailed him cheerily.

"Here you are, then," said he, "all figged out in your new togs, too. But we're in a bit of a difficulty, d'ye see. We've got to pull up to Whitstable this morning, so I can't send a man out with you and I can't spare a boat."

"Have I got to swim out, then?" asked Brown.

The coast-guard grinned. "Not in them new clothes, mate," he answered. "No, but there's old Willett's boat; he isn't using her to-day; he's going over to Minster to see his daughter, and he'll let us have the loan of the boat. But there's no one to go with you, and I'm responsible to Willett."

"Well, what about it?" asked Brown, with the deep-sea sailor's (usually misplaced) confidence in his power to handle a sailing-boat. "D'ye think I can't manage a tub of a boat? Me what's used the sea since I was a kid of ten?"

"Yes," said the coast-guard; "but who's to bring her back?"

"Why, the man that I'm going to relieve," answered Brown. "He don't want to swim no more than what I do."

The coast-guard reflected with his telescope pointed at a passing barge. "Well, I suppose it'll be all right," he concluded; "but it's a pity they couldn't send the tender round. However, if you undertake to send the boat back, we'll get her afloat. It's time you were off."

He strolled away to the back of the cottages, whence he presently returned with two of his mates, and the four men proceeded along the shore to where Willett's boat lay just above the high-water mark.

The *Emily* was a beamy craft of the type locally known as a "half-share skiff," solidly built of oak, with varnished planking and fitted with main and mizzen lugs. She was a good handful for four men, and, as she slid over the soft chalk rocks with a hollow rumble, the coast-guards debated the advisability of lifting out the bags of shingle with which she was ballasted. However, she was at length dragged down, ballast and all, to the water's edge, and then, while Brown stepped the mainmast, the petty-officer gave him his directions. "What you've got to do," said he, "is to make use of the flood-tide. Keep her nose nor'-east, and with this trickle of nor'-westerly breeze you ought to make the lighthouse in one board. Anyhow, don't let her get east of the lighthouse, or, when the ebb sets in, you'll be in a fix."

To these admonitions Brown listened with jaunty indifference as he hoisted the sails and watched the incoming tide creep over the level shore. Then the boat lifted on the gentle swell. Putting out an oar, he gave a vigorous shove off that sent the boat, with a final scrape, clear of the beach, and then, having dropped the rudder onto its pintles, he seated himself and calmly belayed the main-sheet.

"There he goes," growled the coast-guard; "makin' fast his sheet. They *will* do it" (he invariably did it himself), "and that's how accidents happen. I hope old Willett 'll see his boat back all right."

He stood for some time watching the dwindling boat as it sidled across the smooth water; then he turned and followed his mates towards the station.

Out on the south-western edge of the Girdler Sand, just inside the two fathom line, the spindle-shanked lighthouse stood a-straddle on its long screw-piles like some uncouth red-bodied wading-bird. It was now nearly half-flood tide. The highest shoals were long since covered, and the lighthouse rose above the smooth sea as solitary as a slaver becalmed in the "middle passage."

On the gallery outside the lantern were two men, the entire staff of the building, of whom one sat huddled in a chair with his left leg propped up with pillows on another, while his companion rested a telescope on the rail and peered at the faint grey line of the distant land and the two tiny points that marked the twin spires of Reculver.

"I don't see any signs of the boat, Harry," said he.

The other man groaned. "I shall lose the tide," he complained, "and then there's another day gone."

"They can pull you down to Birchington and put you in the train," said the first man.

"I don't want no trains," growled the invalid. "The boat 'll be bad enough. I suppose there's nothing coming our way, Tom?"

Tom turned his face eastward and shaded his eyes. "There's a brig coming across the tide from the north," he said. "Looks like a collier." He pointed his telescope at the approaching vessel, and added: "She's got two new cloths in her upper fore top-sail, one on each leech."

The other man sat up eagerly. "What's her trysail like, Tom?" he asked.

"Can't see it," replied Tom. "Yes, I can now: it's tanned. Why, that'll be the old *Utopia*, Harry; she's the only brig I know that's got a tanned trysail."

"Look here, Tom," exclaimed the other, "if that's the *Utopia*, she's going to my home and I'm going aboard of her. Captain Mockett 'll give me a passage, I know."

"You oughtn't to go until you're relieved, you know, Barnett," said Tom doubtfully; "it's against regulations to leave your station."

"Regulations be blowed!" exclaimed Barnett. "My leg's more to me than the regulations. I don't want to be a cripple all my life. Besides, I'm no good here, and this new chap, Brown, will be coming out presently. You run up the signal, Tom, like a good comrade, and hail the brig."

"Well, it's your look-out," said Tom, "and I don't mind saying that if I was in your place I should cut off home and see a doctor, if I got the chance." He sauntered off to the flag-locker, and, selecting the two code-flags, deliberately toggled them onto the halyards. Then, as the brig swept up within range, he hoisted the little balls of bunting to the flagstaff-head and jerked the halyards, when the two flags blew out making the signal "Need assistance."

Promptly a coal-soiled answering pennant soared to the brig's main-truck; less promptly the collier went about, and, turning her nose down stream, slowly drifted stern-forwards towards the lighthouse. Then a boat slid out through her gangway, and a couple of men plied the oars vigorously.

"Lighthouse ahoy!" roared one of them, as the boat came within hail. "What's amiss?"

"Harry Barnett has broke his leg," shouted the lighthouse keeper "and he wants to know if Captain Mockett will give him a passage to Whitstable."

The boat turned back to the brig, and after a brief and bellowed consultation, once more pulled towards the lighthouse.

"Skipper says yus," roared the sailor, when he was within ear-shot, "and he says look alive, 'cause he don't want to miss his tide."

The injured man heaved a sigh of relief. "That's good news," said he, "though, how the blazes I'm going to get down the ladder is more than I can tell. What do you say, Jeffreys?"

"I say you'd better let me lower you with the tackle," replied Jeffreys. "You can sit in the bight of a rope and I'll give you a line to steady yourself with."

"Ah, that'll do, Tom," said Barnett; "but, for the Lord's sake, pay out the fall-rope gently."

The arrangements were made so quickly that by the time the boat was fast alongside everything was in readiness, and a minute later the injured man, dangling like a gigantic spider from the end of the tackle, slowly descended, cursing volubly to the accompaniment of the creaking of the blocks. His chest and kit-bag followed, and, as soon as these were unhooked from the tackle, the boat pulled off to the brig, which was now slowly creeping stern-foremost past the lighthouse. The sick man was hoisted up the side, his chest handed up after him, and then the brig was put on her course due south across the Kentish Flats.

Jeffreys stood on the gallery watching the receding vessel and listening to the voices of her crew as they grew small and weak in the increasing distance. Now that his gruff companion was gone, a strange loneliness had fallen on the lighthouse. The last of the home-ward-bound ships had long since passed up the Princes Channel and left the calm sea desolate and blank. The distant buoys, showing as tiny black dots on the glassy surface, and the spindly shapes of the beacons which stood up from invisible shoals, but emphasized the solitude of the empty sea, and the tolling of the bell buoy on the Shivering Sand, stealing faintly down the wind, sounded weird and mournful. The day's work was already done. The lenses were polished, the lamps had been trimmed, and the little motor that worked the fog-horn had been cleaned and oiled. There were several odd jobs, it is true, waiting to be done, as there always are in a lighthouse; but, just now, Jeffreys was not in a working humour. A new comrade was coming into his life to-day, a stranger with whom he was to be shut up alone, night and day, for a month on end, and whose temper and tastes and habits might mean for him pleasant companionship or jangling and discord without end. Who was this man Brown? What had be been? and what was he like? These were the questions that passed, naturally enough, through the lighthouse keeper's mind and distracted him from his usual thoughts and occu-pations.

Presently a speck on the landward horizon caught his eye. He snatched up the telescope eagerly to inspect it. Yes, it was a boat; but not the coast-guard's cutter, for which he was looking. Evidently a fisherman's boat and with only one man in it. He laid down the telescope with a sigh of disappointment, and, filling his pipe, leaned on the rail with a dreamy eye bent on the faint grey line of the land.

Three long years had he spent in this dreary solitude, so repugnant to his active, restless nature: three blank, interminable years, with nothing to look back on but the endless succession of summer calms, stormy nights and the chilly fogs of winter, when the unseen steamers hooted from the void and the fog-horn bellowed its hoarse warning.

Why had he come to this God-forsaken spot? and why did he stay, when the wide world called to him? And then memory painted him a picture on which his mind's eye had often looked before and which once again rose before him, shutting out the vision of the calm sea and the distant land. It was a brightly-coloured picture. It showed a cloudless sky brooding over the deep blue tropic sea; and in the middle of the picture, sea-sawing gently on the quiet swell, a white-painted barque.

Her sails were clewed up untidily, her swinging yards jerked at the slack braces and her untended wheel revolved to and fro to the oscillations of the rudder.

She was not a derelict, for more than a dozen men were on her deck; but the men were all drunk and mostly asleep, and there was never an officer among them.

Then he saw the interior of one of her cabins. The chart-rack, the tell-tale compass and the chronometers marked it as the captain's cabin. In it were four men, and two of them lay dead on the deck. Of the other two, one was a small, cunning-faced man, who was, at the moment, kneeling, beside one of the corpses to wipe a knife upon its coat. The fourth man was himself.

Again, he saw the two murderers stealing off in a quarter-boat, as the barque with her drunken crew drifted towards the spouting surf of a river-bar. He saw the ship melt away in the surf like an icicle in the sunshine; and, later, two shipwrecked mariners, picked up in an open boat and set ashore at an American port.

That was why he was here. Because he was a murderer. The other scoundrel, Amos Todd, had turned Queen's Evidence and denounced him, and he had barely managed to escape. Since then he had hidden himself from the great world, and here he must continue to hide, not from the law—for his person was unknown now that his shipmates were dead—but from the partner of his crime. It was the fear of Todd that had changed him from Jeffrey Rorke to Tom Jeffreys and had sent him to the Girdler, a prisoner for life. Todd might die—might even now be dead—but he would never hear of it: would never hear the news of his release.

He roused himself and once more pointed his telescope at the distant boat. She was considerably nearer now and seemed to be heading out towards the lighthouse. Perhaps the man in her was bringing a message; at any rate, there was no sign of the coast-guard's cutter.

He went in and, betaking himself to the kitchen, busied himself with a few simple preparations for dinner. But there was nothing to cook, for there remained the cold meat from yesterday's cooking, which he would make sufficient, with some biscuit in place of potatoes. He felt restless and unstrung; the solitude irked him, and the everlasting wash of the water among the piles jarred on his nerves.

When he went out again into the gallery the ebb-tide had set in strongly and the boat was little more than a mile distant; and now, through the glass, he could see that the man in her wore the uniform cap of the Trinity House. Then the man must be his future comrade, Brown; but this was very extraordinary. What were they to do with the boat? There was no one to take her back.

The breeze was dying away. As he watched the boat, he saw the man lower the sail and take to his oars; and something of hurry in the way the man pulled over the gathering tide, caused Jeffreys to look round the horizon. And then, for the first time, he noticed a bank of fog creeping up from the east and already so near that the beacon on the East Girdler had faded out of sight. He hastened in to start the little motor that compressed the air for the fog-horn and waited awhile to see that the mechanism was running properly. Then, as the deck vibrated to the roar of the horn, he went out once more into the gallery.

The fog was now all round the lighthouse and the boat was hidden from view. He listened intently. The enclosing wall of vapour seemed to have shut out sound as well as vision. At intervals the horn bellowed its note of warning, and then all was still save the murmur of the water among the piles below, and, infinitely faint and far away, the mournful tolling of the bell on the Shivering Sand.

At length there came to his ear the muffled sound of oars working in the tholes; then, at the very edge of the circle of grey water that was visible, the boat appeared through the fog, pale and spectral, with a shadowy figure pulling furiously. The horn emitted a hoarse growl; the man looked round, perceived the lighthouse and altered his course towards it.

Jeffreys descended the iron stairway, and, walking along the lower gallery, stood at the head of the ladder earnestly watching the approaching stranger. Already he was tired of being alone. The yearning for human companionship had been growing ever since Barnett left. But what sort of comrade was this stranger who was coming into his life? And coming to occupy so dominant a place in it. It was a momentous question.

The boat swept down swiftly athwart the hurrying tide. Nearer it came and yet nearer: and still Jeffreys could catch no glimpse of his new comrade's face. At length it came fairly alongside and bumped against the fender-posts; the stranger whisked in an oar and grabbed a rung of the ladder, and Jeffreys dropped a coil of rope into the boat. And still the man's face was hidden.

Jeffreys leaned out over the ladder and watched him anxiously, as he made fast the rope, unhooked the sail from the traveller and unstepped the mast. When he had set all in order, the stranger picked up a small chest, and, swinging it over his shoulder, stepped onto the ladder. Slowly, by reason of his encumbrance, he mounted, rung by rung, with never an upward glance, and Jeffreys gazed down at the top of his head with growing curiosity. At last he reached the top of the ladder and Jeffreys stooped to lend him a hand. Then, for the first time, he looked up, and Jeffreys started back with a blanched face.

"God Almighty!" he gasped. "It's Amos Todd!"

As the newcomer stepped on the gallery, the fog-horn emitted a roar like that of some hungry monster. Jeffreys turned abruptly without a word, and walked to the stairs, followed by Todd, and the two men ascended with never a sound but the hollow clank of their footsteps on the iron plates. Silently Jeffreys stalked into the living-room and, as his companion followed, he turned and motioned to the latter to set down his chest.

"You ain't much of a talker, mate," said Todd, looking round the room in some surprise; "ain't you going to say 'good-morning'? We're going to be good comrades, I hope. I'm Jim Brown, the new hand, I am; what might your name be?"

Jeffreys turned on him suddenly and led him to the window. "Look at me carefully, Amos Todd," he said sternly, "and then ask yourself what my name is."

At the sound of his voice Todd looked up with a start and turned pale as death. "It can't be," he whispered, "it can't be Jeff Rorke!"

The other man laughed harshly, and, leaning forward, said in a low voice: "Hast thou found me, O mine enemy!"

"Don't say that!" exclaimed Todd. "Don't call me your enemy, Jeff. Lord knows but I'm glad to see you, though I'd never have known you without your beard and with that grey hair. I've been to blame, Jeff, and I know it; but it ain't no use raking up old grudges. Let bygones be bygones, Jeff, and let us be pals as we used to be." He wiped his face with his handkerchief and watched his companion apprehensively.

"Sit down," said Rorke, pointing to a shabby, rep-covered arm-chair; "sit down and tell me what you've done with all that money. You've blued it all, I suppose, or you wouldn't be here."

"Robbed, Jeff," answered Todd; "robbed of every penny. Ah! that was an unfortunate affair, that job on board the old *Sea-flower*. But it's over and done with and we'd best forget it. They're all dead but us, Jeff, so we're safe enough so long as we keep our mouths shut; all at the bottom of the sea—and the best place for 'em, too."

"Yes," Rorke replied fiercely, "that's the best place for your ship-mates when they know too much; at the bottom of the sea or swing-ing at the end of a rope." He paced up and down the little room with rapid strides, and each time that he approached Todd's chair the latter shrank back with an expression of alarm.

"Don't sit there staring at me," said Rorke. "Why don't you smoke or do something?"

Todd hastily produced a pipe from his pocket, and having filled it from a moleskin pouch, stuck it in his mouth while he searched for a match. Apparently he carried his matches loose in his pocket, for he presently brought one forth—a red-headed match, which, when he struck it on the wall, lighted with a pale-blue flame. He applied it to his pipe, sucking in his cheeks while he kept his eyes fixed on his companion. Rorke, meanwhile, halted in his walk to cut some shavings from a cake of hard tobacco with a large clasp-knife; and, as he stood, he gazed with frowning abstraction at Todd.

"This pipe's stopped," said the latter, sucking ineffectually at the mouthpiece. "Have you got such a thing as a piece of wire, Jeff?"

"No, I haven't," replied Rorke; "not up here. I'll get a bit from the store presently. Here, take this pipe till you can clean your own: I've got another in the rack there." The sailor's natural hospitality overcoming for the moment his animosity, he thrust the pipe that he had just filled towards Todd, who took it with a mumbled "Thank you" and an anxious eye on the open knife. On the wall beside the chair was a roughly-carved pipe-rack containing several pipes, one of which Rorke lifted out; and, as he leaned over the chair to reach it, Todd's face went several shades paler.

"Well, Jeff," he said, after a pause, while Rorke cut a fresh "fill" of tobacco, "are we going to be pals same as what we used to be?"

Rorke's animosity lighted up afresh. "Am I going to be pals with the man who tried to swear away my life?" he said sternly; and after a pause he added: "That wants thinking about, that does; and meantime I must go and look at the engine."

When Rorke had gone the new hand sat, with the two pipes in his hands, reflecting deeply. Abstractedly he stuck the fresh pipe into his mouth, and, dropping the stopped one into the rack, felt for a match. Still with an air of abstraction he lit the pipe, and, having smoked for a minute or two, rose from the chair and began softly to creep across the room, looking about him and listening intently. At the door he paused to look out into the fog, and then, having again listened attentively, he stepped on tip-toe out onto the gallery and along towards the stairway. Of a sudden the voice of Rorke brought him up with a start.

"Hallo, Todd! where are you off to?"

"I'm just going down to make the boat secure," was the reply.

"Never you mind about the boat," said Rorke. "I'll see to her."

"Right-o, Jeff," said Todd, still edging towards the stairway. "But, I say, mate, where's the other man—the man that I'm to relieve?"

"There ain't any other man," replied Rorke; "he went off aboard a collier."

Todd's face suddenly became grey and haggard. "Then there's no one here but us two!" he gasped; and then, with an effort to conceal his fear, he asked: "But who's going to take the boat back?"

"We'll see about that presently," replied Rorke; "you get along in and unpack your chest."

He came out on the gallery as he spoke, with a lowering frown on his face. Todd cast a terrified glance at him, and then turned and ran for his life towards the stairway.

"Come back!" roared Rorke, springing forward along the gallery; but Todd's feet were already clattering down the iron steps. By the time Rorke reached the head of the stairs, the fugitive was near the bottom; but here, in his haste, he stumbled, barely saving himself by the handrail, and when he recovered his balance Rorke was upon him. Todd darted to the head of the ladder, but, as he grasped the stanchion, his pursuer seized him by the collar. In a moment he had turned with his hand under his coat. There was a quick blow, a loud curse from Rorke, an answering yell from Todd, and a knife fell spinning through the air and dropped into the fore-peak of the boat below.

"You murderous little devil!" said Rorke in an ominously quiet
voice, with his bleeding hand gripping his captive by the throat.
"Handy with your knife as ever, eh? So you were off to give information, were you?"

"No, I wasn't, Jeff," replied Todd in a choking voice; "I wasn't,
s'elp me, God. Let go, Jeff. I didn't mean no harm. I was only——"
With a sudden wrench he freed one hand and struck out frantically
at his captor's face. But Rorke warded off the blow, and, grasping
the other wrist, gave a violent push and let go. Todd staggered
backward a few paces along the staging, bringing up at the extreme
edge; and here, for a sensible time, he stood with wide-open mouth
and staring eye-balls, swaying and clutching wildly at the air. Then,
with a shrill scream, he toppled backwards and fell, striking a pile
in his descent and rebounding into the water.

In spite of the audible thump of his head on the pile, he was not
stunned, for, when he rose to the surface, he struck out vigorously,
uttering short, stifled cries for help. Rorke watched him with set
teeth and quickened breath, but made no move. Smaller and still
smaller grew the head with its little circle of ripples, swept away on
the swift ebb-tide, and fainter the bubbling cries that came across
the smooth water. At length as the small black spot began to fade
in the fog, the drowning man, with a final effort, raised his head
clear of the surface and sent a last, despairing shriek towards the
lighthouse. The fog-horn sent back an answering bellow; the head
sank below the surface and was seen no more; and in the dreadful
stillness that settled down upon the sea there sounded faint and
far away the muffled tolling of a bell.

Rorke stood for some minutes immovable, wrapped in thought.
Presently the distant hoot of a steamer's whistle aroused him. The
ebb-tide shipping was beginning to come down and the fog might
lift at any moment; and there was the boat still alongside. She must
be disposed of at once. No one had seen her arrive and no one
must see her made fast to the lighthouse. Once get rid of the boat
and all traces of Todd's visit would be destroyed.

He ran down the ladder and stepped into the boat. It was perfectly
simple. She was heavily ballasted and would go down like a stone
if she filled.

He shifted some of the bags of shingle, and, lifting the bottom
boards, pulled out the plug. Instantly a large jet of water spouted
up into the bottom. Rorke looked at it critically, and, deciding that

it would fill her in a few minutes, replaced the bottom boards; and having secured the mast and sail with a few turns of the sheet round a thwart, to prevent them from floating away, he cast off the mooring-rope and stepped on the ladder.

As the released boat began to move away on the tide, he ran up and mounted to the upper gallery to watch her disappearance. Suddenly he remembered Todd's chest. It was still in the room below. With a hurried glance around into the fog, he ran down to the room, and snatching up the chest, carried it out on the lower gallery. After another nervous glance around to assure himself that no craft was in sight, he heaved the chest over the handrail, and, when it fell with a loud splash into the sea, he waited to watch it float away after its owner and the sunken boat. But it never rose; and presently he returned to the upper gallery.

The fog was thinning perceptibly now, and the boat remained plainly visible as she drifted away. But she sank more slowly than he had expected, and presently, as she drifted farther away, he fetched the telescope and peered at her with growing anxiety. It would be unfortunate if any one saw her; if she should be picked up here, with her plug out, it would be disastrous.

He was beginning to be really alarmed. Through the glass he could see that the boat was now rolling in a sluggish, water-logged fashion, but she still showed some inches of free-board, and the fog was thinning every moment.

Presently the blast of a steamer's whistle sounded close at hand. He looked round hurriedly, and, seeing nothing, again pointed the telescope eagerly at the dwindling boat. Suddenly he gave a gasp of relief. The boat had rolled gunwale under; had staggered back for a moment and then rolled again, slowly, finally, with the water pouring in over the submerged gunwale.

In a few more seconds she had vanished. Rorke lowered the telescope and took a deep breath. Now he was safe. The boat had sunk unseen. But he was better than safe: he was free. His evil spirit, the standing menace of his life, was gone, and the wide world, the world of life, of action, of pleasure, called to him.

In a few minutes the fog lifted. The sun shone brightly on the red-funnelled cattle-boat whose whistle had startled him just now, the summer blue came back to sky and sea, and the land peeped once more over the edge of the horizon.

He went in, whistling cheerfully, and stopped the motor; returned to coil away the rope that he had thrown to Todd; and, when he had hoisted a signal for assistance, he went in once more to eat his solitary meal in peace and gladness.

PART II—THE SINGING BONE

(*Related by Christopher Jervis, M.D.*)

To every kind of scientific work a certain amount of manual labour naturally appertains, labour that cannot be performed by the scientist himself, since art is long but life is short. A chemical analysis involves a laborious "clean up" of apparatus and laboratory, for which the chemist has no time; the preparation of a skeleton —the maceration, bleaching, "assembling," and riveting together of bones—must be carried out by some one whose time is not too precious. And so with other scientific activities. Behind the man of science with his outfit of knowledge is the indispensable mechanic with his outfit of manual skill.

Thorndyke's laboratory assistant, Polton, was a fine example of the latter type, deft, resourceful, ingenious and untiring. He was somewhat of an inventive genius, too; and it was one of his inventions that connected us with the singular case that I am about to record.

Though by trade a watchmaker, Polton was, by choice, an optician. Optical apparatus was the passion of his life, and when, one day, he produced for our inspection an improved prism for increasing the efficiency of gas-buoys, Thorndyke at once brought the invention to the notice of a friend at the Trinity House.

As a consequence, we three—Thorndyke, Polton and I—found ourselves early on a fine July morning making our way down Middle Temple Lane bound for the Temple Pier. A small oil-launch lay alongside the pontoon, and, as we made our appearance, a red-faced, white-whiskered gentleman stood up in the cockpit.

"Here's a delightful morning, doctor," he sang out in a fine, brassy, resonant, sea-faring voice; "sort of day for a trip to the lower river, hey? Hallo, Polton! Coming down to take the bread out of our mouths, are you? Ha, ha!" The cheery laugh rang out over the river and mingled with the throb of the engine as the little launch moved off from the pier.

Captain Grumpass was one of the Elder Brethren of the Trinity House. Formerly a client of Thorndyke's, he had subsided, as Thorndyke's clients were apt to do, into the position of a personal friend, and his hearty regard included our invaluable assistant.

"Nice state of things," continued the captain, with a chuckle, "when a body of nautical experts have got to be taught their business by a parcel of lawyers or doctors, what? I suppose trade's slack and 'Satan findeth mischief still,' hey, Polton?"

"There isn't much doing on the civil side, sir," replied Polton, with a quaint, crinkly smile, "but the criminals are still going strong."

"Ha! mystery department still flourishing, what? And, by Jove! talking of mysteries, doctor, our people have got a queer problem to work out; something quite in your line—quite. Yes, and, by the Lord Moses, since I've got you here, why shouldn't I suck your brains?"

"Exactly," said Thorndyke. "Why shouldn't you?"

"Well, then, I will," said the captain, "so here goes. All hands to the pump!" He lit a cigar, and, after a few preliminary puffs, began: "The mystery, shortly stated, is this: one of our lighthouse-men has disappeared—vanished off the face of the earth and left no trace. He may have bolted, he may have been drowned accidentally or he may have been murdered. But I'd rather give you the particulars in order. At the end of last week a barge brought into Ramsgate a letter from the screw-pile lighthouse on the Girdler. There are only two men there, and it seems that one of them, a man named Barnett, had broken his leg, and he asked that the tender should be sent to bring him ashore. Well, it happened that the local tender, the *Warden*, was up on the slip in Ramsgate Harbour, having a scrape down, and wouldn't be available for a day or two, so, as the case was urgent, the officer at Ramsgate sent a letter to the lighthouse by one of the pleasure steamers saying that the man should be relieved by boat on the following morning, which was Saturday. He also wrote to a new hand who had just been taken on, a man named James Brown, who was lodging near Reculver, waiting his turn, telling him to go out on Saturday morning in the coast-guard's boat; and he sent a third letter to the coast-guard at Reculver asking him to take Brown out to the lighthouse and bring Barnett ashore. Well, between them, they made a fine muddle of it. The coast-guard couldn't spare either a boat or a man, so they borrowed a fisher-man's boat, and in this the man Brown started off alone, like an idiot, on the chance that Barnett would be able to sail the boat back in spite of his broken leg.

"Meanwhile Barnett, who is a Whitstable man, had signalled a collier bound for his native town, and got taken off; so that the other keeper, Thomas Jeffreys, was left alone until Brown should turn up.

"But Brown never did turn up. The coast-guard helped him to put off and saw him well out to sea, and the keeper, Jeffreys, saw a sailing-boat with one man in her making for the lighthouse. Then a bank of fog came up and hid the boat, and when the fog cleared she was nowhere to be seen. Man and boat had vanished and left no sign."

"He may have been run down in the fog," Thorndyke suggested.

"He may," agreed the captain, "but no accident has been reported. The coast-guards think he may have capsized in a squall—they saw him make the sheet fast. But there weren't any squalls: the weather was quite calm."

"Was he all right and well when he put off?" inquired Thorndyke.

"Yes," replied the captain, "the coast-guards' report is highly circumstantial; in fact, it's full of silly details that have no bearing on anything. This is what they say." He pulled out an official letter and read: " 'When last seen, the missing man was seated in the boat's stern to windward of the helm. He had belayed the sheet. He was holding a pipe and tobacco-pouch in his hands and steering with his elbow. He was filling the pipe from the tobacco-pouch.' There! 'He was holding the pipe in his hand,' mark you! not with his toes; and he was filling it from a tobacco-pouch, whereas you'd have expected him to fill it from a coal-scuttle or a feeding-bottle. Bah!" The captain rammed the letter back in his pocket and puffed scornfully at his cigar.

"You are hardly fair to the coast-guard," said Thorndyke, laughing at the captain's vehemence. "The duty of a witness is to give *all* the facts, not a judicious selection."

"But, my dear sir," said Captain Grumpass, "what the deuce can it matter what the poor devil filled his pipe from?"

"Who can say?" answered Thorndyke. "It may turn out to be a highly material fact. One never knows before-hand. The value of a particular fact depends on its relation to the rest of the evidence."

"I suppose it does," grunted the captain; and he continued to smoke in reflective silence until we opened Blackwall Point, when he suddenly stood up.

"There's a steam trawler alongside our wharf," he announced. "Now what the deuce can she be doing there?" He scanned the little steamer attentively, and continued; "They seem to be landing something, too. Just pass me those glasses, Polton. Why, hang me! it's a dead body! But why on earth are they landing it on our wharf? They must have known you were coming, doctor."

As the launch swept alongside the wharf, the captain sprang up lightly and approached the group gathered round the body. "What's this?" he asked. "Why have they brought this thing here?"

The master of the trawler, who had superintended the landing, proceeded to explain.

"It's one of your men, sir," said he. "We saw the body lying on the edge of the South Shingles Sand, close to the beacon, as we passed at low water, so we put off the boat and fetched it aboard. As there was nothing to identify the man by, I had a look in his pocket and found this letter." He handed the captain an official envelope addressed to "Mr. J. Brown, c/o Mr. Solly, Shepherd, Reculver, Kent."

"Why, this is the man we were speaking about, doctor," exclaimed Captain Grumpass. "What a very singular coincidence. But what are we to do with the body?"

"You will have to write to the coroner," replied Thorndyke. "By the way, did you turn out all the pockets?" he asked, turning to the skipper of the trawler.

"No, sir," was the reply. "I found the letter in the first pocket that I felt in, so I didn't examine any of the others. Is there anything more that you want to know, sir?"

"Nothing but your name and address, for the coroner," replied Thorndyke, and the skipper, having given this information and expressed the hope that the coroner would not keep him "hanging about," returned to his vessel and pursued his way to Billingsgate.

"I wonder if you would mind having a look at the body of this poor devil, while Polton is showing us his contraptions," said Captain Grumpass.

"I can't do much without a coroner's order," replied Thorndyke; "but if it will give you any satisfaction, Jervis and I will make a preliminary inspection with pleasure."

"I should be glad if you would," said the captain. "We should like to know that the poor begger met his end fairly."

The body was accordingly moved to a shed, and, as Polton was led away, carrying the black bag that contained his precious model, we entered the shed and commenced our investigation.

The deceased was a small, elderly man, decently dressed in a somewhat nautical fashion. He appeared to have been dead only two or three days, and the body, unlike the majority of sea-borne corpses, was uninjured by fish or crabs. There were no fractured bones or other gross injuries, and no wounds, excepting a rugged tear in the scalp at the back of the head.

"The general appearance of the body," said Thorndyke, when he had noted these particulars, "suggests death by drowning, though, of course, we can't give a definite opinion until a *post mortem* has been made."

"You don't attach any significance to that scalp-wound, then?" I asked.

"As a cause of death? No. It was obviously inflicted during life, but it seems to have been an oblique blow that spent its force on the scalp, leaving the skull uninjured. But it is very significant in another way."

"In what way?" I asked.

Thorndyke took out his pocket-case and extracted a pair of forceps. "Consider the circumstances," said he. "This man put off from the shore to go to the lighthouse, but never arrived there. The question is, where did he arrive?" As he spoke he stooped over the corpse and turned back the hair round the wound with the beak of the forceps. "Look at those white objects among the hair, Jervis, and inside the wound. They tell us something, I think."

I examined, through my lens, the chalky fragments to which he pointed. "These seem to be bits of shells and the tubes of some marine worms," I said.

"Yes," he answered; "the broken shells are evidently those of the acorn barnacle, and the other fragments are mostly pieces of the tubes of the common serpula. The inference that these objects suggest is an important one. It is that this wound was produced by some body encrusted by acorn barnacles and serpulae; that is to say, by a body that is periodically submerged. Now, what can that body be, and how can the deceased have knocked his head against it?"

"It might be the stem of a ship that ran him down," I suggested.

"I don't think you would find many serpulae on the stem of a ship," said Thorndyke. "The combination rather suggests some stationary object between tide-marks, such as a beacon. But one doesn't see how a man could knock his head against a beacon, while, on the other hand, there are no other stationary objects out in the estuary to knock against except buoys, and a buoy presents a flat surface that could hardly have produced this wound. By the way, we may as well see what there is in his pockets, though it is not likely that robbery had anything to do with his death."

"No," I agreed, "and I see his watch is in his pocket; quite a good silver one," I added, taking it out. "It has stopped at 12.13."

"That may be important," said Thorndyke, making a note of the fact, "but we had better examine the pockets one at a time, and put the things back when we have looked at them."

The first pocket that we turned out was the left hip-pocket of the monkey jacket. This was apparently the one that the skipper had rifled, for we found in it two letters, both bearing the crest of the Trinity House. These, of course, we returned without reading, and then passed on to the right pocket. The contents of this were common-place enough, consisting of a briar pipe, a moleskin pouch and a number of loose matches.

"Rather a casual proceeding, this," I remarked, "to carry matches loose in the pocket, and a pipe with them, too."

"Yes," agreed Thorndyke; "especially with these very inflammable matches. You notice that the sticks had been coated at the upper end with sulphur before the red phosphorus heads were put on. They would light with a touch, and would be very difficult to extinguish; which, no doubt, is the reason that this type of match is so popular among seamen, who have to light their pipes in all sorts of weather." As he spoke he picked up the pipe and looked at it reflectively, turning it over in his hand and peering into the bowl. Suddenly he glanced from the pipe to the dead man's face and then, with the forceps, turned back the lips to look into the mouth.

"Let us see what tobacco he smokes," said he.

I opened the sodden pouch and displayed a mass of dark, fine-cut tobacco. "It looks like shag," I said.

"Yes, it is shag," he replied; "and now we will see what is in the pipe. "It has been only half-smoked out." He dug out the "dottle" with his pocket-knife onto a sheet of paper, and we both inspected it. Clearly it was not shag, for it consisted of coarsely-cut shreds and was nearly black.

"Shavings from a cake of 'hard,' " was my verdict, and Thorndyke agreed as he shot the fragments back into the pipe.

The other pockets yielded nothing of interest, except a pocket-knife, which Thorndyke opened and examined closely. There was not much money, though as much as one would expect, and enough to exclude the idea of robbery.

"Is there a sheath-knife on that strap?" Thorndyke asked, pointing to a narrow leather belt. I turned back the jacket and looked.

"There is a sheath," I said, "but no knife. It must have dropped out."

"That is rather odd," said Thorndyke. "A sailor's sheath-knife takes a deal of shaking out as a rule. It is intended to be used in working on the rigging when the man is aloft, so that he can get it out with one hand while he is holding on with the other. It has to be and usually is very secure, for the sheath holds half the handle as well as the blade. What makes one notice the matter in this case is that the man, as you see, carried a pocket-knife; and, as this would serve all the ordinary purposes of a knife, it seems to suggest that the sheath-knife was carried for defensive purposes: as a weapon, in fact. However, we can't get much further in the case without a *post mortem*, and here comes the captain."

Captain Grumpass entered the shed and looked down commiseratingly at the dead seaman.

"Is there anything, doctor, that throws any light on the man's disappearance?" he asked.

"There are one or two curious features in the case," Thorndyke replied; "but, oddly enough, the only really important point arises out of that statement of the coast-guard's, concerning which you were so scornful."

"You don't say so!" exclaimed the captain.

"Yes," said Thorndyke; "the coast-guard states that when last seen deceased was filling his pipe from his tobacco-pouch. Now his pouch contains shag; but the pipe in his pocket contains hard cut."

"Is there no cake tobacco in any of the pockets?"

"Not a fragment. Of course, it is possible that he might have had a piece and used it up to fill the pipe; but there is no trace of any on the blade of his pocket-knife, and you know how this juicy black cake stains a knife-blade. His sheath-knife is missing, but he would hardly have used that to shred tobacco when he had a pocket-knife."

"No," assented the captain; "but are you sure he hadn't a second pipe?"

"There was only one pipe," replied Thorndyke, "and that was not his own."

"Not his own!" exclaimed the captain, halting by a huge, chequered buoy to stare at my colleague. "How do you know it was not his own?"

"By the appearance of the vulcanite mouthpiece," said Thorndyke. "It showed deep tooth-marks; in fact, it was nearly bitten through. Now a man who bites through his pipe usually presents certain definite physical peculiarities, among which is, necessarily, a fairly good set of teeth. But the dead man had not a tooth in his head."

The captain cogitated a while, and then remarked: "I don't quite see the bearing of this."

"Don't you?" said Thorndyke. "It seems to me highly suggestive. Here is a man who, when last seen, was filling his pipe with a particular kind of tobacco. He is picked up dead, and his pipe contains a totally different kind of tobacco. Where did that tobacco come from? The obvious suggestion is that he had met some one."

"Yes, it does look like it," agreed the captain.

"Then," continued Thorndyke, "there is the fact that his sheath-knife is missing. That may mean nothing, but we have to bear it in mind. And there is another curious circumstance: there is a wound on the back of the head caused by a heavy bump against some body that was covered with acorn barnacles and marine worms. Now there are no piers or stages out in the open estuary. The question is, what could he have struck?"

"Oh, there is nothing in that," said the captain. "When a body has been washing about in a tide-way for close on three days——"

"But this is not a question of a body," Thorndyke interrupted. "The wound was made during life."

"The deuce it was!" exclaimed the captain. "Well, all I can suggest is that he must have fouled one of the beacons in the fog, stove in his boat and bumped his head, though, I must admit, that's rather a lame explanation." He stood for a minute gazing at his toes with a cogitative frown and then looked up at Thorndyke.

"I have an idea," he said. "From what you say, this matter wants looking into pretty carefully. Now, I am going down on the tender to-day to make inquiries on the spot. What do you say to coming with me as adviser—as a matter of business, of course—you and Dr. Jervis? I shall start about eleven; we shall be at the lighthouse by three o'clock, and you can get back to town to-night, if you want to. What do you say?"

"There's nothing to hinder us," I put in eagerly, for even at

Bugsby's Hole the river looked very alluring on this summer morning.

"Very well," said Thorndyke, "we will come. Jervis is evidently hankering for a sea-trip, and so am I, for that matter."

"It's a business engagement, you know," the captain stipulated.

"Nothing of the kind," said Thorndyke; "it's unmitigated pleasure; the pleasure of the voyage and your high well-born society."

"I didn't mean that," grumbled the captain, "but, if you are coming as guests, send your man for your night-gear and let us bring you back to-morrow evening."

"We won't disturb Polton," said my colleague; "we can take the train from Blackwall and fetch our things ourselves. Eleven o'clock, you said?"

"Thereabouts," said Captain Grumpass; "but don't put yourselves out."

The means of communication in London have reached an almost undesirable state of perfection. With the aid of the snorting train and the tinkling, two-wheeled "gondola," we crossed and re-crossed the town with such celerity that it was barely eleven when we re-appeared on Trinity Wharf with a joint Gladstone and Thorndyke's little green case.

The tender had hauled out of Bow Creek, and now lay alongside the wharf with a great striped can buoy dangling from her derrick, and Captain Grumpass stood at the gangway, his jolly, red face beaming with pleasure. The buoy was safely stowed forward, the derrick hauled up to the mast, the loose shrouds rehooked to the screw-lanyards, and the steamer, with four jubilant hoots, swung round and shoved her sharp nose against the incoming tide.

For near upon four hours the ever-widening stream of the "London River" unfolded its moving panorama. The smoke and smell of Woolwich Reach gave place to lucid air made soft by the summer haze; the grey huddle of factories fell away and green levels of cattle-spotted marsh stretched away to the high land bordering the river valley. Venerable training ships displayed their chequered hulls by the wooden shore, and whispered of the days of oak and hemp, when the tall three-decker, comely and majestic, with her soaring heights of canvas, like towers of ivory, had not yet given place to the mud-coloured saucepans that fly the white ensign now-a-days and devour the substance of the British taxpaper: when a sailor was a sailor and not a mere seafaring mechanic. Sturdily breasting the flood tide, the tender threaded her way through the endless procession of shipping; barges, billy-boys, schooners, brigs; lumpish Black-seamen, blue-funnelled China tramps, rickety Baltic barques with twirling windmills, gigantic liners, staggering under a mountain of top-hamper. Erith, Purfleet, Greenhithe, Grays greeted us and passed astern. The chimneys of Northfleet, the clustering roofs of Gravesend, the populous anchorage and the lurking batteries, were left behind, and, as we swung out of the Lower Hope, the wide expanse of sea reach spread out before us like a great sheet of blue-shot satin.

About half-past twelve the ebb overtook us and helped us on our way, as we could see by the speed with which the distant land slid past, and the freshening of the air as we passed through it.

But sky and sea were hushed in a summer calm. Balls of fleecy cloud hung aloft, motionless in the soft blue; the barges drifted on the tide with drooping sails, and a big, striped bell buoy—surmounted by a staff and cage and labelled "Shivering Sand"—sat dreaming in the sun above its motionless reflection, to rouse for a moment as it met our wash, nod its cage drowsily, utter a solemn ding-dong, and fall asleep again.

It was shortly after passing the buoy that the gaunt shape of a screw-pile lighthouse began to loom up ahead, its dull-red paint turned to vermillion by the early afternoon sun. As we drew nearer, the name *Girdler*, painted in huge, white letters, became visible, and two men could be seen in the gallery around the lantern, inspecting us through a telescope.

"Shall you be long at the lighthouse, sir?" the master of the tender inquired of Captain Grumpass; "because we're going down to the North-East Pan Sand to fix this new buoy and take up the old one."

"Then you'd better put us off at the lighthouse and come back for us when you've finished the job," was the reply. "I don't know how long we shall be."

The tender was brought to, a boat lowered, and a couple of hands pulled us across the intervening space of water.

"It will be a dirty climb for you in your shore-going clothes," the captain remarked—he was as spruce as a new pin himself, "but the stuff will all wipe off." We looked up at the skeleton shape. The falling tide had exposed some fifteen feet of the piles, and piles and ladder alike were swathed in sea-grass and encrusted with barnacles and worm-tubes. But we were not such town-sparrows as the captain seemed to think, for we both followed his lead without difficulty up the slippery ladder, Thorndyke clinging tenaciously to his little green case, from which he refused to be separated even for an instant.

"These gentlemen and I," said the captain, as we stepped on the stage at the head of the ladder, "have come to make inquiries about the missing man, James Brown. Which of you is Jeffreys?"

"I am, sir," replied a tall, powerful, square-jawed, beetle-browed man, whose left hand was tied up in a rough bandage.

"What have you been doing to your hand?" asked the captain.

"I cut it while I was peeling some potatoes," was the reply. "It isn't much of a cut, sir."

"Well, Jeffreys," said the captain. "Brown's body has been picked up and I want particulars for the inquest. You'll be summoned as a witness, I suppose, so come in and tell us all you know."

We entered the living-room and seated ourselves at the table. The captain opened a massive pocket-book, while Thorndyke, in his attentive, inquisitive fashion, looked about the odd, cabin-like room as if making a mental inventory of its contents.

Jeffreys' statement added nothing to what we already knew. He had seen a boat with one man in it making for the lighthouse. Then the fog had drifted up and he had lost sight of the boat. He started the fog-horn and kept a bright look-out, but the boat never arrived. And that was all he knew. He supposed that the man must have missed the lighthouse and been carried away on the ebb-tide, which was running strongly at the time.

"What time was it when you last saw the boat?" Thorndyke asked.

"About half-past eleven," replied Jeffreys.

"What was the man like?" asked the captain.

"I don't know, sir; he was rowing, and his back was towards me."

"Had he any kit-bag or chest with him?" asked Thorndyke.

"He'd got his chest with him," said Jeffreys.

"What sort of chest was it?" inquired Thorndyke.

"A small chest, painted green, with rope beckets."

"Was it corded?"

"It had a single cord round, to hold the lid down."

"Where was it stowed?"

"In the stern-sheets, sir."

"How far off was the boat when you last saw it?"

"About half-a-mile."

"Half-a-mile!" exclaimed the captain. "Why, how the deuce could you see what the chest was like half-a-mile away?"

The man reddened and cast a look of angry suspicion at Thorndyke. "I was watching the boat through the glass, sir," he replied sulkily.

"I see," said Captain Grumpass. "Well, that will do, Jeffreys. We shall have to arrange for you to attend the inquest. Tell Smith I want to see him."

The examination concluded, Thorndyke and I moved our chairs to the window, which looked out over the sea to the east. But it was not the sea or the passing ships that engaged my colleague's attention. On the wall, beside the window, hung a rudely-carved pipe-rack containing five pipes. Thorndyke had noted it when we entered the room, and now, as we talked, I observed him regarding it from time to time with speculative interest.

"You men seem to be inveterate smokers," he remarked to the keeper, Smith, when the captain had concluded the arrangements for the "shift."

"Well, we do like our bit of 'baccy, sir, and that's a fact," answered Smith. "You see, sir," he continued, "it's a lonely life, and tobacco's cheap out here."

"How is that?" asked Thorndyke.

"Why, we get it given to us. The small craft from foreign parts, especially the Dutchmen, generally heave us a cake or two when they pass close. We're not ashore, you see, so there's no duty to pay."

"So you don't trouble the tobacconists much? Don't go in for cut tobacco?"

"No, sir; we'd have to buy it, and then the cut stuff wouldn't keep. No, it's hard-tack to eat out here and hard tobacco to smoke."

"I see you've got a pipe-rack, too, quite a stylish affair."

"Yes," said Smith, "I made it in my off-time. Keeps the place tidy and looks more ship-shape than letting the pipes lay about anywhere."

"Some one seems to have neglected his pipe," said Thorndyke, pointing to one at the end of the rack which was coated with green mildew.

"Yes; that's Parsons, my mate. He must have left it when he went off near a month ago. Pipes do go mouldy in the damp air out here."

"How soon does a pipe go mouldy if it is left untouched?" Thorndyke asked.

"It's according to the weather," said Smith. "When it's warm and damp they'll begin to go in about a week. Now here's Barnett's pipe that he's left behind—the man that broke his leg, you know, sir—it's just beginning to spot a little. He couldn't have used it for a day or two before he went."

"And are all these other pipes yours?"

"No, sir. This here one is mine. The end one is Jeffreys', and I suppose the middle one is his too, but I don't know it."

"You're a demon for pipes, doctor," said the captain, strolling up at this moment; "you seem to make a special study of them."

" 'The proper study of mankind is man,' " replied Thorndyke, as the keeper retired, "and 'man' includes those objects on which his personality is impressed. Now a pipe is a very personal thing. Look at that row in the rack. Each has its own physiognomy which, in a measure, reflects the peculiarities of the owner. There is Jeffreys' pipe at the end, for instance. The mouth-piece is nearly bitten through, the bowl scraped to a shell and scored inside and the brim battered and chipped. The whole thing speaks of rude strength and rough handling. He chews the stem as he smokes, he scrapes the bowl violently, and he bangs the ashes out with unnecessary force. And the man fits the pipe exactly: powerful, square-jawed and, I should say, violent on occasion."

"Yes, he looks a tough customer, does Jeffreys," agreed the captain.

"Then," continued Thorndyke, "there is Smith's pipe, next to it; 'coked' up until the cavity is nearly filled and burnt all round the edge; a talker's pipe, constantly going out and being relit. But the one that interests me most is the middle one."

"Didn't Smith say that was Jeffreys' too?" I said.

"Yes," replied Thorndyke, "but he must be mistaken. It is the very opposite of Jeffreys' pipe in every respect. To begin with, although it is an old pipe, there is not a sign of any tooth-mark on the mouth-piece. It is the only one in the rack that is quite unmarked. Then the brim is quite uninjured: it has been handled gently, and the silver band is jet-black, whereas the band on Jeffreys' pipe is quite bright."

"I hadn't noticed that it had a band," said the captain. "What has made it so black?"

Thorndyke lifted the pipe out of the rack and looked at it closely. "Silver sulphide," said he, "the sulphur no doubt derived from something carried in the pocket."

"I see," said Captain Grumpass, smothering a yawn and gazing out of the window at the distant tender. "Incidentally it's full of tobacco. What moral do you draw from that?"

Thorndyke turned the pipe over and looked closely at the mouth-piece. "The moral is," he replied, "that you should see that your pipe is clear before you fill it." He pointed to the mouth-piece, the bore of which was completely stopped up with fine fluff.

"An excellent moral too," said the captain, rising with another yawn. "If you'll excuse me a minute, I'll just go and see what the tender is up to. She seems to be crossing to the East Girdler." He reached the telescope down from its brackets and went out onto the gallery.

As the captain retreated, Thorndyke opened his pocket-knife, and, sticking the blade into the bowl of the pipe, turned the tobacco out into his hand.

"Shag, by Jove!" I exclaimed.

"Yes," he answered, poking it back into the bowl. "Didn't you expect it to be shag?"

"I don't know that I expected anything," I admitted. "The silver band was occupying my attention."

"Yes, that is an interesting point," said Thorndyke, "but let us see what the obstruction consists of." He opened the green case, and, taking out a dissecting needle, neatly extracted a little ball of fluff from the bore of the pipe. Laying this on a glass slide, he teased it out in a drop of glycerine and put on a cover-glass while I set up the microscope.

"Better put the pipe back in the rack," he said, as he laid the slide on the stage of the instrument. I did so and then turned, with no little excitement, to watch him as he examined the specimen. After a brief inspection he rose and waved his hand towards the microscope.

"Take a look at it Jervis," he said, "and let us have your learned opinion."

I applied my eye to the instrument, and, moving the slide about, identified the constituents of the little mass of fluff. The ubiquitous cotton fibre was, of course, in evidence, and a few fibres of wool, but the most remarkable objects were two or three hairs—very minute hairs of a definite zigzag shape and having a flat expansion near the free end like the blade of a paddle.

"These are the hairs of some small animal," I said; "not a mouse or rat or any rodent, I should say. Some small insectivorous animal, I fancy. Yes! Of course! They are the hairs of a mole." I stood up, and, as the importance of the discovery flashed on me, I looked at my colleague in silence.

"Yes," he said, "they are unmistakable; and they furnish the keystone of the argument."

"You think that this is really the dead man's pipe, then?" I said.

"According to the law of multiple evidence," he replied. "it is practically a certainty. Consider the facts in sequence. Since there is no sign of mildew on it, this pipe can have been here only a short time, and must belong either to Barnett, Smith, Jeffreys or Brown. It is an old pipe, but it has no tooth-marks on it. Therefore it has been used by a man who has no teeth. But Barnett, Smith and Jeffreys all had teeth and mark their pipes, whereas Brown had no teeth. The tobacco in it is shag. But these three men do not smoke shag, whereas Brown had shag in his pouch. The silver band is encrusted with sulphide; and Brown carried sulphur-tipped matches loose in his pocket with his pipe. We find hairs of a mole in the bore of the pipe; and Brown carried a moleskin pouch in the pocket in which he appears to have carried his pipe. Finally, Brown's pocket contained a pipe which was obviously not his and which closely resembled that of Jeffreys; it contained tobacco similar to that which Jeffreys smokes and different from that in Brown's pouch. It appears to me quite conclusive, especially when we add to this evidence the other items that are in our possession."

"What items are they?" I asked.

"First there is the fact that the dead man had knocked his head heavily against some periodically submerged body covered with acorn barnacles and serpulæ. Now the piles of this lighthouse answer to the description exactly, and there are no other bodies in the neighbourhood that do: for even the beacons are too large to have produced that kind of wound. Then the dead man's sheath-knife is missing, and Jeffreys has a knife-wound on his hand. You must admit that the circumstantial evidence is overwhelming."

At this moment the captain bustled into the room with the telescope in his hand. "The tender is coming up towing a strange boat," he said. "I expect it's the missing one, and, if it is, we may learn something. You'd better pack up your traps and get ready to go on board."

We packed the green case and went out into the gallery, where the two keepers were watching the approaching tender; Smith frankly curious and interested, Jeffreys restless, fidgety and noticeably pale. As the steamer came opposite the lighthouse, three men dropped into the boat and pulled across, and one of them—the mate of the tender—came climbing up the ladder.

"Is that the missing boat?" the captain sang out.

"Yes, sir," answered the officer, stepping onto the staging and wiping his hands on the reverse aspect of his trousers, "we saw her lying on the dry patch of the East Girdler. There's been some hanky-panky in this job, sir."

"Foul play, you think, hey?"

"Not a doubt of it, sir. The plug was out and lying loose in the bottom, and we found a sheath-knife sticking into the kelson forward among the coils of the painter. It was stuck in hard as if it had dropped from a height."

"That's odd," said the captain. "As to the plug, it might have got out by accident."

"But it hadn't, sir," said the mate. "The ballast-bags had been shifted along to get the bottom boards up. Besides, sir, a seaman wouldn't let the boat fill; he'd have put the plug back and baled out."

"That's true," replied Captain Grumpass; "and certainly the presence of the knife looks fishy. But where the deuce could it have dropped from, out in the open sea? Knives don't drop from the clouds—fortunately. What do you say, doctor?"

"I should say that it is Brown's own knife, and that it probably fell from this staging."

Jeffreys turned swiftly, crimson with wrath. "What d'ye mean?" he demanded. "Haven't I said that the boat never came here?"

"You have," replied Thorndyke; "but if that is so, how do you explain the fact that your pipe was found in the dead man's pocket and that the dead man's pipe is at this moment in your pipe-rack?"

The crimson flush on Jeffreys' face faded as quickly as it had come. "I don't know what you're talking about," he faltered.

"I'll tell you," said Thorndyke. "I will relate what happened and you shall check my statements. Brown brought his boat alongside and came up into the living-room, bringing his chest with him. He filled his pipe and tried to light it, but it was stopped and wouldn't draw. Then you lent him a pipe of yours and filled it for him. Soon afterwards you came out on this staging and quarrelled. Brown defended himself with his knife, which dropped from his hand into the boat. You pushed him off the staging and he fell, knocking his head on one of the piles. Then you took the plug out of the boat and sent her adrift to sink, and you flung the chest into the sea. This happened about ten minutes past twelve. Am I right?"

Jeffreys stood staring at Thorndyke, the picture of amazement and consternation; but he uttered no word in reply.

"Am I right?" Thorndyke repeated.

"Strike me blind!" muttered Jeffreys. "Was you here, then? You talk as if you had been. Anyhow," he continued, recovering somewhat, "you seem to know all about it. But you're wrong about one thing. There was no quarrel. This chap, Brown, didn't take to me and he didn't mean to stay out here. He was going to put off and go ashore again and I wouldn't let him. Then he hit out at me with his knife and I knocked it out of his hand and he staggered backwards and went overboard."

"And did you try to pick him up?" asked the captain.

"How could I," demanded Jeffreys, "with the tide racing down and me alone on the station? I'd never have got back."

"But what about the boat, Jeffreys? Why did you scuttle her?"

"The fact is," replied Jeffreys, "I got in a funk, and I thought the simplest plan was to send her to the cellar and know nothing about it. But I never shoved him over. It was an accident, sir; I swear it!"

"Well, that sounds a reasonable explanation," said the captain. "What do you say, doctor?"

"Perfectly reasonable," replied Thorndyke, "and, as to its truth, that is no affair of ours."

"No. But I shall have to take you off, Jeffreys, and hand you over to the police. You understand that?"

"Yes, sir, I understand," answered Jeffreys.

"That was a queer case, that affair on the Girdler," remarked Captain Grumpass, when he was spending an evening with us some six months later. "A pretty easy let off for Jeffreys, too—eighteen months, wasn't it?"

"Yes, it was a very queer case indeed," said Thorndyke. "There was something behind that 'accident,' I should say. Those men had probably met before "

"So I thought," agreed the captain. "But the queerest part of it to me was the way you nosed it all out. I've had a deep respect for briar pipes since then. It was a remarkable case," he continued. "The way in which you made that pipe tell the story of the murder seems to me like sheer enchantment."

"Yes," said I; "it spoke like the magic pipe—only that wasn't a tobacco-pipe—in the German folk-story of the 'Singing Bone.' Do you remember it? A peasant found the bone of a murdered man and fashioned it into a pipe. But when he tried to play on it, it burst into a song of its own—

'My brother slew me and buried my bones
Beneath the sand and under the stones.' "

"A pretty story," said Thorndyke. "and one with an excellent moral. The inanimate things around us have each of them a song to sing to us if we are but ready with attentive ears."

The Mandarin's Pearl

Mr. Brodribb stretched out his toes on the curb before the blazing fire with the air of a man who is by no means insensible to physical comfort.

"You are really an extraordinarily polite fellow, Thorndyke," said he.

He was an elderly man, rosy-gilled, portly, and convivial, to whom a mass of bushy, white hair, an expansive double chin, and a certain prim sumptuousness of dress imparted an air of old-world distinction. Indeed, as he dipped an amethystine nose into his wine-glass, and gazed thoughtfully at the glowing end of his cigar, he looked the very type of the well-to-do lawyer of an older generation.

"You are really an extraordinarily polite fellow, Thorndyke," said Mr. Brodribb.

"I know," replied Thorndyke. "But why this reference to an admitted fact?"

"The truth has just dawned on me," said the solicitor. "Here am I, dropping in on you, uninvited and unannounced, sitting in your own armchair before your fire, smoking your cigars, drinking your Burgundy—and deuced good Burgundy, too, let me add—and you have not dropped a single hint of curiosity as to what has brought me here."

"I take the gifts of the gods, you see, and ask no questions," said Thorndyke.

"Devilish handsome of you, Thorndyke—unsociable beggar like you, too," rejoined Mr. Brodribb, a fan of wrinkles spreading out genially from the corners of his eyes; "but the fact is I have come, in a sense, on business—always glad of a pretext to look you up, as you know—but I want to take your opinion on a rather queer case. It is about young Calverley. You remember Horace Calverley? Well, this is his son. Horace and I were schoolmates, you know, and after his death the boy, Fred, hung on to me rather. We're near neighbors down at Weybridge, and very good friends. I like Fred. He's a good fellow, though cranky, like all his people."

"What has happened to Fred Calverley?" Thorndyke asked, as the solicitor paused.

"Why, the fact is," said Mr. Brodribb, "just lately he seems to be going a bit queer—not mad, mind you—at least, I think not—but undoubtedly queer. Now, there is a good deal of property, and a good many highly interested relatives, and, as a natural consequence, there is some talk of getting him certified. They're afraid he may do something involving the estate or develop homicidal tendencies, and they talk of possible suicide—you remember his father's death— but I say that's all bunkum. The fellow is just a bit cranky, and nothing more."

"What are his symptoms?" asked Thorndyke.

"Oh, he thinks he is being followed about and watched, and he has delusions; sees himself in the glass with the wrong face, and that sort of thing, you know."

"You are not highly circumstantial," Thorndyke remarked.

Mr. Brodribb looked at me with a genial smile.

"What a glutton for facts this fellow is, Jervis. But you're right, Thorndyke; I'm vague. However, Fred will be here presently. We travelled down together, and I took the liberty of asking him to call for me. We'll get him to tell you about his delusions, if you don't mind. He's not shy about them. And meanwhile I'll give you a few preliminary facts. The trouble began about a year ago. He was in a railway accident, and that knocked him all to pieces. Then he went for a voyage to recruit, and the ship broke her propeller-shaft in a storm and became helpless. That didn't improve the state of his nerves. Then he went down the Mediterranean, and after a month or two, back he came, no better than when he started. But here he is, I expect."

He went over to the door and admitted a tall, frail young man whom Thorndyke welcomed with quiet geniality, and settled in a chair by the fire. I looked curiously at our visitor. He was a typical neurotic—slender, fragile, eager. Wide-open blue eyes with broad pupils, in which I could plainly see the characteristic "hippus"— that incessant change of size that marks the unstable nervous equilibrium—parted lips, and wandering taper fingers, were as the stigmata of his disorder. He was of the stuff out of which prophets and devotees, martyrs, reformers, and third-rate poets are made.

"I have been telling Dr. Thorndyke about these nervous troubles of yours," said Mr. Brodribb presently. "I hope you don't mind. He is an old friend, you know, and he is very much interested."

"It is very good of him," said Calverley. Then he flushed deeply, and added: "But they are not really nervous, you know. They can't be merely subjective."

"You think they can't be?" said Thorndyke.

"No, I am sure they are not." He flushed again like a girl, and looked earnestly at Thorndyke with his big, dreamy eyes. "But you doctors," he said, "are so dreadfully sceptical of all spiritual phenomena. You are such materialists."

"Yes," said Mr. Brodribb; "the doctors are not hot on the supernatural, and that's the fact."

"Supposing you tell us about your experiences," said Thorndyke persuasively. "Give us a chance to believe, if we can't explain away."

Calverley reflected for a few moments; then, looking earnestly at Thorndyke, he said:

"Very well; if it won't bore you, I will. It is a curious story."

"I have told Dr. Thorndyke about your voyage and your trip down the Mediterranean," said Mr. Brodribb.

"Then," said Calverley, "I will begin with the events that are actually connected with these strange visitations. The first of these occurred in Marseilles. I was in a curio-shop there, looking over some Algerian and Moorish things, when my attention was attracted by a sort of charm or pendant that hung in a glass case. It was not particularly beautiful, but its appearance was quaint and curious, and took my fancy. It consisted of an oblong block of ebony in which was set a single pear-shaped pearl more than three-quarters of an inch long. The sides of the ebony block were lacquered— probably to conceal a joint—and bore a number of Chinese characters, and at the top was a little gold image with a hole through it, presumably for a string to suspend it by. Excepting for the pearl, the whole thing was uncommonly like one of those ornamental tablets of Chinese ink.

"Now, I had taken a fancy to the thing, and I can afford to indulge my fancies in moderation. The man wanted five pounds for it; he assured me that the pearl was a genuine one of fine quality, and obviously did not believe it himself. To me, however, it looked like a real pearl, and I determined to take the risk; so I paid the money, and he bowed me out with a smile—I may almost say a grin—of satisfaction. He would not have been so well pleased if he had followed me to a jeweller's to whom I took it for an expert opinion; for the jeweller pronounced the pearl to be undoubtedly genuine, and worth anything up to a thousand pounds.

"A day to two later, I happened to show my new purchase to some men whom I knew, who had dropped in at Marseilles in their yacht. They were highly amused at my having bought the thing, and when I told them what I had paid for it, they positively howled with derision.

" 'Why, you silly guffin,' said one of them, a man named Halliwell, 'I could have had it ten days ago for half a sovereign, or probably five shillings. I wish now I had bought it; then I could have sold it to you.'

"It seemed that a sailor had been hawking the pendant round the harbor, and had been on board the yacht with it.

" 'Deuced anxious the beggar was to get rid of it, too,' said Halliwell, grinning at the recollection. 'Swore it was a genuine pearl of priceless value, and was willing to deprive himself of it for the trifling sum of half a jimmy. But we'd heard that sort of thing before. However, the curio-man seems to have speculated on the chance of meeting with a greenhorn, and he seems to have pulled it off. Lucky curio-man! '

"I listened patiently to their gibes, and when they had talked themselves out I told them about the jeweller. They were most frightfully sick; and when we had taken the pendant to a dealer in gems who happened to be staying in the town, and he had offered me five hundred pounds for it, their language wasn't fit for a divinity students' debating club. Naturally the story got noised abroad, and when I left, it was the talk of the place. The general opinion was that the sailor, who was traced to a tea-ship that had put into the harbor, had stolen it from some Chinese passenger; and no less than seventeen different Chinamen came forward to claim it as their stolen property.

"Soon after this I returned to England, and, as my nerves were still in a very shaky state, I came to live with my cousin Alfred, who has a large house at Weybridge. At this time he had a friend staying with him, a certain Captain Raggerton, and the two men appeared to be on very intimate terms. I did not take to Raggerton at all.

He was a good-looking man, pleasant in his manners, and remarkably plausible. But the fact is—I am speaking in strict confidence, of course—he was a bad egg. He had been in the Guards, and I don't quite know why he left; but I do know that he played bridge and baccarat pretty heavily at several clubs, and that he had a reputation for being a rather uncomfortably lucky player. He did a good deal at the race-meetings, too, and was in general such an obvious undesirable that I could never understand my cousin's intimacy with him, though I must say that Alfred's habits had changed somewhat for the worse since I had left England.

" The fame of my purchase seems to have preceded me, for when, one day, I produced the pendant to show them, I found that they knew all about it. Raggerton had heard the story from a naval man, and I gathered vaguely that he had heard something that I had not, and that he did not care to tell me; for when my cousin and he talked about the pearl, which they did pretty often, certain-significant looks passed between them, and certain veiled references were made which I could not fail to notice.

"One day I happened to be telling them of a curious incident that occurred on my way home. I had travelled to England on one of Holt's big China boats, not liking the crowd and bustle of the regular passenger-lines. Now, one afternoon, when we had been at sea a couple of days, I took a book down to my berth, intending to have a quiet read till tea-time. Soon, however, I dropped off into a doze, and must have remained asleep for over an hour. I awoke suddenly, and as I opened my eyes, I perceived that the door of the state-room was half-open, and a well-dressed Chinaman, in native costume, was looking in at me. He closed the door immediately, and I remained for a few moments paralyzed by the start that he had given me. Then I leaped from my bunk, opened the door, and looked out. But the alley-way was empty. The Chinaman had vanished as if by magic.

"This little occurrence made me quite nervous for a day or two, which was very foolish of me; but my nerves were all on edge— and I am afraid they are still."

"Yes," said Thorndyke. "There was nothing mysterious about the affair. These boats carry a Chinese crew, and the man you saw was probably a Serang, or whatever they call the gang-captains on these vessels. Or he may have been a native passenger who had strayed into the wrong part of the ship."

"Exactly," agreed our client. "But to return to Raggerton. He listened with quite extraordinary interest as I was telling this story, and when I had finished he looked very queerly at my cousin.

" 'A deuced odd thing, this, Calverley,' said he. 'Of course, it may be only a coincidence, but it really does look as if there was something, after all, in that——'

" 'Shut up, Raggerton,' said my cousin. 'We don't want any of that rot.'

" 'What is he talking about?' I asked.

" 'Oh, it's only a rotten, silly yarn that he has picked up somewhere. You're not to tell him, Raggerton.'

" 'I don't see why I am not to be told,' I said, rather sulkily. 'I'm not a baby.'

" 'No,' said Alfred, 'but you're an invalid. You don't want any horrors.'

"In effect, he refused to go into the matter any further, and I was left on tenter-hooks of curiosity.

"However, the very next day I got Raggerton alone in the smoking-room, and had a little talk with him. He had just dropped a hundred pounds on a double event that hadn't come off, and I expected to find him pliable. Nor was I disappointed, for, when we had negotiated a little loan, he was entirely at my service, and willing to tell me everything, on my promising not to give him away to Alfred.

" 'Now, you understand,' he said, 'that this yarn about your pearl is nothing but a damn silly fable that's been going the round in Marseilles. I don't know where it came from, or what sort of demented rotter invented it; I had it from a Johnnie in the Mediterranean Squadron, and you can have a copy of his letter if you want it.'

"I said that I did want it. Accordingly, that same evening he handed me a copy of the narrative extracted from his friend's letter, the substance of which was this:

"About four months ago there was lying in Canton Harbor a large English barque. Her name is not mentioned, but that is not material to the story. She had got her cargo stowed and her crew signed on, and was only waiting for certain official formalities to be completed before putting to sea on her homeward voyage. Just ahead of her, at the same quay, was a Danish ship that had been in collision outside, and was now laid up pending the decision of the Admiralty Court. She had been unloaded, and her crew paid off, with the exception of one elderly man, who remained on board as ship-keeper.

Now, a considerable part of the cargo of the English barque was the property of a certain wealthy mandarin, and this person had been about the vessel a good deal while she was taking in her lading.

"One day, when the mandarin was on board the barque, it happened that three of the seamen were sitting in the galley smoking and chatting with the cook—an elderly Chinaman named Wo-li— and the latter, pointing out the mandarin to the sailors, expatiated on his enormous wealth, assuring them that he was commonly believed to carry on his person articles of sufficient value to buy up the entire lading of a ship.

"Now, unfortunately for the mandarin, it chanced that these three sailors were about the greatest rascals on board; which is saying a good deal when one considers the ordinary moral standard that prevails in the forecastle of a sailing-ship. Nor was Wo-li himself an angel; in fact, he was a consummate villain, and seems to have been the actual originator of the plot which was presently devised to rob the mandarin.

"This plot was as remarkable for its simplicity as for its cold-blooded barbarity. On the evening before the barque sailed, the three seamen, Nilsson, Foucault, and Parratt, proceeded to the Danish ship with a supply of whisky, made the ship-keeper royally drunk, and locked him up in an empty berth. Meanwhile Wo-li made a secret communication to the mandarin to the effect that certain stolen property, believed to be his, had been secreted in the hold of the empty ship. Thereupon the mandarin came down hot-foot to the quay-side, and was received on board by the three seamen, who had got the covers off the after-hatch in readiness. Parratt now ran down the iron ladder to show the way, and the mandarin followed; but when he reached the lower deck, and looked down the hatch into the black darkness of the lower hold, he seems to have taken fright, and begun to climb up again. Meanwhile Nilsson had made a running bow-line in the end of a loose halyard that was rove through a block aloft, and had been used for hoisting out the cargo. As the mandarin came up, he leaned over the coaming of the hatch, dropped the noose over the Chinaman's head, jerked it tight, and then he and Foucault hove on the fall of the rope. The unfortunate Chinaman was dragged from the ladder, and, as he swung clear, the two rascals let go the rope, allowing him to drop through the hatches into the lower hold. Then they belayed the rope, and went down below. Parratt had already lighted a slush-lamp, by the glimmer of which they could see the mandarin swinging to and fro like a pendulum within a few feet of the ballast, and still quivering and twitching in his death-throes. They were now joined by Wo-li, who had watched the proceedings from the quay, and the four villains proceeded, without loss of time, to rifle the body as it hung. To their surprise and disgust, they found nothing of value excepting an ebony pendant set with a single large pearl; but Wo-li, though evidently disappointed at the nature of the booty, assured his comrades that this alone was well worth the hazard, pointing out the great size and exceptional beauty of the pearl. As to this, the seamen knew nothing about pearls, but the thing was done, and had to be made the best of; so they made the rope fast to the lower deck-beams, cut off the remainder and unrove it from the block, and went back to their ship.

"It was twenty-four hours before the ship-keeper was sufficiently sober to break out of the berth in which he had been locked, by which time the barque was well out to sea; and it was another three days before the body of the mandarin was found. An active search was then made for the murderers, but as they were strangers to the ship-keeper, no clues to their whereabouts could be discovered.

"Meanwhile, the four murderers were a good deal exercised as to the disposal of the booty. Since it could not be divided, it was evident that it must be entrusted to the keeping of one of them. The choice in the first place fell upon Wo-li, in whose chest the pendant was deposited as soon as the party came on board, it being arranged that the Chinaman should produce the jewel for inspection by his confederates whenever called upon.

"For six weeks nothing out of the common occurred; but then a very singular event befell. The four conspirators were sitting outside the galley one evening, when suddenly the cook uttered a cry of amazement and horror. The other three turned to see what it was that had so disturbed their comrade, and then they, too, were struck dumb with consternation; for, standing at the door of the companion-hatch—the barque was a flush-decked vessel—was the mandarin whom they had left for dead. He stood quietly regarding them for fully a minute, while they stared at him transfixed with terror. Then he beckoned to them, and went below.

"So petrified were they with astonishment and mortal fear that they remained for a long time motionless and dumb. At last they plucked up courage, and began to make furtive inquiries among the crew; but no one—not even the steward—knew anything of any passengers, or, indeed, of any Chinaman, on board the ship, excepting Wo-li.

"At daybreak the next morning, when the cook's mate went to the galley to fill the coppers, he found Wo-li hanging from a hook in the ceiling. The cook's body was stiff and cold, and had evidently been hanging several hours. The report of the tragedy quickly spread through the ship, and the three conspirators hurried off to remove the pearl from the dead man's chest before the officers should come to examine it. The cheap lock was easily picked with a bent wire, and the jewel abstracted; but now the question arose as to who should take charge of it. The eagerness to be the actual custodian of the precious bauble, which had been at first displayed, now gave place to equally strong reluctance. But someone had to take charge of it, and after a long and angry discussion, Nilsson was prevailed upon to stow it in his chest.

"A fortnight passed. The three conspirators went about their duties soberly, like men burdened with some secret anxiety, and in their leisure moments they would sit and talk with bated breath of the apparition at the companion-hatch, and the mysterious death of their late comrade.

"At last the blow fell.

"It was at the end of the second dog-watch that the hands were gathered on the forecastle, preparing to make sail after a spell of bad weather. Suddenly Nilsson gave a husky shout, and rushed at Parratt, holding out the key of his chest.

" 'Here you, Parratt,' he exclaimed, 'go below and take that accursed thing out of my chest.'

" 'What for?' demanded Parratt; and then he and Foucault, who was standing close by, looked aft to see what Nilsson was staring at.

"Instantly they both turned white as ghosts, and fell trembling so that they could hardly stand; for there was the mandarin, standing calmly by the companion, returning with a steady, impassive gaze their looks of horror. And even as they looked he beckoned and went below.

" 'D'ye hear, Parratt?' gasped Nilsson; 'take my key and do what I say, or else——'

"But at this moment the order was given to go aloft and set all plain sail; the three men went off to their respective posts, Nilsson going up the fore-topmast rigging, and the other two to the main-top. Having finished their work aloft, Foucault and Parratt, who were both in the port watch, came down on deck, and then, it being their watch below, they went and turned in.

"When they turned out with their watch at midnight, they looked about for Nilsson, who was in the starboard watch, but he was nowhere to be seen. Thinking he might have slipped below unobserved, they made no remark, though they were very uneasy about him; but when the starboard watch came on deck at four o'clock, and Nilsson did not appear with his mates, the two men became alarmed, and made inquiries about him. It was now discovered that no one had seen him since eight o'clock on the previous evening, and, this being reported to the officer of the watch, the latter ordered all hands to be called. But still Nilsson did not appear. A thorough search was now instituted, both below and aloft, and as there was still no sign of the missing man, it was concluded that he had fallen overboard.

"But at eight o'clock two men were sent aloft to shake out the fore-royal. They reached the yard almost simultaneously, and were just stepping on to the foot-ropes when one of them gave a shout; then the pair came sliding down a backstay, with faces as white as tallow. As soon as they reached the deck, they took the officer of the watch forward, and, standing on the heel of the bowsprit, pointed aloft. Several of the hands, including Foucault and Parratt, had followed, and all looked up; and there they saw the body of Nilsson, hanging on the front of the fore-topgallant sail. He was dangling at the end of a gasket, and bouncing up and down on the taut belly of the sail as the ship rose and fell to the send of the sea.

"The two survivors were now in some doubt about having anything further to do with the pearl. But the great value of the jewel, and the consideration that it was now to be divided between two instead of four, tempted them. They abstracted it from Nilsson's chest, and then, as they could not come to an agreement in any other way, they decided to settle who should take charge of it by tossing a coin. The coin was accordingly spun, and the pearl went to Foucault's chest.

"From this moment Foucault lived in a state of continual apprehension. When on deck, his eyes were forever wandering towards the companion hatch, and during his watch below, when not asleep, he would sit moodily on his chest, lost in gloomy reflection. But a fortnight passed, then three weeks, and still nothing happened. Land was sighted, the Straits of Gibraltar passed, and the end of the voyage was but a matter of days. And still the dreaded mandarin made no sign.

"At length the ship was within twenty-four hours of Marseilles, to which port a large part of the cargo was consigned. Active preparations were being made for entering the port, and among other things the shore tackle was being overhauled. A share in this latter work fell to Foucault and Parratt, and about the middle of the second dog-watch—seven o'clock in the evening—they were sitting on the deck working an eye-splice in the end of a large rope. Suddenly Foucault, who was facing forward, saw his companion turn pale and stare aft with an expression of terror. He immediately turned and looked over his shoulder to see what Parratt was staring at. It was the mandarin, standing by the companion, gravely watching them; and as Foucault turned and met his gaze, the Chinaman beckoned and went below.

"For the rest of the day Parratt kept close to his terrified comrade, and during their watch below he endeavoured to remain awake, that he might keep his friend in view. Nothing happened through the night, and the following morning, when they came on deck for the forenoon watch, their port was well in sight. The two men now separated for the first time, Parratt going aft to take his trick at the wheel, and Foucault being set to help in getting ready the ground tackle.

"Half an hour later Parratt saw the mate stand on the rail and lean outboard, holding on to the mizzen-shrouds while he stared along the ship's side. Then he jumped on to the deck and shouted angrily: 'Forward, there! What the deuce is that man up to under the starboard cat-head?'

"The men on the forecastle rushed to the side and looked over; two of them leaned over the rail with the bight of a rope between them, and a third came running aft to the mate. 'It's Foucault, sir,' Parratt heard him say. 'He's hanged hisself from the cat-head.'

"As soon as he was off duty, Parratt made his way to his dead comrade's chest, and, opening it with his pick-lock, took out the pearl. It was now his sole property, and, as the ship was within an hour or two of her destination, he thought he had little to fear from its murdered owner. As soon as the vessel was alongside the wharf, he would slip ashore and get rid of the jewel, even if he sold it at a comparatively low price. The thing looked perfectly simple.

"In actual practice, however, it turned out quite otherwise. He began by accosting a well-dressed stranger and offering the pendant for fifty pounds, but the only reply that he got was a knowing smile and a shake of the head. When this experience had been repeated a dozen times or more, and he had been followed up and down the streets for nearly an hour by a suspicious gendarme, he began to grow anxious. He visited quite a number of ships and yachts in the harbor, and at each refusal the price of his treasure came down, until he was eager to sell it for a few francs. But still no one would have it. Everyone took it for granted that the pearl was a sham, and most of the persons whom he accosted assumed that it had been stolen. The position was getting desperate. Evening was approaching—the time of the dreaded dog-watches—and still the pearl was in his possession. Gladly would he now have given it away for nothing, but he dared not try, for this would lay him open to the strongest suspicion.

"At last, in a by-street, he came upon the shop of a curio-dealer. Putting on a careless and cheerful manner, he entered and offered the pendant for ten francs. The dealer looked at it, shook his head, and handed it back.

" 'What will you give me for it?' demanded Parratt, breaking out into a cold sweat at the prospect of a final refusal.

"The dealer felt in his pocket, drew out a couple of francs, and held them out.

" 'Very well,' said Parratt. He took the money as calmly as he could, and marched out of the shop, with a gasp of relief, leaving the pendant in the dealer's hand.

"The jewel was hung up in a glass case, and nothing more was thought about it until some ten days later, when an English tourist, who came into the shop, noticed it and took a liking to it. Thereupon the dealer offered it to him for five pounds, assuring him that it was a genuine pearl, a statement that, to his amazement, the stranger evidently believed. He was then deeply afflicted at not having asked a higher price, but the bargain had been struck, and the Englishman went off with his purchase.

"This was the story told by Captain Raggerton's friend, and I have given it to you in full detail, having read the manuscript over many times since it was given to me. No doubt you will regard it as a mere traveller's tale, and consider me a superstitious idiot for giving any credence to it."

"It certainly seems more remarkable for picturesqueness than for credibility," Thorndyke agreed. "May I ask," he continued, "whether Captain Raggerton's friend gave any explanation as to how this singular story came to his knowledge, or to that of anybody else?"

"Oh yes," replied Calverley; "I forgot to mention that the seaman, Parratt, very shortly after he had sold the pearl, fell down the hatch into the hold as the ship was unloading, and was very badly injured. He was taken to the hospital, where he died on the following day; and it was while he was lying there in a dying condition that he confessed to the murder, and gave this circumstantial account of it."

"I see," said Thorndyke; "and I understand that you accept the story as literally true?"

"Undoubtedly." Calverley flushed defiantly as he returned Thorndyke's look, and continued: "You see, I am not a man of science; therefore my beliefs are not limited to things that can be weighed and measured. There are things, Dr. Thorndyke, which are outside the range of our puny intellects; things that science, with its arrogant materialism, puts aside and ignores with close-shut eyes. I prefer to believe in things which obviously exist, even though I cannot explain them. It is the humbler and, I think, the wiser attitude."

"But, my dear Fred," protested Mr. Brodribb, "this is a rank fairy-tale."

Calverley turned upon the solicitor. "If you had seen what I have seen, you would not only believe: you would *know*."

"Tell us what you have seen, then," said Mr. Brodribb.

"I will, if you wish to hear it," said Calverley. "I will continue the strange history of the Mandarin's Pearl."

He lit a fresh cigarette and continued:

"The night I came to Beech-hurst—that is my cousin's house, you know—a rather absurd thing happened, which I mention on account of its connection with what has followed. I had gone to my room early, and sat for some time writing letters before getting ready for bed. When I had finished my letters, I started on a tour of inspection of my room. I was then, you must remember, in a very nervous state, and it had become my habit to examine the room in which I was to sleep before undressing, looking under the bed, and in any cupboards and closets that there happened to be. Now, on looking round my new room, I perceived that there was a second door, and I at once proceeded to open it to see where it led to. As soon as I opened the door, I got a terrible start. I found myself looking into a narrow closet or passage, lined with pegs, on which the servant had hung some of my clothes; at the farther end was another door, and, as I stood looking into the closet, I observed, with startled amazement, a man standing holding the door half-open, and silently regarding me. I stood for a moment staring at him, with my heart thumping and my limbs all of a tremble; then I slammed the door and ran off to look for my cousin.

"He was in the billiard-room with Raggerton, and the pair looked up sharply as I entered.

" 'Alfred,' I said, 'where does that passage lead to out of my room?'

" 'Lead to?' said he. 'Why, it doesn't lead anywhere. It used to open into a cross corridor, but when the house was altered, the corridor was done away with, and this passage closed up. It is only a cupboard now.'

" 'Well, there's a man in it—or there was just now.'

"'Nonsense!' he exclaimed: 'impossible! Let us go and look at the place.'

"He and Raggerton rose, and we went together to my room. As we flung open the door of the closet and looked in, we all three burst into a laugh. There were three men now looking at us from the open door at the other end, and the mystery was solved. A large mirror had been placed at the end of the closet to cover the partition which cut it off from the cross corridor.

"This incident naturally exposed me to a good deal of chaff from my cousin and Captain Raggerton; but I often wished that the mirror had not been placed there, for it happened over and over again that, going to the cupboard hurriedly, and not thinking of the mirror, I got quite a bad shock on being confronted by a figure apparently coming straight at me through an open door. In fact, it annoyed me so much, in my nervous state, that I even thought of asking my cousin to give me a different room; but, happening to refer to the matter when talking to Raggerton, I found the Captain so scornful of my cowardice that my pride was touched, and I let the affair drop.

"And now I come to a very strange occurrence, which I shall relate quite frankly, although I know beforehand that you will set me down as a liar or a lunatic. I had been away from home for a fortnight, and as I returned rather late at night, I went straight to my room. Having partly undressed, I took my clothes in one hand

and a candle in the other, and opened the cupboard door. I stood for a moment looking nervously at my double, standing, candle in hand, looking at me through the open door at the other end of the passage; then I entered, and, setting the candle on a shelf, proceeded to hang up my clothes. I had hung them up, and had just reached up for the candle, when my eye was caught by something strange in the mirror. It no longer reflected the candle in my hand, but, instead of it, a large colored paper lantern. I stood petrified with astonishment, and gazed into the mirror; and then I saw that my own reflection was changed, too; that, in place of my own figure, was that of an elderly Chinaman, who stood regarding me with stony calm.

"I must have stood for near upon a minute, unable to move and scarce able to breathe, face to face with that awful figure. At length I turned to escape, and, as I turned, he turned also, and I could see him, over my shoulder, hurrying away. As I reached the door, I halted for a moment, looking back with the door in my hand, holding the candle above my head; and even so *he* halted, looking back at me, with his hand upon the door and his lantern held above his head.

"I was so much upset that I could not go to bed for some hours, but continued to pace the room, in spite of my fatigue. Now and again I was impelled, irresistibly, to peer into the cupboard, but nothing was to be seen in the mirror save my own figure, candle in hand, peeping in at me through the half-open door. And each time that I looked into my own white, horror-stricken face, I shut the door hastily and turned away with a shudder; for the pegs, with the clothes hanging on them, seemed to call to me. I went to bed at last, and before I fell asleep I formed the resolution that, if I was spared until the next day, I would write to the British Consul at Canton, and offer to restore the pearl to the relatives of the murdered mandarin.

"On the following day I wrote and despatched the letter, after which I felt more composed, though I was haunted continually by the recollection of that stony, impassive figure; and from time to time I felt an irresistible impulse to go and look in at the door of the closet, at the mirror and the pegs with the clothes hanging from them. I told my cousin of the visitation that I had received, but he merely laughed, and was frankly incredulous; while the Captain bluntly advised me not to be a superstitious donkey.

"For some days after this I was left in peace, and began to hope that my letter had appeased the spirit of the murdered man; but on the fifth day, about six o'clock in the evening, happening to want some papers that I had left in the pocket of a coat which was hanging in the closet, I went in to get them. I took in no candle, as it was not yet dark, but left the door wide open to light me. The coat that I wanted was near the end of the closet, not more than four paces from the mirror, and as I went towards it I watched my reflection rather nervously as it advanced to meet me. I found my coat, and as I felt for the papers, I still kept a suspicious eye on my double. And, even as I looked, a most strange phenomenon appeared: the mirror seemed for an instant to darken or cloud over, and then, as it cleared again, I saw, standing dark against the light of the open door behind him, the figure of the mandarin. After a single glance, I ran out of the closet, shaking with agitation; but as I turned to shut the door, I noticed that it was my own figure that was reflected in the glass. The Chinaman had vanished in an instant.

"It now became evident that my letter had not served its purpose, and I was plunged in despair; the more so since, on this day, I felt again the dreadful impulse to go and look at the pegs on the walls of the closet. There was no mistaking the meaning of that impulse, and each time that I went, I dragged myself away reluctantly, though shivering with horror. One circumstance, indeed, encouraged me a little; the mandarin had not, on either occasion, beckoned to me as he had done to the sailors, so that perhaps some way of escape yet lay open to me.

"During the next few days I considered very earnestly what measures I could take to avert the doom that seemed to be hanging over me. The simplest plan, that of passing the pearl on to some other person, was out of the question; it would be nothing short of murder. On the other hand, I could not wait for an answer to my letter; for even if I remained alive, I felt that my reason would have given way long before the reply reached me. But while I was debating what I should do, the mandarin appeared to me again; and then, after an interval of only two days, he came to me once more. That was last night. I remained gazing at him, fascinated, with my flesh creeping, as he stood, lantern in hand, looking steadily in my face. At last he held out his hand to me, as if asking me to give him the pearl; then the mirror darkened, and he vanished in a flash; and in the place where he had stood there was my own reflection looking at me out of the glass.

"That last visitation decided me. When I left home this morning the pearl was in my pocket, and as I came over Waterloo Bridge, I leaned over the parapet and flung the thing into the water. After that I felt quite relieved for a time; I had shaken the accursed thing off without involving anyone in the curse that it carried. But presently I began to feel fresh misgivings, and the conviction has been growing upon me all day that I have done the wrong thing. I have only placed it forever beyond the reach of its owner, whereas I ought to have burnt it, after the Chinese fashion, so that its nonmaterial essence could have joined the spiritual body of him to whom it had belonged when both were clothed with material substance.

"But it can't be altered now. For good or for evil, the thing is done, and God alone knows what the end of it will be."

As he concluded, Calverley uttered a deep sigh, and covered his face with his slender, delicate hands. For a space we were all silent and, I think, deeply moved; for, grotesquely unreal as the whole thing was, there was a pathos, and even a tragedy, in it that we all felt to be very real indeed.

Suddenly Mr. Brodribb started and looked at his watch.

"Good gracious, Calverley, we shall lose our train."

The young man pulled himself together and stood up. "We shall just do it if we go at once," he said. "Good-bye," he added, shaking Thorndyke's hand and mine. "You have been very patient, and I have been rather prosy, I am afraid. Come along, Mr. Brodribb."

Thorndyke and I followed them out on to the landing, and I heard my colleague say to the solicitor in a low tone, but very earnestly: "Get him away from that house, Brodribb, and don't let him out of your sight for a moment."

I did not catch the solicitor's reply, if he made any, but when we were back in our room I noticed that Thorndyke was more agitated than I had ever seen him.

"I ought not to have let them go," he exclaimed. "Confound me! If I had had a grain of wit, I should have made them lose their train."

He lit his pipe and fell to pacing the room with long strides, his eyes bent on the floor with an expression sternly reflective. At last, finding him hopelessly taciturn, I knocked out my pipe and went to bed.

As I was dressing on the following morning, Thorndyke entered my room. His face was grave even to sternness, and he held a telegram in his hand.

"I am going to Weybridge this morning," he said shortly, holding the "flimsy" out to me. "Shall you come?"

I took the paper from him, and read:

"Come, for God's sake! F. C. is dead. You will understand.

BRODRIBB."

I handed him back the telegram, too much shocked for a moment to speak. The whole dreadful tragedy summed up in that curt message rose before me in an instant, and a wave of deep pity swept over me at this miserable end to the sad, empty life.

"What an awful thing, Thorndyke!" I exclaimed at length. "To be killed by a mere grotesque delusion."

"Do you think so?" he asked dryly. "Well, we shall see; but you will come?"

"Yes," I replied; and as he retired, I proceeded hurriedly to finish dressing.

Half an hour later, as we rose from a rapid breakfast, Polton came into the room, carrying a small roll-up case of tools and a bunch of skeleton keys.

"Will you have them in a bag, sir?" he asked.

"No," replied Thorndyke; "in my overcoat pocket. Oh, and here is a note, Polton, which I want you to take round to Scotland Yard. It is to the Assistant Commissioner, and you are to make sure that it is in the right hands before you leave. And here is a telegram to Mr. Brodribb."

He dropped the keys and the tool-case into his pocket, and we went down together to the waiting hansom.

At Weybridge Station we found Mr. Brodribb pacing the platform in a state of extreme dejection. He brightened up somewhat when he saw us, and wrung our hands with emotional heartiness.

"It was very good of you both to come at a moment's notice," he said warmly, "and I feel your kindness very much. You understood, of course, Thorndyke?"

"Yes," Thorndyke replied. "I suppose the mandarin beckoned to him."

Mr. Brodribb turned with a look of surprise. "How did you guess that?" he asked; and then, without waiting for a reply, he took from his pocket a note, which he handed to my colleague. "The poor old fellow left this for me," he said. "The servant found it on his dressing-table."

Thorndyke glanced through the note and passed it to me. It consisted of but a few words, hurriedly written in a tremulous hand.

"He has beckoned to me, and I must go. Good-bye, dear old friend."

"How does his cousin take the matter?" asked Thorndyke.

"He doesn't know of it yet," replied the lawyer. "Alfred and Raggerton went out after an early breakfast, to cycle over to Guildford on some business or other, and they have not returned yet. The catastrophe was discovered soon after they left. The maid went to his room with a cup of tea, and was astonished to find that his bed had not been slept in. She ran down in alarm and reported to the butler, who went up at once and searched the room; but he could find no trace of the missing one, except my note, until it occurred to him to look in the cupboard. As he opened the door he got rather a start from his own reflection in the mirror; and then he saw poor Fred hanging from one of the pegs near the end of the closet, close to the glass. It's a melancholy affair—but here is the house, and here is the butler waiting for us. Mr. Alfred is not back yet, then, Stevens?"

"No, sir." The white-faced, frightened-looking man had evidently been waiting at the gate from distaste of the house, and he now walked back with manifest relief at our arrival. When we entered the house, he ushered us without remark up on to the first-floor, and preceding us along a corridor, halted near the end. "That's the room, sir," said he; and without another word he turned and went down the stairs.

We entered the room, and Mr. Brodribb followed on tiptoe, looking about him fearfully, and casting awe-struck glances at the shrouded form on the bed. To the latter Thorndyke advanced, and gently drew back the sheet.

"You'd better not look, Brodribb," said he, as he bent over the corpse. He felt the limbs and examined the cord, which still remained round the neck, its raggedly-severed end testifying to the terror of the servants who had cut down the body. Then he replaced the sheet and looked at his watch. "It happened at about three o'clock in the morning," said he. "He must have struggled with the impulse for some time, poor fellow! Now let us look at the cupboard."

We went together to a door in the corner of the room, and, as we opened it, we were confronted by three figures, apparently looking in at us through an open door at the other end.

"It is really rather startling," said the lawyer, in a subdued voice, looking almost apprehensively at the three figures that advanced to meet us. "The poor lad ought never to have been here."

It was certainly an eerie place, and I could not but feel, as we walked down the dark, narrow passage, with those other three dimly-seen figures silently coming towards us, and mimicking our every gesture, that it was no place for a nervous, supersitious man like poor Fred Calverley. Close to the end of the long row of pegs was one from which hung an end of stout box-cord, and to this Mr. Brodribb pointed with an awe-struck gesture. But Thorndyke gave it only a brief glance, and then walked up to the mirror, which he proceeded to examine minutely. It was a very large glass, nearly seven feet high, extending the full width of the closet, and reaching to within a foot of the floor; and it seemed to have been let into the partition from behind, for, both above and below, the woodwork was in front of it. While I was making these observations, I watched Thorndyke with no little curiosity. First he rapped his knuckles on the glass; then he lighted a wax match, and, holding it close to the mirror, carefully watched the reflection of the flame. Finally, laying his cheek on the glass, he held the match at arm's length, still close to the mirror, and looked at the reflection along the surface. Then he blew out the match and walked back into the room, shutting the cupboard door as we emerged.

"I think," said he, "that as we shall all undoubtedly be sub-poenaed by the coroner, it would be well to put together a few notes of the facts. I see there is a writing-table by the window, and I would propose that you, Brodribb, just jot down a *précis* of the statement that you heard last night, while Jervis notes down the exact condition of the body. While you are doing this, I will take a look round."

"We might find a more cheerful place to write in," grumbled Mr. Brodribb; "however——"

Without finishing the sentence, he sat down at the table, and, having found some sermon paper, dipped a pen in the ink by way of encouraging his thoughts. At this moment Thorndyke quietly slipped out of the room, and I proceeded to make a detailed examination of the body; in which occupation I was interrupted at intervals by requests from the lawyer that I should refresh his memory.

We had been occupied thus for about a quarter of an hour, when a quick step was heard outside, the door was opened abruptly, and a man burst into the room. Brodribb rose and held out his hand.

"This is a sad home-coming for you, Alfred," said he.

"Yes, my God!" the newcomer exclaimed. "It's awful."

He looked askance at the corpse on the bed, and wiped his forehead with his handkerchief. Alfred Calverley was not extremely prepossessing. Like his cousin, he was obviously neurotic, but there were signs of dissipation in his face, which, just now, was pale and ghastly, and wore an expression of abject fear. Moreover, his entrance was accompanied by that of a perceptible odor of brandy.

He had walked over, without noticing me, to the writing-table, and as he stood there, talking in subdued tones with the lawyer, I suddenly found Thorndyke at my side. He had stolen in noiselessly through the door that Calverley had left open.

"Show him Brodribb's note," he whispered, "and then make him go in and look at the peg."

With this mysterious request, he slipped out of the room as silently as he had come, unperceived either by Calverley or the lawyer.

"Has Captain Raggerton returned with you?" Brodribb was inquiring.

"No, he has gone into the town," was the reply; "but he won't be long. This will be a frightful shock to him."

At this point I stepped forward. "Have you shown Mr. Calverley the extraordinary letter that the deceased left for you?" I asked.

"What letter was that?" demanded Calverley, with a start.

Mr. Brodribb drew forth the note and handed it to him. As he read it through, Calverley turned white to the lips, and the paper trembled in his hand.

" 'He has beckoned to me, and I must go,' " he read. Then, with a furtive glance at the lawyer: "Who had beckoned? What did he mean?"

Mr. Brodribb briefly explained the meaning of the allusion, adding: "I thought you knew all about it."

"Yes, yes," said Calverley, with some confusion; "I remember the matter now you mention it. But it's all so dreadful and bewildering."

At this point I again interposed. "There is a question," I said, "that may be of some importance. It refers to the cord with which the poor fellow hanged himself. Can you identify that cord, Mr. Calverley?"

"I!" he exclaimed, staring at me, and wiping the sweat from his white face; "how should I? Where is the cord?"

"Part of it is still hanging from the peg in the closet. Would you mind looking at it?"

"If you would very kindly fetch it—you know I—er—naturally—have a——"

"It must not be disturbed before the inquest," said I; "but surely you are not afraid——"

"I didn't say I was afraid," he retorted angrily. "Why should I be?"

With a strange, tremulous swagger, he strode across to the closet, flung open the door, and plunged in.

A moment later we heard a shout of horror, and he rushed out, livid and gasping.

"What is it, Calverley?" exclaimed Mr. Brodribb, starting up in alarm.

But Calverley was incapable of speech. Dropping limply into a chair, he gazed at us for a while in silent terror; then he fell back uttering a wild shriek of laughter.

Mr. Brodribb looked at him in amazement. "What is it, Calverley?" he asked again.

As no answer was forthcoming, he stepped across to the open door of the closet and entered, peering curiously before him. Then he, too, uttered a startled exclamation, and backed out hurriedly, looking pale and flurried.

"Bless my soul!" he ejaculated. "Is the place bewitched?"

He sat down heavily and stared at Calverley, who was still shaking with hysteric laughter; while I, now consumed with curiosity, walked over to the closet to discover the cause of their singular behavior. As I flung open the door, which the lawyer had closed, I must confess to being very considerably startled; for though the reflection of the open door was plain enough in the mirror, my own reflection was replaced by that of a Chinaman. After a momentary pause of astonishment, I entered the closet and walked towards the mirror; and simultaneously the figure of the Chinaman entered and walked towards me. I had advanced more than halfway down the closet when suddenly the mirror darkened; there was a whirling flash, the Chinaman vanished in an instant, and, as I reached the glass, my own reflection faced me.

I turned back into the room pretty completely enlightened, and looked at Calverley with a new-born distaste. He still sat facing the bewildered lawyer, one moment sobbing convulsively, the next yelping with hysteric laughter. He was not an agreeable spectacle, and when, a few moments later, Thorndyke entered the room, and halted by the door with a stare of disgust, I was moved to join him. But at this juncture a man pushed past Thorndyke, and, striding up to Calverley, shook him roughly by the arm.

"Stop that row!" he exclaimed furiously. "Do you hear? Stop it!"

"I can't help it, Raggerton," gasped Calverley. "He gave me such a turn—the mandarin, you know."

"What!" ejaculated Raggerton.

He dashed across to the closet, looked in, and turned upon Calverley with a snarl. Then he walked out of the room.

"Brodribb," said Thorndyke. "I should like to have a word with you and Jervis outside." Then, as we followed him out on to the landing, he continued: "I have something rather interesting to show you. It is in here."

He softly opened an adjoining door, and we looked into a small unfurnished room. A projecting closet occupied one side of it, and at the door of the closet stood Captain Raggerton, with his hand upon the key. He turned upon us fiercely, though with a look of alarm, and demanded:

"What is the meaning of this intrusion? and who the deuce are you? Do you know that this is my private room?"

"I suspected that it was," Thorndyke replied quietly. "Those will be your properties in the closet, then?"

Raggerton turned pale, but continued to bluster. "Do I understand that you have dared to break into my private closet?" he demanded.

"I have inspected it," replied Thorndyke, "and I may remark that it is useless to wrench at that key, because I have hampered the lock."

"The devil you have!" shouted Raggerton.

"Yes; you see, I am expecting a police-officer with a search warrant, so I wished to keep everything intact."

Raggerton turned livid with mingled fear and rage. He stalked up to Thorndyke with a threatening air, but, suddenly altering his mind, exclaimed, "I must see to this!" and flung out of the room.

Thorndyke took a key from his pocket, and, having locked the door, turned to the closet. Having taken out the key to unhamper the lock with a stout wire, he reinserted it and unlocked the door. As we entered, we found ourselves in a narrow closet, similar to the one in the other room, but darker, owing to the absence of a mirror. A few clothes hung from the pegs, and when Thorndyke had lit a candle that stood on a shelf, we could see more of the details.

"Here are some of the properties," said Thorndyke. He pointed to a peg from which hung a long, blue silk gown of Chinese make, a mandarin's cap, with a pigtail attached to it, and a beautifully-made papier-mâché mask. "Observe," said Thorndyke, taking the latter down and exhibiting a label on the inside, marked "Renouard à Paris," "no trouble has been spared."

He took off his coat, slipped on the gown, the mask, and the cap, and was, in a moment, in that dim light, transformed into the perfect semblance of a Chinaman.

"By taking a little more time," he remarked, pointing to a pair of Chinese shoes and a large paper lantern, "the make-up could be rendered more complete; but this seems to have answered for our friend Alfred."

"But," said Mr. Brodribb, as Thorndyke shed the disguise, "still, I don't understand——"

"I will make it clear to you in a moment," said Thorndyke. He walked to the end of the closet, and, tapping the right-hand wall, said: "This is the back of the mirror. You see that it is hung on massive well-oiled hinges, and is supported on this large, rubber-tired castor, which evidently has ball bearings. You observe three black cords running along the wall, and passing through those pulleys above. Now, when I pull this cord, notice what happens."

He pulled one cord firmly, and immediately the mirror swung noiselessly inwards on its great castor, until it stood diagonally across the closet, where it was stopped by a rubber buffer.

"Bless my soul!" exclaimed Mr. Brodribb. "What an extraordinary thing!"

The effect was certainly very strange, for, the mirror being now exactly diagonal to the two closets, they appeared to be a single, continuous passage, with a door at either end. On going up to the mirror, we found that the opening which it had occupied was filled by a sheet of plain glass, evidently placed there as a precaution to prevent any person from walking through from one closet into the other, and so discovering the trick.

"It's all very puzzling," said Mr. Brodribb; "I don't clearly understand it now."

"Let us finish here," replied Thorndyke, "and then I will explain. Notice this black curtain. When I pull the second cord, it slides across the closet and cuts off the light. The mirror now reflects nothing into the other closet; it simply appears dark. And now I pull the third cord."

He did so and the mirror swung noiselessly back into its place.

"There is only one other thing to observe before we go out," said Thorndyke, "and that is this other mirror standing with its face to the wall. This, of course, is the one that Fred Calverley originally saw at the end of the closet; it has since been removed, and the larger swinging glass put in its place. And now," he continued, when we came out into the room, "let me explain the mechanism in detail. It was obvious to me, when I heard poor Fred Calverley's story, that the mirror was 'faked,' and I drew a diagram of the probable arrangement, which turns out to be correct. Here it is."

He took a sheet of paper from his pocket and handed it to the lawyer. "There are two sketches. Sketch 1 shows the mirror in its ordinary position, closing the end of the closet. A person standing at A, of course, sees his reflection facing him at, apparently, A1. Sketch 2 shows the mirror swung across. Now a person standing at A does not see his own reflection at all; but if some other person is standing in the other closet at B, A sees the reflection of B apparently at B1—that is, in the identical position that his own reflection occupied when the mirror was straight across."

"I see now," said Brodribb; "but who set up this apparatus, and why was it done?"

"Let me ask you a question," said Thorndyke. "Is Alfred Calverley the next-of-kin?"

"No; there is Fred's younger brother. But I may say that Fred has made a will quite recently very much in Alfred's favor."

"There is the explanation, then," said Thorndyke. "These two scoundrels have conspired to drive the poor fellow to suicide, and Raggerton was clearly the leading spirit. He was evidently concocting some story with which to work on poor Fred's superstitions when the mention of the Chinaman on the steamer gave him his cue. He then invented the very picturesque story of the murdered mandarin and the stolen pearl. You remember that these 'visitations' did not begin until after that story had been told, and Fred had been absent from the house on a visit. Evidently, during his absence, Raggerton took down the original mirror, and substituted this swinging arrangement; and at the same time procured the Chinaman's dress and mask from the theatrical property dealers. No doubt he reckoned on being able quietly to remove the swinging glass and other properties and replace the original mirror before the inquest."

"By God!" exclaimed Mr. Brodribb, "it's the most infamous, cowardly plot I have ever heard of. They shall go to jail for it, the villains, as sure as I am alive."

But in this Mr. Brodribb was mistaken; for immediately on finding themselves detected, the two conspirators had left the house, and by nightfall were safely across the Channel; and the only satisfaction that the lawyer obtained was the setting aside of the will on facts disclosed at the inquest.

As to Thorndyke, he has never to this day forgiven himself for having allowed Fred Calverley to go home to his death.

The Blue Sequin

Thorndyke stood looking up and down the platform with anxiety that increased as the time drew near for the departure of the train.

"This is very unfortunate," he said, reluctantly stepping into an empty smoking compartment as the guard executed a flourish with his green flag. "I am afraid we have missed our friend." He closed the door, and, as the train began to move, thrust his head out of the window.

"Now I wonder if that will be he," he continued. "If so, he has caught the train by the skin of his teeth, and is now in one of the rear compartments."

The subject of Thorndyke's speculations was Mr. Edward Stopford, of the firm of Stopford and Myers, of Portugal Street, solicitors, and his connection with us at present arose out of a telegram that had reached our chambers on the preceding evening. It was reply-paid, and ran thus:

"Can you come here to-morrow to direct defence? Important case. All costs undertaken by us.—STOPFORD AND MYERS."

Thorndyke's reply had been in the affirmative, and early on this present morning a further telegram—evidently posted overnight—had been delivered:

"Shall leave for Woldhurst by 8.25 from Charing Cross. Will call for you if possible.—EDWARD STOPFORD."

He had not called, however, and, since he was unknown personally to us both, we could not judge whether or not he had been among the passengers on the platform.

"It is most unfortunate," Thorndyke repeated, "for it deprives us of that preliminary consideration of the case which is so invaluable." He filled his pipe thoughtfully, and, having made a fruitless inspection of the platform at London Bridge, took up the paper that he had bought at the bookstall, and began to turn over the leaves, running his eye quickly down the columns, unmindful of the journalistic baits in paragraph or article.

"It is a great disadvantage," he observed, while still glancing through the paper, "to come plump into an inquiry without preparation—to be confronted with the details before one has a chance of considering the case in general terms. For instance——"

He paused, leaving the sentence unfinished, and as I looked up inquiringly I saw that he had turned over another page, and was now reading attentively.

"This looks like our case, Jervis," he said presently, handing me the paper and indicating a paragraph at the top of the page. It was quite brief, and was headed "Terrible Murder in Kent," the account being as follows:

"A shocking crime was discovered yesterday morning at the little town of Woldhurst, which lies on the branch line from Halbury Junction. The discovery was made by a porter who was inspecting the carriages of the train which had just come in. On opening the door of a first-class compartment, he was horrified to find the body of a fashionably-dressed woman stretched upon the floor. Medical aid was immediately summoned, and on the arrival of the divisional surgeon, Dr. Morton, it was ascertained that the woman had not been dead more than a few minutes.

"The state of the corpse leaves no doubt that a murder of a most brutal kind has been perpetrated, the cause of death being a penetrating wound of the head, inflicted with some pointed implement, which must have been used with terrible violence, since it has perforated the skull and entered the brain. That robbery was not the motive of the crime is made clear by the fact that an expensively fitted dressing-bag was found on the rack, and that the dead woman's jewellery, including several valuable diamond rings, was untouched. It is rumoured that an arrest has been made by the local police."

"A gruesome affair," I remarked as I handed back the paper, "but the report does not give us much information."

"It does not," Thorndyke agreed, "and yet it gives us something to consider. Here is a perforating wound of the skull, inflicted with some pointed implement—that is, assuming that it is not a bullet wound. Now, what kind of implement would be capable of inflicting such an injury? How would such an implement be used in the confined space of a railway-carriage, and what sort of person would be in possession of such an implement? These are preliminary questions that are worth considering, and I commend them to you, together with the further problems of the possible motive—excluding robbery—and any circumstances other than murder which might account for the injury."

"The choice of suitable implements is not very great," I observed.

"It is very limited, and most of them, such as a plasterer's pick or a geological hammer, are associated with certain definite occupations. You have a notebook?"

I had, and, accepting the hint, I produced it and pursued my further reflections in silence, while my companion, with his notebook also on his knee, gazed steadily out of the window. And thus he remained, wrapped in thought, jotting down an entry now and again in his book, until the train slowed down at Halbury Junction, where we had to change on to a branch line.

As we stepped out, I noticed a well-dressed man hurrying up the platform from the rear and eagerly scanning the faces of the few passengers who had alighted. Soon he espied us, and, approaching quickly, asked, as he looked from one of us to the other:

"Dr. Thorndyke?"

"Yes," replied my colleague, adding: "And you, I presume, are Mr. Edward Stopford?"

The solicitor bowed. "This is a dreadful affair," he said, in an agitated manner. "I see you have the paper. A most shocking affair. I am immensely relieved to find you here. Nearly missed the train, and feared I should miss you."

"There appears to have been an arrest," Thorndyke began.

"Yes—my brother. Terrible business. Let us walk up the platform; our train won't start for a quarter of an hour yet."

We deposited our joint Gladstone and Thorndyke's travelling-case in an empty first-class compartment, and then, with the solicitor between us, strolled up to the unfrequented end of the platform.

"My brother's position," said Mr. Stopford, "fills me with dismay—but let me give you the facts in order, and you shall judge for yourself. This poor creature who has been murdered so brutally was a Miss Edith Grant. She was formerly an artist's model, and as such was a good deal employed by my brother, who is a painter—Harold Stopford, you know, A.R.A. now——"

"I know his work very well, and charming work it is."

"I think so, too. Well, in those days he was quite a youngster—about twenty—and he became very intimate with Miss Grant, in quite an innocent way, though not very discreet; but she was a nice respectable girl, as most English models are, and no one thought any harm. However, a good many letters passed between them, and some little presents, among which was a beaded chain carrying a locket, and in this he was fool enough to put his portrait and the inscription, 'Edith, from Harold.'

"Later on Miss Grant, who had a rather good voice, went on the stage, in the comic opera line, and, in consequence, her habits and associates changed somewhat; and, as Harold had meanwhile become engaged, he was naturally anxious to get his letters back, and especially to exchange the locket for some less compromising gift. The letters she eventually sent him, but refused absolutely to part with the locket.

"Now, for the last month Harold has been staying at Halbury, making sketching excursions into the surrounding country, and yesterday morning he took the train to Shinglehurst, the third station from here, and the one before Woldhurst.

"On the platform here he met Miss Grant, who had come down from London, and was going to Worthing. They entered the branch train together, having a first-class compartment to themselves. It seems she was wearing his locket at the time, and he made another appeal to her to make an exchange, which she refused, as before. The discussion appears to have become rather heated and angry on both sides, for the guard and a porter at Munsden both noticed that they seemed to be quarrelling; but the upshot of the affair was that the lady snapped the chain, and tossed it together with the locket to my brother, and they parted quite amiably at Shinglehurst, where Harold got out. He was then carrying his full sketching kit, including a large holland umbrella, the lower joint of which is an ash staff fitted with a powerful steel spike for driving into the ground.

"It was about half-past ten when he got out at Shinglehurst; by eleven he had reached his pitch and got to work, and he painted steadily for three hours. Then he packed up his traps, and was just starting on his way back to the station, when he was met by the police and arrested.

"And now, observe the accumulation of circumstantial evidence against him. He was the last person seen in company with the murdered woman—for no one seems to have seen her after they left Munsden; he appeared to be quarrelling with her when she was last seen alive, he had a reason for possibly wishing for her death, he was provided with an implement—a spiked staff—capable of inflicting the injury which caused her death, and, when he was searched, there was found in his possession the locket and broken chain, apparently removed from her person with violence.

"Against all this is, of course, his known character—he is the gentlest and most amiable of men—and his subsequent conduct—imbecile to the last degree if he had been guilty; but, as a lawyer, I can't help seeing that appearances are almost hopelessly against him."

"We won't say 'hopelessly,' " replied Thorndyke, as we took our places in the carriage, "though I expect the police are pretty cocksure. When does the inquest open?"

"To-day at four. I have obtained an order from the coroner for you to examine the body and be present at the *post-mortem*."

"Do you happen to know the exact position of the wound?"

"Yes; it is a little above and behind the left ear—a horrible round hole, with a ragged cut or tear running from it to the side of the forehead."

"And how was the body lying?"

"Right along the floor, with the feet close to the off-side door."

"Was the wound on the head the only one?"

"No; there was a long cut or bruise on the right cheek—a contused wound the police surgeon called it, which he believes to have been inflicted with a heavy and rather blunt weapon. I have not heard of any other wounds or bruises."

"Did anyone enter the train yesterday at Shinglehurst?" Thorndyke asked.

"No one entered the train after it left Halbury."

Thorndyke considered these statements in silence, and presently fell into a brown study, from which he roused only as the train moved out of Shinglehurst station.

"It would be about here that the murder was committed," said Mr. Stopford; "at least, between here and Woldhurst."

Thorndyke nodded rather abstractedly, being engaged at the moment in observing with great attention the objects that were visible from the windows.

"I notice," he remarked presently, "a number of chips scattered about between the rails, and some of the chair-wedges look new. Have there been any plate-layers at work lately?"

"Yes," answered Stopford, "they are on the line now, I believe—at least, I saw a gang working near Woldhurst yesterday, and they are said to have set a rick on fire; I saw it smoking when I came down."

"Indeed; and this middle line of rails is, I suppose, a sort of siding?"

"Yes; they shunt the goods trains and empty trucks on to it. There are the remains of the rick—still smouldering, you see."

Thorndyke gazed absently at the blackened heap until an empty cattle-truck on the middle track hid it from view. This was succeeded by a line of goods-wagons, and these by a passenger coach, one compartment of which—a first-class—was closed up and sealed. The train now began to slow down rather suddenly, and a couple of minutes later we brought up in Woldhurst station.

It was evident that rumors of Thorndyke's advent had preceded us, for the entire staff—two porters, an inspector, and the station-master—were waiting expectantly on the platform, and the latter came forward, regardless of his dignity, to help us with our luggage.

"Do you think I could see the carriage?" Thorndyke asked the solicitor.

"Not the inside, sir," said the station-master, on being appealed to. "The police have sealed it up. You would have to ask the inspector."

"Well, I can have a look at the outside, I suppose?" said Thorndyke, and to this the station-master readily agreed, and offered to accompany us.

"What other first-class passengers were there?" Thorndyke asked.

"None, sir. There was only one first-class coach, and the deceased was the only person in it. It has given us all a dreadful turn, this affair has," he continued, as we set off up the line. "I was on the platform when the train came in. We were watching a rick that was burning up the line, and a rare blaze it made, too; and I was just saying that we should have to move the cattle-truck that was on the mid-track, because, you see, sir, the smoke and sparks were blowing across, and I thought it would frighten the poor beasts. And Mr. Felton he don't like his beasts handled roughly. He says it spoils the meat."

"No doubt he is right," said Thorndyke. "But now, tell me, do you think it is possible for any person to board or leave the train on the off-side unobserved? Could a man, for instance, enter a compartment on the off-side at one station and drop off as the train was slowing down at the next, without being seen?"

"I doubt it," replied the station-master. "Still, I wouldn't say it is impossible."

"Thank you. Oh, and there's another question. You have a gang of men at work on the line, I see. Now, do those men belong to the district?"

"No, sir; they are strangers, every one, and pretty rough diamonds some of 'em are. But I shouldn't say there was any real harm in 'em. If you was suspecting any of 'em of being mixed up in this——"

"I am not," interrupted Thorndyke rather shortly. "I suspect nobody; but I wish to get all the facts of the case at the outset."

"Naturally, sir," replied the abashed official; and we pursued our way in silence.

"Do you remember, by the way," said Thorndyke, as we approached the empty coach, "whether the off-side door of the compartment was closed and locked when the body was discovered?"

"It was closed, sir, but not locked. Why, sir, did you think——?"

"Nothing, nothing. The sealed compartment is the one, of course?"

Without waiting for a reply, he commenced his survey of the coach, while I gently restrained our two companions from shadowing him, as they were disposed to do. The off-side footboard occupied his attention specially, and when he had scrutinized minutely the part opposite the fatal compartment, he walked slowly from end to end with his eyes but a few inches from its surface, as though he was searching for something.

Near what had been the rear end he stopped, and drew from his pocket a piece of paper; then, with a moistened finger-tip he picked up from the footboard some evidently minute object, which he carefully transferred to the paper, folding the latter and placing it in his pocket-book.

He next mounted the footboard, and, having peered in through the window of the sealed compartment, produced from his pocket a small insufflator or powder-blower, with which he blew a stream of impalpable smoke-like powder on to the edges of the middle window, bestowing the closest attention on the irregular dusty patches in which it settled, and even measuring one on the jamb of the window with a pocket-rule. At length he stepped down, and, having carefully looked over the near-side footboard, announced that he had finished for the present.

As we were returning down the line, we passed a working man, who seemed to be viewing the chairs and sleepers with more than casual interest.

"That, I suppose, is one of the plate-layers?" Thorndyke suggested to the station-master.

"Yes, the foreman of the gang," was the reply.

"I'll just step back and have a word with him, if you will walk on slowly." And my colleague turned back briskly and overtook the man, with whom he remained in conversation for some minutes.

"I think I see the police-inspector on the platform," remarked Thorndyke, as we approached the station.

"Yes, there he is," said our guide. "Come down to see what you are after, sir, I expect," Which was doubtless the case, although the officer professed to be there by the merest chance.

"You would like to see the weapon, sir, I suppose?" he remarked when he had introduced himself.

"The umbrella-spike," Thorndyke corrected. "Yes, if I may. We are going to the mortuary now."

"Then you'll pass the station on the way; so, if you care to look in, I will walk up with you."

This proposition being agreed to, we all proceeded to the police-station, including the station-master, who was on the very tiptoe of curiosity.

"There you are, sir," said the inspector, unlocking his office, and ushering us in. "Don't say we haven't given every facility to the defence. There are all the effects of the accused, including the very weapon the deed was done with."

"Come, come," protested Thorndyke; "we mustn't be premature." He took the stout ash staff from the officer, and, having examined the formidable spike through a lens, drew from his pocket a steel calliper-gauge, with which he carefully measured the diameter of the spike, and the staff to which it was fixed. "And now," he said, when he had made a note of the measurements in his book, "we will look at the color-box and the sketch. Ha! a very orderly man, your brother, Mr. Stopford. Tubes all in their places, palette-knives wiped clean, palette cleaned off and rubbed bright, brushes wiped— they ought to be washed before they stiffen—all this is very significant." He unstrapped the sketch from the blank canvas to which it was pinned, and, standing it on a chair in a good light, stepped back to look at it.

"And you tell me that that is only three hours' work!" he exclaimed, looking at the lawyer. "It is really a marvellous achievement."

"My brother is a very rapid worker," replied Stopford dejectedly.

"Yes, but this is not only amazingly rapid; it is in his very happiest vein—full of spirit and feeling. But we mustn't stay to look at it longer." He replaced the canvas on its pins, and having glanced at the locket and some other articles that lay in a drawer, thanked the inspector for his courtesy and withdrew.

"That sketch and the color-box appear very suggestive to me," he remarked, as we walked up the street.

"To me also," said Stopford gloomily, "for they are under lock and key, like their owner, poor old fellow."

He sighed heavily, and we walked on in silence.

The mortuary-keeper had evidently heard of our arrival, for he was waiting at the door with the key in his hand, and, on being shown the coroner's order, unlocked the door, and we entered together; but, after a momentary glance at the ghostly, shrouded figure lying upon the slate table, Stopford turned pale and retreated, saying that he would wait for us outside with the mortuary-keeper.

As soon as the door was closed and locked on the inside, Thorndyke glanced curiously round the bare, whitewashed building. A stream of sunlight poured in through the skylight, and fell upon the silent form that lay so still under its covering-sheet, and one stray beam glanced into a corner by the door, where, on a row of pegs and a deal table, the dead woman's clothing was displayed.

"There is something unspeakably sad in these poor relics, Jervis," said Thorndyke, as we stood before them. "To me they are more tragic, more full of pathetic suggestion, than the corpse itself. See the smart, jaunty hat, and the costly skirts hanging there, so desolate and forlorn; the dainty *lingerie* on the table, neatly folded—by the mortuary-man's wife, I hope—the little French shoes and open-work silk stockings. How pathetically eloquent they are of harmless, womanly vanity, and the gay, careless life, snapped short in the twinkling of an eye. But we must not give way to sentiment. There is another life threatened, and it is in our keeping."

He lifted the hat from its peg, and turned it over in his hand. It was, I think, what is called a "picture-hat"—a huge, flat, shapeless mass of gauze and ribbon and feather, spangled over freely with dark-blue sequins. In one part of the brim was a ragged hole, and from this the glittering sequins dropped off in little showers when the hat was moved.

"This will have been worn tilted over on the left side," said Thorndyke, "judging by the general shape and the position of the hole."

"Yes," I agreed. "Like that of the Duchess of Devonshire in Gainsborough's portrait."

"Exactly."

He shook a few of the sequins into the palm of his hand, and, replacing the hat on its peg, dropped the little discs into an envelope, on which he wrote, "From the hat," and slipped it into his pocket. Then, stepping over to the table, he drew back the sheet reverently and even tenderly from the dead woman's face, and looked down at it with grave pity. It was a comely face, white as marble, serene and peaceful in expression, with half-closed eyes, and framed with a mass of brassy, yellow hair; but its beauty was marred by a long linear wound, half cut, half bruise, running down the right cheek from the eye to the chin.

"A handsome girl," Thorndyke commented—"a dark-haired blonde. What a sin to have disfigured herself so with that horrible peroxide." He smoothed the hair back from her forehead, and added: "She seems to have applied the stuff last about ten days ago. There is about a quarter of an inch of dark hair at the roots. What do you make of that wound on the cheek?"

"It looks as if she had struck some sharp angle in falling, though, as the seats are padded in first-class carriages, I don't see what she could have struck."

"No. And now let us look at the other wound. Will you note down the description?" He handed me his notebook, and I wrote down as he dictated: "A clean-punched circular hole in skull, an inch behind and above margin of left ear—diameter, an inch and seven-sixteenths; starred fracture of parietal bone; membranes perforated, and brain entered deeply; ragged scalp-wound, extending forward to margin of left orbit; fragments of gauze and sequins in edges of wound. That will do for the present. Dr. Morton will give us further details if we want them."

He pocketed his callipers and rule, drew from the bruised scalp one or two loose hairs, which he placed in the envelope with the sequins, and, having looked over the body for other wounds or bruises (of which there were none), replaced the sheet, and prepared to depart.

As we walked away from the mortuary, Thorndyke was silent and deeply thoughtful, and I gathered that he was piecing together the facts that he had acquired. At length Mr. Stopford, who had several times looked at him curiously, said:

"The *post-mortem* will take place at three, and it is now only half-past eleven. What would you like to do next?"

Thorndyke, who, in spite of his mental preoccupation, had been looking about him in his usual keen, attentive way, halted suddenly.

"Your reference to the *post-mortem*," said he, "reminds me that I forgot to put the ox-gall into my case."

"Ox-gall!" I exclaimed, endeavoring vainly to connect this substance with the technique of the pathologist. "What were you going to do with——"

But here I broke off, remembering my friend's dislike of any discussion of his methods before strangers.

"I suppose," he continued, "there would hardly be an artist's colorman in a place of this size?"

"I should think not," said Stopford. "But couldn't you get the stuff from a butcher? There's a shop just across the road."

"So there is," agreed Thorndyke, who had already observed the shop. "The gall ought, of course, to be prepared, but we can filter it ourselves—that is, if the butcher has any. We will try him, at any rate."

He crossed the road towards the shop, over which the name "Felton" appeared in gilt lettering, and, addressing himself to the proprietor, who stood at the door, introduced himself and explained his wants.

"Ox-gall?" said the butcher. "No, sir, I haven't any just now; but I am having a beast killed this afternoon, and I can let you have some then. In fact," he added, after a pause, "as the matter is of importance, I can have one killed at once if you wish it."

"That is very kind of you," said Thorndyke, "and it would greatly oblige me. Is the beast perfectly healthy?"

"They're in splendid condition, sir. I picked them out of the herd myself. But you shall see them—ay, and choose the one that you'd like killed."

"You are really very good," said Thorndyke warmly. "I will just run into the chemist's next door, and get a suitable bottle, and then I will avail myself of your exceedingly kind offer."

He hurried into the chemist's shop, from which he presently emerged, carrying a white paper parcel; and we then followed the butcher down a narrow lane by the side of his shop. It led to an enclosure containing a small pen, in which were confined three handsome steers, whose glossy, black coats contrasted in a very striking manner with their long, greyish-white, nearly straight horns.

"These are certainly very fine beasts, Mr. Felton," said Thorndyke, as we drew up beside the pen, "and in excellent condition, too."

He leaned over the pen and examined the beasts critically, especially as to their eyes and horns; then, approaching the nearest one, he raised his stick and bestowed a smart tap on the under-side of the right horn, following it by a similar tap on the left one, a proceeding that the beast viewed with stolid surprise.

"The state of the horns," explained Thorndyke, as he moved on to the next steer, "enables one to judge, to some extent, of the beast's health."

"Lord bless you, sir," laughed Mr. Felton, "they haven't got no feeling in their horns, else what good 'ud their horns be to 'em?"

Apparently he was right, for the second steer was as indifferent to a sounding rap on either horn as the first. Nevertheless, when Thorndyke approached the third steer, I unconsciously drew nearer to watch; and I noticed that, as the stick struck the horn, the beast drew back in evident alarm, and that when the blow was repeated, it became manifestly uneasy.

"He don't seem to like that," said the butcher. "Seems as if—— Hullo, that's queer!"

Thorndyke had just brought his stick up against the left horn, and immediately the beast had winced and started back, shaking his head and moaning. There was not, however, room for him to back out of reach, and Thorndyke, by leaning into the pen, was able to inspect the sensitive horn, which he did with the closest attention, while the butcher looked on with obvious perturbation.

"You don't think there's anything wrong with this beast, sir, I hope," said he.

"I can't say without a further examination," replied Thorndyke. "It may be the horn only that is affected. If you will have it sawn off close to the head, and sent up to me at the hotel, I will look at it and tell you. And, by way of preventing any mistakes, I will mark it and cover it up, to protect it from injury in the slaughter-house."

He opened his parcel and produced from it a wide-mouthed bottle labelled "Ox-gall," a sheet of gutta-percha tissue, a roller bandage, and a stick of sealing-wax. Handing the bottle to Mr. Felton, he encased the distal half of the horn in a covering by means of the tissue and the bandage, which he fixed securely with the sealing-wax.

"I'll saw the horn off and bring it up to the hotel myself, with the ox-gall," said Mr. Felton. "You shall have them in half an hour."

He was as good as his word, for in half an hour Thorndyke was seated at a small table by the window of our private sitting-room in the Black Bull Hotel. The table was covered with newspaper, and on it lay the long grey horn and Thorndyke's travelling-case, now open and displaying a small microscope and its accessories. The butcher was seated solidly in an armchair waiting, with a half-suspicious eye on Thorndyke, for the report; and I was endeavoring by cheerful talk to keep Mr. Stopford from sinking into utter despondency, though I, too, kept a furtive watch on my colleague's rather mysterious proceedings.

I saw him unwind the bandage and apply the horn to his ear, bending it slightly to and fro. I watched him, as he scanned the surface closely through a lens, and observed him as he scraped some substance from the pointed end on to a glass slide, and, having applied a drop of some reagent, began to tease out the scraping with a pair of mounted needles. Presently he placed the slide under the microscope, and, having observed it attentively for a minute or two, turned round sharply.

"Come and look at this, Jervis," said he.

I wanted no second bidding, being on tenter-hooks of curiosity, but came over and applied my eye to the instrument.

"Well, what is it?" he asked.

"A multipolar nerve corpuscle—very shrivelled, but unmistakable."

"And this?"

He moved the slide to a fresh spot.

"Two pyramidal nerve corpuscles and some portions of fibres."

"And what do you say the tissue is?"

"Cortical brain substance, I should say, without a doubt."

"I entirely agree with you. And that being so," he added, turning to Mr. Stopford, "we may say that the case for the defence is practically complete."

"What, in Heaven's name, do you mean?" exclaimed Stopford, starting up.

"I mean that we can now prove when and where and how Miss Grant met her death. Come and sit down here, and I will explain.

No, you needn't go away, Mr. Felton. We shall have to subpœna you. Perhaps," he continued, "we had better go over the facts and see what they suggest. And first we note the position of the body, lying with the feet close to the off-side door, showing that, when she fell, the deceased was sitting, or more probably standing, close to that door. Next there is this." He drew from his pocket a folded paper, which he opened, displaying a tiny blue disc. "It is one of the sequins with which her hat was trimmed, and I have in this envelope several more which I took from the hat itself.

"This single sequin I picked up on the rear end of the off-side footboard, and its presence there makes it nearly certain that at some time Miss Grant had put her head out of the window on that side.

"The next item of evidence I obtained by dusting the margins of the off-side window with a light powder, which made visible a greasy impression three and a quarter inches long on the sharp corner of the right-hand jamb (right-hand from the inside, I mean).

"And now as to the evidence furnished by the body. The wound in the skull is behind and above the left ear, is roughly circular, and measures one inch and seven-sixteenths at most, and a ragged scalp-wound runs from it towards the left eye. On the right cheek is a linear contused wound three and a quarter inches long. There are no other injuries.

"Our next facts are furnished by this." He took up the horn and tapped it with his finger, while the solicitor and Mr. Felton stared at him in speechless wonder. "You notice it is a left horn, and you remember that it was highly sensitive. If you put your ear to it while I strain it, you will hear the grating of a fracture in the bony core. Now look at the pointed end, and you will see several deep scratches running lengthwise, and where those scratches end the diameter of the horn is, as you see by this calliper-gauge, one inch and seven-sixteenths. Covering the scratches is a dry blood-stain, and at the extreme tip is a small mass of a dried substance which Dr. Jervis and I have examined with the microscope and are satisfied is brain tissue."

"Good God!" exclaimed Stopford eagerly. "Do you mean to say——"

"Let us finish with the facts, Mr. Stopford," Thorndyke interrupted. "Now, if you look closely at that blood-stain, you will see a short piece of hair stuck to the horn, and through this lens you can make out the root-bulb. It is a golden hair, you notice, but near the root it is black, and our calliper-gauge shows us that the black portion is fourteen sixty-fourths of an inch long. Now, in this envelope are some hairs that I removed from the dead woman's head. They are also golden hairs, black at the roots, and when I measure the black portion I find it to be fourteen sixty-fourths of an inch long. Then, finally, there is this."

He turned the horn over, and pointed to a small patch of dried blood. Embedded in it was a blue sequin.

Mr. Stopford and the butcher both gazed at the horn in silent amazement; then the former drew a deep breath and looked up at Thorndyke.

"No doubt," said he, "you can explain this mystery, but for my part I am utterly bewildered, though you are filling me with hope."

"And yet the matter is quite simple," returned Thorndyke, "even with these few facts before us, which are only a selection from the body of evidence in our possession. But I will state my theory, and you shall judge." He rapidly sketched a rough plan on a sheet of paper, and continued: "These were the conditions when the train was approaching Woldhurst: Here was the passenger-coach, here was the burning rick, and here was a cattle-truck. This steer was in that truck. Now my hypothesis is that at that time Miss Grant was standing with her head out of the off-side window, watching the burning rick. Her wide hat, worn on the left side, hid from her view the cattle-truck which she was approaching, and then this is what happened." He sketched another plan to a larger scale. "One of the steers—this one—had thrust its long horn out through the bars. The point of that horn struck the deceased's head, driving her face violently against the corner of the window, and then, in disengaging, ploughed its way through the scalp, and suffered a fracture of its core from the violence of the wrench. This hypothesis is inherently probable, it fits all the facts, and those facts admit of no other explanation."

The solicitor sat for a moment as though dazed, then he rose impulsively and seized Thorndyke's hands.

"I don't know what to say to you," he exclaimed huskily, "except that you have saved my brother's life, and for that may God reward you!"

The butcher rose from his chair with a slow grin.

"It seems to me," said he, "as if that ox-gall was what you might call a blind, eh, sir?"

And Thorndyke smiled an inscrutable smile.

When we returned to town on the following day we were a party of four, which included Mr. Harold Stopford. The verdict of "Death by misadventure," promptly returned by the coroner's jury, had been shortly followed by his release from custody, and he now sat with his brother and me, listening with rapt attention to Thorndyke's analysis of the case.

"So, you see," the latter concluded, "I had six possible theories of the cause of death worked out before I reached Halbury, and it only remained to select the one that fitted the facts. And when I had seen the cattle-truck, had picked up that sequin, had heard the description of the steers, and had seen the hat and the wounds, there was nothing left to do but the filling in of details."

"And you never doubted my innocence?" asked Harold Stopford.

Thorndyke smiled at his quondam client.

"Not after I had seen your color-box and your sketch," said he, "to say nothing of the spike."

The Moabite Cipher

A large and motley crowd lined the pavements of Oxford Street as Thorndyke and I made our way leisurely eastward. Floral decorations and dropping bunting announced one of those functions inaugurated from time to time by a benevolent Government for the entertainment of fashionable loungers and the relief of distressed pickpockets. For a Russian Grand Duke, who had torn himself away, amidst valedictory explosions, from a loving if too demonstrative people, was to pass anon on his way to the Guildhall; and a British Prince, heroically indiscreet, was expected to occupy a seat in the ducal carriage.

Near Rathbone Place Thorndyke halted and drew my attention to a smart-looking man who stood lounging in a doorway, cigarette in hand.

"Our old friend Inspector Badger," said Thorndyke. "He seems mightily interested in that gentleman in the light overcoat. How d'ye do, Badger?" for at this moment the detective caught his eye and bowed. "Who is your friend?"

"That's what I want to know, sir," replied the inspector. "I've been shadowing him for the last half-hour, but I can't make him out, though I believe I've seen him somewhere. He don't look like a foreigner, but he has got something bulky in his pocket, so I must keep him in sight until the Duke is safely past. I wish," he added gloomily, "these beastly Russians would stop at home. They give us no end of trouble."

"Are you expecting any—occurrences, then?" asked Thorndyke.

"Bless you, sir," exclaimed Badger, "the whole route is lined with plain-clothes men. You see, it is known that several desperate characters followed the Duke to England, and there are a good many exiles living here who would like to have a rap at him. Hallo! What's he up to now?"

The man in the light overcoat had suddenly caught the inspector's too inquiring eye, and forthwith dived into the crowd at the edge of the pavement. In his haste he trod heavily on the foot of a big, rough-looking man, by whom he was in a moment hustled out into the road with such violence that he fell sprawling face downwards. It was an unlucky moment. A mounted constable was just then backing in upon the crowd, and before he could gather the meaning of the shout that arose from the by-standers, his horse had set down one hind-hoof firmly on the prostrate man's back.

The inspector signalled to a constable, who forthwith made a way for us through the crowd; but even as we approached the injured man, he rose stiffly and looked round with a pale, vacant face.

"Are you hurt?" Thorndyke asked gently, with an earnest look into the frightened, wondering eyes.

"No sir," was the reply; "only I feel queer—sinking—just here."

He laid a trembling hand on his chest, and Thorndyke, still eyeing him anxiously, said in a low voice to the inspector: "Cab or ambulance, as quickly as you can."

A cab was led round from Newman Street, and the injured man put into it. Thorndyke, Badger, and I entered, and we drove off up Rathbone Place. As we proceeded, our patient's face grew more and more ashen, drawn, and anxious; his breathing was shallow and uneven, and his teeth chattered slightly. The cab swung round into Goodge Street, and then—suddenly, in the twinkling of an eye—there came a change. The eyelids and jaw relaxed, the eyes became filmy, and the whole form subsided into the corner in a shrunken heap, with the strange gelatinous limpness of a body that is dead as a whole, while its tissues are still alive.

"God save us! The man's dead!" exclaimed the inspector in a shocked voice—for even policeman have their feelings. He sat staring at the corpse, as it nodded gently with the jolting of the cab, until we drew up inside the courtyard of the Middlesex Hospital, when he got out briskly, with suddenly renewed cheerfulness, to help the porter to place the body on the wheeled couch.

"We shall know who he is now, at any rate," said he, as we followed the couch to the casualty-room. Thorndyke nodded unsympathetically. The medical instinct in him was for the moment stronger than the legal.

The house-surgeon leaned over the couch, and made a rapid examination as he listened to our account of the accident. Then he straightened himself up and looked at Thorndyke.

"Internal hæmorrhage, I expect," said he. "At any rate, he's dead, poor beggar!—as dead as Nebuchadnezzar. Ah! here comes a bobby; it's his affair now."

A sergeant came into the room, breathing quickly, and looked in surprise from the corpse to the inspector. But the latter, without loss of time, proceeded to turn out the dead man's pockets, commencing with the bulky object that had first attracted his attention; which proved to be a brown-paper parcel tied up with red tape.

"Pork-pie, begad!" he exclaimed with a crestfallen air as he cut the tape and opened the package. "You had better go through his other pockets, sergeant."

The small heap of odds and ends that resulted from this process tended, with a single exception, to throw little light on the man's identity; the exception being a letter, sealed, but not stamped, addressed in an exceedingly illiterate hand to Mr. Adolf Schönberg, 213, Greek Street, Soho.

"He was going to leave it by hand, I expect," observed the inspector, with a wistful glance at the sealed envelope. "I think I'll take it round myself, and you had better come with me, sergeant."

He slipped the letter into his pocket, and, leaving the sergeant to take possession of the other effects, made his way out of the building.

"I suppose, Doctor," said he, as we crossed into Berners Street, "you are not coming our way? Don't want to see Mr. Schönberg, h'm?"

Thorndyke reflected for a moment. "Well, it isn't very far, and we may as well see the end of the incident. Yes; let us go together."

No. 213, Greek Street, was one of those houses that irresistibly suggest to the observer the idea of a church organ, either jamb of the doorway being adorned with a row of brass bell-handles corresponding to the stop-knobs.

These the sergeant examined with the air of an expert musician, and having, as it were, gauged the capacity of the instrument, selected the middle knob on the right-hand side and pulled it briskly; whereupon a first-floor window was thrown up and a head protruded. But it afforded us a momentary glimpse only, for, having caught the sergeant's upturned eye, it retired with surprising precipitancy, and before we had time to speculate on the apparition, the street-door was opened and a man emerged. He was about to close the door after him when the inspector interposed.

"Does Mr. Adolf Schönberg live here?"

The newcomer, a very typical Jew of the red-haired type, surveyed us thoughtfully through his gold-rimmed spectacles as he repeated the name.

"Schönberg—Schönberg? Ah, yes! I know. He lives on the third-floor. I saw him go up a short time ago. Third-floor back"; and indicating the open door with a wave of the hand, he raised his hat and passed into the street.

"I suppose we had better go up," said the inspector, with a dubious glance at the row of bell-pulls. He accordingly started up the stairs, and we all followed in his wake.

There were two doors at the back on the third-floor, but as the one was open, displaying an unoccupied bedroom, the inspector rapped smartly on the other. It flew open almost immediately, and a fierce-looking little man confronted us with a hostile stare.

"Well?" said he.

"Mr. Adolf Schönberg?" inquired the inspector.

"Well? What about him?" snapped our new acquaintance.

"I wished to have a few words with him," said Badger.

"Then what the deuce do you come banging at *my* door for?" demanded the other.

"Why, doesn't he live here?"

"No. First-floor front," replied our friend, preparing to close the door.

"Pardon me," said Thorndyke, "but what is Mr. Schönberg like? I mean——"

"Like?" interrupted the resident. "He's like a blooming Sheeny, with a carroty beard and gold gig-lamps!" and, having presented this impressionist sketch, he brought the interview to a definite close by slamming the door and turning the key.

With a wrathful exclamation, the inspector turned towards the stairs, down which the sergeant was already clattering in hot haste, and made his way back to the ground-floor, followed, as before, by Thorndyke and me. On the doorstep we found the sergeant breathlessly interrogating a smartly-dressed youth, whom I had seen alight from a hansom as we entered the house, and who now stood with a notebook tucked under his arm, sharpening a pencil with deliberate care.

"Mr James saw him come out, sir," said the sergeant. "He turned up towards the Square."

"Did he seem to hurry?" asked the inspector.

"Rather," replied the reporter. "As soon as you were inside, he went off like a lamplighter. You won't catch him now."

"We don't want to catch him," the detective rejoined gruffly; then, backing out of earshot of the eager pressman, he said in a lower tone: "That was Mr. Schönberg, beyond a doubt, and it is clear that he has some reason for making himself scarce; so I shall consider myself justified in opening that note."

He suited the action to the word, and, having cut the envelope open with official neatness, drew out the enclosure.

"My hat!" he exclaimed, as his eye fell upon the contents. "What in creation is this? It isn't shorthand, but what the deuce is it?"

He handed the document to Thorndyke, who, having held it up to the light and felt the paper critically, proceeded to examine it with keen interest. It consisted of a single half-sheet of thin notepaper, both sides of which were covered with strange, crabbed characters, written with a brownish-black ink in continuous lines, without any spaces to indicate the divisions into words; and, but for the modern material which bore the writing, it might have been a portion of some ancient manuscript or forgotten codex.

"What do you make of it, Doctor?" inquired the inspector anxiously, after a pause, during which Thorndyke had scrutinized the strange writing with knitted brows.

"Not a great deal," replied Thorndyke. "The character is the Moabite or Phœnician—primitive Semitic, in fact—and reads from right to left. The language I take to be Hebrew. At any rate, I can find no Greek words, and I see here a group of letters which *may* form one of the few Hebrew words that I know—the word *badim*, 'lies.' But you had better get it deciphered by an expert."

"If it is Hebrew," said Badger, "we can manage it all right. There are plenty of Jews at our disposal."

"You had much better take the paper to the British Museum," said Thorndyke, "and submit it to the keeper of the Phœnician antiquities for decipherment."

Inspector Badger smiled a foxy smile as he deposited the paper in his pocket-book. "We'll see what we can make of it ourselves first," he said; "but many thanks for your advice, all the same, Doctor. No, Mr. James, I can't give you any information just at present; you had better apply at the hospital."

"I suspect," said Thorndyke, as we took our way homewards,

"that Mr. James has collected enough material for his purpose already. He must have followed us from the hospital, and I have no doubt that he has his report, with 'full details,' mentally arranged at this moment. And I am not sure that he didn't get a peep at the mysterious paper, in spite of the inspector's precautions."

"By the way," I said, "what do you make of the document?"

"A cipher, most probably," he replied. "It is written in the primitive Semitic alphabet, which, as you know, is practically identical with primitive Greek. It is written from right to left, like the Phœnician, Hebrew, and Moabite, as well as the earliest Greek, inscriptions. The paper is common cream-laid notepaper, and the ink is ordinary indelible Chinese ink, such as is used by draughtsmen. Those are the facts, and without further study of the document itself, they don't carry us very far."

"Why do you think it is a cipher rather than a document in straightforward Hebrew?"

"Because it is obviously a secret message of some kind. Now, every educated Jew knows more or less Hebrew, and, although he is able to read and write only the modern square Hebrew character, it is so easy to transpose one alphabet into another that the mere language would afford no security. Therefore, I expect that, when the experts translate this document, the translation or transliteration will be a mere farrago of unintelligible nonsense. But we shall see, and meanwhile the facts that we have offer several interesting suggestions which are well worth consideration."

"As, for instance——?"

"Now, my dear Jervis," said Thorndyke, shaking an admonitory forefinger at me, "don't, I pray you, give way to mental indolence. You have these few facts that I have mentioned. Consider them separately and collectively, and in their relation to the circumstances. Don't attempt to suck my brain when you have an excellent brain of your own to suck."

On the following morning the papers fully justified my colleague's opinion of Mr. James. All the events which had occurred, as well as a number that had not, were given in the fullest and most vivid detail, a lengthy reference being made to the paper "found on the person of the dead anarchist," and "written in a private shorthand or cryptogram."

The report concluded with the gratifying—though untrue—statement that "in this intricate and important case, the police have wisely secured the assistance of Dr. John Thorndyke, to whose acute intellect and vast experience the portentous cryptogram will doubtless soon deliver up its secret."

"Very flattering," laughed Thorndyke, to whom I read the extract on his return from the hospital, "but a little awkward if it should induce our friends to deposit a few trifling mementoes in the form of nitro-compounds on our main staircase or in the cellars. By the way, I met Superintendent Miller on London Bridge. The 'cryptogram,' as Mr. James calls it, has set Scotland Yard in a mighty ferment."

"Naturally. What have they done in the matter?"

"They adopted my suggestion, after all, finding that they could make nothing of it themselves, and took it to the British Museum. The Museum people referred them to Professor Poppelbaum, the great palæographer, to whom they accordingly submitted it."

"Did he express any opinion about it?"

"Yes, provisionally. After a brief examination, he found it to consist of a number of Hebrew words sandwiched between apparently meaningless groups of letters. He furnished the Superintendent off-hand with a translation of the words, and Miller forthwith struck off a number of hectograph copies of it, which he has distributed among the senior officials of his department; so that at present"—here Thorndyke gave vent to a soft chuckle—"Scotland Yard is engaged in a sort of missing word—or, rather, missing sense—competition. Miller invited me to join the sport, and to that end presented me with one of the hectograph copies on which to exercise my wits, together with a photograph of the document."

"And shall you?" I asked.

"Not I," he replied, laughing. "In the first place, I have not been formally consulted, and consequently am a passive, though interested, spectator. In the second place, I have a theory of my own which I shall test if the occasion arises. But if you would like to take part in the competition, I am authorized to show you the photograph and the translation. I will pass them on to you, and I wish you joy of them."

He handed me the photograph and a sheet of paper that he had just taken from his pocket-book, and watched me with grim amusement as I read out the first few lines.

"Woe, city, lies, robbery, prey, noise, whip, rattling, wheel, horse, chariot, day, darkness, gloominess, clouds, darkness, morning, mountain, people, strong, fire, them, flame."

The Cipher

"It doesn't look very promising at first sight," I remarked. "What is the Professor's theory?"

"His theory—provisionally, of course—is that the words form the message, and the groups of letters represent mere filled-up spaces before the words."

"But surely," I protested, "that would be a very transparent device."

Thorndyke laughed. "There is a childlike simplicity about it," said he, "that is highly attractive—but discouraging. It is much more probable that the words are dummies, and that the letters contain the message. Or, again, the solution may lie in an entirely different direction. But listen! Is that cab coming here?"

It was. It drew up opposite our chambers, and a few moments later a brisk step ascending the stairs heralded a smart rat-tat at our door. Flinging open the latter, I found myself confronted by a well-dressed stranger, who, after a quick glance at me, peered inquisitively over my shoulder into the room.

"I am relieved, Dr. Jervis," said he, "to find you and Dr. Thorndyke at home, as I have come on somewhat urgent professional business. My name," he continued, entering in response to my invitation, "is Barton, but you don't know me, though I know you both by sight. I have come to ask you if one of you—or, better still, both—could come to-night and see my brother."

"That," said Thorndyke, "depends on the circumstances and on the whereabouts of your brother."

"The circumstances," said Mr. Barton, "are, in my opinion, highly suspicious, and I will place them before you—of course, in strict confidence."

Thorndyke nodded and indicated a chair.

"My brother," continued Mr. Barton, taking the proffered seat, "has recently married for the second time. His age is fifty-five, and that of this wife twenty-six, and I may say that the marriage has been—well, by no means a success. Now, within the last fortnight, my brother has been attacked by a mysterious and extremely painful affection of the stomach, to which his doctor seems unable to give a name. It has resisted all treatment hitherto. Day by day the pain and distress increase, and I feel that, unless something decisive is done, the end cannot be far off."

"Is the pain worse after taking food?" inquired Thorndyke.

"That's just it!" exclaimed our visitor. "I see what is in your mind, and it has been in mine, too; so much so that I have tried repeatedly to obtain samples of the food that he is taking. And this morning I succeeded." Here he took from his pocket a wide-mouthed bottle, which, disengaging from its paper wrappings, he laid on the table. "When I called, he was taking his breakfast of arrowroot, which he complained had a gritty taste, supposed by his wife to be due to the sugar. Now I had provided myself with this bottle, and, during the absence of his wife, I managed unobserved to convey a portion of the arrowroot that he had left into it, and I should be greatly obliged if you would examine it and tell me if this arrowroot contains anything that it should not."

He pushed the bottle across to Thorndyke, who carried it to the window, and, extracting a small quantity of the contents with a glass rod, examined the pasty mass with the aid of a lens; then, lifting the bell-glass cover from the microscope, which stood on its table by the window, he smeared a small quantity of the suspected matter on to a glass slip, and placed it on the stage of the instrument.

"I observe a number of crystalline particles in this," he said, after a brief inspection, "which have the appearance of arsenious acid."

"Ah!" ejaculated Mr. Barton, "just what I feared. But are you certain?"

"No," replied Thorndyke; "but the matter is easily tested."

He pressed the button of the bell that communicated with the laboratory, a summons that brought the laboratory assistant from his lair with characteristic promptitude.

"Will you please prepare a Marsh's apparatus, Polton," said Thorndyke.

"I have a couple ready, sir," replied Polton.

"Then pour the acid into one and bring it to me, with a tile."

As his familiar vanished silently, Thorndyke turned to Mr. Barton.

"Supposing we find arsenic in this arrowroot, as we probably shall, what do you want us to do?"

"I want you to come and see my brother," replied our client.

"Why not take a note from me to his doctor?"

"No, no; I want you to come—I should like you both to come—and put a stop at once to this dreadful business. Consider! It's a matter of life and death. You won't refuse! I beg you not to refuse me your help in these terrible circumstances."

"Well," said Thorndyke, as his assistant reappeared, "let us first see what the test has to tell us."

Polton advanced to the table, on which he deposited a small flask, the contents of which were in a state of brisk effervescence, a bottle labelled "calcium hypochlorite," and a white porcelain tile. The flask was fitted with a safety-funnel and a glass tube drawn out to a fine jet, to which Polton cautiously applied a lighted match. Instantly there sprang from the jet a tiny, pale violet flame. Thorndyke now took the tile, and held it in the flame for a few seconds, when the appearance of the surface remained unchanged save for a small circle of condensed moisture. His next proceeding was to thin the arrowroot with distilled water until it was quite fluid, and then pour a small quantity into the funnel. It ran slowly down the tube into the flask, with the bubbling contents of which it became speedily mixed. Almost immediately a change began to appear in the character of the flame, which from a pale violet turned gradually to a sickly blue, while above it hung a faint cloud of white smoke. Once more Thorndyke held the tile above the jet, but this time, no sooner had the pallid flame touched the cold surface of the porcelain, than there appeared on the latter a glistening black stain.

"That is pretty conclusive," observed Thorndyke, lifting the stopper out of the reagent bottle, "but we will apply the final test." He dropped a few drops of the hypochlorite solution on to the tile, and immediately the black stain faded away and vanished. "We can now answer your question, Mr. Barton," said he, replacing the stopper as he turned to our client. "The specimen that you brought us certainly contains arsenic, and in very considerable quantities."

"Then," exclaimed Mr. Barton, starting from his chair, "you will come and help me to rescue my brother from this dreadful peril. Don't refuse me, Dr. Thorndyke, for mercy's sake, don't refuse."

Thorndyke reflected for a moment.

"Before we decide," said he, "we must see what engagements we have."

With a quick, significant glance at me, he walked into the office, whither I followed in some bewilderment, for I knew that we had no engagements for the evening.

"Now, Jervis," said Thorndyke, as he closed the office door, "what are we to do?"

"We must go, I suppose," I replied. "It seems a pretty urgent case."

"It does," he agreed. "Of course, the man may be telling the truth, after all."

"You don't think he is, then?"

"No. It is a plausible tale, but there is too much arsenic in that arrowroot. Still, I think I ought to go. It is an ordinary professional risk. But there is no reason why you should put your head into the noose."

"Thank you," said I, somewhat huffily. "I don't see what risk there is, but if any exists I claim the right to share it,"

"Very well," he answered with a smile, "we will both go. I think we can take care of ourselves."

He re-entered the sitting-room, and announced his decision to Mr. Barton, whose relief and gratitude were quite pathetic.

"But," said Thorndyke, "you have not yet told us where your brother lives."

"Rexford," was the reply—"Rexford, in Essex. It is an out-of-the-way place, but if we catch the seven-fifteen train from Liverpool Street, we shall be there in an hour and a half."

"And as to the return? You know the trains, I suppose?"

"Oh, yes," replied our client; "I will see that you don't miss your train back."

"Then I will be with you in a minute," said Thorndyke; and, taking the still-bubbling flask, he retired to the laboratory, whence he returned in a few minutes carrying his hat and overcoat.

The cab which had brought our client was still waiting, and we were soon rattling through the streets towards the station, where we arrived in time to furnish ourselves with dinner-baskets and select our compartment at leisure.

During the early part of the journey our companion was in excellent spirits. He despatched the cold fowl from the basket and quaffed the rather indifferent claret with as much relish as if he had not had a single relation in the world, and after dinner he became genial to the verge of hilarity. But, as time went on, there crept into his manner a certain anxious restlessness. He became silent and preoccupied, and several times furtively consulted his watch.

"The train is confoundedly late!" he exclaimed irritably. "Seven minutes behind time already!"

"A few minutes more or less are not of much consequence," said Thorndyke.

"No, of course not; but still—— Ah, thank Heaven, here we are!"

He thrust his head out of the off-side window, and gazed eagerly down the line; then, leaping to his feet, he bustled out on to the platform while the train was still moving.

Even as we alighted a warning bell rang furiously on the up-platform, and as Mr. Barton hurried us through the empty booking-office to the outside of the station, the rumble of the approaching train could be heard above the noise made by our own train moving off.

"My carriage doesn't seem to have arrived yet," exclaimed Mr. Barton, looking anxiously up the station approach. "If you will wait here a moment, I will go and make inquiries."

He darted back into the booking office and through it on to the platform, just as the up-train roared into the station. Thorndyke followed him with quick but stealthy steps, and, peering out of the booking-office door, watched his proceedings; then he turned and beckoned to me.

"There he goes," said he, pointing to an iron foot-bridge that spanned the line; and, as I looked, I saw, clearly defined against the dim night sky, a flying figure racing towards the "up" side.

It was hardly two-thirds across when the guard's whistle sang out its shrill warning.

"Quick, Jervis," exclaimed Thorndyke; "She's off!"

He leaped down on to the line, whither I followed instantly, and, crossing the rails, we clambered up together on to the footboard opposite an empty first-class compartment. Thorndyke's magazine knife, containing, among other implements, a railway-key, was already in his hand. The door was speedily unlocked, and, as we entered, Thorndyke ran through and looked out on to the platform.

"Just in time!" he exclaimed. "He is in one of the forward compartments."

He relocked the door, and, seating himself, proceeded to fill his pipe.

"And now," said I, as the train moved out of the station, "perhaps you will explain this little comedy."

"With pleasure," he replied, "if it needs any explanation. But you can hardly have forgotten Mr. James's flattering remarks in his report of the Greek Street incident, clearly giving the impression that the mysterious document was in my possession. When I read that, I knew I must look out for some attempt to recover it, though I hardly expected such promptness. Still, when Mr. Barton called without credentials or appointment, I viewed him with some suspicion. That suspicion deepened when he wanted us both to come. It deepened further when I found an impossible quantity of arsenic in his sample, and it gave place to certainty when, having allowed him to select the trains by which we were to travel, I went up to the laboratory and examined the time-table; for I then found that the last train for London left Rexford ten minutes after we were due to arrive. Obviously this was a plan to get us both safely out of the way while he and some of his friends ransacked our chambers for the missing document."

"I see; and that accounts for his extraordinary anxiety at the lateness of the train. But why did you come, if you knew it was a 'plant'?"

"My dear fellow," said Thorndyke, "I never miss an interesting experience if I can help it. There are possibilities in this, too, don't you see?"

"But supposing his friends have broken into our chambers already?"

"That contingency has been provided for; but I think they will wait for Mr. Barton—and us."

Our train, being the last one up, stopped at every station, and crawled slothfully in the intervals, so that it was past eleven o'clock when we reached Liverpool Street. Here we got out cautiously, and, mingling with the crowd, followed the unconscious Barton up the platform, through the barrier, and out into the street. He seemed in no special hurry, for, after pausing to light a cigar, he set off at an easy pace up New Broad Street.

Thorndyke hailed a hansom, and, motioning me to enter, directed the cabman to drive to Clifford's Inn Passage.

"Sit well back," said he, as we rattled away up New Broad Street. "We shall be passing our gay deceiver presently—in fact, there he is, a living, walking illustration of the folly of underrating the intelligence of one's adversary."

At Clifford's Inn Passage we dismissed the cab, and, retiring into the shadow of the dark, narrow alley, kept an eye on the gate of Inner Temple Lane. In about twenty minutes we observed our friend approaching on the south side of Fleet Street. He halted at the gate, plied the knocker, and after a brief parley with the night-porter, vanished through the wicket. We waited yet five minutes more, and then, having given him time to get clear of the entrance, we crossed the road.

The porter looked at us with some surprise.

"There's a gentleman just gone down to your chambers, sir," said he. "He told me you were expecting him."

"Quite right," said Thorndyke, with a dry smile, "I was. Good-night."

We slunk down the lane, past the church, and through the gloomy cloisters, giving a wide berth to all lamps and lighted entries, until, emerging into Paper Buildings, we crossed at the darkest part to King's Bench Walk, where Thorndyke made straight for the chambers of our friend Anstey, which were two doors above our own.

"Why are we coming here?" I asked, as we ascended the stairs.

But the question needed no answer when we reached the landing, for through the open door of our friend's chambers I could see in the darkened room Anstey himself with two uniformed constables and a couple of plain-clothes men.

"There has been no signal yet, sir," said one of the latter, whom I recognized as a detective-sergeant of our division.

"No," said Thorndyke, "but the M.C. has arrived. He came in five minutes before us."

"Then," exclaimed Anstey, "the ball will open shortly, ladies and gents. The boards are waxed, the fiddlers are tuning up, and——"

"Not quite so loud, if you please, sir," said the sergeant. "I think there is somebody coming up Crown Office Row."

The ball had, in fact, opened. As we peered cautiously out of the open window, keeping well back in the darkened room, a stealthy figure crept out of the shadow, crossed the road, and stole noiselessly into the entry of Thorndyke's chambers. It was quickly followed by a second figure, and then by a third, in which I recognized our elusive client.

"Now listen for the signal," said Thorndyke. "They won't waste time. Confound that clock!"

The soft-voiced bell of the Inner Temple clock, mingling with the harsher tones of St. Dunstan's and the Law Courts, slowly told out the hour of midnight; and as the last reverberations were dying away, some metallic object, apparently a coin, dropped with a sharp clink on to the pavement under our window.

At the sound the watchers simultaneously sprang to their feet.

"You two go first," said the sergeant, addressing the uniformed men, who thereupon stole noiselessly, in their rubber-soled boots, down the stone stairs and along the pavement. The rest of us followed, with less attention to silence, and as we ran up to Thorndyke's chambers, we were aware of quick but stealthy footsteps on the stairs above.

"They've been at work, you see," whispered one of the constables, flashing his lantern on to the iron-bound outer door of our sitting-room, on which the marks of a large jimmy were plainly visible.

The sergeant nodded grimly, and bidding the constables to remain on the landing, led the way upwards.

As we ascended, faint rustlings continued to be audible from above, and on the second-floor landing we met a man descending briskly, but without hurry, from the third. It was Mr. Barton, and I could not but admire the composure with which he passed the two detectives. But suddenly his glance fell on Thorndyke, and his composure vanished. With a wild stare of incredulous horror, he halted as if petrified; then he broke away and raced furiously down the stairs, and a moment later a muffled shout and the sound of a scuffle told us that he had received a check. On the next flight we met two more men, who, more hurried and less self-possessed, endeavoured to push past; but the sergeant barred the way.

"Why, bless me!" exclaimed the latter, "it's Moakey; and isn't that Tom Harris?"

"It's all right, sergeant," said Moakey plaintively, striving to escape from the officer's grip. "We've come to the wrong house, that's all."

The sergeant smiled indulgently. "I know," he replied. "But you're always coming to the wrong house, Moakey; and now you're just coming along with me to the right house."

He slipped his hand inside his captive's coat, and adroitly fished out a large, folding jimmy; whereupon the discomfited burglar abandoned all further protest.

On our return to the first-floor, we found Mr. Barton sulkily awaiting us, handcuffed to one of the constables, and watched by Polton with pensive disapproval.

"I needn't trouble you to-night, Doctor," said the sergeant, as he marshalled his little troop of captors and captives. "You'll hear from us in the morning. Goodnight, sir."

The melancholy procession moved off down the stairs, and we retired into our chambers with Anstey to smoke a last pipe.

"A capable man, that Barton," observed Thorndyke—"ready, plausible, and ingenious, but spoiled by prolonged contact with fools. I wonder if the police will perceive the significance of this little affair."

"They will be more acute than I am if they do," said I.

"Naturally," interposed Anstey, who loved to "cheek" his revered senior, "because there isn't any. It's only Thorndyke's bounce. He is really in a deuce of a fog himself."

However this may have been, the police were a good deal puzzled by the incident, for, on the following morning, we received a visit from no less a person than Superintendent Miller, of Scotland Yard.

"This is a queer business," said he, coming to the point at once— "this burglary, I mean. Why should they want to crack your place, right here in the Temple, too? You've got nothing of value here, have you? No 'hard stuff,' as they call it, for instance?"

"Not so much as a silver teaspoon," replied Thorndyke, who had a conscientious objection to plate of all kinds.

"It's odd," said the superintendent, "deuced odd. When we got your note, we thought these anarchist idiots had mixed you up with the case—you saw the papers, I suppose—and wanted to go through your rooms for some reason. We thought we had our hands on the gang, instead of which we find a party of common crooks that we're sick of the sight of. I tell you, sir, it's annoying when you think you've hooked a salmon, to bring up a blooming eel."

"It must be a great disappointment," Thorndyke agreed, suppressing a smile.

"It is," said the detective. "Not but what we're glad enough to get these beggars, especially Halkett, or Barton, as he calls himself —a mighty slippery customer is Halkett, and mischievous, too—but we're not wanting any disappointments just now. There was that big jewel job in Piccadilly, Taplin and Horne's; I don't mind telling you that we've not got the ghost of a clue. Then there's this anarchist affair. We're all in the dark there, too."

"But what about the cipher?" asked Thorndyke.

"Oh, hang the cipher!" exclaimed the detective irritably. "This Professor Poppelbaum may be a very learned man, but he doesn't help *us* much. He says the document is in Hebrew, and he has translated it into Double Dutch. Just listen to this!" He dragged out of his pocket a bundle of papers, and, dabbing down a photograph of the document before Thorndyke, commenced to read the Professor's report. " 'The document is written in the characters of the well-known inscription of Mesha, King of Moab' (who the devil's he? Never heard of him. Well known, indeed!) 'The language is Hebrew, and the words are separated by groups of letters, which are meaningless, and obviously introduced to mislead and confuse the reader. The words themselves are not strictly consecutive, but, by the interpolation of certain other words, a series of intelligible sentences is obtained, the meaning of which is not very clear, but is no doubt allegorical. The method of decipherment is shown in the accompanying tables, and the full rendering suggested on the enclosed sheet. It is to be noted that the writer of this document was apparently quite unacquainted with the Hebrew language, as appears from the absence of any grammatical construction.' That's the Professor's report, Doctor, and here are the tables showing how he worked it out. It makes my head spin to look at 'em."

He handed to Thorndyke a bundle of ruled sheets, which my colleague examined attentively for a while, and then passed on to me.

"This is very systematic and thorough," said he. "But now let us see the final result at which he arrives."

"It may be all very systematic," growled the superintendent, sorting out his papers, "but I tell you, sir, it's all BOSH!" The latter word he jerked out viciously, as he slapped down on the table the final product of the Professor's labors. "There," he continued, "that's what he calls the 'full rendering,' and I reckon it'll make your hair curl. It might be a message from Bedlam."

Thorndyke took up the first sheet, and as he compared the constructed renderings with the literal translation, the ghost of a smile stole across his usually immovable countenance.

"The meaning is certainly a little obscure," he observed, "though the reconstruction is highly ingenious; and, moreover, I think the Professor is probably right. That is to say, the words which he has supplied are probably the omitted parts of the passages from which the words of the cryptogram were taken. What do you think, Jervis?"

He handed me the two papers, of which one gave the actual words of the cryptogram, and the other a suggested reconstruction, with omitted words supplied. The first read:

"Woe　　city　　lies　　robbery　　prey　　noise　　whip

Analysis of the cipher with transliteration into modern square Hebrew characters and a translation into English. N. B. The cipher reads from right to left.

	Space	Word	Space	Word	Space	Word
Moabite	Y3	YJA9	A1	470	9A	ZYA
Hebrew		בבים		עיר		אוי
Translation		LIES		CITY		WOE
Moabite	5.ꞁ	6YP	6Y7	74X	HI	6Z1
Hebrew		קֹל		טרף		גַן
Translation		NOISE		PREY		ROBBERY
Moabite	w4	57Y&	9P	wo4	70$	XYW
Hebrew		אוֹפָן		רָעַשׁ		שׁוֹט
Translation		WHEEL		RATTLING		WHIP
Moabite	Y3	JY7	A1	39Y47	9&X	Y
Hebrew		יוֹם		מֶרְכָּבָה		סוּס
Translation		DAY		CHARIOT		HORSE

The Professor's Analysis

rattling   wheel   horse   chariot   day   darkness
gloominess   cloud   darkness   morning   mountain
people   strong   fire   them   flame."

Turning to the second paper, I read out the suggested rendering:

" 'Woe *to the bloody* city! *It is full of* lies *and* robbery; *the* prey *departeth not. The* noise *of a* whip, *and the noise of the* rattling *of the* wheel*s, and of the prancing* horse*s, and of the jumping* chariots.

" '*A* day *of* darkness *and of* gloominess, *a day of* cloud*s, and of thick* darkness, *as the* morning *spread upon the* mountains, *a great* people *and a* strong.

" '*A* fire *devoureth before* them, *and behind them a* flame *burneth.' *"

Here the first sheet ended, and, as I laid it down, Thorndyke looked at me inquiringly.

"There is a good deal of reconstruction in proportion to the original matter," I objected. "The Professor has 'supplied' more than three-quarters of the final rendering."

"Exactly," burst in the superintendent; "it's all Professor and no cryptogram."

"Still, I think the reading is correct," said Thorndyke. "As far as it goes, that is."

"Good Lord!" exclaimed the dismayed detective. "Do you mean to tell me, sir, that that balderdash is the real meaning of the thing?"

"I don't say that," replied Thorndyke. "I say it is correct as far as it goes; but I doubt its being the solution of the cryptogram."

"Have you been studying that photograph that I gave you?" demanded Miller, with sudden eagerness.

"I have looked at it," said Thorndyke evasively, "but I should like to examine the original if you have it with you."

"I have," said the detective. "Professor Poppelbaum sent it back with the solution. You can have a look at it, though I can't leave it with you without special authority."

He drew the document from his pocket-book and handed it to Thorndyke, who took it over to the window and scrutinized it closely. From the window he drifted into the adjacent office, closing the door after him; and presently the sound of a faint explosion told me that he had lighted the gas-fire.

"Of course," said Miller, taking up the translation again, "this gibberish is the sort of stuff you might expect from a parcel of crack-brained anarchists; but it doesn't seem to mean anything."

"Not to us," I agreed; "but the phrases may have some

prearranged significance. And then there are the letters between the words. It is possible that they may really form a cipher."

"I suggested that to the Professor," said Miller, "but he wouldn't hear of it. He is sure they are only dummies."

"I think he is probably mistaken, and so, I fancy, does my colleague. But we shall hear what he has to say presently."

"Oh, I know what he will say," growled Miller. "He will put the thing under the microscope, and tell us who made the paper, and what the ink is composed of, and then we shall be just where we were." The superintendent was evidently deeply depressed.

We sat for some time pondering in silence on the vague sentences of the Professor's translation, until, at length, Thorndyke reappeared, holding the document in his hand. He laid it quietly on the table by the officer, and then inquired:

"Is this an official consultation?"

"Certainly," replied Miller. "I was authorized to consult you respecting the translation, but nothing was said about the original. Still, if you want it for further study, I will get it for you."

"No, thank you," said Thorndyke. "I have finished with it. My theory turned out to be correct."

"Your theory!" exclaimed the superintendent, eagerly. "Do you mean to say——?"

"And, as you are consulting me officially, I may as well give you this."

He held out a sheet of paper, which the detective took from him and began to read.

"What is this?" he asked, looking up at Thorndyke with a puzzled frown. "Where did it come from?"

"It is the solution to the cryptogram," replied Thorndyke.

The detective re-read the contents of the paper, and, with the frown of perplexity deepening, once more gazed at my colleague.

"This is a joke, sir; you are fooling me," he said sulkily.

"Nothing of the kind," answered Thorndyke. "That is the genuine solution."

"But it's impossible! "exclaimed Miller. "Just look at it, Dr. Jervis."

I took the paper from his hand, and, as I glanced at it, I had no difficulty in understanding his surprise. It bore a short inscription in printed Roman capitals, thus:

"THE PICKERDILLEY STUF IS UP THE CHIMBLY 416 WARDOUR ST

2ND FLOUR BACK IT WAS HID BECOS OF OLD MOAKEYS JOOD MOAKEY
IS A BLITER."

"Then that fellow wasn't an anarchist at all!" I exclaimed.

"No," said Miller. "He was one of Moakey's gang. We suspected
Moakey of being mixed up with that job, but we couldn't fix it on
him. By Jove!" he added, slapping his thigh, "if this is right, and
I can lay my hands on the loot! Can you lend me a bag, Doctor?
I'm off to Wardour Street this very moment."

We furnished him with an empty suit-case, and, from the window,
watched him making for Mitre Court at a smart double.

"I wonder if he will find the booty," said Thorndyke. "It just
depends on whether the hiding-place was known to more than one of
the gang. Well, it has been a quaint case, and instructive, too. I
suspect our friend Barton and the evasive Schönberg were the colla-
borators who produced that curiosity of literature."

"May I ask how you deciphered the thing?" I said "It didn't
appear to take long."

"It didn't. It was merely a matter of testing a hypothesis; and
you ought not to have to ask that question," he added, with mock
severity, "seeing that you had what turn out to have been all the
necessary facts, two days ago. But I will prepare a document and
demonstrate to you to-morrow morning."

"So Miller was successful in his quest," said Thorndyke, as we
smoked our morning pipes after breakfast. "The 'entire swag', as
he calls it, was 'up the chimbly,' undisturbed."

He handed me a note which had been left, with the empty suit-
case, by a messenger, shortly before, and I was about to read it
when an agitated knock was heard at our door. The visitor, whom I
admitted, was a rather haggard and dishevelled elderly gentleman,
who, as he entered, peered inquisitively through his concave
spectacles from one of us to the other.

"Allow me to introduce myself, gentlemen," said he. "I am
Professor Poppelbaum."

Thorndyke bowed and offered a chair.

"I called yesterday afternoon," our visitor continued, "at Scotland Yard, where I heard of your remarkable decipherment and
of the convincing proof of its correctness. Thereupon I borrowed the
cryptogram, and have spent the entire night in studying it, but I
cannot connect your solution with any of the characters. I wonder

if you would do me the great favor of enlightening me as to your method of decipherment, and so save me further sleepless nights? You may rely on my discretion."

"Have you the document with you?" asked Thorndyke.

The Professor produced it from his pocket-book, and passed it to my colleague.

"You observe, Professor," said the latter, "that this is a laid paper, and has no water-mark?"

"Yes, I noticed that."

"And that the writing is in indelible Chinese ink?"

"Yes, yes," said the savant impatiently; "but it is the inscription that interests me, not the paper and ink."

"Precisely," said Thorndyke. "Now, it was the ink that interested me when I caught a glimpse of the document three days ago. 'Why,' I asked myself, 'should anyone use this troublesome medium'—for this appears to be stick ink—'when good writing ink is to be had?' What advantages has Chinese ink over writing ink? It has several advantages as a drawing ink, but for writing purposes it has only one: it is quite unaffected by wet. The obvious inference, then, was that this document was, for some reason, likely to be exposed to wet. But this inference instantly suggested another, which I was yesterday able to put to the test—thus."

He filled a tumbler with water, and, rolling up the document, dropped it in. Immediately there began to appear on it a new set of characters of a curious grey color. In a few seconds Thorndyke lifted out the wet paper, and held it up to the light, and now there was plainly visible an inscription in transparent lettering, like a very distinct water-mark. It was in printed Roman capitals, written across the other writing, and read:

"THE PICKERDILLEY STUF IS UP THE CHIMBLY 416 WARDOUR ST 2ND FLOUR BACK IT WAS HID BECOS OF OLD MOAKEYS JOOD MOAKEY IS A BLITER."

The Professor regarded the inscription with profound disfavor. "How do you suppose this was done?" he asked gloomily.

"I will show you," said Thorndyke. "I have prepared a piece of paper to demonstrate the process to Dr. Jervis. It is exceedingly simple."

He fetched from the office a small plate of glass, and a photographic dish in which a piece of thin notepaper was soaking in water.

"This paper," said Thorndyke, lifting it out and laying it on the glass, "has been soaking all night, and is now quite pulpy."

He spread a dry sheet of paper over the wet one, and on the former wrote heavily with a hard pencil, "Moakey is a bliter." On lifting the upper sheet, the writing was seen to be transferred in a deep grey to the wet paper, and when the latter was held up to the light the inscription stood out clear and transparent as if written with oil.

"When this dries," said Thorndyke, "the writing will completely disappear, but it will reappear whenever the paper is again wetted."

The Professor nodded.

"Very ingenious," said he—"a sort of artificial palimpsest, in fact. But I do not understand how that illiterate man could have written in the difficult Moabite script."

"He did not," said Thorndyke. "The 'cryptogram' was probably written by one of the leaders of the gang, who, no doubt, supplied copies to the other members to use instead of blank paper for secret communications. The object of the Moabite writing was evidently to divert attention from the paper itself, in case the communication fell into the wrong hands, and I must say it seems to have answered its purpose very well."

The Professor started, stung by the sudden recollection of his labors.

"Yes," he snorted; "but I am a scholar, sir, not a policeman. Every man to his trade."

He snatched up his hat, and with a curt "Good-morning," flung out of the room in dudgeon.

Thorndyke laughed softly.

"Poor Professor!" he murmured. "Our playful friend Barton has much to answer for."

The Aluminium Dagger

The "urgent call"—the instant, peremptory summons to professional duty—is an experience that appertains to the medical rather than the legal practitioner, and I had supposed, when I abandoned the clinical side of my profession in favor of the forensic, that henceforth I should know it no more; that the interrupted meal, the broken leisure, and the jangle of the night-bell, were things of the past; but in practice it was otherwise. The medical jurist is, so to speak, on the borderland of the two professions, and exposed to the vicissitudes of each calling, and so it happened from time to time that the professional services of my colleague or myself were demanded at a moment's notice. And thus it was in the case that I am about to relate.

The sacred rite of the "tub" had been duly performed, and the freshly-dried person of the present narrator was about to be insinuated into the first instalment of clothing, when a hurried step was heard upon the stair, and the voice of our laboratory assistant, Polton, arose at my colleague's door.

"There's a gentleman downstairs, sir, who says he must see you instantly on most urgent business. He seems to be in a rare twitter, sir——"

Polton was proceeding to descriptive particulars, when a second and more hurried step became audible, and a strange voice addressed Thorndyke.

"I have come to beg your immediate assistance, sir; a most dreadful thing has happened. A horrible murder has been committed. Can you come with me now?"

"I will be with you almost immediately," said Thorndyke. "Is the victim quite dead?"

"Quite. Cold and stiff. The police think——"

"Do the police know that you have come for me?" interrupted Thorndyke.

"Yes. Nothing is to be done until you arrive."

"Very well. I will be ready in a few minutes."

"And if you would wait downstairs, sir," Polton added persuasively, "I could help the doctor to get ready."

With this crafty appeal, he lured the intruder back to the sitting-room, and shortly after stole softly up the stairs with a small break-fast-tray, the contents of which he deposited firmly in our respective rooms, with a few timely words on the folly of "undertaking murders on an empty stomach." Thorndyke and I had meanwhile clothed ourselves with a celerity known only to medical practitioners and quick-change artists, and in a few minutes descended the stairs together, calling in at the laboratory for a few appliances that Thorndyke usually took with him on a vist of investigation.

As we entered the sitting-room, our visitor, who was feverishly pacing up and down, seized his hat with a gasp of relief. "You are ready to come?" he asked. "My carriage is at the door;" and, without waiting for an answer, he hurried out, and rapidly preceded us down the stairs.

The carriage was a roomy brougham, which fortunately accommodated the three of us, and as soon as we had entered and shut the door, the coachman whipped up his horse and drove off at a smart trot.

"I had better give you some account of the circumstances, as we go," said our agitated friend. "In the first place, my name is Curtis, Henry Curtis; here is my card. Ah! and here is another card, which I should have given you before. My solicitor, Mr. Marchmont, was with me when I made this dreadful discovery, and he sent me to you. He remained in the rooms to see that nothing is disturbed until you arrive."

"That was wise of him," said Thorndyke. "But now tell us exactly what has occurred."

"I will," said Mr. Curtis. "The murdered man was my brother-in-law, Alfred Hartridge, and I am sorry to say he was—well, he was a bad man. It grieves me to speak of him thus—*de mortuis,* you know—but, still, we must deal with the facts, even though they be painful."

"Undoubtedly," agreed Thorndyke.

"I have had a great deal of very unpleasant correspondence with him—Marchmont will tell you about that—and yesterday I left a note for him, asking for an interview, to settle the business, naming eight o'clock this morning as the hour, because I had to leave town before noon. He replied, in a very singular letter, that he would see me at that hour, and Mr. Marchmont very kindly consented to accompany me. Accordingly, we went to his chambers together this morning, arriving punctually at eight o'clock. We rang the bell several times, and knocked loudly at the door, but as there was no response, we went down and spoke to the hall-porter. This man, it seems, had already noticed, from the courtyard, that the electric lights were full on in Mr. Hartridge's sitting-room, as they had been all night, according to the statement of the night-porter; so now, suspecting that something was wrong, he came up with us, and rang the bell and battered at the door. Then, as there was still no sign of life within, he inserted his duplicate key and tried to open the door—unsuccessfully, however, as it proved to be bolted on the inside. Thereupon the porter fetched a constable, and, after a consultation, we decided that we were justified in breaking open the door; the porter produced a crowbar, and by our united efforts the door was eventually burst open. We entered, and—my God! Dr. Thorndyke, what a terrible sight it was that met our eyes! My brother-in-law was lying dead on the floor of the sitting-room. He had been stabbed—stabbed to death; and the dagger had not even been withdrawn. It was still sticking out of his back."

He mopped his face with his handkerchief, and was about to continue his account of the catastrophe when the carriage entered a quiet side-street between Westminster and Victoria, and drew up before a block of tall, new, red-brick buildings. A flurried hall-porter ran out to open the door, and we alighted opposite the main entrance.

"My brother-in-law's chambers are on the second-floor," said Mr. Curtis. "We can go up in the lift."

The porter had hurried before us, and already stood with his hand upon the rope. We entered the lift, and in a few seconds were discharged on to the second-floor, the porter, with furtive curiosity, following us down the corridor. At the end of the passage was a half-open door, considerably battered and bruised. Above the door, painted in white lettering, was the inscription, "Mr. Hartridge"; and through the doorway protruded the rather foxy countenance of Inspector Badger.

"I am glad you have come, sir," said he, as he recognized my colleague. "Mr. Marchmont is sitting inside like a watch-dog, and he growls if any of us even walks across the room."

The words formed a complaint, but there was a certain geniality in the speaker's manner which made me suspect that Inspector Badger was already navigating his craft on a lee shore.

We entered a small lobby or hall, and from thence passed into the sitting-room, where we found Mr. Marchmont keeping his vigil, in company with a constable and a uniformed inspector. The three rose softly as we entered, and greeted us in a whisper; and then, with one accord, we all looked towards the other end of the room, and so remained for a time without speaking.

There was, in the entire aspect of the room, something very grim and dreadful. An atmosphere of tragic mystery enveloped the most commonplace objects; and sinister suggestions lurked in the most familiar appearances. Especially impressive was the air of suspense —of ordinary, every-day life suddenly arrested—cut short in the twinkling of an eye. The electric lamps, still burning dim and red, though the summer sunshine streamed in through the windows; the half-emptied tumbler and open book by the empty chair, had each its whispered message of swift and sudden disaster, as had the hushed voices and stealthy movements of the waiting men, and, above all, an awesome shape that was but a few hours since a living man, and that now sprawled, prone and motionless on the floor.

"This is a mysterious affair," observed Inspector Badger, breaking the silence at length, "though it is clear enough up to a certain point. The body tells its own story."

We stepped across and looked down at the corpse. It was that of a somewhat elderly man, and lay, on an open space of floor before the fireplace, face downwards, with the arms extended. The slender hilt of a dagger projected from the back below the left shoulder, and, with the exception of a trace of blood upon the lips, this was the only indication of the mode of death. A little way from the body a clock-key lay on the carpet, and, glancing up at the clock on the mantelpiece, I perceived that the glass front was open.

"You see," pursued the inspector, noting my glance, "he was standing in front of the fireplace, winding the clock. Then the murderer stole up behind him—the noise of the turning key must have covered his movements—and stabbed him. And you see, from the position of the dagger on the left side of the back, that the murderer must have been left-handed. That is all clear enough. What is not clear is how he got in, and how he got out again."

"The body has not been moved, I suppose," said Thorndyke.

"No. We sent for Dr. Egerton, the police-surgeon, and he certified that the man was dead. He will be back presently to see you and arrange about the post-mortem."

"Then," said Thorndyke, "we will not disturb the body till he comes, except to take the temperature and dust the dagger-hilt."

He took from his bag a long, registering chemical thermometer and an insufflator or powder-blower. The former he introduced under the dead man's clothing against the abdomen, and with the latter blew a stream of fine yellow powder on to the black leather handle of the dagger. Inspector Badger stooped eagerly to examine the handle, as Thorndyke blew away the powder that had settled evenly on the surface.

"No finger-prints," said he, in a disappointed tone. "He must have worn gloves. But that inscription gives a pretty broad hint."

He pointed, as he spoke, to the metal guard of the dagger, on which was engraved, in clumsy lettering, the single word, "TRADITORE."

"That's the Italian for 'traitor,' " continued the inspector, "and I got some information from the porter that fits in with that suggestion. We'll have him in presently, and you shall hear."

"Meanwhile," said Thorndyke, "as the position of the body may be of importance in the inquiry, I will take one or two photographs and make a rough plan to scale. Nothing has been moved, you say? Who opened the windows?"

"They were open when we came in," said Mr. Marchmont. "Last night was very hot, you remember. Nothing whatever has been moved."

Thorndyke produced from his bag a small folding camera, a telescopic tripod, a surveyor's measuring-tape, a boxwood scale, and a sketch-block. He set up the camera in a corner, and exposed a plate, taking a general view of the room, and including the corpse. Then he moved to the door and made a second exposure.

"Will you stand in front of the clock, Jervis," he said, "and raise your hand as if winding it? Thanks; keep like that while I expose a plate."

I remained thus, in the position that the dead man was assumed to have occupied at the moment of the murder, while the plate was exposed, and then, before I moved, Thorndyke marked the position of my feet with a blackboard chalk. He next set up the tripod over the chalk marks, and took two photographs from that position, and finally photographed the body itself.

The photographic operations being concluded, he next proceeded, with remarkable skill and rapidity, to lay out on the sketch-block a ground plan of the room, showing the exact position of the various objects, on a scale of a quarter of an inch to the foot—a process that the inspector was inclined to view with some impatience.

"You don't spare trouble, Doctor," he remarked: "nor time either," he added, with a significant glance at his watch.

"No," answered Thorndyke, as he detached the finished sketch from the block; "I try to collect all the facts that may bear on a case. They may prove worthless, or they may turn out of vital importance; one never knows beforehand, so I collect them all. But here, I think, is Dr. Egerton."

The police-surgeon greeted Thorndyke with respectful cordiality, and we proceeded at once to the examination of the body. Drawing out the thermometer, my colleague noted the reading, and passed the instrument to Dr. Egerton.

"Dead about ten hours," remarked the latter, after a glance at it. "This was a very determined and mysterious murder."

"Very," said Thorndyke. "Feel that dagger, Jervis."

I touched the hilt, and felt the characteristic grating of bone.

"It is through the edge of a rib!" I exclaimed.

"Yes; it must have been used with extraordinary force. And you notice that the clothing is screwed up slightly, as if the blade had been rotated as it was driven in. That is a very peculiar feature, especially when taken together with the violence of the blow."

"It is singular, certainly," said Dr. Egerton, "though I don't know that it helps us much. Shall we withdraw the dagger before moving the body?"

"Certainly," replied Thorndyke, "or the movement may produce fresh injuries. But wait." He took a piece of string from his pocket, and, having drawn the dagger out a couple of inches, stretched the string in a line parallel to the flat of the blade. Then, giving me the ends to hold, he drew the weapon out completely. As the blade emerged, the twist in the clothing disappeared. "Observe," said he, "that the string gives the direction of the wound, and that the cut in the clothing no longer coincides with it. There is quite a consider- able angle, which is the measure of the rotation of the blade."

"Yes, it is odd," said Dr. Egerton, "though, as I said, I doubt that it helps us."

"At present," Thorndyke rejoined dryly, "we are noting the facts."

"Quite so," agreed the other, reddening slightly; "and perhaps we had better move the body to the bedroom, and make a preliminary inspection of the wound."

We carried the corpse into the bedroom, and, having examined the wound without eliciting anything new, covered the remains with a sheet, and returned to the sitting-room.

"Well, gentlemen," said the inspector, "you have examined the body and the wound, and you have measured the floor and the furniture, and taken photographs, and made a plan, but we don't seem much more forward. Here's a man murdered in his rooms. There is only one entrance to the flat, and that was bolted on the inside at the time of the murder. The windows are some forty feet from the ground; there is no rain-pipe near any of them; they are set flush in the wall, and there isn't a foothold for a fly on any part of that wall. The grates are modern, and there isn't room for a good-sized cat to crawl up any of the chimneys. Now, the question is, How did the murderer get in, and how did he get out again?"

"Still," said Mr. Marchmont, "the fact is that he did get in, and that he is not here now; and therefore he must have got out; and therefore it must have been possible for him to get out. And, further, it must be possible to discover how he got out."

The inspector smiled sourly, but made no reply.

"The circumstances," said Thorndyke, "appear to have been these: The deceased seems to have been alone; and there is no trace of a second occupant of the room, and only one half-emptied tumbler on the table. He was sitting reading when apparently he noticed that the clock had stopped—at ten minutes to twelve; he laid his book, face downwards, on the table, and rose to wind the clock, and as he was winding it he met his death."

"By a stab dealt by a left-handed man, who crept up behind him on tiptoe," added the inspector.

Thorndyke nodded. "That would seem to be so," he said. "But now let us call in the porter, and hear what he has to tell us."

The custodian was not difficult to find, being, in fact, engaged at that moment in a survey of the premises through the slit of the letter-box.

"Do you know what persons visited these rooms last night?" Thorndyke asked him, when he entered, looking somewhat sheepish.

"A good many were in and out of the building," was the answer, "but I can't say if any of them came to this flat. I saw Miss Curtis pass in about nine.

"My daughter!" exclaimed Mr. Curtis, with a start. "I didn't know that."

"She left about nine-thirty," the porter added.

"Do you know what she came about?" asked the inspector.

"I can guess," replied Mr. Curtis.

"Then don't say," interrupted Mr. Marchmont. "Answer no questions."

"You're very close, Mr. Marchmont," said the inspector; "we are not suspecting the young lady. We don't ask, for instance, if she is left-handed."

He glanced craftily at Mr. Curtis as he made this remark, and I noticed that our client suddenly turned deathly pale, whereupon the inspector looked away again quickly, as though he had not observed the change.

"Tell us about those Italians again," he said, addressing the porter. "When did the first of them come here?"

"About a week ago," was the reply. "He was a common-looking man—looked like an organ-grinder—and he brought a note to my lodge. It was in a dirty envelope, and was addressed 'Mr. Hartridge, Esq., Brackenhurst Mansions,' in a very bad handwriting. The man gave me the note and asked me to give it to Mr. Hartridge; then he went away, and I took the note up and dropepd it into the letter-box."

"What happened next?"

"Why, the very next day an old hag of an Italian woman—one of them fortune-telling swines with a cage of birds on a stand—came and set up just by the main doorway. I soon sent her packing, but, bless you! she was back again in ten minutes, birds and all. I sent her off again—I kept on sending her off, and she kept on coming back, until I was reg'lar wore to a thread."

"You seem to have picked up a bit since then," remarked the inspector with a grin and a glance at the sufferer's very pronounced bow-window.

"Perhaps I have," the custodian replied haughtily. "Well, the next day there was a ice-cream man—a reg'lar waster, *he* was. Stuck outside as if he was froze to the pavement. Kept giving the errand-boys tasters, and when I tried to move him on, he told me not to obstruct his business. Business, indeed! Well, there them boys stuck, one after the other, wiping their tongues round the bottoms of them glasses, until I was fit to bust with aggravation. And *he* kept me going all day.

"Then, the day after that there was a barrel-organ, with a mangy-looking monkey on it. He was the worst of all. Profane, too, *he* was. Kept mixing up sacred tunes and comic songs: 'Rock of Ages,' 'Bill Bailey,' 'Cujus Animal,' and 'Over the Garden Wall'. And when I tried to move him on, that little blighter of a monkey made a run at my leg; and then the man grinned and started playing 'Wait Till the Clouds Roll By'. I tell you, it was fair sickening."

He wiped his brow at the recollection, and the inspector smiled appreciatively.

"And that was the last of them?" said the latter; and as the porter nodded sulkily, he asked: "Should you recognize the note that the Italian gave you?"

"I should," answered the porter with frosty dignity.

The inspector bustled out of the room, and returned a minute later with a letter-case in his hand.

"This was in his breast-pocket," said he, laying the bulging case on the table, and drawing up a chair. "Now, here are three letters tied together. Ah! this will be the one." He untied the tape, and held out a dirty envelope addressed in a sprawling, illiterate hand to "Mr. Hartridge, Esq." "Is that the note the Italian gave you?"

The porter examined it critically. "Yes," said he; "that is the one."

The inspector drew the letter out of the envelope, and, as he opened it, his eyebrows went up.

"What do you make of that, Doctor?" he said, handing the sheet to Thorndyke.

Thorndyke regarded it for a while in silence, with deep attention. Then he carried it to the window, and, taking his lens from his pocket, examined the paper closely, first with the low power, and then with the highly magnifying Coddington attachment.

"I should have thought you could see that with the naked eye," said the inspector, with a sly grin at me. "It's a pretty bold design."

"Yes," replied Thorndyke; "a very interesting production. What do you say, Mr. Marchmont?"

The solicitor took the note, and I looked over his shoulder. It was certainly a curious production. Written in red ink, on the commonest notepaper, and in the same sprawling hand as the address, was the following message: "You are given six days to do what is just. By the sign above, know what to expect if you fail." The sign referred to was a skull and cross-bones, very neatly, but rather unskilfully, drawn at the top of the paper.

"This," said Mr. Marchmont, handing the document to Mr. Curtis, "explains the singular letter that he wrote yesterday. You have it with you, I think?"

"Yes," replied Mr. Curtis; "here it is."

He produced a letter from his pocket, and read aloud:

"'Yes: come if you like, though it is an ungodly hour. Your threatening letters have caused me great amusement. They are worthy of Sadler's Wells in its prime.

"'ALFRED HARTRIDGE.'"

"Was Mr. Hartridge ever in Italy?" asked Inspector Badger.

"Oh yes," replied Mr. Curtis. "He stayed at Capri nearly the whole of last year."

"Why, then, that gives us our clue. Look here. Here are these two other letters; E.C. postmark—Saffron Hill is E.C. And just look at that!"

He spread out the last of the mysterious letters, and we saw that, besides the *memento mori,* it contained only three words: "Beware! Remember Capri!"

"If you have finished, Doctor, I'll be off and have a look round Little Italy. Those four Italians oughtn't to be difficult to find, and we've got the porter to identify them."

"Before you go," said Thorndyke, "there are two little matters that I should like to settle. One is the dagger: it is in your pocket, I think. May I have a look at it?"

The inspector rather reluctantly produced the dagger and handed it to my colleague.

"A very singular weapon, this," said Thorndyke, regarding the dagger thoughtfully, and turning it about to view its different parts. "Singular both in shape and material. I have never seen an aluminium hilt before, and bookbinder's morocco is a little unusual."

"The aluminium was for lightness," explained the inspector,

"and it was made narrow to carry up the sleeve, I expect."

"Perhaps so," said Thorndyke.

He continued his examination, and presently, to the inspector's delight, brought forth his pocket lens.

"I never saw such a man!" exclaimed the jocose detective. "His motto ought to be, 'We magnify thee.' I suppose he'll measure it next."

The inspector was not mistaken. Having made a rough sketch of the weapon on his block, Thorndyke produced from his bag a folding rule and a delicate calliper-gauge. With these instruments he proceeded, with extraordinary care and precision, to take the dimensions of the various parts of the dagger, entering each measurement in its place on the sketch, with a few brief, descriptive details.

"The other matter," said he at length, handing the dagger back to the inspector, "refers to the houses opposite."

He walked to the window, and looked out at the backs of a row of tall buildings similar to the one we were in. They were about thirty yards distant, and were separated from us by a piece of ground, planted with shrubs and intersected by gravel paths.

"If any of those rooms were occupied last night," continued Thorndyke, "we might obtain an actual eyewitness of the crime. This room was brilliantly lighted, and all the blinds were up, so that an observer at any of those windows could see right into the room, and very distinctly, too. It might be worth inquiring into."

"Yes, that's true," said the inspector; "though I expect, if any of them have seen anything, they will come forward quick enough when they read the report in the papers. But I must be off now, and I shall have to lock you out of the rooms."

As we went down the stairs, Mr. Marchmont announced his intention of calling on us in the evening, "unless," he added, "you want any information from me now."

"I do," said Thorndyke. "I want to know who is interested in this man's death."

"That," replied Marchmont, "is rather a queer story. Let us take a turn in that garden that we saw from the window. We shall be quite private there."

He beckoned to Mr. Curtis, and, when the inspector had departed with the police-surgeon, we induced the porter to let us into the garden.

"The question that you asked," Mr. Marchmont began, looking up curiously at the tall houses opposite, "is very simply answered. The only person immediately interested in the death of Alfred Hartridge is his executor and sole legatee, a man named Leonard Wolfe. He is no relation of the deceased, merely a friend, but he inherits the entire estate—about twenty thousand pounds. The circumstances are these: Alfred Hartridge was the elder of two brothers, of whom the younger, Charles, died before his father, leaving a widow and three children. Fifteen years ago the father died, leaving the whole of his property to Alfred, with the understanding that he should support his brother's family and make the children his heirs."

"Was there no will?" asked Thorndyke.

"Under great pressure from the friends of his son's widow, the old man made a will shortly before he died; but he was then very old and rather childish, so the will was contested by Alfred, on the grounds of undue influence, and was ultimately set aside. Since then Alfred Hartridge has not paid a penny towards the support of his brother's family. If it had not been for my client, Mr. Curtis, they might have starved; the whole burden of the support of the widow and the education of the children has fallen upon him.

"Well, just lately the matter has assumed an acute form, for two reasons. The first is that Charles's eldest son, Edmund, has come of age. Mr. Curtis had him articled to a solicitor, and, as he is now fully qualified, and a most advantageous proposal for a partnership has been made, we have been putting pressure on Alfred to supply the necessary capital in accordance with his father's wishes. This he had refused to do, and it was with reference to this matter that we were calling on him this morning. The second reason involves a curious and disgraceful story. There is a certain Leonard Wolfe, who has been an intimate friend of the deceased. He is, I may say, a man of bad character, and their association has been of a kind creditable to neither. There is also a certain woman named Hester Greene, who had certain claims upon the deceased, which we need not go into at present. Now, Leonard Wolfe and the deceased, Alfred Hartridge, entered into an agreement, the terms of which were these: (1) Wolfe was to marry Hester Greene, and in consideration of this service (2) Alfred Hartridge was to assign to Wolfe the whole of his property, absolutely, the actual transfer to take place on the death of Hartridge."

"And has this transaction been completed?" asked Thorndyke.
"Yes, it has, unfortunately. But we wished to see if anything could be done for the widow and the children during Hartridge's lifetime. No doubt, my client's daughter, Miss Curtis, called last night on a similar mission—very indiscreetly, since the matter was in our hands; but, you know, she is engaged to Edmund Hartridge—and I expect the inteview was a pretty stormy one."

Thorndyke remained silent for a while, pacing slowly along the gravel path, with his eyes bent on the ground: not abstractedly, however, but with a searching attentive glance that roved amongst the shrubs and bushes, as though he were looking for something.

"What sort of man," he asked presently, "is this Leonard Wolfe? Obviously he is a low scoundrel, but what is he like in other respects? Is he a fool, for instance?"

"Not at all, I should say," said Mr. Curtis. "He was formerly an engineer, and, I believe, a very capable mechanician. Latterly he has lived on some property that came to him, and has spent both his time and his money in gambling and dissipation. Consequently, I expect he is pretty short of funds at present."

"And in appearance?"

"I only saw him once," replied Mr. Curtis, "and all I can remember of him is that he is rather short, fair, thin, and clean-shaven, and that he has lost the middle finger of his left hand."

"And he lives at——?"

"Eltham, in Kent. Morton Grange, Eltham," said Mr. Marchmont. "And now, if you have all the information that you require, I must really be off, and so must Mr. Curtis."

The two men shook our hands and hurried away, leaving Thorndyke gazing meditatively at the dingy flower-beds.

"A strange and interesting case, this, Jervis," said he, stooping to peer under a laurel-bush. "The inspector is on a hot scent—a most palpable red herring on a most obvious string; but that is his business. Ah, here comes the porter, intent, no doubt, on pumping us, whereas——" He smiled genially at the approaching custodian, and asked: "Where did you say those houses fronted?"

"Cotman Street, sir," answered the porter. "They are nearly all offices."

"And the numbers? That open second-floor window, for instance?"

"That is number six; but the house opposite Mr. Hartridge's rooms is number eight."

"Thank you."

Thorndyke was moving away, but suddenly turned again to the porter.

"By the way," said he. "I dropped something out of the window just now—a small flat piece of metal, like this." He made on the back of his visiting card a neat sketch of a circular disc, with a hexagonal hole through it, and handed the card to the porter. "I can't say where it fell," he continued; "these flat things scale about so; but you might ask the gardener to look for it. I will give him a sovereign if he brings it to my chambers, for, although it is of no value to anyone else, it is of considerable value to me."

The porter touched his hat briskly, and as we turned out at the gate, I looked back and saw him already wading among the shrubs.

The object of the porter's quest gave me considerable mental occupation. I had not seen Thorndyke drop anything, and it was not his way to finger carelessly any object of value. I was about to question him on the subject, when, turning sharply round into Cotman Street, he drew up at the doorway of number six, and began attentively to read the names of the occupants.

"'Third-floor,'" he read out, "'Mr. Thomas Barlow, Commission Agent.' Hum! I think we will look in on Mr. Barlow."

He stepped quickly up the stone stairs, and I followed, until we arrived, somewhat out of breath, on the third-floor. Outside the Commission Agent's door he paused for a moment, and we both listened curiously to an irregular sound of shuffling feet from within. Then he softly opened the door and looked into the room. After remaining thus for nearly a minute, he looked round at me with a broad smile, and noiselessly set the door wide open. Inside, a lanky youth of fourteen was practising, with no mean skill, the manipulation of an appliance known by the appropriate name of diabolo; and so absorbed was he in his occupation that we entered and shut the door without being observed. At length the shuttle missed the string and flew into a large waste-paper basket; the boy turned and confronted us, and was instantly covered with confusion.

"Allow me," said Thorndyke, rooting rather unnecessarily in the waste-paper basket, and handing the toy to its owner. "I need not ask if Mr. Barlow is in," he added, "nor if he is likely to return shortly."

"He won't be back to-day," said the boy, perspiring with embarrassment; "he left before I came. I was rather late."

"I see," said Thorndyke. "The early bird catches the worm, but the late bird catches the diabolo. How did you know he would not be back?"

"He left a note. Here it is."

He exhibited the document, which was neatly written in red ink. Thorndyke examined it attentively, and then asked:

"Did you break the inkstand yesterday?"

The boy stared at him in amazement. "Yes, I did," he answered. "How did you know?"

"I didn't, or I should not have asked. But I see that he has used his stylo to write this note."

The boy regarded Thorndyke distrustfully, as he continued:

"I really called to see if your Mr. Barlow was a gentleman whom I used to know; but I expect you can tell me. My friend was tall and thin, dark, and clean-shaved."

"This ain't him, then," said the boy. "He's thin, but he ain't tall or dark. He's got a sandy beard and he wears spectacles and a wig. I know a wig when I see one," he added cunningly, " 'cause my father wears one. He puts it on a peg to comb it, and he swears at me when I larf."

"My friend had injured his left hand," pursued Thorndyke.

"I dunno about that," said the youth. "Mr. Barlow nearly always wears gloves; he always wears one on his left hand, anyhow."

"Ah well! I'll just write him a note on the chance, if you will give me a piece of notepaper. Have you any ink?"

"There's some in the bottle. I'll dip the pen in for you."

He produced, from the cupboard, an opened packet of cheap notepaper and a packet of similar envelopes, and, having dipped the pen to the bottom of the ink-bottle, handed it to Thorndyke, who sat down and hastily scribbled a short note. He had folded the paper, and was about to address the envelope, when he appeared suddenly to alter his mind.

"I don't think I will leave it, after all," he said, slipping the folded paper into his pocket. "No. Tell him I called—Mr. Horace Budge— and say I will look in again in a day or two."

The youth watched our exit with an air of perplexity, and he even came out on to the landing, the better to observe us over the balusters; until, unexpectedly catching Thorndyke's eye, he withdrew his head with remarkable suddenness, and retired in disorder.

To tell the truth, I was now little less perplexed than the office-boy by Thorndyke's proceedings; in which I could discover no relevancy to the investigation that I presumed he was engaged upon: and the last straw was laid upon the burden of my curiosity when he stopped at a staircase window, drew the note out of his pocket, examined it with his lens, held it up to the light, and chuckled aloud.

"Luck," he observed, "though no substitute for care and intelligence, is a very pleasant addition. Really, my learned brother, we are doing uncommonly well."

When we reached the hall, Thorndyke stopped at the housekeeper's box, and looked in with a genial nod.

"I have just been up to see Mr. Barlow," said he. "He seems to have left quite early."

"Yes, sir," the man replied. "He went away about half-past eight."

"That was very early; and presumably he came earlier still?"

"I suppose so," the man assented, with a grin; "but I had only just come on when he left."

"Had he any luggage with him?"

"Yes, sir. There was two cases, a square one and a long, narrow one, about five foot long. I helped him to carry them down to the cab."

"Which was a four-wheeler, I suppose?"

"Yes, sir."

"Mr. Barlow hasn't been here very long, has he?" Thorndyke inquired.

"No, He only came in last quarter-day—about six weeks ago."

"Ah well! I must call another day. Good-morning"; and Thorndyke strode out of the building, and made directly for the cab-rank in the adjoining street. Here he stopped for a minute or two to parley with the driver of a four-wheeled cab, whom he finally commissioned to convey us to a shop in New Oxford Street. Having dismissed the cabman with his blessing and a half-sovereign, he vanished into the shop, leaving me to gaze at the lathes, drills, and bars of metal displayed in the window. Presently he emerged with a small parcel, and explained, in answer to my inquiring look: "A strip of tool steel and a block of metal for Polton."

His next purchase was rather more eccentric. We were proceeding along Holborn when his attention was suddenly arrested by the window of a furniture shop, in which was displayed a collection of obsolete French small-arms—relics of the tragedy of 1870—which were being sold for decorative purposes. After a brief inspection,

he entered the shop, and shortly reappeared carrying a long sword-
bayonet and an old Chassepôt rifle.

"What may be the meaning of this martial display?" I asked, as
we turned down Fetter Lane.

"House protection," he replied promptly. "You will agree that
a discharge of musketry, followed by a bayonet charge, would dis-
concert the boldest of burglars."

I laughed at the absurd picture thus drawn of the strenuous
house-protector, but nevertheless continued to speculate on the
meaning of my friend's eccentric proceedings, which I felt sure were
in some way related to the murder in Brackenhurst Chambers,
though I could not trace the connection.

After a late lunch, I hurried out to transact such of my business
as had been interrupted by the stirring events of the morning, leaving Thorndyke busy with a drawing-board, squares, scale, and compasses, making accurate, scaled drawings from his rough sketches;
while Polton, with the brown-paper parcel in his hand, looked on
at him with an air of anxious expectation.

As I was returning homeward in the evening by way of Mitre
Court, I overtook Mr. Marchmont, who was also bound for our
chambers, and we walked on together.

"I had a note from Thorndyke," he explained, "asking for a
specimen of handwriting, so I thought I would bring it along myself,
and hear if he has any news."

When we entered the chambers, we found Thorndyke in earnest
consultation with Polton, and on the table before them I observed
to my great surprise, the dagger with which the murder had been
committed.

"I have got you the specimen that you asked for," said Marchmont. "I didn't think I should be able to, but, by a lucky chance,

The Aluminium Dagger

Curtis kept the only letter he ever received from the party in
question."

He drew the letter from his wallet, and handed it to Thorndyke,
who looked at it attentively and with evident satisfaction.

"By the way," said Marchmont, taking up the dagger, "I thought the inspector took this away with him."

"He took the original," replied Thorndyke. "This is a duplicate, which Polton has made, for experimental purposes, from my drawings."

"Really!" exclaimed Marchmont, with a glance of respectful admiration at Polton; "it is a perfect replica—and you have made it so quickly, too."

"It was quite easy to make," said Polton, "to a man accustomed to work in metal."

"Which," added Thorndyke, "is a fact of some evidential value."

At this moment a hansom drew up outside. A moment later flying footsteps were heard on the stairs. There was a furious battering at the door, and, as Polton threw it open, Mr. Curtis burst wildly into the room.

"Here is a frightful thing, Marchmont!" he gasped. "Edith—my daughter—arrested for the murder. Inspector Badger came to our house and took her. My God! I shall go mad!"

Thorndyke laid his hand on the excited man's shoulder. "Don't distress yourself, Mr. Curtis," said he. "There is no occasion, I assure you. I suppose," he added, "your daughter is left-handed?"

"Yes, she is, by a most disastrous coincidence. But what are we to do? Good God! Dr. Thorndyke, they have taken her to prison—to prison—think of it! My poor Edith!"

"We'll soon have her out," said Thorndyke. "But listen; there is someone at the door."

A brisk rat-tat confirmed his statement, and when I rose to open the door, I found myself confronted by Inspector Badger. There was a moment of extreme awkwardness, and then both the detective and Mr. Curtis proposed to retire in favor of the other.

"Don't go, inspector," said Thorndyke; "I want to have a word with you. Perhaps Mr. Curtis would look in again, say, in an hour. Will you? We shall have news for you by then, I hope."

Mr. Curtis agreed hastily, and dashed out of the room with his characteristic impetuosity. When he had gone, Thorndyke turned to the detective, and remarked dryly:

"You seem to have been busy, inspector?"

"Yes," replied Badger; "I haven't let the grass grow under my feet; and I've got a pretty strong case against Miss Curtis already. You see, she was the last person seen in the company of the deceased;

she had a grievance against him; she is left-handed, and you remember that the murder was committed by a left-handed person."

"Anything else?"

"Yes. I have seen those Italians, and the whole thing was a put-up job. A woman, in a widow's dress and veil, paid them to go and play the fool outside the building, and she gave them the letter that was left with the porter. They haven't identified her yet, but she seems to agree in size with Miss Curtis."

"And how did she get out of the chambers, with the door bolted on the inside?"

"Ah, there you are! That's a mystery at present—unless you can give us an explanation." The inspector made this qualification with a faint grin, and added: "As there was no one in the place when we broke into it, the murderer must have got out somehow. You can't deny that."

"I do deny it, nevertheless," said Thorndyke. "You look surprised," he continued (which was undoubtedly true), "but yet the whole thing is exceedingly obvious. The explanation struck me directly I looked at the body. There was evidently no practicable exit from the flat, and there was certainly no one in it when you entered. Clearly, then, *the murderer had never been in the place at all.*"

"I don't follow you in the least," said the inspector.

"Well," said Thorndyke, "as I have finished with the case, and am handing it over to you, I will put the evidence before you *seriatim*. Now, I think we are agreed that, at the moment when the blow was struck, the deceased was standing before the fireplace, winding the clock. The dagger entered obliquely from the left, and, if you recall its position, you will remember that its hilt pointed directly towards an open window."

"Which was forty feet from the ground."

"Yes. And now we will consider the very peculiar character of the weapon with which the crime was committed."

He had placed his hand upon the knob of a drawer, when we were interrupted by a knock at the door. I sprang up, and, opening it, admitted no less a person than the porter of Brackenhurst Chambers. The man looked somewhat surprised on recognizing our visitors, but advanced to Thorndyke, drawing a folded paper from his pocket.

"I've found the article you were looking for, sir," said he, "and a rare hunt I had for it. It had stuck in the leaves of one of them shrubs."

Thorndyke opened the packet, and, having glanced inside, laid it on the table.

"Thank you," said he, pushing a sovereign across to the gratified official. "The inspector has your name, I think?"

"He have, sir," replied the porter; and, pocketing his fee, he departed, beaming.

"To return to the dagger," said Thorndyke, opening the drawer. "It was a very peculiar one, as I have said, and as you will see from this model, which is an exact duplicate." Here he exhibited Polton's production to the astonished detective. "You see that it is extraordinarily slender, and free from projections, and of unusual materials. You also see that it was obviously not made by an ordinary dagger-maker; that, in spite of the Italian word scrawled on it, there is plainly written all over it 'British mechanic.' The blade is made from a strip of common three-quarter-inch tool steel; the hilt is turned from an aluminium rod; and there is not a line of engraving on it that could not be produced in a lathe by any engineer's apprentice. Even the boss at the top is mechanical, for it is just like an ordinary hexagon nut. Then, notice the dimensions, as shown on my drawing. The parts A and B, which just project beyond the blade, are exactly similar in diameter—and such exactness could hardly be accidental. They are each parts of a circle having a diameter of 10.9 millimetres—a dimension which happens, by a singular coincidence, to be exactly the calibre of the old Chassepôt rifle, specimens of which are now on sale at several shops in London. Here is one, for instance."

He fetched the rifle that he had bought, from the corner in which it was standing, and, lifting the dagger by its point, slipped the hilt into the muzzle. When he let go, the dagger slid quietly down the barrel, until its hilt appeared in the open breech.

"Good, God!" exclaimed Marchmont. "You don't suggest that the dagger was shot from a gun?"

"I do, indeed; and you now see the reason for the aluminium hilt—to diminish the weight of the already heavy projectile—and also for this hexagonal boss on the end?"

"No, I do not," said the inspector; "but I say that you are suggesting an impossibility."

"Then," replied Thorndyke, "I must explain and demonstrate.

To begin with, this projectile had to travel point foremost; therefore it had to be made to spin—and it certainly was spinning when it entered the body, as the clothing and the wound showed us. Now, to make it spin, it had to be fired from a rifled barrel; but as the hilt would not engage in the rifling, it had to be fitted with something that would. That something was evidently a soft metal washer, which fitted on to this hexagon, and which would be pressed into the grooves of the rifling, and so spin the dagger, but would drop off as soon as the weapon left the barrel. Here is such a washer, which Polton has made for us."

He laid on the table a metal disc, with a hexagonal hole through it.

"This is all very ingenious," said the inspector, "but I say it is impossible and fantastic."

"It certainly sounds rather improbable," Marchmont agreed.

"We will see," said Thorndyke. "Here is a makeshift cartridge of Polton's manufacture, containing an eighth charge of smokeless powder for a 20-bore gun."

He fitted the washer on to the boss of the dagger in the open breech of the rifle, pushed it into the barrel, inserted the cartridge, and closed the breech. Then, opening the office-door, he displayed a target of padded strawboard against the wall.

"The length of the two rooms," said he, "gives us a distance of thirty-two feet. Will you shut the windows, Jervis?"

I complied, and he then pointed the rifle at the target. There was a dull report—much less loud than I had expected—and when we looked at the target, we saw the dagger driven in up to its hilt at the margin of the bull's-eye.

"You see," said Thorndyke, laying down the rifle, "that the thing is practicable. Now for the evidence as to the actual occurrence. First, on the original dagger there are linear scratches which exactly correspond with the grooves of the rifling. Then there is the fact that the dagger was certainly spinning from left to right—in the direction of the rifling, that is—when it entered the body. And then there is this, which, as you heard, the porter found in the garden."

He opened the paper packet. In it lay a metal disc, perforated by a hexagonal hole. Stepping into the office, he picked up from the floor the washer that he had put on the dagger, and laid it on the paper beside the other. The two discs were identical in size, and the margin of each was indented with identical markings, corresponding to the rifling of the barrel.

The inspector gazed at the two discs in silence for a while; then, looking up at Thorndyke, he said:

"I give in, Doctor. You're right, beyond all doubt; but how you came to think of it beats me into fits. The only question now is, who fired the gun, and why wasn't the report heard?"

"As to the latter," said Thorndyke, "it is probable that he used a compressed-air attachment, not only to diminish the noise, but also to prevent any traces of the explosive being left on the dagger. As to the former, I think I can give you the murderer's name; but we had better take the evidence in order. You may remember," he continued, "that when Dr. Jervis stood as if winding the clock, I chalked a mark on the floor where he stood. Now, standing on that marked spot, and looking out of the open window, I could see two of the windows of a house nearly opposite. They were the second- and third-floor windows of No. 6, Cotman Street. The second-floor is occupied by a firm of architects; the third-floor by a commission agent named Thomas Barlow. I called on Mr. Barlow, but before describing my visit, I will refer to another matter. You haven't those threatening letters about you, I suppose?"

"Yes, I have," said the inspector; and he drew forth a wallet from his breast-pocket.

"Let us take the first one, then," said Thorndyke. "You see that the paper and envelope are of the very commonest, and the writing illiterate. But the ink does not agree with this. Illiterate people usually buy their ink in penny bottles. Now, this envelope is addressed with Draper's dichroic ink—a superior office ink, sold only in large bottles—and the red ink in which the note is written is an unfixed, scarlet ink, such as is used by draughtsmen, and has been used, as you can see, in a stylographic pen. But the most interesting thing about this letter is the design drawn at the top. In an artistic sense, the man could not draw, and the anatomical details of the skull are ridiculous. Yet the drawing is very neat. It has the clean, wiry line of a machine drawing, and is done with a steady, practised hand. It is also perfectly symmetrical; the skull, for instance, is exactly in the centre, and, when we examine it through a lens, we see why it is so, for we discover traces of a pencilled centre-line and ruled cross-lines. Moreover, the lens reveals a tiny particle of draughts-man's soft, red rubber, with which the pencil lines were taken out; and all these facts, taken together, suggest that the drawing was made by someone accustomed to making accurate mechanical drawings. And now we will return to Mr. Barlow. He was out when I called, but I took the liberty of glancing round the office, and this is what I saw. On the mantel-shelf was a twelve-inch flat boxwood rule, such as engineers use, a piece of soft, red rubber, and a stone bottle of Draper's dichroic ink. I obtained, by a simple ruse, a specimen of the office notepaper and the ink. We will examine it presently. I found that Mr. Barlow is a new tenant, that he is rather short, wears a wig and spectacles, and always wears a glove on his left hand. He left the office at 8.30 this morning, and no one saw him arrive. He had with him a square case, and a narrow, oblong one about five feet in length; and he took a cab to Victoria, and apparently caught the 8.51 train to Chatham."

"Ah!" exclaimed the inspector.

"But," continued Thorndyke, "now examine those three letters, and compare them with this note that I wrote in Mr. Barlow's office. You see that the paper is of the same make, with the same water-mark, but that is of no great significance. What is of crucial importance is this: You see, in each of these letters, two tiny indentations near the bottom corner. Somebody has used compasses or drawing-pins over the packet of notepaper, and the points have made little indentations, which have marked several of the sheets. Now, notepaper is cut to its size after it is folded, and if you stick a pin into the top sheet of a section, the indentations on all the underlying sheets will be at exactly similar distances from the edges and corners of the sheet. But you see that these little dents are all at the same distance from the edges and the corner." He demonstrated the fact with a pair of compasses. "And now look at this sheet, which I obtained at Mr. Barlow's office. There are two little indentations—rather faint, but quite visible—near the bottom corner, and when we measure them with the compasses, we find that they are exactly the same distance apart as the others, and the same distance from the edges and the bottom corner. The irresistible conclusion is that these four sheets came from the same packet."

The inspector started up from his chair, and faced Thorndyke. "Who is this Mr. Barlow?" he asked.

"That," replied Thorndyke, "is for you to determine; but I can give you a useful hint. There is only one person who benefits by the death of Alfred Hartridge, but he benefits to the extent of twenty thousand pounds. His name is Leonard Wolfe, and I learn from Mr. Marchmont that he is a man of indifferent character—a gambler and a spendthrift. By profession he is an engineer, and he is a capable mechanician. In appearance he is thin, short, fair, and clean-shaven, and he has lost the middle finger of his left hand. Mr. Barlow is also short, thin, and fair, but wears a wig, a beard, and spectacles, and always wears a glove on his left hand. I have seen the handwriting of both these gentlemen, and should say that it would be difficult to distinguish one from the other."

"That's good enough for me," said the inspector. "Give me his address, and I'll have Miss Curtis released at once."

The same night Leonard Wolfe was arrested at Eltham, in the very act of burying in his garden a large and powerful compressed-air rifle. He was never brought to trial, however, for he had in his pocket a more portable weapon—a large-bore Derringer pistol—with which he managed to terminate an exceedingly ill-spent life.

"And, after all," was Thorndyke's comment, when he heard of the event, "he had his uses. He has relieved society of two very bad men, and he has given us a most instructive case. He has shown us how a clever and ingenious criminal may take endless pains to mislead and delude the police, and yet, by inattention to trivial details, may scatter clues broadcast. We can only say to the criminal class generally, in both respects, 'Go thou and do likewise'."

31 New Inn

CHAPTER I—THE MYSTERIOUS PATIENT

The hour of nine was approaching—the blessed hour of release when the casual patient ceases from troubling (or is expected to do so) and the weary practitioner may put on his slippers and turn down the surgery gas.

The fact was set forth with needless emphasis by the little American clock on the mantel-shelf, which tick-tacked frantically, as though it were eager to get the day over and be done with it; indeed, the approaching hour might have been ninety-nine from the to-do the little clock made about the matter.

The minute-hand was creeping up to the goal and the little clock had just given a kind of preliminary cough to announce its intention of striking the hour, when the bell on the door of the outer surgery rang to announce the arrival of a laggard visitor. A moment later the office-boy thrust his head in at my door and informed me that a gentleman wished to see me.

They were all gentlemen in Kennington Lane—unless they were ladies or children. Sweeps, milkmen, bricklayers, costermongers, all were impartially invested with rank and title by the democratic office-boy, and I was not, therefore, surprised or disappointed when the open door gave entrance to a man in the garb of a cabman or coachman.

As he closed the door behind him, he drew from his coat pocket a note, which he handed to me without remark. It was not addressed to me, but to my principal—to the doctor, that is to say, of whose practise I was taking charge in his absence.

"You understand, I suppose," I said, as I prepared to open the envelope, "that I am not Dr. Pike? He is out of town at present, and I am looking after his patients."

"It's of no consequence," the man replied. "You'll do just as well as him, I expect."

On this I opened the note and read the contents, which were quite brief and, at first sight, in no way remarkable.

Dear Sir:
Could you come at once and see my brother? The bearer of this will give you further particulars and convey you to the house.
Yours truly,
J. MORGAN.

There was no address on the paper and no date, and the name of the writer was, of course, unknown to me.

"This note speaks of some further particulars," I said to the messenger. "What are the particulars referred to?"

"Why, sir, the fact is," he replied, "it's a most ridic'lous affair altogether. The sick gentleman don't seem to me to be quite right in his head; at any rate, he's got some very peculiar ideas. He's been ailing now for some time, and the master, Mr. Morgan, has tried everything he knew to get him to see a doctor. But he wouldn't. However, at last it seems he gave way, but only on one condition. He said the doctor was to come from a distance and was not to be told who he was or where he lived or anything about him; and he made the master promise to keep to these conditions before he would let him send for advice. Do you think you could come and see him on them conditions, sir?"

I considered the question for a while before replying. We doctors all know the kind of idiot who is possessed with an insane dislike and distrust of the members of our profession and we like to have as little to do with him as possible. If this had been my own practise I would have declined the case off-hand; but I could not lightly refuse work that would bring profit to my principal.

As I turned the matter over in my mind I half-unconsciously scrutinized my visitor—rather to his embarrassment—and I liked his appearance as little as I liked his message. He kept his hat on, which I resented, and he stood near the door where the light was dim, for the illumination was concentrated on the table and the patient's chair; but I could see that he had a sly, unprepossessing face and a greasy red mustache that seemed out of character with his livery, though this was mere prejudice. Moreover, his voice was disagreeable, having that dull, snuffling quality that, to the medical ear, suggests a nasal polypus. Altogether I was unpleasantly impressed, but decided, nevertheless, to undertake the case.

"I suppose," I answered at length, "it is no affair of mine who the sick man is or where he lives; but how do you propose to manage the business? Am I to be blindfolded like the visitor to the bandits' cave?"

"No, sir," he replied with a forced smile and with evident relief at my agreement. "I have a carriage waiting to take you."

"Very well," I rejoined, opening the door to let him out, "I will be with you in a minute."

I slipped into a bag a small supply of emergency drugs and a few diagnostic instruments, turned down the gas and passed out through the surgery. The carriage was standing by the curb and I viewed it with mingled curiosity and disfavor; it was a kind of large brougham, such as is used by some commercial travelers, the usual glass windows being replaced by wooden shutters intended to conceal the piles of sample-boxes, and the doors capable of being locked from outside.

As I emerged, the coachman unlocked the door and held it open.

"How long will the journey take?" I asked, pausing with my foot on the step.

"Nigh upon half an hour," was the reply.

I glanced at my watch and, reflecting gloomily that my brief hour of leisure would be entirely absorbed by this visit, stepped into the uninviting vehicle. Instantly the coachman slammed the door and turned the key, leaving me in total darkness.

As the carriage rattled along, now over the macadam of quiet side-streets and now over the granite of the larger thoroughfares, I meditated on the oddity of this experience and on the possible issues of the case. For one moment a suspicion arose in my mind that this might be a trick to lure me to some thieves' den where I might be robbed and possibly murdered; but I immediately dismissed this idea, reflecting that so elaborate a plan would not have been devised for so unremunerative a quarry as an impecunious general practitioner.

CHAPTER II—I MEET MR. MORGAN

My reflections were at length brought to an end by the carriage slowing down and passing under an archway—as I could tell by the hollow sound—where it presently stopped. Then I distinguished the clang of heavy wooden gates closed behind me, and a moment later the carriage door was unlocked and opened. I stepped out into a covered way that seemed to lead down to a stable; but it was all in darkness and I had no time to make any detailed observations, for the carriage had drawn up opposite a side door which was open, and in which stood an elderly woman holding a candle.

"Is that the doctor?" she inquired, shading the candle with her hand and peering at me with screwed-up eyes. Then, with evident relief: "I am glad you have come, sir. Will you please to step in?"

I followed her across a dark passage into a large room almost destitute of furniture, where she set down the candle on a chest of drawers and turned to depart.

"The master will see you in a moment," she said. "I will go and tell him you are here."

With that she left me in the twilight of the solitary candle to gaze curiously at the bare and dismal apartment with its three rickety chairs, its unswept floor, its fast-closed shutters and the dark drapery of cobwebs that hung from the ceiling to commemorate a long and illustrious dynasty of spiders.

Presently the door opened and a shadowy figure appeared, standing close by the threshold.

"Mr. Morgan, I presume?" said I, advancing toward the stranger as he remained standing by the doorway.

"Quite right, sir," he answered, and as he spoke I started, for his voice had the same thick, snuffling quality that I had already noticed in that of the coachman. The coincidence was certainly an odd one, and it caused me to look at the stranger narrowly. He appeared somewhat shorter than his servant, but then he had a pronounced stoop, whereas the coachman was stiff and upright in his carriage; then the coachman had short hair of a light brown and a reddish mustache, whereas this man appeared, so far as I could see in the gloom, to have a shock head of black hair and a voluminous black beard. Moreover he wore spectacles. "Quite right, sir," said this individual, "and I thought I had better give you an outline of the case before you go up to the patient. My brother is, as my man has probably told you, very peculiar in some of his ideas, whence these rather foolish proceedings, for which I trust you will not hold me responsible, though I feel obliged to carry out his wishes. He returned a week or two ago from New York and, being then in rather indifferent health, he asked me to put him up for a time, as he had no settled home of his own. From that time he has gradually become worse and has really caused me a good deal of anxiety, for until now I have been quite unable to prevail on him to seek medical advice. And even now he has only consented subject to the ridiculous conditions that my man has probably explained to you."

"What is the nature of his illness?" I asked. "Does he complain of any definite symptoms?"

"No," was the reply. "Indeed, he makes very few complaints of any kind, although he is obviously ill, but the fact is that he is hardly ever more than half awake. He lies in a kind of dreamy stupor from morning to night."

This struck me as excessively odd and by no means in agreement with the patient's energetic refusal to see a doctor.

"But does he never rouse completely?" I asked.

"Oh, yes," Mr. Morgan answered quickly; "he rouses occasionally and is then quite rational and, as you may have gathered, rather obstinate. But perhaps you had better see for yourself what his condition is. Follow me, please: the stairs are rather dark."

The stairs were very dark and were, moreover, without any covering of carpet, so that our footsteps resounded on the bare boards as though we were in an empty house. I stumbled up after my guide, feeling my way by the hand-rail, and on the first floor followed him into a room similar in size to the one below and very barely furnished, though less squalid than the other. A single candle at the farther end threw its feeble light on a figure in the bed, leaving the rest of the room in a dim twilight.

"Here is the doctor, Henry," Mr. Morgan called out as we entered, and, receiving no answer, he added: "He seems to be dozing as usual."

I stepped forward to look at my patient while Mr. Morgan remained at the other end of the room, pacing noiselessly backward and forward in the semi-obscurity. By the light of the candle I saw an elderly man with good features and an intelligent and even attractive face, but dreadfully emaciated, bloodless and yellow. He lay with half-closed eyes and seemed to be in a dreamy, somnolent state, although not actually asleep. I advanced to the bedside and addressed him somewhat loudly by name, but the only response was a slight lifting of the eyelids which, after a brief, drowsy glance at me, slowly subsided to their former position.

I now proceeded to feel his pulse, grasping his wrist with intentional bruskness in the hope of rousing him from his stupor. The beats were slow and feeble and slightly irregular, giving clear evidence, if any were wanted, of his generally lowered vitality. My attention was next directed to the patient's eyes, which I examined closely with the aid of the candle, raising the lids somewhat roughly so as to expose the whole of the iris. He submitted without resistance to my rather ungentle handling, and showed no signs of discomfort even when I brought the flame of the candle to within a couple of inches of his eyes.

His extreme tolerance of light, however, was in no way surprising when one came to examine the pupils, for they were contracted to such a degree as to present only the minutest point of black upon the gray iris.

But the excessive contraction of the pupils was not the only singular feature in the sick man's eyes. As he lay on his back, the right iris sagged down slightly toward its center, showing a distinctly concave surface and, whenever any slight movement of the eyeball took place, a perceptible undulatory movement could be detected in it.

The patient had, in fact, what is known as a tremulous iris, a condition that is seen in cases where the crystalline lens has been extracted for the cure of cataract, or where it has become accidentally displaced, leaving the iris unsupported. Now, in the present case the complete condition of the iris made it clear that the ordinary extraction operation had not been performed, nor was I able, on the closest inspection with the aid of a lens, to find any signs of the less common "needle operation." The inference was that the patient had suffered from the accident known as dislocation of the lens, and this led to the further inference that he was almost or completely blind in the right eye.

This conclusion was, indeed, to some extent negatived by a deep indentation on the bridge of the nose, evidently produced by spectacles habitually worn, for if only one eye were useful, a monocle would answer the purpose. Yet this objection was of little weight, for many men, under the circumstances, would elect to wear spectacles rather than submit to the inconvenience and disfigurement of the single eyeglass.

As to the nature of the patient's illness, only one opinion seemed possible; it was a clear case of opium or morphia poisoning. To this conclusion all his symptoms seemed to point plainly enough. His coated tongue, which he protruded slowly and tremulously in response to a command bawled in his ear; his yellow skin and ghastly expression; his contracted pupils and the stupor from which he could be barely roused by the roughest handling, and which yet did not amount to actual insensibility—these formed a distinct and coherent group of symptoms, not only pointing plainly to the nature of the drug, but also suggesting a very formidable dose.

The only question that remained was: How and by whom that dose had been administered. The closest scrutiny of his arms and legs failed to reveal a single mark such as would be made by a hypodermic needle, and there was, of course, nothing to show or suggest whether the drug had been taken voluntarily by the patient himself or administered by some one else.

And then there remained the possibility that I might, after all, be mistaken in my diagnosis—a reflection that, in view of the obviously serious condition of the patient, I found eminently disturbing. As I pocketed my stethoscope and took a last look at my patient I realized that my position was one of extraordinary difficulty and perplexity. On the one hand my suspicions inclined me to extreme reticence, while, on the other, it was evidently my duty to give any information that might prove serviceable to the patient.

CHAPTER III—FOUL PLAY?

"Well, Doctor, what do you think of my brother?" Mr. Morgan asked as I joined him at the darkened end of the room. His manner, in asking the question, struck me as anxious and eager, but of course there was nothing remarkable in this.

"I think rather badly of him, Mr. Morgan," I replied. "He is certainly in a very low state."

"But you are able to form an opinion as to the nature of the disease?" he asked, still in a tone of suppressed eagerness.

"I can not give a very definite opinion at present," I replied guardedly. "The symptoms are decidedly obscure and might equally well indicate several different affections. They might be due to congestion of the brain and, in the absence of any other explanation, I am inclined to adopt that view. The most probable alternative is some narcotic drug such as opium, if it were possible for him to obtain access to it without your knowledge—but I suppose it is not?"

"I should say decidedly not," he replied. "You see, my brother is not very often left alone, and he never leaves the room, so I don't see how he could obtain anything. My housekeeper is absolutely trustworthy."

"Is he often as drowsy as he seems now?"

"Oh, very often. In fact, that is his usual condition. He rouses now and again and is quite lucid and natural for perhaps half an hour, and then he dozes off again and remains asleep for hours on end. You don't think this can be a case of sleeping-sickness, I suppose?"

"I think not," I answered, making a mental note, nevertheless, to look up the symptoms of this rare and curious disease as soon as I reached home. "Besides, he has not been in Africa, has he?"

"I can't say where he has been," was the reply. "He has just come from New York, but where he was before going there I have no idea."

"Well," I said, "we will give him some medicine and attend to his general condition, and I think I had better see him again very shortly. Meanwhile you must watch him closely, and perhaps you may have something to report to me at my next visit."

I then gave him some general directions as to the care of the patient, to which he listened attentively, and I once more suggested that I ought to see the sick man again quite soon.

"Very well, Doctor," Mr. Morgan replied, "I will send for you again in a day or two if he does not get better; and now if you will allow me to pay your fee, I will go and order the carriage while you write the prescription."

He handed me the fee and, having indicated some writing materials on a table near the bed, wished me good-evening and left the room.

As soon as I was left alone, I drew from my bag the hypodermic syringe with its little magazine of drugs that I always carried with me on my rounds. Charging the syringe with a full dose of atropin, I approached the patient once more, and, slipping up the sleeve of his night-shirt, injected the dose under the skin of his forearm. The prick of the needle roused him for a moment and he gazed at me with dull curiosity, mumbling some indistinguishable words. Then he relapsed once more into silence and apathy while I made haste to put the syringe back into its receptacle. I had just finished writing the prescription (a mixture of permanganate of potash to destroy any morphia that might yet remain in the patient's stomach) and was watching the motionless figure on the bed, when the housekeeper looked in at the door.

"The carriage is ready, doctor," said she, whereupon I rose and followed her downstairs.

The vehicle was drawn up in the covered way, as I perceived by the glimmer of the housekeeper's candle, which also enabled me dimly to discern the coachman standing close by in the shadow. I entered the carriage, the door was banged to and locked, and I then heard the heavy bolts of the gates withdrawn and the loud creaking of hinges. Immediately after, the carriage passed out and started off at a brisk pace, which was never relaxed until we reached our destination.

My reflections during the return journey were the reverse of pleasant, for I could not rid myself of the conviction that I was being involved in some very suspicious proceedings. And yet it was possible that I might be entirely mistaken—that the case might in reality be one of some brain affection accompanied by compression such as slow hemorrhage, abscess, tumor or simple congestion. Again, the patient might be a confirmed opium-eater, unknown to his brother. The cunning of these unfortunates is proverbial, and it would be quite possible for him to feign profound stupor so long as he was watched and then, when left alone for a few minutes, to nip out of bed and help himself from some secret store of the drug.

Still I did not believe this to be the true explanation. In spite of all the various possibilities, my suspicions came back to Mr. Morgan and refused to be dispelled. All the circumstances of the case itself were suspicious; so was the strange and sinister resemblance between the coachman and his employer; and so, most of all, was the fact that Mr. Morgan had told me a deliberate lie.

For he had lied, beyond all doubt. His statement as to the almost continuous stupor was absolutely irreconcilable with his other statement as to his brother's wilfulness and obstinacy; and even more irreconcilable with the deep and comparatively fresh marks of the spectacles on the patient's nose. The man had certainly worn spectacles within twenty-four hours, which he would hardly have done if he had been in a state bordering on coma.

My reflections were, for the moment, interrupted by the stopping of the carriage. The door was unlocked and thrown open and I emerged from my dark and stuffy prison.

"You seem to have a good fresh horse," I remarked, as a pretext for having another look at the coachman.

"Ay," he answered, "he can go, he can. Good-night, sir."

He slammed the carriage door, mounted the box and drove off as if to avoid further conversation; and as I again compared his voice with those of his master, and his features with those I had seen so imperfectly in the darkened rooms, I was still inclined to entertain my suspicion that the coachman and Mr. Morgan were one and the same person.

Over my frugal supper I found myself taking up anew the thread of my meditations, and afterward, as I smoked my last pipe by the expiring surgery fire, the strange and sinister features of the case continued to obtrude themselves on my notice. Especially was I puzzled as to what course of action I ought to follow. Should I maintain the professional secrecy to which I was tacitly committed, or ought I to convey a hint to the police?

Suddenly, and with a singular feeling of relief, I bethought me of my old friend and fellow student, John Thorndyke, now an eminent authority on medical jurisprudence. Thorndyke was a barrister in extensive special practise and so would be able to tell me at once what was my duty from a legal point of view, and, as he was also a doctor of medicine, he would understand the exigencies of medical practise. If I could only find time to call at the Temple and put the case before him, all my doubts and difficulties would be resolved.

Anxiously I opened my visiting-list to see what kind of day's work was in store for me on the morrow. It was not a heavy day, but I was doubtful whether it would allow of my going so far from my district, until my eye caught, near the foot of the page, the name of Burton. Now Mr. Burton lived in one of the old houses on the east side of Bouverie Street—less than five minutes' walk from Thorndyke's chambers in King's Bench Walk, and he was, moreover, a "chronic" who could safely be left for the last. When I had done with Mr. Burton, I could look in on my friend with a good chance of catching him on his return from the hospital.

Having thus arranged my program, I rose, in greatly improved spirits, and knocked out my pipe just as the little clock banged out the hour of midnight.

CHAPTER IV—I CONSULT THORNDYKE

"And so," said Thorndyke, eyeing me critically as we dropped into our respective easy chairs by the fire with the little tea-table between us, "you are back once more on the old trail?"

"Yes," I answered, with a laugh, " 'the old trail, the long trail, the trail that is always new.' "

"And leads nowhere," added Thorndyke grimly.

I laughed again—not very heartily, for there was an uncomfortable element of truth in my friend's remark, to which my own experience bore only too complete testimony. The medical practitioner whose lack of means forces him to subsist by taking temporary charge of other men's practises is likely to find that the passing years bring him little but gray hairs and a wealth of disagreeable experience.

"You will have to drop it, Jervis, you will, indeed," Thorndyke resumed after a pause. "This casual employment is preposterous for a man of your class and professional attainments. Besides, are you not engaged to be married, and to a most charming girl?"

"Juliet has just been exhorting me in similar terms—except as to the last particular," I replied. "She threatens to buy a practise and put me in at a small salary and batten on the proceeds. Moreover, she seems to imply that my internal charge of pride, vanity and egotism is equal to about four hundred pounds to the square inch and is rapidly approaching bursting-point. I am not sure that she is not right, too."

"Her point of view is eminently reasonable, at any rate," said Thorndyke. "But as to buying a practise, before you commit yourself to any such thing I would ask you to consider the suggestion that I have made more than once—that you join me here as my junior. We worked together with excellent results in the 'Red Thumbmark' case, as the newspapers called it, and we could do as well in many another. Of course, if you prefer general practise, well and good; only remember that I should be glad to have you as my junior, and that in that capacity and with your abilities you would have an opening for something like a career."

"My dear Thorndyke," I answered, not without emotion. "I am more rejoiced at your offer and more grateful than I can tell you, and I should like to go into the matter this very moment. But I must not, for I have only a very short time now before I must go back to my work, and I have not yet touched upon the main object of my visit."

"I supposed that you had come to see me," remarked Thorndyke.

"So I did. I came to consult you professionally. The fact is, I am in a dilemma, and I want you to tell me what you think I ought to do." Thorndyke paused in the act of refilling my cup and glanced at me anxiously.

"It is nothing that affects me personally at all," I continued. "But perhaps I had better give you an account of the whole affair from the beginning."

Accordingly I proceeded to relate in detail the circumstances connected with my visit to the mysterious patient of the preceding evening, to all of which Thorndyke listened with close attention and evident interest.

"A very remarkable story, Jervis," he said, as I concluded my narrative. "In fact, quite a fine mystery of the good, old-fashioned Adelphi drama type. I particularly like the locked carriage. You have obviously formed certain hypotheses on the subject?"

"Yes; but I have come to you to hear yours."

"Well," said Thorndyke, "I expect yours and mine are pretty much alike, for there are two obvious alternative explanations of the affair."

"As for instance——"

"That Mr. Morgan's account of his brother's illness may be perfectly true and straightforward. The patient may be an opium-eater or morphinomaniac hitherto unsuspected. The secrecy and reticence attributed to him are quite consistent with such a supposition. On the other hand, Mr. J. Morgan's story may be untrue—which is certainly more probable—and he may be administering morphia for his own ends.

"The objection to this view is that morphia is a very unusual and inconvenient poison, except in a single fatal dose, on account of the rapidity with which tolerance of the drug is established. Nevertheless we must not forget that slow morphia poisoning might prove eminently suitable in certain cases. The prolonged use of morphia in large doses enfeebles the will, confuses the judgment and debilitates the body, and so might be adopted by a poisoner whose aim was to get some instrument or document executed, such as a will or assignment, after which, death might, if necessary, be brought about by other means. Did it seem to you as if Mr. Morgan was sounding you as to your willingness to give a death-certificate?"

"He said nothing to that effect, but the matter was in my mind, which was one reason for my extreme reticence."

"Yes, you showed excellent judgment in circumstances of

considerable difficulty," said Thorndyke, "and, if our friend is up to mischief, he has not made a happy selection in his doctor. Just consider what would have happened—assuming the man to be bent on murder—if some blundering, cocksure idiot had rushed in, jumped to a diagnosis, called the case, let us say, an erratic form of Addison's disease, and predicted a fatal termination. Thenceforward the murderer's course would be clear; he could compass his victim's death at any moment, secure of getting a death-certificate. As it is, he will have to move cautiously for the present—always assuming that we are not doing him a deep injustice."

"Yes," I answered, "we may take it that nothing fatal will happen just at present, unless some more easy-going practitioner is called in. But the question that is agitating me is, What ought I to do? Should I, for instance, report the case to the police?"

"I should say certainly not," replied Thorndyke. "In the first place, you can give no address, nor even the slightest clue to the whereabouts of the house, and, in the second, you have nothing definite to report. You certainly could not swear an information and, if you made any statement, you might find, after all, that you had committed a gross and ridiculous breach of professional confidence. No, if you hear no more from Mr. J. Morgan, you must watch the reports of inquests carefully and attend if necessary. If Mr. Morgan sends for you again, you ought undoubtedly to fix the position of the house. That is your clear duty for many and obvious reasons, and especially in view of your finding it necessary to communicate with the coroner or the police."

"That is all very well," I exclaimed, "but will you kindly tell me, my dear Thorndyke, how a man, boxed up in a pitch-dark carriage, is going to locate any place to which he may be conveyed?"

"I don't think the task presents any difficulties," he replied. "You would be prepared to take a little trouble, I suppose?"

"Certainly," I rejoined. "I will do my utmost to carry out any plan you may suggest."

"Very well, then. Can you spare me a few minutes?"

"It must be only a few," I answered, "for I ought to be getting back to my work."

"I won't detain you more than five minutes," said Thorndyke. "I will just run up to the workshop and get Polton to prepare what you will want, and when I have shown you how to get to work I will let you go."

He hurried away, leaving the door open, and returned in less than a couple of minutes.

"Come into the office," said he, and I followed him into the adjoining room—a rather small but light apartment of which the walls were lined with labeled deed-boxes. A massive safe stood in one corner and, in another, close to a window, was a great roll-top table surmounted by a nest of over a hundred labeled drawers. From one of the latter he drew a paper-covered pocket note-book and, sitting down at the table, began to rule the pages each into three columns, two quite narrow and one broad.

He was just finishing the last page when there came a very gentle tap at the door.

"Is that you, Polton? Come in," said my friend.

The dry, shrewd-looking, little elderly man entered and I was at once struck by the incongruity of his workman's apron and rolled-up sleeves with his refined and intellectual face.

"Will this do?" he asked, holding out a little thin board about seven inches by five, to one corner of which a pocket compass had been fixed with shellac.

"The very thing, Polton, thank you."

"What a wonderful old fellow that is, Jervis!" my friend observed, as his assistant retired with a friendly smile at me. "He took in the idea instantly and he seems to have produced the finished article by magic, as the conjurors bring forth bowls of goldfish at a moment's notice. And now as to the use of this appliance. Can you read a compass?"

"Oh, yes," I replied. "I used to sail a small yacht at one time."

"Good, then you will have no difficulty, though I expect the compass needle will jig about a good deal in the carriage. Here is a pocket reading-lamp, which you can hook on to the carriage lining. This note-book can be fixed to the board with an india-rubber band —so. You observe that the thoughtful Polton has stuck a piece of thread on the glass of the compass to serve as a lubber's line. Now this is how you will proceed: As soon as you are locked in the carriage, light your lamp—better have a book with you in case the light is seen—get out your watch and put the board on your knee. Then enter in one narrow column of your note-book the time; in the other, the direction shown by the compass and, in the broad column, any particulars, including the number of steps the horse makes in a minute. Thus:—"

He opened the note-book and made one or two sample entries in pencil as follows:

9:40—S.E.   Start from home.
9:41—S.W.   Granite blocks.
9:43—S.W.   Wood pavement.   Hoofs 104.
9:47—W. by S.   Granite crossing Macadam.

"And so on. You follow the process, Jervis?"

"Perfectly," I answered. "It is quite clear and simple, though, I must say, highly ingenious. But I must really go now."

"Good-by, then," said Thorndyke, slipping a well-sharpened pencil through the rubber band that fixed the note-book to the board. Let me know how you get on, and come and see me again as soon as you can, in any case."

He handed me the board and the lamp, and when I had slipped them into my pocket we shook hands and I hurried away, a little uneasy at having left my charge so long.

CHAPTER V—THE MYSTERY DEEPENS

A couple of days passed without my receiving any fresh summons from Mr. Morgan, a circumstance that occasioned me some little disappointment, for I was now eager to put into practise Thorndyke's ingenious plan for discovering the whereabouts of the house of mystery. When the evening of the third day was well advanced and Mr. Morgan still made no sign, I began to think that I had seen the last of my mysterious patient and that the elaborate preparations for tracking him to his hiding-place had been made in vain.

It was therefore with a certain sense of relief and gratification that I received, at about ten minutes to nine, the office-boy's laconic announcement of "Mr. Morgan's carriage," followed by the inevitable "Wants you to go and see him at once."

The two remaining patients were of the male sex—an important time-factor in medical practise—and, as they were both cases of simple and common ailments, I was able to dispatch their business in about ten minutes.

Then, bidding the boy close up the surgery, I put on my overcoat, slipped the little board and the lamp into the pocket, tucked a newspaper under my arm and went out.

The coachman was standing by the horse's head and touched his hat as he came forward to open the door.

"I have fortified myself for the long drive, you see," I remarked, exhibiting the newspaper as I stepped into the carriage.

"But you can't read in the dark," said he.

"No, but I have a lamp," I replied, producing it and striking a match.

"Oh, I see," said the coachman, adding, as I hooked the lamp on to the back cushion, "I suppose you found it rather a dull ride last time?" Then, without waiting for a reply, he slammed and locked the door and mounted the box.

I laid the board on my knee, looked at my watch and made the first entry.

9:05—S.W. Start from home. Horse 13 hands.

As on the previous occasion, the carriage was driven at a smart and regular pace, but as I watched the compass I became more and more astonished at the extraordinarily indirect manner in which it proceeded. For the compass needle, though it oscillated continually with the vibration, yet remained steady enough to show the main direction quite plainly, and I was able to see that our course zigzagged in a way that was difficult to account for.

Once we must have passed close to the river, for I heard a steamer's whistle—apparently a tug's—quite near at hand, and several times we passed over bridges or archways. All these meanderings I entered carefully in my note-book, and mightily busy the occupation kept me; for I had hardly time to scribble down one entry before the compass needle would swing round sharply, showing that we had, once more, turned a corner.

At length the carriage slowed down and turned into the covered way, whereupon, having briefly noted the fact and the direction, I smuggled the board and the note-book—now nearly half-filled with hastily scrawled memoranda—into my pocket; and when the door was unlocked and thrown open, I was deep in the contents of the evening paper.

I was received, as before, by the housekeeper, who, in response to my inquiry as to the patient's condition, informed me that he had seemed somewhat better. "As, indeed, he ought to," she added, "with all the care and watching he gets from the master. But you'll see that for yourself, sir, and, if you will wait here, I will go and tell Mr. Morgan you have come."

An interval of about five minutes elapsed before she returned to usher me up the dark staircase to the sick-room, and, on entering, I perceived Mr. Morgan, stooping over the figure on the bed. He rose, on seeing me, and came to meet me with his hand extended.

"I had to send for you again, you see, Doctor," he said. "The fact is, he is not quite so well this evening, which is extremely disappointing, for he had begun to improve so much that I hoped recovery had fairly set in. He has been much brighter and more wakeful the last two days, but this afternoon he sank into one of his dozes and has seemed to be getting more and more heavy ever since."

"He has taken his medicine?" I asked.

"Quite regularly," replied Mr. Morgan, indicating with a gesture the half-empty bottle on the table by the bedside.

"And as to food?"

"Naturally he takes very little; and, of course, when these attacks of drowsiness come on, he is without food for rather long periods."

I stepped over to the bed, leaving Mr. Morgan in the shadow, as before, and looked down at the patient. His aspect was, if anything, more ghastly and corpse-like than before; he lay quite motionless and relaxed, the only sign of life being the slight rise and fall of his chest and the soft gurgling snore at each shallow breath. At the first glance I should have said that he was dying, and indeed, with my previous knowledge of the case, I viewed him with no little anxiety, even now.

He opened his eyes, however, when I shouted in his ear, and even put out his tongue when asked in similar stentorian tones, but I could get no answer to any of my questions—not even the half-articulate mumble I had managed to elicit on the previous occasion. His stupor was evidently more profound now than then and, whatever might be the cause of his symptoms, he was certainly in a condition of extreme danger. Of that I had no doubt.

"I am afraid you don't find him any better to-night," remarked Mr. Morgan as I joined him at the other end of the room.

"No," I answered. "His condition appears to me to be very critical. I should say it is very doubtful whether he will rouse at all."

"You don't mean that you think he is dying?" Mr. Morgan spoke in tones of very unmistakable anxiety—even of terror.

"I think he might die at any moment," I replied.

"Good God!" exclaimed Morgan. "You horrify me!"

He evidently spoke the truth, for his appearance and manner denoted the most extreme agitation.

"I really think," he continued, "——at least I hope that you take an unnecessarily serious view of his condition. He has been like this before, you know."

"Possibly," I answered. "But there comes a last time, and it may have come now."

"Have you been able to form any more definite opinion as to the nature of this dreadful complaint?" he asked.

I hesitated for a moment and he continued:

"As to your suggestion that his symptoms might be due to drugs, I think we may consider that disposed of. He has been watched, practically without cessation, since you came last and, moreover, I have myself turned out the room and examined the bed, and not a trace of any drug was to be found. Have you considered the question of sleeping-sickness?"

I looked at the man narrowly before answering, and distrusted him more than ever. Still, my concern was with the patient and his present needs; I was, after all, a doctor, not a detective, and the circumstances called for straightforward speech and action on my part.

"His symptoms are not those of sleeping-sickness," I replied. "They are brain symptoms and are, in my opinion, due to morphia poisoning."

CHAPTER VI—MR. MORGAN'S SPECTACLES

"But, my dear sir," he exclaimed, "the thing is impossible! Haven't I just told you that he has been watched continuously?"

"I can judge only by the appearances I find," I answered. Then, seeing that he was about to offer fresh objections, I continued: "Don't let us waste precious time in discussion, or your brother may be dead before we have reached a conclusion. If you will get some strong coffee made, I will take the other necessary measures, and perhaps we may manage to pull him round."

The decision of my manner cowed him; besides which he was manifestly alarmed. Replying stiffly that I "must do as I thought best," he hurried from the room, leaving me to carry out my part of the cure. And as soon as he was gone I set to work without further loss of time.

Having injected a full dose of atropin, I took down from the mantelshelf the bottle containing the mixture that I had prescribed—a solution of potassium permanganate. The patient's lethargic condition made me fear that he might be unable to swallow, so that I could not take the risk of pouring the medicine into his mouth for fear of suffocating him. A stomach-tube would have solved the difficulty, but of course I had none with me.

I had, however, a mouth-speculum, which also acted as a gag, and, having propped the patient's mouth open with this, I hastily slipped off one of the rubber tubes from my stethoscope and inserted into one end of it a vulcanite ear-speculum to act as a funnel. Then, introducing the other end of the tube into the gullet, I cautiously poured a small quantity of the medicine into the extemporized funnel.

To my great relief, a movement of the throat showed that the swallowing reflex still existed, and, thus encouraged, I poured down the tube as much of the fluid as I thought it wise to administer at one time.

I had just withdrawn the tube and was looking round for some means of cleansing it when Mr. Morgan returned and, contrary to his usual practise, came close up to the bed. He glanced anxiously from the prostrate figure to the tube that I was holding and then announced that the coffee was being prepared. As he spoke, I was able, for the first time, to look him fairly in the face by the light of the candle.

Now it is a curious fact—though one that most persons must have observed—that there sometimes occurs a considerable interval between the reception of a visual impression and its transfer to the consciousness. A thing may be seen, as it were, unconsciously, and the impression consigned, apparently, to instant oblivion, and yet the picture may be subsequently revived by memory with such completeness that its details can be studied as though the object were still actually visible. Something of that kind must have happened to me now, for, preoccupied as I was by the condition of the patient, the professional habit of rapid and close observation caused me to direct a searching glance at the man before me. It was only a brief glance, for Mr. Morgan, perhaps embarrassed by my intent regard of him, almost immediately withdrew into the shadow, but it revealed two facts of which I took no conscious note at the time, but which came back to me later and gave me much food for speculation.

One fact thus observed was that Mr. Morgan's eyes were of a

bluish-gray, like those of his brother, and were surmounted by light-coloured eyebrows, entirely incongruous with his black hair and beard.

But the second fact was much more curious. As he stood, with his head slightly turned, I was able to look through one glass of his spectacles at the wall beyond. On the wall was a framed print, and the edge of the frame, seen through the spectacle-glass, appeared unaltered and free from distortion, as though seen through plain window-glass; and yet the reflections of the candle-flame in the spectacles showed the flame inverted, clearly proving that the glasses were concave on one surface at least.

These two apparently irreconcilable appearances, when I subsequently recalled them, puzzled me completely, and it was not until some time afterward that the explanation of the mystery came to me.

For the moment, however, the sick man occupied my attention to the exclusion of all else. As the atropin took effect he became somewhat less lethargic, for when I spoke loudly in his ear and shook him gently by the arm he opened his eyes and looked dreamily into my face; but the instant he was left undisturbed, he relapsed into his former condition. Presently the housekeeper arrived with a jug of strong black coffee, which I proceeded to administer in spoonfuls, giving the patient a vigorous shake-up between whiles and talking loudly into his ear.

Under this treatment he revived considerably and began to mumble and mutter in reply to my questions, at which point Mr. Morgan suggested that he should continue the treatment while I wrote a prescription.

"It seems as if you were right, after all, Doctor," he conceded, as he took his place by the bedside, "but it is a complete mystery to me. I shall have to watch him more closely than ever, that is evident."

His relief at the improvement of his brother's condition was most manifest and, as the invalid continued to revive apace, I thought it now safe to take my departure.

"I am sorry to have kept you so long," he said, "but I think the patient will be all right now. If you will take charge of him for a moment, I will go and call the coachman; and perhaps, as it is getting late, you could make up the prescription yourself and send the medicine back with the carriage."

To this request I assented and, as he left the room, I renewed my assaults upon the unresisting invalid.

In about five minutes the housekeeper made her appearance to tell me that the carriage was waiting and that she would stay with the patient until the master returned.

"If you take my candle, you will be able to find your way down, sir," she said.

To this I agreed and took my departure, candle in hand, leaving her shaking the patient's hand with pantomimic cordiality and squalling into his ear shrill exhortations to "wake up and pull himself together."

As soon as I was shut in the carriage, I lighted my lamp and drew forth the little board and note-book, but the notes that I jotted down on the return journey were must less complete than before, for the horse, excelling his previous performances, rattled along at a pace that rendered writing almost impossible, and indeed more than once he broke into a gallop.

The incidents of that evening made me resolve to seek the advice of Thorndyke on the morrow and place the note-book in his hands, if the thing could possibly be done, and with this comforting resolution I went to bed. But

> The best-laid schemes o' mice and men
> Gang aft a-gley,

and my schemes, in this respect, went "a-gley" with a vengeance. In the course of the following morning a veritable avalanche of urgent messages descended on the surgery, piling up a visiting-list at which I stood aghast.

Later on, it appeared that a strike in the building trade had been followed immediately by a general failure of health on the part of the bricklayers who were members of the benefit clubs, accompanied by symptoms of the most alarming and unclassical character, ranging from "sciatica of the blade-bones," which consigned one horny-handed sufferer to an armchair by the kitchen fire, to "windy spavins," which reduced another to a like piteous plight. Moreover, the sufferings of these unfortunates were viewed with callous skepticism by their fellow members (not in the building trade) who called aloud for detailed reports from the medical officer.

And, as if this were not enough, a local milkman, having secretly indulged in an attack of scarlatina, proceeded to shed microbes into the milk-cans, with the result that a brisk epidemic swept over the neighborhood.

From these causes I was kept hard at work from early morning to late at night, with never an interval for repose or reflection. Not only was I unable to call upon Thorndyke, but the incessant round of visits, consultations and reports kept my mind so preoccupied that the affairs of my mysterious patient almost faded from my recollection. Now and again, indeed, I would give a passing thought to the silent figure in the dingy house, and, as the days passed and the carriage came no more, I would wonder whether I ought not to communicate my deepening suspicions to the police. But, as I have said, my time was spent in an unceasing rush of work and the matter was allowed to lapse.

CHAPTER VII—JEFFREY BLACKMORE'S WILL

The hurry and turmoil continued without abatement during the three weeks that remained before my employer was due to return. Long harassing days spent in tramping the dingy streets of Kennington, or scrambling up and down narrow stairways, alternated with nights made hideous by the intolerable jangle of the night-bell, until I was worn out with fatigue. Nor was the labor made more grateful by the incessant rebuffs that fall to the lot of the "substitute," or by the reflection that for all this additional toil and anxiety I should reap not a farthing of profit.

As I trudged through the dreary thoroughfares of this superannuated suburb with its once rustic villas and its faded gardens, my thoughts would turn enviously to the chambers in King's Bench Walk and I would once again register a vow that this should be my last term of servitude.

From all of which it will be readily understood that when one morning there appeared opposite our house a four-wheeled cab laden with trunks and portmanteaux I hurried out with uncommon cordiality to greet my returning principal. He was not likely to grumble at the length of the visiting-list, for he was, as he once told me, a glutton for work, and a full day-book makes a full ledger. And, in fact, when he ran his eye down the crowded pages of my list he chuckled aloud and expressed himself as more than eager to get to work at once.

In this I was so far from thwarting him that by two o'clock I had fairly closed my connection with the practise, and half-an-hour later found myself strolling across Waterloo Bridge with the sensations of a newly-liberated convict and a check for twenty-five guineas in my pocket. My objective was the Temple, for I was now eager to hear more of Thorndyke's proposal, and wished, also, to consult him as to where in his neighborhood I might find lodgings in which I could put up for a few days.

The "oak" of my friend's chambers stood open and when I plied the knocker the inner door was opened by Polton.

"Why, it's Dr. Jervis," said he, peering up at me in his quick birdlike manner. "The Doctor is out just now, but I am sure he wouldn't like to miss you. Will you come in and wait? He will be in very shortly."

I entered and found two strangers seated by the fire, one an elderly professional-looking man—a lawyer as I guessed; the other a man of about twenty-five, fresh-faced, sunburnt and decidedly prepossessing in appearance. As I entered, the latter rose and made a place for me by the fire, for the day was chilly, though it was late Spring.

"You are one of Thorndyke's colleagues, I gather," said the elder man after we had exchanged a few remarks on the weather. "Since I have known him I have acquired a new interest in and respect for doctors. He is a most remarkable man, sir, a positive encyclopedia of out-of-the-way and unexpected knowledge."

"His acquirements certainly cover a very wide area," I agreed.

"Yes, and the way in which he brings his knowledge to bear on intricate cases is perfectly astonishing," my new acquaintance continued. "I seldom abandon an obscure case or let it go into court until I have taken his opinion. An ordinary counsel looks at things from the same point of view as I do myself and has the same kind of knowledge, if rather more of it, but Thorndyke views things from a radically different standpoint and brings a new and totally different kind of knowledge into the case. He is a lawyer and a scientific specialist in one, and the combination of the two types of culture in one mind, let me tell you emphatically, is an altogether different thing from the same two types in separate minds."

"I can well believe that," I said and was about to illustrate my opinion when a key was heard in the latch and the subject of our discourse entered the room.

"Why, Jervis," he exclaimed cheerily, "I thought you had given me the slip again. Where have you been?"

"Up to my eyes in work," I replied. "But I am free—my engagement is finished."

"Good!" said he. "And how are you, Mr. Marchmont?"

"Well, not so young as I was at your age," answered the solicitor with a smile. "I have brought a client of mine to see you," he continued—"Mr. Stephen Blackmore."

Thorndyke shook hands with the younger man and hoped that he might be of service to him.

"Shall I take a walk and look in a little later?" I suggested.

"Oh, no," answered Thorndyke. "We can talk over our business in the office."

"For my part," said Mr. Blackmore, "I see no necessity for Dr. Jervis to go away. We have nothing to tell that is not public property."

"If Mr. Marchmont agrees to that," said Thorndyke, "I shall have the advantage of being able to consult with my colleague if necessary."

"I leave the matter in your hands, Doctor," said the solicitor. "Your friend is no doubt used to keeping his own counsel."

"He is used to keeping mine, as a matter of fact," replied Thorndyke. "He was with me in the Hornby case, you may remember, Marchmont, and a most trusty colleague I found him; so, with your permission, we will consider your case with the aid of a cup of tea." He pressed an electric bell three times, in response to which signal Polton presently appeared with a teapot and, having set out the tea-service with great precision and gravity, retired silently to his lair on the floor above.

"Now," said Mr. Marchmont, "let me explain at the outset that ours is a forlorn hope. We have no expectations whatever."

"Blessed are they who expect nothing," murmured Thorndyke.

"Quite so—by the way, what delicious tea you brew in these chambers! Well, as to our little affair. Legally speaking, we have no case—not the ghost of one. Yet I have advised my client to take your opinion on the matter, on the chance that you may perceive some point that we have overlooked. The circumstances, briefly stated, are these: My client, who is an orphan, had two uncles, John Blackmore, and Jeffrey, his younger brother. Some two years ago—to be exact, on the twenty-third of July, 1898—Jeffrey executed a will by which he made my client his executor and sole legatee. He had a pension from the Foreign Office, on which he lived, and he possessed personal property to the extent of about two thousand pounds.

"Early last year he left the rooms in Jermyn Street, where he had lived for some years, stored his furniture and went to Nice, where he remained until November. In that month, it appears, he returned to England and at once took chambers in New Inn, which he furnished with some of the things from his old rooms. He never communicated with any of his friends, so that the fact of his being in residence at the Inn only became known to them when he died.

"This was all very strange and different from his customary conduct, as was also the fact that he seems to have had no one to cook for him or look after his rooms.

"About a fortnight ago he was found dead in his chambers— under slightly peculiar circumstances, and a more recent will was then discovered, dated the ninth of December, 1899. Now no change had taken place in the circumstances of the testator to account for the new will, nor was there any material change in the disposition of the property. The entire personalty, with the exception of fifty pounds, was bequeathed to my client, but the separate items were specified, and the testator's brother, John Blackmore, was named as the executor and residuary legatee."

"I see," said Thorndyke. "So that your client's interest in the will would appear to be practically unaffected by the change."

"There it is!" exclaimed the solicitor, slapping the table to add emphasis to his words. "Apparently his interest is unaffected; but actually the change in the form of the will affects him in the most vital manner."

"Indeed!"

"Yes. I have said that no change had taken place in the testator's circumstances at the time the new will was executed. But only two days before his death, his sister, Mrs. Edmund Wilson, died and, on her will being proved, it appears that she had bequeathed to him her entire personalty, estimated at nearly thirty thousand pounds."

Thorndyke gave a low whistle.

"You see the point," continued Mr. Marchmont. "By the original will this great sum would have accrued to my client, whereas by the second will it goes to the residuary legatee, Mr. John Blackmore; and this, it appears to us, could not have been in accordance with the wishes and intentions of Mr. Jeffrey, who evidently desired his nephew to inherit his property."

"The will is perfectly regular?" inquired Thorndyke.

"Perfectly. Not a flaw in it."

"There seem to be some curious features in the case," said Thorn-dyke. "Perhaps we had better have a narrative of the whole affair from the beginning."

He fetched from the office a small note-book and a blotting-pad which he laid on his knee as he reseated himself.

"Now let us have the facts in their order," said he.

CHAPTER VIII—THORNDYKE TAKES EVIDENCE

"Well," said Mr. Marchmont, "we will begin with the death of Mr. Jeffrey Blackmore. It seems that about eleven o'clock in the morning of the twenty-seventh of March, that is, about a fortnight ago, a builder's man was ascending a ladder to examine a gutter on one of the houses in New Inn when, on passing a window that was open at the top, he looked in and perceived a gentleman lying on the bed. The gentleman was fully dressed and had apparently lain down to rest, but, looking again, the workman was struck by the remark-able pallor of the face and by the entire absence of movement. On coming down, he reported the matter to the porter at the lodge.

"Now the porter had already that morning knocked at Mr. Blackmore's door to hand him the receipt for the rent and, receiving no answer, had concluded that the tenant was absent. When he received the workman's report, therefore, he went to the door of the chambers, which were on the second floor, and knocked loudly and repeatedly, but there was still no answer.

"Considering the circumstances highly suspicious, he sent for a constable, and when the latter arrived the workman was directed to enter the chambers by the window and open the door from the inside. This was done, and the porter and the constable, going into the bedroom, found Mr. Blackmore lying upon the bed, dressed in his ordinary clothes, and quite dead."

"How long had be been dead?" asked Thorndyke.

"Less than twenty-four hours, for the porter saw him on the previous day. He came to the Inn about half-past six in a four-wheeled cab."

"Was any one with him?"

"That the porter can not say. The glass window of the cab was drawn up and he saw Mr. Blackmore's face through it only by the light of the lamp outside the lodge as the cab passed through the archway. There was a dense fog at the time—you may remember that very foggy day about a fortnight ago?"

"I do," replied Thorndyke. "Was that the last time the porter saw Mr. Blackmore?"

"No. The deceased came to the lodge at eight o'clock and paid the rent."

"By a check?" asked Thorndyke.

"Yes, a crossed check. That was the last time the porter saw him."

"You said, I think, that the circumstances of his death were suspicious."

"No, I said 'peculiar,' not 'suspicious'; it was a clear case of suicide. The constable reported to his inspector, who came to the chambers at once and brought the divisional surgeon with him. On examining the body they found a hypodermic syringe grasped in the right hand, and at the post-mortem a puncture was found in the right thigh. The needle had evidently entered vertically and deeply instead of being merely passed through the skin, which was explained by the fact that it had been driven in through the clothing.

"The syringe contained a few drops of a concentrated solution of strophanthin, and there were found on the dressing-table two empty tubes labeled 'Hypodermic Tabloids; Strophanthin 1-500 grain,' and a tiny glass mortar and pestle containing crystals of strophanthin. It was concluded that the entire contents of both tubes, each of which was proved to have contained twenty tabloids, had been dissolved to charge the syringe. The post-mortem showed, naturally, that death was due to poisoning by strophanthin.

"It was also proved that the deceased had been in the habit of taking morphia, which was confirmed by the finding in the chamber of a large bottle half full of morphia pills, each containing half a grain."

"The verdict was suicide, of course?" said Thorndyke.

"Yes. The theory of the doctors was that the deceased had taken morphia habitually and that, in a fit of depression caused by reaction from the drug, he had taken his life by means of the more rapidly acting poison."

"A very reasonable explanation," agreed Thorndyke. "And now to return to the will. Had your Uncle Jeffrey any expectations from his sister, Mr. Blackmore?"

"I can't say with certainty," replied Blackmore. I knew very little of my aunt's affairs, and I don't think my uncle knew much more, for he was under the impression that she had only a life interest in her late husband's property."

"Did she die suddenly?" asked Thorndyke.

"No," replied Blackmore. "She died of cancer."

Thorndyke made an entry on his note-book and, turning to the solicitor, said:

"The will, you say, is perfectly regular. Has the signature been examined by an expert?"

"As a matter of form," replied Mr. Marchmont, "I got the head cashier of the deceased's bank to step round and compare the signatures of the two wills. There were, in fact, certain trifling differences; but these are probably to be explained by the drug habit, especially as a similar change was to be observed in the checks that have been paid in during the last few months. In any case the matter is of no moment, owing to the circumstances under which the will was executed."

"Which were——?"

"That on the morning of the ninth of December Mr. Jeffrey Blackmore came into the lodge and asked the porter and his son, a house-painter, who happened to be in the lodge at the time, to witness his signature. 'This is my will,' said he, producing the document, 'and perhaps you had better glance through it, though that is not necessary.' The porter and his son accordingly read through the will and then witnessed the signature and so were able to swear to the document at the inquest."

"Ah, then that disposes of the will," said Thorndyke, "even of the question of undue influence. Now, as to your Uncle Jeffrey, Mr. Blackmore. What kind of man was he?"

"A quiet, studious, gentle-mannered man," answered Blackmore, "very nervous, about fifty-five years of age, and not very robust. He was of medium height—about five feet seven—fair, slightly gray, clean shaven, rather spare, had gray eyes, wore spectacles and stooped slightly as he walked."

"And is now deceased," added Mr. Marchmont dryly, as Thorndyke noted down these apparently irrelevant particulars.

"How came he to be a civil-service pensioner at fifty-five?" asked Thorndyke.

"He had a bad fall from a horse, which left him, for a time, a complete wreck. Moreover, his eyesight, which was never very good, became much worse. In fact, he practically lost the sight of one eye altogether—it was the right one, I think—and as this had been his good eye, he felt the loss very much."

"You mentioned that he was a studious man. Of what nature were the subjects that occupied him?"

"He was an Oriental scholar of some position, I believe. He had been attached to the legations at Bagdad and Tokyo and had given a good deal of attention to Oriental languages and literature. He was also much interested in Babylonian and Assyrian archeology and assisted, for a time, in the excavations at Birs Nimroud."

"I see," said Thorndyke; "a man of considerable attainments. And now as to your Uncle John?"

"I can't tell you much about him," answered Blackmore. "Until I saw him at the inquest I had not met him since I was a boy, but he is as great a contrast to Uncle Jeffrey in character as in appearance."

"The two brothers were very unlike in exterior, then?"

"Well, perhaps I am exaggerating the difference. They were of much the same height, though John was a shade taller, and their features were, I suppose, not unlike; and their coloring was similar, but, you see, John is a healthy man with good eyesight and a brisk, upright carriage and he wears a large beard and mustache. He is rather stout, too, as I noticed when I met him at the inquest. As to his character, I am afraid he has not been a great credit to his family. He started in life as a manufacturing chemist, but of late years he has been connected with what they call, I think, a bucket-shop, though he describes himself as a stock broker."

"I see—an outside broker. Was he on good terms with his brother?"

"Not very, I think. At any rate, they saw very little of each other."

"And what were his relations with your aunt?"

"Not friendly at all. I think Uncle John had done something shady —let Mr. Wilson in, in some way, over a bogus investment, but I don't know the details."

"Would you like a description of the lady, Thorndyke?" asked Mr. Marchmont with genial sarcasm.

"Not just now, thanks," answered Thorndyke with a quiet smile, "but I will note down her full name."

"Julia Elizabeth Wilson."

"Thank you. There is just one more point—what were your uncle's habits and manner of life at New Inn?"

"According to the porter's evidence at the inquest," said Mr.

Blackmore, "he lived in a very secluded manner. He had no one to look after his rooms, but did everything for himself, and no one is known to have visited the chambers. He was seldom seen about the Inn and the porter thinks that he must have spent most of his time indoors or else he must have been away a good deal—he can not say which."

"By the way, what has happened to the chambers since your uncle's death?"

"I understand that the porter has been instructed by the executor to let them."

"Thank you, Mr. Blackmore. I think that is all I have to ask at present. If anything fresh occurs to me, I will communicate with you through Mr. Marchmont."

The two men rose and prepared to depart.

"I am afraid there is little to hope for," said the solicitor as he shook my friend's hand, "but I thought it worth while to give you a chance of working a miracle."

"You would like to set aside the second will, of course?" said Thorndyke.

"Naturally; and a more unlikely case I never met with."

"It is not promising, I must admit. However, I will digest the material and let you have my views after due reflection."

The lawyer and his client took their departure, and Thorndyke, with a thoughtful and abstracted air, separated the written sheets from his note-book, made two perforations in the margins by means of a punch, and inserted them into a small Stolzenburg file, on the outside of which he wrote, "Jeffrey Blackmore's Will."

"There," said he, depositing the little folio in a drawer labeled "B,"—"there is the nucleus of the body of data on which our investigations must be based; and I am afraid it will not receive any great additions, though there are some very singular features in the case, as you doubtless observed."

"I observed that the will seemed as simple and secure as a will could be made," I answered, "and I should suppose the setting of it aside to be a wild impossibility."

"Perhaps you are right," rejoined Thorndyke, "but time will show. Meanwhile I understand that you are a gentleman at large now; what are your plans?"

"My immediate purpose is to find lodgings for a week or so, and I came to you for guidance as to their selection."

"You had better let me put you up for the night, at any rate. Your old bedroom is at your service and you can pursue your quest in the morning, if you wish to. Give me a note and I will send Polton with it to bring up your things in a cab."

"It is exceedingly good of you, Thorndyke, but I hardly like to——"

"Now don't raise obstacles, my dear fellow," urged Thorndyke. "Say yes, and let us have a long chat to-night over old times."

I was glad enough to be persuaded to so pleasant an arrangement, so I wrote a few lines on one of my cards, which was forthwith dispatched by the faithful Polton.

CHAPTER IX—THE CUNEIFORM INSCRIPTION

"We have an hour and a half to dispose of before dinner," said Thorndyke, looking at his watch. "What say you, my dear Jervis— shall we wander over the breezy uplands of Fleet Street or shall we seek the leafy shades of New Inn? I incline to New Inn, if that sylvan retreat commends itself to you."

"Very well," said I, "let it be New Inn. I suppose you want to nose around the scene of the tragedy, though what you expect to find is a mystery to me."

"A man of science," replied Thorndyke, "expects nothing. He collects facts and keeps an open mind. As for me, I am a mere legal snapper-up of unconsidered trifles of evidence. When I have accumulated a few facts I arrange them and reason from them. It is a capital error to decide beforehand what data are to be sought for."

"But surely," said I, as we emerged from the doorway and turned up toward Mitre Court, "you can not see any possible grounds for disputing that will?"

"I don't," he answered, "or I should have said so; but I am engaged to look into the case and I shall do so, as I said just now with an open mind. Moreover, the circumstances of the case are so singular, so full of strange coincidences and improbabilities, that they call for the closest and most searching examination."

"I hadn't observed anything so very abnormal in the case," I said. "Of course, I can see that the second will was unnecessary— that a codicil would have answered all purposes; that, as things have turned out, it does not seem to carry out the wishes of the testator; but then, if he had lived, Jeffrey Blackmore would probably have made a new will."

"Which would not have suited Brother John. But have you considered the significance of the order in which the events occurred and the strange coincidences in the dates?"

"I am afraid I missed that point," I replied. "How do the dates run?"

"The second will," replied Thorndyke, "was made on the ninth of December 1899; Mrs. Wilson died of cancer on the twenty-fourth of March, 1900; Jeffrey Blackmore was seen alive on the twenty-sixth of March, thus establishing the fact that he survived Mrs. Wilson, and his body was found on the twenty-seventh of March. Does that group of dates suggest nothing to you?"

I reflected for awhile and then had to confess that it suggested nothing at all.

"Then make a note of it and consider it at your leisure," said Thorndyke; "or I will write out the dates for you later, for here we are at our destination."

It was a chilly day, and a cold wind blew through the archway leading into New Inn. Halting at the half-door of the lodge we perceived a stout, purple-faced man crouching over the fire, coughing violently. He held up his hand to intimate that he was fully occupied for the moment, so we waited for his paroxysm to subside.

"Dear, dear!" exclaimed Thorndyke sympathetically, "you ought not to be sitting in this drafty lodge with your delicate chest. You should make them fit a glass door with a pigeonhole."

"Bless you," said the porter, wiping his eyes, "I daren't make any complaints. There's plenty of younger men ready to take the job. But it's terrible work for me in the Winter, especially when the fogs are about."

"It must be," rejoined Thorndyke, and then, rather to my surprise, he proceeded to inquire with deep interest into the sufferer's symptoms and the history of the attack, receiving in reply a wealth of detail and discursive reminiscence delivered with the utmost gusto. To all of this I listened a little impatiently, for chronic bronchitis is not, medically speaking, an entertaining complaint, and consultations out of business hours are an abomination to doctors. Something of this perhaps appeared in my manner, for the man broke off suddenly with an apology:

"But I mustn't detain you gentlemen talking about my health. It can't interest you, though it's serious enough for me."

"I am sure it is," said Thorndyke, "and I hope we may be able to do something for you. I am a medical man and so is my friend. We came to ask if you had any chambers to let."

"Yes, we've got three sets empty."

"Not furnished, I suppose?"

"Yes, one set is furnished. It is the one," he added, lowering his voice, "that the gentleman committed suicide in—but you wouldn't mind that, being a doctor?"

"Oh, no," laughed Thorndyke, "the disease is not catching. What is the rent?"

"Twenty-three pounds, but the furniture would have to be taken at a valuation. There isn't much of it."

"May I see the rooms?"

"Certainly. Here's the key; I've only just had it back from the police. There's no need for me to come with gentlemen like you; it's such a drag up all those stairs. The gas hasn't been cut off because the tenancy has not expired. It's Number 31, second floor."

We made our way across the Inn to the doorway of Number 31, the ground floor of which was occupied by solicitors' offices. The dusk was just closing in and a man was lighting a lamp on the first-floor landing as we came up the stairs.

"Who occupies the chambers on the third floor?" Thorndyke asked him as we turned on to the next flight.

"The third floor has been empty for about three months," was the reply.

"We are looking at the chambers on the second floor," said Thorndyke. "Are they pretty quiet?"

"Quiet!" exclaimed the man. "Lord bless you! the place is like a deaf and dumb cemetery. There's the solicitors on the ground floor and the architects on the first floor. They both clear out at about six, and then the 'ouse is as empty as a blown hegg. I don't wonder poor Mr. Blackmore made away with hisself; he must 'ave found it awful dull."

"So," said Thorndyke, as the man's footsteps echoed down the stairs, "when Jeffrey Blackmore came home that last evening the house was empty."

He inserted the key into the door, above which was painted in white letters the deceased man's name, and we entered, my companion striking a wax vesta and lighting the gas in the sitting-room.

"Spare and simple," remarked Thorndyke, looking round critically, "but well enough for a solitary bachelor. A cupboard of a kitchen—never used, apparently, and a small bedroom opening out of the sitting-room. Why, the bed hasn't been made since the catastrophe! There is the impression of the body! Rather gruesome for a new tenant, eh?"

He wandered round the sitting-room, looking at the various objects it contained as though he would question them as to what they had witnessed. The apartment was bare and rather comfortless and its appointments were all old and worn. A small glass-fronted bookcase held a number of solid-looking volumes—proceedings of the Asiatic Society and works on Oriental literature for the most part; and a half-dozen framed photographs of buildings and objects of archeological interest formed the only attempts at wall decoration.

Before one of these latter Thorndyke halted and, having regarded it for a few moments with close attention, uttered an exclamation.

"Here is a very strange thing, Jervis," said he.

I stepped across the room and looked over his shoulder at an oblong frame enclosing a photograph of an inscription in the weird and cabalistic arrow-head character.

"Yes," I agreed; "the cuneiform writing is surely the most un-canny-looking script that was ever invented. I wonder if poor Blackmore was able to read this stuff; I suppose he was, or it wouldn't be here."

"I should say there is no doubt that he was able to read the cuneiform character; and that is just what constitutes the strangeness of this," and Thorndyke pointed, as he spoke, to the framed photograph on the wall.

"I don't follow you at all," I said. "It would seem to me much more odd if a man were to hang upon his wall an inscription that he could *not* read."

"No doubt," replied Thorndyke. "But you will agree with me that it would be still more odd if a man should hang upon his wall an inscription that he *could* read—and hang it *upside-down!*"

"You don't mean to say that this is up-side-down!" I exclaimed.

"I do indeed," he replied.

"But how can you tell that? I didn't know that Oriental scholarship was included in your long list of accomplishments."

Thorndyke chuckled. "It isn't," he replied; "but I have read with very keen interest the wonderful history of the decipherment of the cuneiform characters, and I happen to remember one or two of the main facts. This particular inscription is in the Persian cuneiform, a much more simple form of the script than the Babylonian or Assyrian; in fact, I suspect that this is the famous inscription from the gateway at Persepolis—the first to be deciphered, which would account for its presence here in a frame.

"Now this script reads, like our own writing, from left to right, and the rule is that all the wedge-shaped characters point to the right or downward, while the arrow-head forms are open toward the right. But if you examine this inscription you will see that the wedges point upward and to the left, and that the arrow-head characters are open toward the left. Obviously the photograph is upside-down."

"But this is really mysterious!" I exclaimed. "What do you suppose can be the explanation? Do you think poor Blackmore's eyesight was failing him, or were his mental faculties decaying?"

"I think," replied Thorndyke, "we may perhaps get a suggestion from the back of the frame. Let us see." He disengaged the frame from the two nails on which it hung and, turning it round, glanced for a moment at the back, which he then presented toward me with a quaint, half-quizzical smile. A label on the backing-paper bore the words: "J. Budge, Frame-maker and Gilder, Gt. Anne St., W.C."

"Well?" I said, when I had read the label without gathering from it anything fresh.

"The label, you observe, is the right way up."

"So it is," I rejoined hastily, a little annoyed that I had not been quicker to observe so obvious a fact. "I see your point. You mean that the frame-maker hung the thing upside-down and Blackmore never noticed the mistake."

"No, I don't think that is the explanation," replied Thorndyke. "You will notice that the label is an old one; it must have been on some years, to judge by its dingy appearance, whereas the two mirror-plates look to me comparatively new. But we can soon put that matter to the test, for the label was evidently stuck on when the frame was new, and if the plates were screwed on at the same time, the wood which they cover will be clean and new-looking."

He drew from his pocket a "combination" knife containing, among other implements, a screw-driver, with which he carefully extracted the screws from one of the little brass plates by which the frame had been suspended from the nails.

"You see," he said, when he had removed the plate and carried the photograph over to the gas-jet, "the wood covered by the plate is as dirty and time-stained as the rest of the frame. The plates have been put on recently."

"And what are we to infer from that?"

"Well, since there are no other marks of plates or rings upon the frame, we may safely infer that the photograph was never hung up until it came to these rooms."

"Yes, I suppose we may. But what is the suggestion that this photograph makes to you? I know you have something in mind that bears upon the case you are investigating. What is it?"

"Come, come, Jervis," said Thorndyke, playfully, "I am not going to wet-nurse you in this fashion! You are a man of ingenuity and far from lacking in the scientific imagination; you must work out the rest of the train of deduction by yourself."

"That is how you always tantalize me!" I complained. "You take out the stopper from your bottle of wisdom and present the mouth to my nose; and then, when I have taken a hearty sniff and got my appetite fairly whetted, you clap in the stopper again and leave me, metaphorically speaking, with my tongue hanging out."

Thorndyke chuckled as he replaced the little brass plate and inserted the screws.

"You must learn to take out the stopper for yourself," said he; "then you will be able to slake your divine thirst to your satisfaction. Shall we take a look round the bedroom?"

CHAPTER X—WE RENT 31 NEW INN

He hung the photograph upon its nails and we passed on to the little chamber, glancing once more at the depression on the narrow bed, which seemed to make the tragedy so real.

"The syringe and the rest of the lethal appliances and material have been removed, I see," remarked Thorndyke. "I suppose the police or the coroner's officers have kept them."

He looked keenly about the bare, comfortless apartment, taking mental notes, apparently, of its general aspect and the few details it presented.

"Jeffrey Blackmore would seem to have been a man of few needs," he observed presently. "I have never seen a bedroom in which less attention seemed to be given to the comfort of the occupant."

He pulled at the drawer of the dressing-table, disclosing a solitary hair-brush; peeped into a cupboard, where an overcoat surmounted by a felt hat hung from a peg like an attenuated suicide; he even picked up and examined the cracked and shrunken cake of soap on the washstand, and he was just replacing this in its dish when his attention was apparently attracted by something in the dark corner close by. As he knelt on the floor to make a close scrutiny, I came over and stooped beside him. I found the object of his regard to be a number of tiny fragments of glass, which had the appearance of having been trodden upon and then scattered by a kick of the foot.

"What have you found?" I asked.

"That is what I am asking myself," he replied. "As far as I can judge from the appearance of these fragments, they appear to be the remains of a small watch-glass. But we can examine them more thoroughly at our leisure."

He gathered up the little splintered pieces with infinite care and bestowed them in the envelope of a letter which he drew from his pocket.

"And now," he said as he rose and dusted his knees, "we had better go back to the lodge, or the porter will begin to think that there has been another tragedy in New Inn."

We passed out into the sitting-room, where Thorndyke once more halted before the inverted photograph.

"Yes," he said, surveying it thoughtfully, "we have picked up a trifle of fact which may mean nothing, or, on the other hand, may be of critical importance."

He paused for a few moments and then said suddenly:

"Jervis, how should you like to be the new tenant of these rooms?"

"It is the one thing necessary for my complete happiness," I replied with a grin.

"I am not joking," said he. "Seriously, these chambers might be very convenient for you, especially in some new circumstances that I, and I hope you also, have in contemplation. But in any case, I should like to examine the premises at my leisure, and I suppose you would not mind appearing as the tenant if I undertake all liabilities?"

"Certainly not," I answered.

"Then let us go down and see what arrangements we can make."

He turned out the gas and we made our way back to the lodge.

"What do you think of the rooms, sir?" asked the porter as I handed him back the key.

"I think they would suit me," I replied, "if the furniture could be had on reasonable terms."

"Oh, that will be all right," said the porter. "The executor—deceased's brother—has written to me saying that the things are to be got rid of for what they will fetch, but as quickly as possible. He wants those chambers off his hands, so, as I am his agent, I shall instruct the valuer to price them low."

"Can my friend have immediate possession?" asked Thorndyke.

"You can have possession as soon as the valuer has seen the effects," said the porter. "The man from the broker's shop down Wych Street will look them over for us."

"I would suggest that we fetch him up at once," said Thorndyke. "Then you can pay over the price agreed on and move your things in without delay—that is, if our friend here has no objection."

"Oh, I have no objection," said the porter. "If you like to pay the purchase-money for the furniture and give me a letter agreeing to take on the tenancy, and a reference, you can have the key at once and sign the regular agreement later."

In a very short time this easy-going arrangement was carried out. The furniture broker was decoyed to the Inn and, having received his instructions from the porter, accompanied us to the vacant chambers.

"Now, gentlemen," said he, looking round disparagingly at the barely furnished rooms, "you tell me what things you are going to take and I will make my estimate."

"We are going to take everything—stock, lock and barrel," said Thorndyke.

"What! clothes and all?" exclaimed the man, grinning.

"Clothes, hats, boots—everything. We can throw out what we don't want afterward, but my friend wishes to have immediate possession of the rooms."

"I understand," said the broker, and without more ado he produced a couple of sheets of foolscap and fell to work on the inventory.

"This gentleman didn't waste much money on clothes," he remarked presently after examining the contents of a cupboard and a chest of drawers. "Why, there's only two suits all told!"

"He doesn't seem to have embarrassed himself with an excessive number of hats or boots either," said Thorndyke. "But I believe he spent most of his time indoors."

"That might account for it," rejoined the broker, and he proceeded to add to his list the meager account of clothing.

The inventory was soon completed and the prices affixed to the items, when it appeared that the value of the entire contents of the rooms amounted to no more than eighteen pounds, twelve shillings. This sum, at Thorndyke's request, I paid to the porter, handing him my recently-acquired check for twenty-five guineas and directing him to drop the change into the letter-box of the chambers.

"That is a good thing done," remarked Thorndyke, as we took our way back toward the Strand. "I will give you a check this evening and you might let me have the key for the present. I will send Polton down with a trunk this evening, to keep up appearances. And now we will go and have some dinner."

"To come back," said Thorndyke, when Polton had set before us our simple meal, with a bottle of sound claret, "to the new arrangement I proposed the other day: You know that Polton gives me a great deal of help in my work, especially by making appliances and photographs and carrying out chemical processes under my directions. But still, clever as he is and wonderfully well-informed, he is not a scientific man, properly speaking, and of course his education and social training do not allow of his taking my place excepting in a quite subordinate capacity. Now there are times when I am greatly pushed for the want of a colleague of my own class, and it occurred to me that you might like to join me as my junior or assistant. We know that we can rub along together in a friendly way, and I know enough of your abilities and accomplishments to feel sure that your help would be of value to me. What do you think of the proposal?"

To exchange the precarious, disagreeable and uninteresting life of a regular "locum" with its miserable pay and utter lack of future prospects, for the freedom and interest of the life thus held out to me with its chances of advancement and success, was to rise at a bound out of the abyss into which misfortune had plunged me, and to cut myself free from the millstone of poverty which had held me down so long. Moreover, with the salary that Thorndyke offered and the position that I should occupy as junior to a famous expert, I could marry without the need of becoming pecuniarily indebted to my wife; a circumstance which I was sure she would regard with as much satisfaction as I did. Hence I accepted joyfully, much to Thorndyke's gratification, and, the few details of our engagement being settled, we filled our glasses and drank to our joint success.

CHAPTER XI—THE EMPTY HOUSE

"By the way, Jervis," said my new principal—or colleague, as he preferred to style himself—when, our dinner over and our chairs drawn up to the fire, we were filling our pipes in preparation for a gossip, "you never told me the end of that odd adventure of yours."

"I went to the house once again," I answered, "and followed your directions to the letter, though how much skill and intelligence I displayed in following them you will be able to judge when you have seen the note-book; it is in my trunk up-stairs with your lamp and compass."

"And what became of the patient?"

"Ah," I replied, "that is what I have often wondered. I don't like to think about it."

"Tell me what happened at the second visit," said Thorndyke.

I gave him a circumstantial description of all that I had seen and all that had happened on that occasion, recalling every detail that I could remember, even to the momentary glimpse I had of Mr. J. Morgan, as he stood in the light of the candle. To all of this my friend listened with rapt attention and asked me so many questions about my first visit that I practically gave him the whole story over again from the beginning.

"It was a fishy business," commented Thorndyke as I concluded, but of course you could do nothing. You had not enough facts to swear an information on. But it would be interesting to plot the route and see where this extremely cautious gentleman resides. I suggest that we do so forthwith."

To this I assented with enthusiasm and, having fetched the note-book from my room, we soon had it spread before us on the table. Thorndyke ran his eye over the various entries, noting the details with an approving smile.

"You seem to the manner born, Jervis," said he with a chuckle, as he came to the end of the first route. "That is quite an artistic touch— 'Passenger station to left.' How did you know there was a station?"

"I heard the guard's whistle and the starting of a train—evidently a long and heavy one, for the engine skidded badly."

"Good!" said Thorndyke. "Have you looked these notes over?"

"No," I answered. "I put the book away when I came in and have never looked at it since."

"It is a quaint document. You seem to be rich in railway bridges in those parts, and the route was certainly none of the most direct. However, we will plot it out and see whither it leads us."

He retired to the laboratory and presently returned with a T-square, a military protractor, a pair of dividers and a large drawing-board, upon which was pinned a sheet of paper.

"I see," said he, "that the horse kept up a remarkably even pace, so we can take the time as representing distance. Let us say that one inch equals one minute—that will give us a fair scale. Now you read out the notes and I will plot the route."

I read out the entries from the note-book—a specimen page of which I present for the reader's inspection—and Thorndyke laid off the lines of direction with the protractor, taking out the distance with the dividers from a scale of equal parts on the back of the instrument.

9.05	S.W.	Start from house. Horse 13 hands.
9.05.30	S.E. by E.	Macadam. Hoofs 110.
9.06	N.E. by N.	Granite.
9.06.25	S.E.	Macadam.
9.07.20	N.	Macadam.
9.08	N.E.	Under bridge. Hoofs 120.
9.08.30	N.E.	Cross granite road. Tram-lines.
9.09.35	N.N.W.	Still macadam. Hoofs 120.
9.10.30	W. by S.	Still macadam. Hoofs 120.
9.11.30	W. by S.	Cross granite road. Tram-lines. Then under bridge.
9.12	S.S.E.	Macadam.
9.12.15	E.N.E.	Macadam.
9.12.30	E.N.E.	Under bridge. Hoofs 116.
9.12.45	S.S.E.	Granite road. Tram-lines.
9.14	E.N.E.	Macadam.

As the work proceeded a smile of quiet amazement spread over his keen, attentive face, and at each new reference to a railway bridge he chuckled softly.

"What! again?" he laughed, as I recorded the passage of the eighth bridge. "Why, it's like a game of croquet! Ah, here we are at last! '9.38—Slow down; enter arched gateway to left; Stop; Wooden gates closed.' Just look at your route, Jervis."

He held up the board with a quizzical smile, when I perceived with astonishment that the middle of the paper was occupied by a single line that zigzagged, crossed and recrossed in the most intricate manner, and terminated at no great distance from its commencement.

"Now," said Thorndyke, "let us get the map and see if we can give to each of these marvelous and erratic lines 'a local habitation and a name.' You started from Lower Kennington Lane, I think?"

"Yes; from this point," indicating the spot with a pencil.

"Then," said Thorndyke, after a careful comparison of the map with the plotted route, "I think we may take it that your gateway was on the north side of Upper Kennington Lane, some three hundred yards from Vauxhall Station. The heavy train that you heard starting was no doubt one of the Southwestern expresses. You see that, rough as was the method of tracing the route, it is quite enough to enable us to identify all the places on the map. The tram-lines and railway bridges are invaluable."

He wrote by the side of the strange crooked lines the names of the streets that its different parts represented and, on comparing the amended sketch with the ordnance map, I saw that the correspondence was near enough to preclude all doubt.

"To-morrow morning," observed Thorndyke, "I shall have an hour or two to spare, and I propose that we take a stroll through Upper Kennington Lane and gaze upon this abode of mystery. This chart has fairly aroused the trailing instinct—although, of course, the affair is no business of mine."

The following morning, after an early breakfast, we pocketed the chart and the note-book and, issuing forth into the Strand, chartered a passing hansom to convey us to Vauxhall Station.

"There should be no difficulty in locating the house," remarked Thorndyke presently, as we bowled along the Albert Embankment. "It is evidently about three hundred yards from the station, and I see you have noted a patch of newly laid macadam about half way."

"That new macadam will be pretty well smoothed down by now," I objected.

"Not so very completely," answered Thorndyke. "It is only three weeks, and there has been no wet weather lately."

A few minutes later the cab drew up at the station and, having alighted and paid the driver, we made our way to the bridge that spans the junction of Harleyford Road and Upper Kennington Lane.

"From here to the house," said Thorndyke, "is three hundred yards—say four hundred and twenty paces, and at about two hundred paces we ought to pass a patch of new road-metal. Now, are you ready? If we keep step we shall average our stride."

We started together at a good pace, stepping out with military regularity, and counting aloud as we went. As we told out the hundred and ninety-fourth pace I observed Thorndyke nod toward the roadway a little ahead and, looking at it attentively as we approached, it was easy to see, by the regularity of the surface and lighter color, that it had recently been remetaled.

Having counted out the four hundred and twenty paces, we halted, and Thorndyke turned to me with a smile of triumph.

"Not a bad estimate, Jervis," said he. "That will be your house if I am not much mistaken." He pointed to a narrow turning a dozen yards ahead, apparently the entrance to a yard and closed by a pair of massive wooden gates.

"Yes," I answered, "there is no doubt that this is the place. But, by Jove!" I added, as we drew nearer, "the nest is empty. Do you see?" I pointed to a small bill that was stuck on the gate announcing, "These premises, including stabling and workshops, to be let," and giving the name and address of an auctioneer in Upper Kennington Lane as the agent.

"Here is a new and startling development," said Thorndyke, "which leads one to wonder still more what has happened to your patient. Now the question is, should we make a few inquiries of the auctioneer or should we get the keys and have a look at the inside of the house? I think we will do both, and the latter first, if Messrs Ryman Brothers will trust us with the keys."

We made our way to the auctioneer's office, and were, without demur, given permission to inspect the premises.

"You will find the place in a very dirty and neglected condition," said the clerk, as he handed us a couple of keys with a wooden label attached. "The house has not been cleaned yet, but is just as it was left when we took out the furniture."

"Was Mr. Morgan sold up then?" inquired Thorndyke.

"Oh, no. But he had to leave rather unexpectedly, and he asked us to dispose of his effects for him."

"He had not been in the house very long, had he?"

"No. Less than six months, I should say."

"Do you know where he has moved to?"

"I don't. He said he should be travelling for a time and he paid us a half-year's rent in advance to be quit. The larger key is that of the wicket in the front gate."

Thorndyke took the keys and we returned together to the house which, with its closed window-shutters, had a very gloomy and desolate aspect. We let ourselves in at the wicket, when I perceived, half-way down the entry, the side door at which I had been admitted by the unknown woman.

"We will look at the bedroom first," said Thorndyke, as we stood in the dark and musty-smelling hall. "That is, if you can remember which room it was."

"It was on the first floor," said I, "and the door was just at the head of the stairs."

We ascended the two flights and as we reached the landing I halted.

"This was the door," I said, and was about to turn the handle when Thorndyke caught me by the arm.

"One moment, Jervis," said he. "What do you make of this?"

He pointed to four screw-holes, neatly filled with putty, near the bottom of the door, and two others on the jamb opposite them.

"Evidently," I answered, "there has been a bolt there, though it seems a queer place to fix one."

"Not at all," rejoined Thorndyke. "If you look up you will see that there was another at the top of the door and, as the lock is in the middle, they must have been highly effective. But there are one or two other things that strike one. First, you will notice that the bolts have been fixed on pretty recently, for the paint that they covered is of the same grimy tint as that on the rest of the door. Next, they have been taken off, which, seeing that they could hardly have been worth the trouble of removal, seems to suggest that the person who fixed them considered that their presence might appear remarkable, while the screw-holes would be less conspicuous.

"They are on the *outside* of the door—an unusual situation for bolts; and if you look closely you can see a slight indentation in the wood of the jamb, made by the sharp edges of the socket-plate, as though at some time a forcible attempt has been made to drag the door open when it was bolted."

"There was a second door, I remember," said I. "Let us see if that was guarded in a similar manner."

We strode through the empty room, awakening dismal echoes as we trod the bar boards, and flung open the other door. At top and bottom similar groups of screw-holes showed that this also had been made secure, the bolts in all cases being of a very substantial size.

"I am afraid these fastenings have a very sinister significance," said Thorndyke gravely, "for I suppose we can have no doubt as to their object or by whom they were fixed."

"No, I suppose not," I answered; "but if the man was really imprisoned, could he not have smashed the window and called for help?"

"The window looks out on the yard, as you see. And I expect it was secured, too."

He drew the massive old-fashioned shutters out of their recess and closed them.

"Yes, here we are!" He pointed to four groups of screw-holes at the corners of the shutters and, lighting a match, narrowly examined the insides of the recesses into which the shutters folded.

"The nature of the fastening is quite evident," said he. "An iron bar passed right across at the top and bottom and was secured by a staple and padlock. You can see the mark the bar made in the recess when the shutters were folded. By heaven, Jervis," he exclaimed as he flung the shutters open again, "this was a diabolical affair, and I would give a good round sum to lay my hand on Mr. J. Morgan!"

CHAPTER XII—IN A LITTLE HEAP OF RUBBISH

"It is a thousand pities we were unable to look round before they moved out the furniture," I remarked. "We might then have found some clue to the scoundrel's identity."

"Yes," replied Thorndyke, gazing round ruefully at the bare walls, "there isn't much information to be gathered here, I am afraid. I see they have swept up the litter under the grate; we may as well turn it over, though it is not likely that we shall find anything of much interest."

He raked out the little heap of rubbish with the crook of his stick and spread it out on the hearth. It certainly looked unpromising enough, being just such a rubbish-heap as may be swept up in any untidy room during a move. But Thorndyke went through it systematically, examining each item attentively, even to the local tradesmen's bills and empty paper bags, before laying them aside. One of the latter he folded up neatly and laid on the mantel-shelf before resuming his investigations.

"Here is something that may give us a hint," said he presently. He held up a battered pair of spectacles of which only one hooked side-bar remained, while both the glasses were badly cracked.

"Left eye a concave cylindrical lens," he continued, peering through the glasses at the window; "right eye plain glass—these must have belonged to your patient, Jervis. You said the tremulous iris was in the right eye, I think?"

"Yes," I replied, "these are his spectacles, no doubt."

"The frames, you notice, are peculiar," he continued. "The shape was invented by Stopford of Moorfields and is made, I believe, by only one optician—Cuxton and Parry of New Bond Street."

"What should you say that is?" I asked, picking up a small object from the rubbish. It was a tiny stick of bamboo furnished with a sheath formed of a shorter length of the same material, which fitted it closely, yet slid easily up and down the little cane.

"Ha!" exclaimed Thorndyke, taking the object eagerly from my hand. "This is really interesting. Have you never seen one of these before? It is a Japanese pocket brush or pencil, and very beautiful little instruments they are, with the most exquisitely delicate and flexible points. They are used principally for writing or drawing with Chinese or, as it is usually called, Indian ink. The bamboo, in this one, is cracked at the end and the hair has fallen out, but the sliding sheath, which protected the point, remains to show what it has been."

He laid the brush-stick on the mantel-shelf and once more turned to the rubbish-heap.

"Now here is a very suggestive thing," he said presently, holding out to me a small wide-mouthed bottle. "Observe the flies sticking to the inside, and the name on the label—'Fox, Russell Street, Covent Garden.' You were right, Jervis, in your surmise; Mr. Morgan and the coachman were one and the same person."

"I don't see how you arrive at that, all the same," I remarked.

"This," said Thorndyke, tapping the bottle with his finger, "contained—and still contains a small quantity of—a kind of cement. Mr. Fox is a dealer in the materials for making-up, theatrical or otherwise. Now your really artistic make-up does not put on an oakum wig nor does he tie on a false beard with strings as if it were a baby's feeder. If he dons a false mustache or beard, the thing is properly made and securely fixed on, and then the ends are finished with ends of loose hair, which are cemented to the skin and afterward trimmed with scissors. This is the kind of cement that is used for that purpose."

He laid the bottle beside his other treasure-trove and returned to his search. But, with the exception of a screw and a trouser-button, he met with no further reward for his industry. At length he rose and, kicking the discarded rubbish back under the grate, gathered up his gleanings and wrapped them in his handkerchief, having first tried the screw in one of the holes in the door, from which he had picked out the putty, and found that it fitted perfectly.

"A poor collection," was his comment, as he pocketed the small parcel of miscellaneous rubbish, "and yet not so poor as I had feared. Perhaps, if we question them closely enough, these unconsidered trifles may be made to tell us something worth hearing, after all. We may as well look through the house and yard before we go."

We did so, but met with nothing that even Thorndyke's inquisitive eye could view with interest and, having returned the keys to the agent, betook ourselves back to the Temple.

CHAPTER XIII—A CHANGE IN SIGNATURE

On our return to Thorndyke's chambers I was inducted forthwith into my new duties, for an inquest of some importance was pending and my friend had been commissioned to examine the body and make a full report upon certain suspected matters.

I entered on the work with a pleasure and revived enthusiasm that tended to drive my recent experiences from my mind. Now and again, indeed, I gave a passing thought to the house in Kennington Lane and its mysterious occupants, but even then it was only the recollection of a strange experience that was past and done with.

Thorndyke, too, I supposed to have dismissed the subject from his mind, in spite of the strong feeling that he had shown and his implied determination to unravel the mystery. But on this point I was mistaken, as was proved to me by an incident that occurred on the fourth day of my residence and which I found, at the time, not a little startling.

We were sitting at breakfast, each of us glancing over the morning's letters, when Thorndyke said rather suddenly:

"Have you a good memory for faces, Jervis?"

"Yes," I answered, "I think I have, rather. Why do you ask?"

"Because I have a photograph here of a man whom I think you may have met. Just look at it and tell me if you remember the face."

He drew a cabinet-size photograph from an envelope that had come by the morning's post and passed it to me.

"I have certainly seen this face somewhere," said I, taking the portrait over to the window to examine it more thoroughly, "but I can not at the moment remember where."

"Try," said Thorndyke. "If you have seen the face before, you should be able to recall the person."

I looked intently at the photograph, and the more I looked, the more familiar did the face appear. Suddenly the identity of the man flashed into my mind and I exclaimed in a tone of astonishment:

"By heaven, Thorndyke, it is the mysterious patient of Kennington Lane!"

"I believe you are right," was the quiet reply, "and I am glad you were able to recognize him. The identification may be of value."

I need not say that the production of this photograph filled me with amazement and that I was seething with curiosity as to how Thorndyke had obtained it; but, as he replaced it impassively in its envelope without volunteering any explanation, I judged it best to ask no questions.

Nevertheless, I pondered upon the matter with undiminished wonder and once again realized that my friend was a man whose powers, alike of observation and inference, were of no ordinary kind. I had myself seen all that he had seen and, indeed, much more. I had examined the little handful of rubbish that he had gathered up so carefully and I would have flung it back under the grate without a qualm. Not a single glimmer of light had I perceived in the cloud of mystery, nor even a hint of the direction in which to seek enlightenment.

And yet Thorndyke had, in some incomprehensible manner, contrived to piece together facts that I had not even observed, and that very completely; for it was evident that he had already, in these few days, narrowed the field of inquiry down to a very small area and must be in possession of the leading facts of the case.

As to the other case—that of Jeffrey Blackmore's will—I had had occasional proofs that he was still engaged upon it, though with what object I could not imagine, for the will seemed to me as incontestable as a will could be. My astonishment may therefore be imagined when, on the very evening of the day on which he had shown me the photograph of my patient, Thorndyke remarked coolly, as we rose from the dinner-table:

"I have nearly finished with the Blackmore case. In fact, I shall write to Marchmont this evening and advise him to enter a caveat at once."

"Why," I exclaimed, "you don't mean to say that you have found a flaw in the second will, after all!"

"A flaw!" repeated Thorndyke. "My dear Jervis, that will is a forgery from beginning to end! Of that I have no doubt whatever. I am only waiting for the final, conclusive verification to institute criminal proceedings."

"You amaze me!" I declared. "I had imagined that your investigations were—well——"

"A demonstration of activity to justify the fee, eh?" suggested Thorndyke, with a mischievous smile.

I laughed a little shamefacedly, for my astute friend had, as usual, shot his bolt very near the mark.

"I haven't shown you the signatures, have I?" he continued. "They are rather interesting and suggestive. I persuaded the bank people to let me photograph the last year's checks in a consecutive series, so as to exhibit the change which was admitted to have occurred in the character of the signature. We pinned the checks to a board in batches, each check overlapping the one below so as to show the signature only and to save space, and the dates were written on a slip of paper at the side. I photographed them full size, a batch at a time, with a tele-photo lens."

"Why a tele-photo?" I asked.

"To enable me to get a full-sized image without bringing the checks close up to the camera," he replied. "If I had used an ordinary lens, the checks could hardly have been much more than a foot from the camera and then the signatures on the margin of the plate would certainly have undergone some distortion from the effects of perspective—even if the lens itself were free from all optical defects. As it is, the photographs are quite reliable, and the enlargements that Polton has made—magnified three diameters—show the characters perfectly."

He brought out from a drawer a number of whole-plate photographs which he laid on the table end to end. Each one contained four of the enlarged signatures and, thus exhibited in series in the order of their dates, it was easy to compare their characters. Further to facilitate the comparison, the signatures of the two wills—also enlarged—had each a card to itself and could thus be laid by the side of any one of the series.

"You will remember," said Thorndyke, "Marchmont referred to a change in the character of Jeffrey Blackmore's signature?"

I nodded.

"It was a very slight change and, though noticed at the bank, it

was not considered to be of any moment. Now if you will cast your
eye over the series, you will be able to distinguish the differences.
They are very small indeed; the later signatures are a little stiffer, a
little more shaky, and the B and the K are both appreciably different
from those in the earlier signatures. But there is another fact which
emerges when the whole series is seen together, and it is so striking
and significant a fact that I am astonished at its having occasioned
no inquiry."

"Indeed!" said I, stooping to examine the photographs with
increased interest. "What is that?"

"It is a very simple matter and very obvious, but yet, as I have
said, very significant. It is this: the change in the characters of the
signatures is not a gradual or insidious change, nor is it progressive.
It occurs at a certain definite point and then continues without
increase or variation. Look carefully at the check dated twenty-
ninth of September and you will see that the signature is in what we
may call the 'old manner,' whereas the next check, dated the
eighteenth of October, is in the new manner.

"Now if you will run your eye through the signatures previous
to the twenty-ninth of September, you will observe that none of
them shows any sign of change whatever; they are all in the 'old
manner'; while the signatures subsequent to the twenty-ninth of
September, from the eighteenth of October onwards, are, without
exception, in the 'new manner.'

"The alteration, slight and trivial as it is, is to be seen in every one of
them; and you will also notice that it does not increase as time goes
on; it is not a progressive change; the signature on the last check—the
one that was drawn on the twenty-sixth of March to pay the rent—
does not differ from the 'old manner' any more than that dated the
eighteenth of October. A rather striking and important fact."

"Yes; and the signatures of the two wills?"

"The first will is signed in the 'old manner,' as you can see for
yourself, while the signature of the second will has the characters
of what we have called the 'new manner.' It is identical in style
with the signatures subsequent to the twenty-ninth of September."

"Yes, I see that it is as you say," I agreed, when I had carefully
made the comparison, "and it is certainly very curious and interesting. But what I do not see is the bearing of all this. The second will
was signed in the presence of witnesses and that seems to dispose
of the whole matter."

"It does," Thorndyke admitted; "but we must not let our data overlap. It is wise always to consider each separate fact on its own merits and work it out to a finish without allowing ourselves to be disturbed or our attention diverted by any seeming incompatibilities with other facts. Then, when we have each datum as complete as we can get it, we may put them all together and consider their relations to one another. It is surprising to see how the incompatibilities become eliminated if we work in this way—how the most (apparently) irreconcilable facts fall into agreement with one another."

"As an academic rule for conducting investigations," I replied, "your principle is, no doubt, entirely excellent. But when you seek to prove by indirect and collateral evidence that Jeffrey Blackmore did not sign a will which two respectable men have sworn they saw him sign, why, I am inclined to think that——"

"That, in the words of the late Captain Bunsby, 'the bearing of these observations lies in their application.' "

"Precisely," I agreed, and we both laughed.

CHAPTER XIV—SOME BITS OF GLASS

"However," I resumed presently, "as you are advising Marchmont to dispute the will, I presume you have some substantial grounds for action, though I can not conceive what they may be."

"You have all the facts that I had to start with and on which I formed the opinion that the will was probably a forgery. Of course I have more data now, for, as 'money makes money,' so knowledge begets knowledge, and I put my original capital out to interest. Shall we tabulate the facts that are in our joint possession and see what they suggest?"

"Yes, do," I replied, "for I am hopelessly in the dark."

Thorndyke produced a note-book from a drawer and, uncapping his fountain pen, wrote down the leading facts, reading each aloud as soon as it was written.

1. The second will was unnecessary, since a codicil would have answered the purpose.

2. The evident intention of the testator was to leave the bulk of his property to Stephen Blackmore.

3. The second will did not, under existing circumstances, give effect to this intention, while the first will did.

4. The signature of the second will differs slightly from that of the first and also from the testator's ordinary signature.

"And as to the very curious group of dates:—

5. Mrs. Wilson made her will at the end of 1897, without acquainting Jeffrey Blackmore, who seems to have been unaware of the existence of this will.

6. His own second will was dated the ninth of December, 1899.

7. Mrs. Wilson died of cancer on the twenty-fourth of March, 1900.

8. Jeffrey Blackmore was last seen alive on the twenty-sixth of March, 1900, *i.e.,* two days after Mrs. Wilson's death.

9. His body was discovered on the twenty-seventh of March, three days after Mrs. Wilson's death.

10. The change in the character of his signature occurred abruptly between the twenty-ninth of September and the eighteenth of October.

"You will find that collection of facts repays careful study, Jervis, especially when considered in relation to the last of our data, which is:

11. We found, in Blackmore's chambers, a framed inscription hung on the wall upside down."

He passed the book to me and I pored over it intently, focusing my attention upon the various items with all the power of my will. But, struggle as I would, no general conclusion could be made to emerge from the mass of apparently disconnected facts.

"Well," said Thorndyke presently, after watching with grave interest my unavailing efforts, "what do you make of it?"

"Nothing!" I exclaimed desperately, slapping the book down upon the table. "Of course I can see that there are some queer features in the case, but you say the will is a forgery. Now I can find nothing in these facts to give the slightest color to such a supposition. You will think me an unmitigated donkey, I have no doubt, but I can't help that." My failure, it will be observed, had put me somewhat out of humor, and, observing this, Thorndyke hastened to reply:

"Not in the least my dear fellow; you merely lack experience.

Wait until you have seen the trained legal intelligence brought to bear on these facts—which you will do, I feel little doubt, very soon after Marchmont gets my letter. You will have a better opinion of yourself then. By the way, here is another little problem for you. What was the object of which these are parts?"

He pushed across the table a little cardboard box, having first removed the lid. In it were a number of very small pieces of broken glass, some of which had been cemented together by their edges.

"These, I suppose, are the pieces of glass that you picked up in poor Blackmore's bedroom," I said, looking at them with considerable curiosity.

"Yes," replied Thorndyke. "You see that Polton has been endeavoring to reconstitute the object, whatever it was; but he has not been very successful, for the fragments were too small and irregular and the collection too incomplete. However, here is a specimen, built up of six small pieces, which exhibits the general character of the object fairly well."

He picked out the little irregular-shaped object and handed it to me, and I could not but admire the neatness with which Polton had joined the little fragments together.

"It was not a lens," I pronounced, holding it up before my eyes and moving it to and fro as I looked through it.

"No, it was not a lens," Thorndyke agreed.

"And so can not have been a spectacle glass. But the surface was curved—one side convex and the other concave—and the little piece that remains of the original edge seems to have been ground to fit a bezel or frame. I should say that these are portions of a small watch-glass."

"That is Polton's opinion," said Thorndyke. "And I think you are both wrong."

"What do you think it is?" I asked.

"I am submitting the problem for solution by my learned brother," he replied with an exasperating smile.

"You had better be careful!" I exclaimed, clapping the lid on to the box and pushing it across to him. "If I am tried beyond endurance I may be tempted to set a booby-trap to catch a medical jurist. And where will your reputation be then?"

Thorndyke's smile broadened, and he broke into an appreciative chuckle.

"Your suggestion has certainly extensive possibilities in the way of farce," he admitted "and I tremble at your threat. But I must write my letter to Marchmont and we will go out and lay the mine in the Fleet Street post-box. I should like to be in his office when it explodes."

"I expect, for that matter," said I, "the explosion will soon be felt pretty distinctly in these chambers."

"I expect so, too," replied Thorndyke. "And that reminds me that I shall be out all day to-morrow, so, if Marchmont calls and seems at all urgent, you might invite him to look in after dinner and talk the case over."

I promised to do so and hoped sincerely that the solicitor would accept the invitation; for I, at any rate, was on tenterhooks of curiosity to hear my colleague's views on Jeffrey Blackmore's will.

CHAPTER XV—A CALL FROM THE LAWYERS

My friend's expectations in respect to Mr. Marchmont were fully realized, for on the following morning, within an hour of his departure from the chambers, the knocker was plied with more than usual emphasis and, on my opening the door, I discovered the solicitor in company with a somewhat older gentleman. Mr. Marchmont appeared rather out of humor, while his companion was obviously in a state of extreme irritation.

"Howdy-do, Dr. Jervis?" said Marchmont, as he entered at my invitation. "Your colleague, I suppose, is not in just now?"

"No, and he will not be returning until the evening."

"Hm; I'm sorry. We wished to see him rather particularly. This is my partner, Mr. Winwood."

The latter gentleman bowed stiffly, and Marchmont continued: "We have had a letter from Mr. Thorndyke, and it is, I may say, a rather curious letter—in fact, a very singular letter indeed."

"It is the letter of a madman!" burst in Mr. Winwood.

"No, no, Winwood, don't say that; but it is really rather incomprehensible. It relates to the will of the late Jeffrey Blackmore—you know the main facts of the case—and we can not reconcile it with those facts."

"This is the letter," exclaimed Mr. Winwood, dragging the document from his wallet and slapping it down on the table. "If you are acquainted with the case, sir, just read that and let us hea▔ what *you* think."

I took up the letter and read:

DEAR MR. MARCHMONT,

Jeffrey Blackmore, decd.: I have gone into this case with some care and have now no doubt that the second will is a forgery. I therefore suggest that, pending the commencement of criminal proceedings, you lose no time in entering a caveat, and I will furnish you with particulars in due course.

Yours truly,

F. C. MARCHMONT, ESQ.   JOHN THORNDYKE.

"Well!" exclaimed Mr. Winwood, glaring ferociously at me, "what do you think of the learned counsel's opinion?"

"I knew that Thorndyke was writing to you to this effect," I replied "but I must frankly confess that I can make nothing of it. Have you acted on his advice?"

"Certainly not!" shouted the irascible lawyer. "Do you suppose we wish to make ourselves the laughing-stock of the courts? The thing is impossible—ridiculously impossible!"

"It can't be that, you know," said I a little stiffly, for I was somewhat nettled by Mr. Winwood's manner, "or Thorndyke would not have written this letter. You had better see him and let him give you the particulars, as he suggests. Could you look in this evening after dinner—say at eight o'clock?"

"It is very inconvenient," grumbled Mr. Winwood; "we should have to dine in town."

"Yes, but it will be the best plan," said Marchmont. "We can bring Mr. Stephen Blackmore with us and hear what Dr. Thorndyke has done. Of course, if what he says is correct, Mr. Stephen's position is totally changed."

"Bah!" exclaimed Winwood, "he has found a mare's-nest, I tell you. However, I suppose we must come, and we will bring Mr. Stephen by all means. The oracle's explanation should be worth hearing—to a man of leisure, at any rate."

With this the two lawyers took their departure, leaving me to meditate upon my colleague's astonishing statement, which I did, considerably to the prejudice of other employment. That Thorndyke would be able to justify the opinion he had given I had no doubt whatever; yet there was no denying that the thing was, upon the face of it, as Mr. Winwood had said, "ridiculously impossible."

When Thorndyke returned I acquainted him with the visit of the two lawyers, and also with the sentiments they had expressed, whereat he smiled with quiet amusement.

"I thought that letter would bring Marchmont to our door before long," said he. "As to Winwood, I have never met him, so he promises to give us what the variety artists would call an 'extra turn.' And what do you think of the affair yourself?"

"I have given it up," I answered, "and feel as if I had taken an overdose of *Cannabis Indica*."

Thorndyke laughed. "Come and dine," said he, "and let us crack a bottle, that our hearts may not turn to water under the frown of the disdainful Winwood."

He rang the bell for Polton, and when that ingenious person made his appearance, said:

"I expect that a man named Walker will call presently, Polton. If he does, take him to your room and detain him till I send for him."

We now betook ourselves to a certain old-world tavern in Fleet Street at which it was our custom occasionally to dine and where on the present occasion certain little extra touches gave a more than unusually festive character to our repast. Thorndyke was in excellent spirits, under the influence of which—and a bottle—he discoursed brilliantly on the evidence of the persistence of ancient racial types in modern populations, until the clock of the Law Courts, chiming three-quarters, warned us to return home.

CHAPTER XVI—SOME SINGULAR FACTS

We had not been back in the chambers more than a few minutes when the little brass knocker announced the arrival of our visitors. Thorndyke himself admitted them and then closed the oak.

"We felt that we must come round and hear a few particulars from you," said Mr. Marchmont, whose manner was now somewhat flurried and uneasy. "We could not quite understand your letter."

"Quite so," said Thorndyke. "The conclusion was a rather unexpected one."

"I should say, rather," exclaimed Mr. Winwood with some heat, "that the conclusion was a palpably ridiculous one."

"That," replied Thorndyke suavely, "can perhaps be better determined after examining all the facts that led up to it."

"No doubt, sir," retorted Mr. Winwood, growing suddenly red and wrathful, "but I speak as a solicitor who was practising in the law when you were an infant in arms! You say that this will is a forgery. I would remind you, sir, that it was executed in broad daylight in the presence of two unimpeachable witnesses, who have not only sworn to their signatures but, one of whom—the house-painter—obligingly left four greasy finger-prints on the document, for subsequent identification, if necessary!"

"After the excellent custom of the Chinese," observed Thorndyke. "Have you verified those finger-prints?"

"No, sir, I have not," replied Mr. Winwood. "Have you?"

"No. The fact is they are of no interest to me, as I am not disputing the witnesses' signatures."

At this, Mr. Winwood fairly danced with irritation.

"Marchmont," he exclaimed fiercely, "this is a mere hoax! This gentleman has brought us here to make fools of us——"

"Pray, my dear Winwood," said Marchmont, "control your temper. No doubt he——"

"But, confound it!" roared Winwood, "you yourself have heard him say that the will is a forgery, but that he doesn't dispute the signatures, which," concluded Winwood, banging his fist down upon the table, "is —— nonsense!"

"May I suggest," interposed Stephen Blackmore, "that we came here to listen to Dr. Thorndyke's explanation of his letter? Perhaps it would be better to postpone any comments until we have heard it."

"Undoubtedly, undoubtedly," said Marchmont. "Let me beg you, Winwood, to listen patiently and refrain from interruption until we have our learned friend's exposition of his opinion."

"Oh, very well," replied Winwood sulkily. "I'll say no more."

He sank into a chair with the manner of a man who shuts himself up and turns the key, and so remained throughout most of the subsequent proceedings, stony and impassive like a seated effigy at the portal of some Egyptian tomb. The other men also seated themselves, as did I, too, and Thorndyke, having laid on the table a small heap of documents, began without preamble.

"There are two ways in which I might lay the case before you," said he. "I might state my theory of the sequence of events and furnish the verification afterward, or I might retrace the actual course of my investigations and give you the facts in the order in which I obtained them myself, with the inferences from them. Which will you have first—the theory or the investigation?"

"Oh, —— the theory!" growled Mr. Winwood, and shut himself up again with a snap.

"Perhaps it would be better," said Marchmont, "if we heard the whole argument from the beginning."

"I think," agreed Thorndyke, "that that method will enable you to grasp the evidence more easily. Now, when you and Mr. Stephen placed the outline of the case before me, there were certain curious features in it which attracted my attention, as they had, no doubt, attracted yours. In the first place, there was the strange circumstance that the second will should have been made at all, its provisions being, under the conditions then existing, practically identical with the first, so that the trifling alteration could have been met easily by a codicil. There was also the fact that the second will—making John Blackmore the residuary legatee—was obviously less in accordance with the intentions of the testator, so far as they may be judged, than the first one.

"The next thing that arrested my attention was the mode of death of Mrs. Wilson. She died of cancer. Now cancer is one of the few diseases of which the fatal termination can be predicted with certainty months before its occurrence, and its date fixed, in suitable cases, with considerable accuracy.

"And now observe the remarkable series of coincidences that are brought into light when we consider this peculiarity of the disease. Mrs. Wilson died on the twenty-fourth of March, 1900, having made her will two years previously. Mr. Jeffrey's second will was signed on the ninth of December, 1899—at a time, that is to say, when the existence of cancer must have been known to Mrs. Wilson's doctor, and might have been known to Mr. Jeffrey himself or any person interested. Yet it is practically certain that Mr. Jeffrey had no intention of bequeathing the bulk of his property to his brother John, as he did by executing this second will.

"Next, you will observe that the remarkable change in Mr. Jeffrey's habits coincides with the same events; for he came over from Nice, where he had been residing for a year—having stored his furniture meanwhile—and took up his residence at New Inn in

September 1899, at a time when the nature of Mrs. Wilson's complaint must almost certainly have been known. At the same time, as I shall presently demonstrate to you, a distinct and quite sudden change took place in the character of his signature.

"I would next draw your attention to the singularly opportune date of his death, in reference to this will. Mrs. Wilson died upon the twenty-fourth of March. Mr. Jeffrey was found dead upon the twenty-seventh of March, and he was seen alive upon the twenty-sixth. If he had died only four days sooner, Mrs. Wilson's property would not have devolved upon him at all. If he had lived a few days longer, it is probable that he would have made a new will in his nephew's favor. Circumstances, therefore, conspired in the most singular manner in favor of Mr. John Blackmore.

"But there is yet another coincidence that you will probably have noticed.

"Mr. Jeffrey's body was found on the twenty-seventh of March, and then by the merest chance. It might have remained undiscovered for weeks—or even months; and if this had happened, it is certain that Mrs. Wilson's next of kin would have disputed John Blackmore's claim—most probably with success—on the grounds that Mr. Jeffrey died before Mrs. Wilson. But all this uncertainty and difficulty was prevented by the circumstance that Mr. Jeffrey paid his rent personally to the porter on the twenty-sixth, so establishing the fact beyond question that he was alive on that date.

"Thus, by a series of coincidences, John Blackmore is enabled to inherit the fortune of a man who, almost certainly, had no intention of bequeathing it to him."

Thorndyke paused, and Mr. Marchmont, who had listened with close attention, nodded as he glanced at his silent partner.

"You have stated the case with remarkable lucidity," he said, "and I am free to confess that some of the points you have raised had escaped my notice."

"Well, then," resumed Thorndyke, "to continue: The facts with which you furnished me, when thus collated, made it evident that the case was a very singular one, and it appeared to me that a case presenting such a series of coincidences in favor of one of the parties should be viewed with some suspicion and subjected to very close examination. But these facts yielded no further conclusion, and it was clear that no progress could be made until we had obtained some fresh data.

"In what direction, however, these new facts were to be looked for did not for the moment appear. Indeed, it seemed as if the inquiry had come to a full stop.

"But there is one rule which I follow religiously in all my investigations, and that is to collect facts of all kinds in any way related to the case in hand, no matter how trivial they may be or how apparently irrelevant."

CHAPTER XVII—THE MAN IN NEW INN

"Now, in pursuance of this rule, I took an opportunity, which offered, of looking over the chambers in New Inn, which had been left untouched since the death of their occupant, and I had hardly entered the rooms when I made a very curious discovery. On the wall hung a framed photograph of an ancient Persian inscription in cuneiform characters."

The expectant look which had appeared on Mr. Marchmont's face changed suddenly to one of disappointment, as he remarked:

"Curious, perhaps, but not of much importance to us, I am afraid."

"My uncle was greatly interested in cuneiform texts, as I think I mentioned," said Stephen Blackmore. "I seem to remember this photograph, too—it used to stand on the mantelpiece in his old rooms, I believe."

"Very probably," replied Thorndyke. "Well, it hung on the wall at New Inn, and it was hung upside-down."

"Upside-down!" exclaimed Blackmore. "That is really very odd."

"Very odd indeed," agreed Thorndyke. "The inscription, I find, was one of the first to be deciphered. From it Grotefend, with incredible patience and skill, managed to construct a number of the hitherto unknown signs. Now is it not an astonishing thing that an Oriental scholar, setting so much store by this monument of human ingenuity that he has a photograph of it framed, should then hang that photograph upon his wall upside-down?"

"I see your point," said Marchmont, "and I certainly agree with you that the circumstance is strongly suggestive of the decay of the mental faculties."

Thorndyke smiled almost imperceptibly as he continued:

"The way in which it came to be inverted is pretty obvious. The photograph had evidently been in the frame some years, but had never been hung up until lately, for the plates by which it was suspended were new; and when I unscrewed one, I found the wood underneath as dark and time-stained as elsewhere; and there were no other marks of plates or rings.

"The frame-maker had, however, pasted his label on the back of the frame, and as this label hung the right way up, it appeared as if the person who fixed on the plates had adopted it as a guide."

"Possibly," said Mr. Marchmont somewhat impatiently. "But these facts, though doubtless very curious and interesting, do not seem to have much bearing upon the genuineness of the late Mr. Blackmore's will."

"On the contrary," replied Thorndyke, "they appeared to me to be full of significance. However, I will return to the chambers presently, and I will now demonstrate to you that the alteration, which you have told me had been noticed at the bank, in the character of Mr. Jeffrey's signature, occurred at the time that I mentioned and was quite an abrupt change."

He drew from his little pile of documents the photogaphs of the checks and handed them to our visitors, by whom they were examined with varying degrees of interest.

"You will see," said he, "that the change took place between the twenty-ninth of September and the eighteenth of October and was, therefore, coincident in time with the other remarkable changes in the habits of the deceased."

"Yes, I see that," replied Mr. Marchmont, "and no doubt the fact would be of some importance if there were any question as to the genuineness of the testator's signature. But there is not. The signature of the will was witnessed, and the witnesses have been produced."

"Whence it follows," added Mr. Winwood, "that all this hair-splitting is entirely irrelevant and, in fact, so much waste of time."

"If you will note the facts that I am presenting to you," said Thorndyke, "and postpone your conclusions and comments until I have finished, you will have a better chance of grasping the case as a whole. I will now relate to you a very strange adventure which befell Dr. Jervis."

He then proceeded to recount the incidents connected with my visits to the mysterious patient in Kennington Lane, including the construction of the chart, presenting the latter for the inspection of his hearers. To this recital our three visitors listened in utter bewilderment, as, indeed, did I also; for I could not conceive in what way my adventures could be related to the affairs of the late Mr. Blackmore. This was manifestly the view taken by Mr. Marchmont, for during a pause, in which the chart was handed to him, he remarked somewhat stiffly:

"I am assuming, Dr. Thorndyke, that the curious story you are telling us has some relevance to the matter in which we are interested."

"You are quite correct in your assumption," replied Thorndyke. "The story is very relevant indeed, as you will presently be convinced."

"Thank you," said Marchmont, sinking back once more into his chair with a sigh of resignation.

"A few days ago," pursued Thorndyke, "Dr. Jervis and I located, with the aid of this chart, the house to which he had been called. We found that it was to let, the recent tenant having left hurriedly, so, when we had obtained the keys, we entered and explored in accordance with the rule that I mentioned just now."

Here he gave a brief account of our visit and the conditions that we observed, and was proceeding to furnish a list of the articles that he had found, when Mr. Winwood started from his chair.

"Good heavens, sir!" he exclaimed, "have I come here, at great personal inconvenience, to hear you read the inventory of a dustheap?"

"You came by your own wish," replied Thorndyke, "and I may add that you are not being forcibly detained."

At this hint Mr. Winwood sat down and shut himself up once more.

"We will now," pursued Thorndyke with unmoved serenity, "consider the significance of these relics and we will begin with this pair of spectacles. They belonged to a person who was near-sighted and astigmatic in the left eye and almost certainly blind in the right. Such a description agrees entirely with Dr. Jervis's account of the sick man."

He paused for a moment, and then, as no one made any comment, proceeded:

"We next come to this little bamboo stick. It is part of a Japanese brush, such as is used for writing in Chinese ink or for making small drawings."

Again he paused as though expecting some remark from his listeners; but no one spoke, and he continued:

"Then there is this bottle with the theatrical wig-maker's label on it, which once contained cement. Its presence suggests some person who was accustomed to 'make up' with a false mustache or beard. You have heard Dr. Jervis's account of Mr. Morgan and his coachman, and will agree with me that the circumstances bear out this suggestion."

He paused once more and looked round expectantly at his audience, none of whom, however, volunteered any remark.

"Do none of these objects that I have described seem to have any suggestion for us?" he asked in a tone of some surprise.

"They convey nothing to me," said Mr. Marchmont, glancing at his partner, who shook his head like a restive horse.

"Nor to you, Mr. Blackmore?"

"No," replied Stephen, "unless you mean to suggest that the sick man was my Uncle Jeffrey."

"That is precisely what I do mean to suggest," rejoined Thorndyke. "I had formed that opinion, indeed, before I saw them and I need not say how much they strengthened it."

"My uncle was certainly blind in the right eye," said Blackmore.

"And," interrupted Thorndyke, "from the same cause—dislocation of the crystalline lens."

"Possibly. And he probably used such a brush as you found, since I know that he corresponded in Japanese with his native friends in Tokyo. But this is surely very slender evidence."

"It is no evidence at all," replied Thorndyke. "It is merely a suggestion."

"Moreover," said Marchmont, "there is the insuperable objection that Mr. Jeffrey was living at New Inn at this time."

"What evidence is there of that?" asked Thorndyke.

"Evidence!" exclaimed Marchmont impatiently. "Why, my dear sir—" he paused suddenly and, leaning forward, regarded Thorndyke with a new and rather startled expression, "—you mean to suggest—" he began.

"I suggest to you what that inverted inscription suggested to me—that *the person who occupied those chambers in New Inn was not Jeffrey Blackmore!*"

CHAPTER XVIII—THORNDYKE EXPLAINS

The lawyer appeared thunderstruck. "This is an amazing proposition!" he exclaimed. "Yet the thing is certainly not impossible, for, now that you recall the fact, no one who had known him previously ever saw him at the Inn! The question of identity was never raised!"

"Excepting," said Mr. Winwood, "in regard to the body; which was certainly that of Jeffrey Blackmore."

"Yes, of course," said Marchmont; "I had forgotten that for the moment. The body was identified beyond doubt. You don't dispute the identity of the body, do you?"

"Certainly not," replied Thorndyke.

"Then for heaven's sake, tell us what you do mean, for I must confess that I am completely bewildered in this tangle of mysteries and contradictions!"

"It is certainly an intricate case," said Thorndyke, "but I think that you will find it comes together very completely. I have described to you my preliminary observations in the order in which I made them and have given you a hint of the nature of my inferences. Now I will lay before you the hypothesis that I have formed as to what were the actual occurrences in this mysterious case.

"It appeared to me probable that John Blackmore must have come to know, in some way, of the will that Mrs. Wilson had made in his brother's favor and that he kept himself informed as to the state of her health. When it became known to him that she was suffering from cancer, and that her death was likely to take place within a certain number of months, I think that he conceived the scheme that he subsequently carried out with such remarkable success.

"In September of 1899, Jeffrey Blackmore returned from Nice, and I think that John must have met him and either drugged him then and there and carried him to Kennington Lane, or induced him to go voluntarily. Once in the house and shut up in that dungeon-like bedroom, it would be easy to administer morphia—in small quantities at first and in larger doses afterward, as toleration of the drug became established."

"But could this be done against the victim's will?" asked Marchmont.

"Certainly. Small doses could be conveyed in food and drink, or administered during sleep, and then, you know, the morphia habit is quickly formed and, once it was established, the unfortunate man would probably take the drug voluntarily. Moreover this drug-habit weakens the will and paralyzes the mental faculties to an extraordinary degree—which was probably the principal object in using it.

"John Blackmore's intention, on this hypothesis, would be to keep his brother in a state of continual torpor and mental enfeeblement as long as Mrs. Wilson remained alive, so that the woman, his accomplice, could manage the prisoner, leaving him, John, free to play his part elsewhere.

"As soon he had thus secured his unfortunate brother, I suggest that this ingenious villain engaged the chambers at New Inn. In order to personate his brother, he must have shaved off his mustache and beard and worn spectacles; and these spectacles introduce a very curious and interesting feature into the case.

"To the majority of people the wearing of spectacles, for the purpose of disguise or personation, seems a perfectly simple and easy proceeding. But to a person of normal eyesight it is nothing of the kind; for if he wears spectacles suited for long sight, he is unable to see distinctly through them at all, while if he wears even weak concave or near-sight glasses, the effort to see through them soon produces such strain and fatigue that his eyes become disabled altogether. On the stage, of course, the difficulty is got over quite simply by using spectacles of plain window-glass, but in ordinary life this would hardly do; the 'property' spectacles would probably be noticed and give rise to suspicion.

"The personator would, therefore, be in this dilemma: if he wore actual spectacles he would not be able to see through them, while if he wore sham spectacles of plain glass his disguise might be detected. There is only one way out of the difficulty, and that not a very satisfactory one, but Mr. J. Morgan seems to have adopted it in lieu of a better.

"We have learned from Dr. Jervis that this gentleman wore spectacles and that these spectacles seemed to have had very peculiar optical properties; for while the image of the candle-flame reflected in them was inverted, showing that one surface at least was concave, my colleague observed that objects seen through them appeared quite free from distortion or change of size, as if seen through plain glass. But there is only one kind of glass which could possess these optical properties, and that is a plain glass with curved surfaces like an ordinary watch-glass."

I started when Thorndyke reached this point, and thought of the contents of the cardboard box, which I now saw was among the objects on the table.

"Do you follow the argument?" my colleague inquired.

"Yes," replied Mr. Marchmont, "I think I follow you, though I do not see the application of all this."

"That will appear presently. For the present we may take it that Mr. J. Morgan wore spectacles of this peculiar character, presumably for the purposes of disguise; and I am assuming, for the purposes of the argument, that Mr. J. Morgan and Mr. John Blackmore are one and the same."

"It is assuming a great deal," grunted Mr. Winwood.

"And now," continued Thorndyke, disregarding the last remark, "to return from this digression to John Blackmore's proceedings. I imagine that he spent very little time at the Inn—for the porter saw him only occasionally and believed him to be frequently absent— and when he was at Kennington Lane or at his office in the city, or elsewhere, he would replace his beard with a false one of the same appearance, which would require to be fixed on securely and finished round the edges with short hairs cemented to the skin— for an ordinary theatrical beard would be detected instantly in daylight.

"He would now commence experiments in forging his brother's handwriting, which he must have practised previously to have obtained Jeffrey's furniture from the repository where it was stored. The difference was observed at the bank, as Mr. Marchmont has told us, but the imitation was close enough not to arouse suspicion.

"The next thing was to make the fresh will and get it witnessed; and this was managed with such adroitness that, although neither of the witnesses had ever seen Jeffrey Blackmore, their identification has been accepted without question. It is evident that, when shaved, John Blackmore must have resembled his brother pretty closely or he would never have attempted to carry out this scheme, and he will have calculated, with much acuteness, that the porter, when called in to identify the body, would observe only the resemblance and would disregard any apparent difference in appearance.

"The position in which John Blackmore was now placed was one of extraordinary difficulty. His brother was immured in Kennington Lane, but, owing to the insecurity of his prison and the frequent absence of his jailer, this confinement could be maintained with safety only by keeping the imprisoned man continuously under the influence of full doses of morphia.

"This constant drugging must have been highly injurious to the health of a delicate man like Jeffery and, as time went on, there must have loomed up the ever-increasing danger that he might die before the appointed time; in which event John would be involved in a double catastrophe, for, on the one hand, the will would now be useless, and, on the other, the crime would be almost inevitably discovered.

"It was, no doubt, with this danger in view that John called in Dr. Jervis—making, as it turned out, a very unsuitable choice. My colleague's assistance was invoked, no doubt, partly to keep the victim alive and partly in the hope that if that were impossible, he might be prepared to cover the crime with a death-certificate.

"We are now approaching the end of the tragedy. Mrs. Wilson died on the twenty-fourth of March. Circumstances point to the conclusion that the murder took place on the evening of the twenty-sixth. Now on that day, about half-past six in the evening, the supposed Jeffrey Blackmore entered New Inn in a four-wheeled cab, as you are aware, his face being seen at the window by the porter as the vehicle passed the lodge under the archway. There was a dense fog at the time, so the cab would be lost to sight as soon as it entered the Square. At this time the offices at No. 31 would be empty and not a soul present in the house to witness the arrival.

"From the first time that my suspicions took definite shape that cab seemed to me to hold the key to the mystery. There can be no doubt that it contained two people—one of them was John Blackmore, whose face was seen at the window, and the other, his victim, the unfortunate Jeffrey.

"As to what happened in that silent house there is no need to speculate. The peculiar vertical manner in which the needle of the syringe was introduced is naturally explained by the fact of its being thrust through the clothing, and we can not but admire the cool calculation with which the appliances of murder were left to give color to the idea of suicide.

"Having committed the crime, the murderer presently walked out and showed himself at the lodge, under the pretext of paying the rent, thus furnishing proof of survival in respect to Mrs. Wilson. After this he returned to the Inn, but not to the chambers, for there is a postern-gate, as you know, opening into Houghton Street. Through this, no doubt, the murderer left the Inn, and vanished, to reappear at the inquest unrecognizable in his beard, his padded clothing and eyes uncovered by spectacles.

"With regard to the identification of the body by the porter there is, as I have said, no mystery. There must have been a considerable resemblance between the two brothers, and the porter, taking it for granted that the body was that of his tenant, would naturally recognize it as such, for even if he had noticed any departure from the usual appearance, he would attribute the difference to changes produced by death.

"Such, gentlemen, is my theory of the circumstances that surrounded the death of Jeffrey Blackmore, and I shall be glad to hear any comments that you may have to make."

CHAPTER XIX—STEP BY STEP

There was an interval of silence after Thorndyke had finished which was at last broken by Mr. Winwood.

"I must admit, sir," said he, "that you have displayed extraordinary ingenuity in the construction of the astonishing story you have told us, and that this story, if it were true, would dispose satisfactorily of every difficulty and obscure point in the case. But is it true? It seems to me to be a matter of pure conjecture, woven most ingeniously around a few slightly suggestive facts. And, seeing that it involves a charge of murder of a most diabolical character against Mr. John Blackmore, nothing but the most conclusive proof would justify us in entertaining it."

"It is not conjecture," said Thorndyke, "although it was so at first. But when I had formed a hypothesis which fitted the facts known to me, I proceeded to test it and have now no doubt that it is correct."

"Would you mind laying before us any new facts that you have discovered which tend to confirm your theory?" said Mr. Marchmont.

"I will place the entire mass of evidence before you," said Thorndyke, "and then I think you will have no more doubts than I have.

"You will observe that there are four points which require to be proved: The first is the identity of Jeffrey with the sick man of Kennington Lane; the second is the identity of Mr. J. Morgan with John Blackmore; the third is the identity of John Blackmore with the tenant of 31 New Inn, and the fourth is the presence together of John and Jeffrey Blackmore at the chambers on the night of the latter gentleman's death.

"We will take the first point. Here are the spectacles I found in the empty house. I tested them optically with great care and measured them minutely and wrote down on this piece of paper their description. I will read it to you:

"Spectacles for distance, curl sides, steel frames, Stopford's pattern, with gold plate under bridge. Distance between centers, 6.2 cm. Right eye plain glass. Left eye—3D spherical—2D cylindrical, axis 35°.

"Now spectacles of this pattern are, I believe, made only by Cuxton & Parry of New Bond Street. I therefore wrote to Mr. Cuxton, who knows me, and asked if he had supplied spectacles to the late Jeffrey Blackmore, Esq., and, if so, whether he would send me a description of them, together with the name of the oculist who prescribed them.

"He replied, in this letter here, that he had supplied spectacles to the late Jeffrey Blackmore and described them thus:

"The spectacles were for distance and had steel frames of Stopford's pattern, with curl sides and a gold plate under the bridge. The formula, which was from Mr. Hindley's prescription, was R. E. plain glass. L.E.—3D sph.—2D cyl., axis 35°.

"You see the descriptions are identical. I then wrote to Mr. Hindley, asking certain questions, to which he replied thus:

" 'You are quite right; Mr. Jeffrey Blackmore had a tremulous iris in his right eye (which was practically blind) due to dislocation of the lens. The pupils were rather large, certainly not contracted.'

"Thus, you see, the description of the deceased tallies with that of the sick man as given by Dr. Jervis, excepting that there was then no sign of his being addicted to taking morphia. One more item of evidence I have on this point, and it is one that will appeal to the legal mind.

"A few days ago, I wrote to Mr. Stephen, asking him whether he possessed a recent photograph of his Uncle Jeffrey. He had one and sent it to me by return. This portrait I showed to Dr. Jervis, asking him if he recognised the person. After examining it attentively, without any hint from me, he identified it as a portrait of the sick man of Kennington Lane."

"Indeed!" exclaimed Mr. Marchmont. "This is most important.

Are you prepared to swear to the resemblance, Dr. Jervis?"
"Perfectly. I have not the slightest doubt," I replied.

"Excellent!" said Mr. Marchmont. "Pray go on, Dr. Thorndyke."

"Well, that is all the evidence I have on the first point," said
Thorndyke, "but, to my mind, it constitutes practically conclusive
proof of identity."

"It is undoubtedly very weighty evidence," Mr. Marchmont agreed.

"Now, as to the second point—the identity of John Blackmore
with Mr. J. Morgan of Kennington Lane. To begin with the *prima
facie* probabilities, in relation to certain assumed data. If we assume:

"1. That the sick man was Jeffrey Blackmore;

"2. That his symptoms were due to the administration of a slow
poison;

"3. That the poison was being administered by J. Morgan, as
suggested by his manifest disguise and the strange secrecy of his
conduct;

"And if we then ask ourselves who could have a motive for causing
the death of Mr. Jeffrey in this manner and at this time, the answer
is John Blackmore, the principal beneficiary under the very unstable
second will. The most obvious hypothesis, then, is that Mr. J.
Morgan and John Blackmore were one and the same person."

"But this is mere surmise," objected Mr. Marchmont.

"Exactly; as every hypothesis must be until it has been tested and
verified. And now for the facts that tend to support this hypothesis.
The first item—a very small one—I picked up when I called on the
doctor who had attended Mrs. Wilson. My object was to obtain
particulars as to her illness and death, but, incidentally, I discovered
that he was well acquainted with John Blackmore and had treated
him—without operation and, therefore, without cure—for a nasal
polypus. You will remember that Mr. J. Morgan appeared to have
a nasal polypus. I may mention, by the way, that John Blackmore
had been aware of Mrs. Wilson's state of health from the onset of
her symptoms and kept himself informed as to her progress. Moreover, at his request a telegram was sent to his office in Copthall
Avenue, announcing her death.

"The next item of evidence is more important. I made a second
visit to the house-agent at Kennington for the purpose of obtaining,
if possible, the names and addresses of the persons who had been
mentioned as references when Mr. Morgan took the house. I
ascertained that only one reference had been given—the intending

tenant's stockbroker; and the name of that stockbroker was John Blackmore of Copthall Avenue."

"That is a significant fact," remarked Mr. Marchmont.

"Yes," answered Thorndyke, "and it would be interesting to confront John Blackmore with this house-agent, who would have seen him with his beard on. Well, that is all the evidence that I have on this point. It is far from conclusive by itself, but, such as it is, it tends to support the hypothesis that J. Morgan and John Blackmore were one and the same.

"I will now pass on to the evidence of the third point—the identity of John Blackmore with the tenant of New Inn.

"With reference to the inverted inscription, that furnishes indirect evidence only. It suggests that the tenant was not Jeffrey. But, if not Jeffrey, it was some one who was personating him; and that some one must have resembled him closely enough for the personation to remain undetected even on the production of Jeffrey's body. But the only person known to us who answers this description is John Blackmore.

"Again, the individual who personated Jeffrey must have had some strong motive for doing do. But the only person known to us who could have had any such motive is John Blackmore.

"The next item of evidence on this point is also merely suggestive and indirect, though to me it was of the greatest value, since it furnished the first link in the chain of evidence connecting Jeffrey Blackmore with the sick man of Kennington. On the floor of the bedroom in New Inn I found the shattered remains of a small glass object which had been trodden on. Here are some of the fragments in this box, and you will see that we have joined a few of them together to help us in our investigations.

"My assistant, who was formerly a watch-maker, judged them to be fragments of the thin crystal glass of a lady's watch, and that, I think, was also Dr. Jervis's opinion. But the small part which remains of the original edge furnishes proof in two respects that this was not a watch-glass. In the first place, on taking a careful tracing of this piece of the edge, I found that its curve was part of an ellipse; but watch-glasses, nowadays, are invariably circular. In the second place, watch-glasses are ground on the edge to a single bevel to snap into the bezel or frame; but the edge of this is ground to a double bevel, like the edge of a spectacle-glass which fits into a groove and is held in position by a screw.

"The unavoidable inference is that this was a spectacle-glass, but, since it had the optical properties of plain glass, it could not have been used to assist vision and was therefore presumably intended for the purpose of disguise. Now you will remember that Mr. J. Morgan wore spectacles having precisely the optical properties of a crystal watch-glass, and it was this fact that first suggested to me a possible connection between New Inn and Kennington Lane."

"By the way," said Stephen Blackmore, "you said that my uncle had plain glass in one side of his spectacles?"

"Yes," replied Thorndyke; "over his blind eye. But that was actually plain glass with flat surfaces, not curved like this one. I should like to observe, with reference to this spectacle-glass, that its importance as a clue is much greater than might, at first sight, appear. The spectacles worn by Mr. Morgan were not merely peculiar or remarkable; they were probably unique. It is exceedingly likely that there is not, in the whole world, another similar pair of spectacles. Hence, the finding of this broken glass does really establish a considerable probability that J. Morgan was, at some time, in the chambers in New Inn. But we have seen that it is highly probable that J. Morgan was, in fact, John Blackmore, wherefore the presence of this glass is evidence suggesting that John Blackmore is the man who personated Jeffrey at New Inn.

"You will have observed, no doubt, that the evidence on the second and third points is by no means conclusive when taken separately, but I think you will agree that the whole body of circumstantial evidence is very strong and might easily be strengthened by further investigation."

"Yes," said Marchmont, "I think we may admit that there is enough evidence to make your theory a possible and even a probable one; and if you can show that there are any good grounds for believing that John and Jeffrey Blackmore were together in the chambers on the evening of the twenty-sixth of March, I should say that you had made out a *prima facie* case. What say you, Winwood?"

"Let us hear the evidence," replied Mr. Winwood gruffly.

"Very well," said Thorndyke, "you shall. And, what is more, you shall have it first-hand."

CHAPTER XX—THE ENEMY DECIDES

He pressed the button of the electric bell three times and, after a short interval, Polton let himself in with his latch-key and beckoned to some one on the landing.

"Here is Walker, sir," said he, and he then retired, shutting the oak after him and leaving a seedy-looking stranger standing near the door and gazing at the assembled company with a mixture of embarrassment and defiance.

"Sit down, Walker," said Thorndyke, placing a chair for him. "I want you to answer a few questions for the information of these gentlemen."

"I know," said Walker with an oracular nod. "You can ask me anything you like."

"Your name, I believe, is James Walker?"

"That's me, sir."

"And your occupation?"

"My occupation, sir, don't agree with my name at all, because I drives a cab—a four-wheeled cab is what I drives—and a uncommon dry job it is, let me tell you."

Acting on this delicate hint, Thorndyke mixed a stiff whisky and soda and passed it across to the cabman, who consumed half at a single gulp and then peered thoughtfully into the tumbler.

"Rum stuff, this soda-water," he remarked. "Makes it taste as if there wasn't no whisky in it."

This hint Thorndyke ventured to ignore and continued his inquiries:

"Do you remember a very foggy day about three weeks ago?"

"Rather. It was the twenty-sixth of March. I remember it because my benefit society came down on me for arrears that morning."

"Will you tell us now what happened to you between six and seven in the evening of that day?"

"I will," replied the cabman, emptying his tumbler by way of bracing himself up for the effort. "I drove a fare to Vauxhall Station and got there a little before six. As I didn't pick up no one there, I drove away and was just turning down Upper Kennington Lane when I see two gentlemen standing at the corner by Harleyford Road, and one of 'em hails me, so I pulls up by the curb. One of 'em seemed to be drunk, for the other one was holding him up, but he might have been feeling queer—it wasn't no affair of mine.

"But the rum thing about 'em was that they was as like as two peas. Their faces was alike, their clothes was alike, they wore the same kind of hats and they both had spectacles. 'Wot O!' says I to myself, ' 'ere's the Siamese Twins out on the jamboree!' Well, the gent what wasn't drunk he opens the door and shoves in the other one what was, and he says to me, he says: 'Do you know New Inn?' he says. Now there was a —— silly question to ask a man what was born and brought up in White Horse Alley, Drury Lane. 'Do I know my grandmother?' says I.

" 'Well,' says he, 'you drive in through the gate in Wych Street,' he says.

" 'Of course I shall,' I says. 'Did you think I was going to drive in the back way down the steps?' I says.

" 'And then,' he says, 'you drive down the Square nearly to the end and you'll see a house with a large brass plate at the corner of the doorway. That's where we want to be set down,' he says. With that he nips in and pulls up the windows and off we goes.

"It took us nigh upon half an hour to get to New Inn through the fog, and as I drove in under the archway I saw it was half-past six by the clock in the porter's lodge. I drove down nearly to the end of the square and drew up opposite a house where there was a large brass plate by the doorway. Then the gent wh:.t was sober jumps out and begins hauling out the other one. I was just getting down off the box to help him when he says, rather short-like:

" 'All right, cabman,' he says, 'I can manage,' and he hands me five bob.

"The other gent seemed to have gone to sleep, and a rare job he had hauling him across the pavement. I see them, by the gas-lamps on the staircase, going up-stairs—regular Pilgrim's Progress it was, I tell you—but they got up at last, for I saw 'em light the gas in a room on the second floor. Then I drove off."

"Could you identify the house?" asked Thorndyke.

"I done it, this morning. You saw me. It was No. 31."

"How was it," said Marchmont, "that you did not come forward at the inquest?"

"What inquest?" inquired the cabman. "I don't know nothing about any inquest. The first I heard of the business was when one of our men told me yesterday about a notice what was stuck up in a shelter offering a reward for information concerning a four-wheel cab what drove to New Inn at six-thirty on the day of the fog at the end of last month. Then I came here and left a message, and this morning this gentleman came to me on the rank and paid up *like* a gentleman."

The latter ceremony was now repeated, and the cabman, having remarked that his services were at the disposal of the present company to an unlimited extent on the same terms, departed, beaming with satisfaction.

When he had gone, our three visitors sat for awhile looking at one another in silence. At length Stephen Blackmore rose with a stern expression on his pale face and said to Thorndyke: "The police must be informed of this at once. I shall never be able to rest until I know that justice has been dealt out to this cold-hearted, merciless villain!"

"The police have already been informed," said Thorndyke. "I completed the case this morning and at once communicated with Superintendent Miller of Scotland Yard. A warrant was obtained immediately and I had expected to hear that the arrest had been made long before this, for Mr. Miller is usually most punctilious in keeping me informed of the progress of cases which I introduce to him. We shall hear to-morrow, no doubt."

"And for the present the case seems to have passed out of our hands," observed Mr. Marchmont.

"I shall enter a caveat, all the same," said Mr. Winwood.

"Why, that doesn't seem very necessary," said Marchmont. "The evidence that we have heard is enough to secure a conviction, and there will be plenty more when the police go into the case. And a conviction would, of course, put an end to the second will."

"I shall enter a caveat, all the same," said Mr. Winwood.

As the two partners showed a disposition to become heated over this question, Thorndyke suggested that they might discuss it at leisure by the light of subsequent events.

Taking this as a hint, for it was now close upon midnight, our visitors prepared to depart and were, in fact, making their way towards the door, when the bell rang.

Thorndyke hastily flung open the door and, as he recognized his visitor, uttered an exclamation of satisfaction.

"Ha! Mr. Miller, we were just speaking˚ of you. This is Mr. Stephen Blackmore, and these gentlemen are Messrs. Marchmont and Winwood, his solicitors, and my colleague, Dr. Jervis."

"Well, Doctor, I have just dropped in to give you the news, which will interest these gentlemen as well as yourself."

"Have you arrested the man?"

"No; he has arrested himself. He is dead!"

"Dead!" we all exclaimed together.

"Yes. It happened this way. We went down to his place at Surbiton early this morning, but it seemed he had just left for town, so we took the next train and went straight to his office. But they must have smoked us and sent him a wire, for, just as we were approaching the office, a man answering the description ran out, jumped into a hansom and drove off like the devil.

"We chanced its being the right man and followed at a run, hailing the first hansom that we met; but he had a good start and his cabby had a good horse, so that we had all our work cut out to keep him in sight. We followed him over Blackfriars Bridge and down Stamford Street to Waterloo; but as we drove up the slope to the station we met a cab coming down and, as the cabby kissed his hand and smiled at us, we concluded it was the one we had been following.

"I remembered that the Southampton Express was due to start about this time, so we made for the platform and, just as the guard was about to blow his whistle, we saw a man bolt through the barrier and run up the platform. We dashed through a few seconds later and just managed to get on the train as it was moving off. But he had seen us, for his head was out of the window when we jumped in, and we kept a sharp lookout on both sides in case he should hop out again before the train got up speed.

"However, he didn't, and nothing more happened until we stopped at Southampton. You may be sure we lost no time in getting out and we ran up the platform, expecting to see him make a rush for the barrier. But there was no sign of him anywhere, and we began to think that he had given us the slip.

"Then, while my inspector watched the barrier, I went down the train until I came to the compartment that I had seen him enter. And there he was, lying back in the off corner, apparently fast asleep. But he wasn't asleep. He was dead. I found this on the floor of the carriage."

He held up a tiny glass tube, labeled "Aconitin Nitrate gr. 1-640."

"Ha!" exclaimed Thorndyke. "This fellow was well up in poisons, it seems! This tube contained twenty tabloids, a thirty-second of a grain altogether, so if he swallowed them all he took about twelve times the medical dose. Well, perhaps he has done the best thing, after all."

"The best thing for you, gentlemen," said Mr. Miller, "for there is no need to raise any questions in detail at the inquest; and publicity would be very unpleasant for Mr. Blackmore. It is a thousand pities that you or Dr. Jervis hadn't put us on the scent in time to prevent the crime—though, of course, we couldn't have entered the premises without a warrant. But it is easy to be wise after the event. Well, good-night, gentlemen; I suppose this accident disposes of your business as far as the will is concerned?"

"I suppose it does," said Mr. Winwood; "but I shall enter a caveat, all the same."

Sources

"The Case of Oscar Brodski," "A Case of Premeditation," "The Echo of a Mutiny" have been taken from *The Singing Bone,* originally published in 1912 by Hodder and Stoughton, London; American edition 1923 by Dodd, Mead & Co., New York.

"The Mandarin's Pearl," "The Blue Sequin," "The Moabite Cipher," "The Aluminium Dagger" have been taken from *John Thorndyke's Cases,* originally published in 1909 by Chatto & Windus, London; the American edition, under the title *Dr. Thorndyke's Cases,* was published by Dodd, Mead & Co., New York, in 1931.

"31 New Inn" has been taken from the January 1911 issue of *Adventure* Magazine, New York.

A CATALOG OF
SELECTED DOVER BOOKS
IN ALL FIELDS OF INTEREST

A CATALOG OF SELECTED DOVER BOOKS IN ALL FIELDS OF INTEREST

CONCERNING THE SPIRITUAL IN ART, Wassily Kandinsky. Pioneering work by father of abstract art. Thoughts on color theory, nature of art. Analysis of earlier masters. 12 illustrations. 80pp. of text. 5⅜ × 8½. 23411-8 Pa. $2.50

LEONARDO ON THE HUMAN BODY, Leonardo da Vinci. More than 1200 of Leonardo's anatomical drawings on 215 plates. Leonardo's text, which accompanies the drawings, has been translated into English. 506pp. 8⅜ × 11¾. 24483-0 Pa. $10.95

GOBLIN MARKET, Christina Rossetti. Best-known work by poet comparable to Emily Dickinson, Alfred Tennyson. With 46 delightfully grotesque illustrations by Laurence Housman. 64pp. 4 × 6¾. 24516-0 Pa. $2.50

THE HEART OF THOREAU'S JOURNALS, edited by Odell Shepard. Selections from *Journal*, ranging over full gamut of interests. 228pp. 5⅜ × 8½. 20741-2 Pa. $4.50

MR. LINCOLN'S CAMERA MAN: MATHEW B. BRADY, Roy Meredith. Over 300 Brady photos reproduced directly from original negatives, photos. Lively commentary. 368pp. 8⅜ × 11¼. 23021-X Pa. $11.95

PHOTOGRAPHIC VIEWS OF SHERMAN'S CAMPAIGN, George N. Barnard. Reprint of landmark 1866 volume with 61 plates: battlefield of New Hope Church, the Etawah Bridge, the capture of Atlanta, etc. 80pp. 9 × 12. 23445-2 Pa. $6.00

A SHORT HISTORY OF ANATOMY AND PHYSIOLOGY FROM THE GREEKS TO HARVEY, Dr. Charles Singer. Thoroughly engrossing non-technical survey. 270 illustrations. 211pp. 5⅜ × 8½. 20389-1 Pa. $4.50

REDOUTE ROSES IRON-ON TRANSFER PATTERNS, Barbara Christopher. Redouté was botanical painter to the Empress Josephine; transfer his famous roses onto fabric with these 24 transfer patterns. 80pp. 8¼ × 10⅞. 24292-7 Pa. $3.50

THE FIVE BOOKS OF ARCHITECTURE, Sebastiano Serlio. Architectural milestone, first (1611) English translation of Renaissance classic. Unabridged reproduction of original edition includes over 300 woodcut illustrations. 416pp. 9⅜ × 12¼. 24349-4 Pa. $14.95

CARLSON'S GUIDE TO LANDSCAPE PAINTING, John F. Carlson. Authoritative, comprehensive guide covers, every aspect of landscape painting. 34 reproductions of paintings by author; 58 explanatory diagrams. 144pp. 8⅜ × 11. 22927-0 Pa. $4.95

101 PUZZLES IN THOUGHT AND LOGIC, C.R. Wylie, Jr. Solve murders, robberies, see which fishermen are liars—purely by reasoning! 107pp. 5⅜ × 8½. 20367-0 Pa. $2.00

TEST YOUR LOGIC, George J. Summers. 50 more truly new puzzles with new turns of thought, new subtleties of inference. 100pp. 5⅜ × 8½. 22877-0 Pa. $2.25

THE MURDER BOOK OF J.G. REEDER, Edgar Wallace. Eight suspenseful stories by bestselling mystery writer of 20s and 30s. Features the donnish Mr. J.G. Reeder of Public Prosecutor's Office. 128pp. 5⅜ × 8½. (Available in U.S. only)
24374-5 Pa. $3.50

ANNE ORR'S CHARTED DESIGNS, Anne Orr. Best designs by premier needlework designer, all on charts: flowers, borders, birds, children, alphabets, etc. Over 100 charts, 10 in color. Total of 40pp. 8¼ × 11. 23704-4 Pa. $2.25

BASIC CONSTRUCTION TECHNIQUES FOR HOUSES AND SMALL BUILDINGS SIMPLY EXPLAINED, U.S. Bureau of Naval Personnel. Grading, masonry, woodworking, floor and wall framing, roof framing, plastering, tile setting, much more. Over 675 illustrations. 568pp. 6½ × 9¼. 20242-9 Pa. $8.95

MATISSE LINE DRAWINGS AND PRINTS, Henri Matisse. Representative collection of female nudes, faces, still lifes, experimental works, etc., from 1898 to 1948. 50 illustrations. 48pp. 8⅜ × 11¼. 23877-6 Pa. $2.50

HOW TO PLAY THE CHESS OPENINGS, Eugene Znosko-Borovsky. Clear, profound examinations of just what each opening is intended to do and how opponent can counter. Many sample games. 147pp. 5⅜ × 8½. 22795-2 Pa. $2.95

DUPLICATE BRIDGE, Alfred Sheinwold. Clear, thorough, easily followed account: rules, etiquette, scoring, strategy, bidding; Goren's point-count system, Blackwood and Gerber conventions, etc. 158pp. 5⅜ × 8½. 22741-3 Pa. $3.00

SARGENT PORTRAIT DRAWINGS, J.S. Sargent. Collection of 42 portraits reveals technical skill and intuitive eye of noted American portrait painter, John Singer Sargent. 48pp. 8¼ × 11⅛. 24524-1 Pa. $2.95

ENTERTAINING SCIENCE EXPERIMENTS WITH EVERYDAY OBJECTS, Martin Gardner. Over 100 experiments for youngsters. Will amuse, astonish, teach, and entertain. Over 100 illustrations. 127pp. 5⅜ × 8½. 24201-3 Pa. $2.50

TEDDY BEAR PAPER DOLLS IN FULL COLOR: A Family of Four Bears and Their Costumes, Crystal Collins. A family of four Teddy Bear paper dolls and nearly 60 cut-out costumes. Full color, printed one side only. 32pp. 9¼ × 12¼.
24550-0 Pa. $3.50

NEW CALLIGRAPHIC ORNAMENTS AND FLOURISHES, Arthur Baker. Unusual, multi-useable material: arrows, pointing hands, brackets and frames, ovals, swirls, birds, etc. Nearly 700 illustrations. 80pp. 8⅜ × 11¼.
24095-9 Pa. $3.75

DINOSAUR DIORAMAS TO CUT & ASSEMBLE, M. Kalmenoff. Two complete three-dimensional scenes in full color, with 31 cut-out animals and plants. Excellent educational toy for youngsters. Instructions; 2 assembly diagrams. 32pp. 9¼ × 12¼. 24541-1 Pa. $3.95

SILHOUETTES: A PICTORIAL ARCHIVE OF VARIED ILLUSTRATIONS, edited by Carol Belanger Grafton. Over 600 silhouettes from the 18th to 20th centuries. Profiles and full figures of men, women, children, birds, animals, groups and scenes, nature, ships, an alphabet. 144pp. 8⅜ × 11¼. 23781-8 Pa. $4.95

25 KITES THAT FLY, Leslie Hunt. Full, easy-to-follow instructions for kites made from inexpensive materials. Many novelties. 70 illustrations. 110pp. 5⅜ × 8½.
22550-X Pa. $2.25

PIANO TUNING, J. Cree Fischer. Clearest, best book for beginner, amateur. Simple repairs, raising dropped notes, tuning by easy method of flattened fifths. No previous skills needed. 4 illustrations. 201pp. 5⅜ × 8½.
23267-0 Pa. $3.50

EARLY AMERICAN IRON-ON TRANSFER PATTERNS, edited by Rita Weiss. 75 designs, borders, alphabets, from traditional American sources. 48pp. 8¼ × 11.
23162-3 Pa. $1.95

CROCHETING EDGINGS, edited by Rita Weiss. Over 100 of the best designs for these lovely trims for a host of household items. Complete instructions, illustrations. 48pp. 8¼ × 11.
24031-2 Pa. $2.25

FINGER PLAYS FOR NURSERY AND KINDERGARTEN, Emilie Poulsson. 18 finger plays with music (voice and piano); entertaining, instructive. Counting, nature lore, etc. Victorian classic. 53 illustrations. 80pp. 6½ × 9¼. 22588-7 Pa. $1.95

BOSTON THEN AND NOW, Peter Vanderwarker. Here in 59 side-by-side views are photographic documentations of the city's past and present. 119 photographs. Full captions. 122pp. 8¼ × 11.
24312-5 Pa. $6.95

CROCHETING BEDSPREADS, edited by Rita Weiss. 22 patterns, originally published in three instruction books 1939-41. 39 photos, 8 charts. Instructions. 48pp. 8¼ × 11.
23610-2 Pa. $2.00

HAWTHORNE ON PAINTING, Charles W. Hawthorne. Collected from notes taken by students at famous Cape Cod School; hundreds of direct, personal *apercus*, ideas, suggestions. 91pp. 5⅜ × 8½.
20653-X Pa. $2.50

THERMODYNAMICS, Enrico Fermi. A classic of modern science. Clear, organized treatment of systems, first and second laws, entropy, thermodynamic potentials, etc. Calculus required. 160pp. 5⅜ × 8½.
60361-X Pa. $4.00

TEN BOOKS ON ARCHITECTURE, Vitruvius. The most important book ever written on architecture. Early Roman aesthetics, technology, classical orders, site selection, all other aspects. Morgan translation. 331pp. 5⅜ × 8½. 20645-9 Pa. $5.50

THE CORNELL BREAD BOOK, Clive M. McCay and Jeanette B. McCay. Famed high-protein recipe incorporated into breads, rolls, buns, coffee cakes, pizza, pie crusts, more. Nearly 50 illustrations. 48pp. 8¼ × 11.
23995-0 Pa. $2.00

THE CRAFTSMAN'S HANDBOOK, Cennino Cennini. 15th-century handbook, school of Giotto, explains applying gold, silver leaf; gesso; fresco painting, grinding pigments, etc. 142pp. 6⅛ × 9¼.
20054-X Pa. $3.50

FRANK LLOYD WRIGHT'S FALLINGWATER, Donald Hoffmann. Full story of Wright's masterwork at Bear Run, Pa. 100 photographs of site, construction, and details of completed structure. 112pp. 9¼ × 10.
23671-4 Pa. $6.50

OVAL STAINED GLASS PATTERN BOOK, C. Eaton. 60 new designs framed in shape of an oval. Greater complexity, challenge with sinuous cats, birds, mandalas framed in antique shape. 64pp. 8¼ × 11.
24519-5 Pa. $3.50

THE BOOK OF WOOD CARVING, Charles Marshall Sayers. Still finest book for beginning student. Fundamentals, technique; gives 34 designs, over 34 projects for panels, bookends, mirrors, etc. 33 photos. 118pp. 7¾ × 10⅝. 23654-4 Pa. $3.95

CARVING COUNTRY CHARACTERS, Bill Higginbotham. Expert advice for beginning, advanced carvers on materials, techniques for creating 18 projects— mirthful panorama of American characters. 105 illustrations. 80pp. 8⅜ × 11. 24135-1 Pa. $2.50

300 ART NOUVEAU DESIGNS AND MOTIFS IN FULL COLOR, C.B. Grafton. 44 full-page plates display swirling lines and muted colors typical of Art Nouveau. Borders, frames, panels, cartouches, dingbats, etc. 48pp. 9⅜ × 12¼. 24354-0 Pa. $6.00

SELF-WORKING CARD TRICKS, Karl Fulves. Editor of *Pallbearer* offers 72 tricks that work automatically through nature of card deck. No sleight of hand needed. Often spectacular. 42 illustrations. 113pp. 5⅜ × 8½. 23334-0 Pa. $3.50

CUT AND ASSEMBLE A WESTERN FRONTIER TOWN, Edmund V. Gillon, Jr. Ten authentic full-color buildings on heavy cardboard stock in H-O scale. Sheriff's Office and Jail, Saloon, Wells Fargo, Opera House, others. 48pp. 9¼ × 12¼. 23736-2 Pa. $3.95

CUT AND ASSEMBLE AN EARLY NEW ENGLAND VILLAGE, Edmund V. Gillon, Jr. Printed in full color on heavy cardboard stock. 12 authentic buildings in H-O scale: Adams home in Quincy, Mass., Oliver Wight house in Sturbridge, smithy, store, church, others. 48pp. 9¼ × 12¼. 23536-X Pa. $3.95

THE TALE OF TWO BAD MICE, Beatrix Potter. Tom Thumb and Hunca Munca squeeze out of their hole and go exploring. 27 full-color Potter illustrations. 59pp. 4¼ × 5½. (Available in U.S. only) 23065-1 Pa. $1.50

CARVING FIGURE CARICATURES IN THE OZARK STYLE, Harold L. Enlow. Instructions and illustrations for ten delightful projects, plus general carving instructions. 22 drawings and 47 photographs altogether. 39pp. 8⅜ × 11. 23151-8 Pa. $2.50

A TREASURY OF FLOWER DESIGNS FOR ARTISTS, EMBROIDERERS AND CRAFTSMEN, Susan Gaber. 100 garden favorites lushly rendered by artist for artists, craftsmen, needleworkers. Many form frames, borders. 80pp. 8¼ × 11. 24096-7 Pa. $3.50

CUT & ASSEMBLE A TOY THEATER/THE NUTCRACKER BALLET, Tom Tierney. Model of a complete, full-color production of Tchaikovsky's classic. 6 backdrops, dozens of characters, familiar dance sequences. 32pp. 9⅜ × 12¼. 24194-7 Pa. $4.50

ANIMALS: 1,419 COPYRIGHT-FREE ILLUSTRATIONS OF MAMMALS, BIRDS, FISH, INSECTS, ETC., edited by Jim Harter. Clear wood engravings present, in extremely lifelike poses, over 1,000 species of animals. 284pp. 9 × 12. 23766-4 Pa. $9.95

MORE HAND SHADOWS, Henry Bursill. For those at their 'finger ends," 16 more effects—Shakespeare, a hare, a squirrel, Mr. Punch, and twelve more—each explained by a full-page illustration. Considerable period charm. 30pp. 6½ × 9¼. 21384-6 Pa. $1.95

SURREAL STICKERS AND UNREAL STAMPS, William Rowe. 224 haunting, hilarious stamps on gummed, perforated stock, with images of elephants, geisha girls, George Washington, etc. 16pp. one side. 8¼ × 11.   24371-0 Pa. $3.50

GOURMET KITCHEN LABELS, Ed Sibbett, Jr. 112 full-color labels (4 copies each of 28 designs). Fruit, bread, other culinary motifs. Gummed and perforated. 16pp. 8¼ × 11.   24087-8 Pa. $2.95

PATTERNS AND INSTRUCTIONS FOR CARVING AUTHENTIC BIRDS, H.D. Green. Detailed instructions, 27 diagrams, 85 photographs for carving 15 species of birds so life-like, they'll seem ready to fly! 8¼ × 11.   24222-6 Pa. $2.75

FLATLAND, E.A. Abbott. Science-fiction classic explores life of 2-D being in 3-D world. 16 illustrations. 103pp. 5⅜ × 8.   20001-9 Pa. $2.00

DRIED FLOWERS, Sarah Whitlock and Martha Rankin. Concise, clear, practical guide to dehydration, glycerinizing, pressing plant material, and more. Covers use of silica gel. 12 drawings. 32pp. 5⅜ × 8½.   21802-3 Pa. $1.00

EASY-TO-MAKE CANDLES, Gary V. Guy. Learn how easy it is to make all kinds of decorative candles. Step-by-step instructions. 82 illustrations. 48pp. 8¼ × 11.   23881-4 Pa. $2.50

SUPER STICKERS FOR KIDS, Carolyn Bracken. 128 gummed and perforated full-color stickers: GIRL WANTED, KEEP OUT, BORED OF EDUCATION, X-RATED, COMBAT ZONE, many others. 16pp. 8¼ × 11.   24092-4 Pa. $2.50

CUT AND COLOR PAPER MASKS, Michael Grater. Clowns, animals, funny faces...simply color them in, cut them out, and put them together, and you have 9 paper masks to play with and enjoy. 32pp. 8¼ × 11.   23171-2 Pa. $2.25

A CHRISTMAS CAROL: THE ORIGINAL MANUSCRIPT, Charles Dickens. Clear facsimile of Dickens manuscript, on facing pages with final printed text. 8 illustrations by John Leech, 4 in color on covers. 144pp. 8⅜ × 11¼.   20980-6 Pa. $5.95

CARVING SHOREBIRDS, Harry V. Shourds & Anthony Hillman. 16 full-size patterns (all double-page spreads) for 19 North American shorebirds with step-by-step instructions. 72pp. 9¼ × 12¼.   24287-0 Pa. $4.95

THE GENTLE ART OF MATHEMATICS, Dan Pedoe. Mathematical games, probability, the question of infinity, topology, how the laws of algebra work, problems of irrational numbers, and more. 42 figures. 143pp. 5⅜ × 8½. (EBE)   22949-1 Pa. $3.50

READY-TO-USE DOLLHOUSE WALLPAPER, Katzenbach & Warren, Inc. Stripe, 2 floral stripes, 2 allover florals, polka dot; all in full color. 4 sheets (350 sq. in.) of each, enough for average room. 48pp. 8¼ × 11.   23495-9 Pa. $2.95

MINIATURE IRON-ON TRANSFER PATTERNS FOR DOLLHOUSES, DOLLS, AND SMALL PROJECTS, Rita Weiss and Frank Fontana. Over 100 miniature patterns: rugs, bedspreads, quilts, chair seats, etc. In standard dollhouse size. 48pp. 8¼ × 11.   23741-9 Pa. $1.95

THE DINOSAUR COLORING BOOK, Anthony Rao. 45 renderings of dinosaurs, fossil birds, turtles, other creatures of Mesozoic Era. Scientifically accurate. Captions. 48pp. 8¼ × 11.   24022-3 Pa. $2.25

JAPANESE DESIGN MOTIFS, Matsuya Co. Mon, or heraldic designs. Over 4000 typical, beautiful designs: birds, animals, flowers, swords, fans, geometrics; all beautifully stylized. 213pp. 11⅜ × 8¼.　　　　　　　　　　22874-6 Pa. $7.95

THE TALE OF BENJAMIN BUNNY, Beatrix Potter. Peter Rabbit's cousin coaxes him back into Mr. McGregor's garden for a whole new set of adventures. All 27 full-color illustrations. 59pp. 4¼ × 5½. (Available in U.S. only)　21102-9 Pa. $1.50

THE TALE OF PETER RABBIT AND OTHER FAVORITE STORIES BOXED SET, Beatrix Potter. Seven of Beatrix Potter's best-loved tales including Peter Rabbit in a specially designed, durable boxed set. 4¼ × 5½. Total of 447pp. 158 color illustrations. (Available in U.S. only)　　　　　　　23903-9 Pa. $10.80

PRACTICAL MENTAL MAGIC, Theodore Annemann. Nearly 200 astonishing feats of mental magic revealed in step-by-step detail. Complete advice on staging, patter, etc. Illustrated. 320pp. 5⅜ × 8½.　　　　　　　　24426-1 Pa. $5.95

CELEBRATED CASES OF JUDGE DEE (DEE GOONG AN), translated by Robert Van Gulik. Authentic 18th-century Chinese detective novel; Dee and associates solve three interlocked cases. Led to van Gulik's own stories with same characters. Extensive introduction. 9 illustrations. 237pp. 5⅜ × 8½.
　　　　　　　　　　　　　　　　　　　　　　23337-5 Pa. $4.50

CUT & FOLD EXTRATERRESTRIAL INVADERS THAT FLY, M. Grater. Stage your own lilliputian space battles.By following the step-by-step instructions and explanatory diagrams you can launch 22 full-color fliers into space. 36pp. 8¼ × 11.　　　　　　　　　　　　　　　　　　　24478-4 Pa. $2.95

CUT & ASSEMBLE VICTORIAN HOUSES, Edmund V. Gillon, Jr. Printed in full color on heavy cardboard stock, 4 authentic Victorian houses in H-O scale: Italian-style Villa, Octagon, Second Empire, Stick Style. 48pp. 9¼ × 12¼.
　　　　　　　　　　　　　　　　　　　　　　23849-0 Pa. $3.95

BEST SCIENCE FICTION STORIES OF H.G. WELLS, H.G. Wells. Full novel *The Invisible Man*, plus 17 short stories: "The Crystal Egg," "Aepyornis Island," "The Strange Orchid," etc. 303pp. 5⅜ × 8½. (Available in U.S. only)
　　　　　　　　　　　　　　　　　　　　　　21531-8 Pa. $4.95

TRADEMARK DESIGNS OF THE WORLD, Yusaku Kamekura. A lavish collection of nearly 700 trademarks, the work of Wright, Loewy, Klee, Binder, hundreds of others. 160pp. 8¾ × 8. (Available in U.S. only)　24191-2 Pa. $5.00

THE ARTIST'S AND CRAFTSMAN'S GUIDE TO REDUCING, ENLARGING AND TRANSFERRING DESIGNS, Rita Weiss. Discover, reduce, enlarge, transfer designs from any objects to any craft project. 12pp. plus 16 sheets special graph paper. 8¼ × 11.　　　　　　　　　　　　　　　24142-4 Pa. $3.25

TREASURY OF JAPANESE DESIGNS AND MOTIFS FOR ARTISTS AND CRAFTSMEN, edited by Carol Belanger Grafton. Indispensable collection of 360 traditional Japanese designs and motifs redrawn in clean, crisp black-and-white, copyright-free illustrations. 96pp. 8¼ × 11.　　　　　　　24435-0 Pa. $3.95

CHANCERY CURSIVE STROKE BY STROKE, Arthur Baker. Instructions and illustrations for each stroke of each letter (upper and lower case) and numerals. 54 full-page plates. 64pp. 8¼ × 11. 24278-1 Pa. $2.50

THE ENJOYMENT AND USE OF COLOR, Walter Sargent. Color relationships, values, intensities; complementary colors, illumination, similar topics. Color in nature and art. 7 color plates, 29 illustrations. 274pp. 5⅜ × 8½. 20944-X Pa. $4.50

SCULPTURE PRINCIPLES AND PRACTICE, Louis Slobodkin. Step-by-step approach to clay, plaster, metals, stone; classical and modern. 253 drawings, photos. 255pp. 8⅛ × 11. 22960-2 Pa. $7.50

VICTORIAN FASHION PAPER DOLLS FROM HARPER'S BAZAR, 1867-1898, Theodore Menten. Four female dolls with 28 elegant high fashion costumes, printed in full color. 32pp. 9¼ × 12¼. 23453-3 Pa. $3.50

FLOPSY, MOPSY AND COTTONTAIL: A Little Book of Paper Dolls in Full Color, Susan LaBelle. Three dolls and 21 costumes (7 for each doll) show Peter Rabbit's siblings dressed for holidays, gardening, hiking, etc. Charming borders, captions. 48pp. 4¼ × 5½. 24376-1 Pa. $2.25

NATIONAL LEAGUE BASEBALL CARD CLASSICS, Bert Randolph Sugar. 83 big-leaguers from 1909-69 on facsimile cards. Hubbell, Dean, Spahn, Brock plus advertising, info, no duplications. Perforated, detachable. 16pp. 8¼ × 11. 24308-7 Pa. $2.95

THE LOGICAL APPROACH TO CHESS, Dr. Max Euwe, et al. First-rate text of comprehensive strategy, tactics, theory for the amateur. No gambits to memorize, just a clear, logical approach. 224pp. 5⅜ × 8½. 24353-2 Pa. $4.50

MAGICK IN THEORY AND PRACTICE, Aleister Crowley. The summation of the thought and practice of the century's most famous necromancer, long hard to find. Crowley's best book. 436pp. 5⅜ × 8½. (Available in U.S. only) 23295-6 Pa. $6.50

THE HAUNTED HOTEL, Wilkie Collins. Collins' last great tale; doom and destiny in a Venetian palace. Praised by T.S. Eliot. 127pp. 5⅜ × 8½. 24333-8 Pa. $3.00

ART DECO DISPLAY ALPHABETS, Dan X. Solo. Wide variety of bold yet elegant lettering in handsome Art Deco styles. 100 complete fonts, with numerals, punctuation, more. 104pp. 8⅛ × 11. 24372-9 Pa. $4.00

CALLIGRAPHIC ALPHABETS, Arthur Baker. Nearly 150 complete alphabets by outstanding contemporary. Stimulating ideas; useful source for unique effects. 154 plates. 157pp. 8⅜ × 11¼. 21045-6 Pa. $4.95

ARTHUR BAKER'S HISTORIC CALLIGRAPHIC ALPHABETS, Arthur Baker. From monumental capitals of first-century Rome to humanistic cursive of 16th century, 33 alphabets in fresh interpretations. 88 plates. 96pp. 9 × 12. 24054-1 Pa. $4.50

LETTIE LANE PAPER DOLLS, Sheila Young. Genteel turn-of-the-century family very popular then and now. 24 paper dolls. 16 plates in full color. 32pp. 9¼ × 12¼. 24089-4 Pa. $3.50

KEYBOARD WORKS FOR SOLO INSTRUMENTS, G.F. Handel. 35 neglected works from Handel's vast oeuvre, originally jotted down as improvisations. Includes Eight Great Suites, others. New sequence. 174pp. 9⅜ × 12¼.
24338-9 Pa. $7.50

AMERICAN LEAGUE BASEBALL CARD CLASSICS, Bert Randolph Sugar. 82 stars from 1900s to 60s on facsimile cards. Ruth, Cobb, Mantle, Williams, plus advertising, info, no duplications. Perforated, detachable. 16pp. 8¼ × 11.
24286-2 Pa. $2.95

A TREASURY OF CHARTED DESIGNS FOR NEEDLEWORKERS, Georgia Gorham and Jeanne Warth. 141 charted designs: owl, cat with yarn, tulips, piano, spinning wheel, covered bridge, Victorian house and many others. 48pp. 8¼ × 11.
23558-0 Pa. $1.95

DANISH FLORAL CHARTED DESIGNS, Gerda Bengtsson. Exquisite collection of over 40 different florals: anemone, Iceland poppy, wild fruit, pansies, many others. 45 illustrations. 48pp. 8¼ × 11.
23957-8 Pa. $1.75

OLD PHILADELPHIA IN EARLY PHOTOGRAPHS 1839-1914, Robert F. Looney. 215 photographs: panoramas, street scenes, landmarks, President-elect Lincoln's visit, 1876 Centennial Exposition, much more. 230pp. 8⅞ × 11¾.
23345-6 Pa. $9.95

PRELUDE TO MATHEMATICS, W.W. Sawyer. Noted mathematician's lively, stimulating account of non-Euclidean geometry, matrices, determinants, group theory, other topics. Emphasis on novel, striking aspects. 224pp. 5⅜ × 8½.
24401-6 Pa. $4.50

ADVENTURES WITH A MICROSCOPE, Richard Headstrom. 59 adventures with clothing fibers, protozoa, ferns and lichens, roots and leaves, much more. 142 illustrations. 232pp. 5⅜ × 8½.
23471-1 Pa. $3.95

IDENTIFYING ANIMAL TRACKS: MAMMALS, BIRDS, AND OTHER ANIMALS OF THE EASTERN UNITED STATES, Richard Headstrom. For hunters, naturalists, scouts, nature-lovers. Diagrams of tracks, tips on identification. 128pp. 5⅜ × 8.
24442-3 Pa. $3.50

VICTORIAN FASHIONS AND COSTUMES FROM HARPER'S BAZAR, 1867-1898, edited by Stella Blum. Day costumes, evening wear, sports clothes, shoes, hats, other accessories in over 1,000 detailed engravings. 320pp. 9⅜ × 12¼.
22990-4 Pa. $9.95

EVERYDAY FASHIONS OF THE TWENTIES AS PICTURED IN SEARS AND OTHER CATALOGS, edited by Stella Blum. Actual dress of the Roaring Twenties, with text by Stella Blum. Over 750 illustrations, captions. 156pp. 9 × 12.
24134-3 Pa. $8.50

HALL OF FAME BASEBALL CARDS, edited by Bert Randolph Sugar. Cy Young, Ted Williams, Lou Gehrig, and many other Hall of Fame greats on 92 full-color, detachable reprints of early baseball cards. No duplication of cards with *Classic Baseball Cards*. 16pp. 8¼ × 11.
23624-2 Pa. $3.50

THE ART OF HAND LETTERING, Helm Wotzkow. Course in hand lettering, Roman, Gothic, Italic, Block, Script. Tools, proportions, optical aspects, individual variation. Very quality conscious. Hundreds of specimens. 320pp. 5⅜ × 8½.
21797-3 Pa. $4.95

HOW THE OTHER HALF LIVES, Jacob A. Riis. Journalistic record of filth, degradation, upward drive in New York immigrant slums, shops, around 1900. New edition includes 100 original Riis photos, monuments of early photography. 233pp. 10 × 7⅞. 22012-5 Pa. $7.95

CHINA AND ITS PEOPLE IN EARLY PHOTOGRAPHS, John Thomson. In 200 black-and-white photographs of exceptional quality photographic pioneer Thomson captures the mountains, dwellings, monuments and people of 19th-century China. 272pp. 9⅜ × 12¼. 24393-1 Pa. $12.95

GODEY COSTUME PLATES IN COLOR FOR DECOUPAGE AND FRAMING, edited by Eleanor Hasbrouk Rawlings. 24 full-color engravings depicting 19th-century Parisian haute couture. Printed on one side only. 56pp. 8¼ × 11. 23879-2 Pa. $3.95

ART NOUVEAU STAINED GLASS PATTERN BOOK, Ed Sibbett, Jr. 104 projects using well-known themes of Art Nouveau: swirling forms, florals, peacocks, and sensuous women. 60pp. 8¼ × 11. 23577-7 Pa. $3.50

QUICK AND EASY PATCHWORK ON THE SEWING MACHINE: Susan Aylsworth Murwin and Suzzy Payne. Instructions, diagrams show exactly how to machine sew 12 quilts. 48pp. of templates. 50 figures. 80pp. 8¼ × 11. 23770-2 Pa. $3.50

THE STANDARD BOOK OF QUILT MAKING AND COLLECTING, Marguerite Ickis. Full information, full-sized patterns for making 46 traditional quilts, also 150 other patterns. 483 illustrations. 273pp. 6⅞ × 9⅝. 20582-7 Pa. $5.95

LETTERING AND ALPHABETS, J. Albert Cavanagh. 85 complete alphabets lettered in various styles; instructions for spacing, roughs, brushwork. 121pp. 8¾ × 8. 20053-1 Pa. $3.75

LETTER FORMS: 110 COMPLETE ALPHABETS, Frederick Lambert. 110 sets of capital letters; 16 lower case alphabets; 70 sets of numbers and other symbols. 110pp. 8⅛ × 11. 22872-X Pa. $4.50

ORCHIDS AS HOUSE PLANTS, Rebecca Tyson Northen. Grow cattleyas and many other kinds of orchids—in a window, in a case, or under artificial light. 63 illustrations. 148pp. 5⅜ × 8½. 23261-1 Pa. $2.95

THE MUSHROOM HANDBOOK, Louis C.C. Krieger. Still the best popular handbook. Full descriptions of 259 species, extremely thorough text, poisons, folklore, etc. 32 color plates; 126 other illustrations. 560pp. 5⅜ × 8½. 21861-9 Pa. $8.50

THE DORÉ BIBLE ILLUSTRATIONS, Gustave Doré. All wonderful, detailed plates: Adam and Eve, Flood, Babylon, life of Jesus, etc. Brief King James text with each plate. 241 plates. 241pp. 9 × 12. 23004-X Pa. $8.95

THE BOOK OF KELLS: Selected Plates in Full Color, edited by Blanche Cirker. 32 full-page plates from greatest manuscript-icon of early Middle Ages. Fantastic, mysterious. Publisher's Note. Captions. 32pp. 9¾ × 12¼. 24345-1 Pa. $4.50

THE PERFECT WAGNERITE, George Bernard Shaw. Brilliant criticism of the Ring Cycle, with provocative interpretation of politics, economic theories behind the Ring. 136pp. 5⅜ × 8½. (Available in U.S. only) 21707-8 Pa. $3.00

THE RIME OF THE ANCIENT MARINER, Gustave Doré, S.T. Coleridge. Doré's finest work, 34 plates capture moods, subtleties of poem. Full text. 77pp. 9¼ × 12. 22305-1 Pa. $4.95

SONGS OF INNOCENCE, William Blake. The first and most popular of Blake's famous "Illuminated Books," in a facsimile edition reproducing all 31 brightly colored plates. Additional printed text of each poem. 64pp. 5¼ × 7. 22764-2 Pa. $3.00

AN INTRODUCTION TO INFORMATION THEORY, J.R. Pierce. Second (1980) edition of most impressive non-technical account available. Encoding, entropy, noisy channel, related areas, etc. 320pp. 5⅜ × 8½. 24061-4 Pa. $4.95

THE DIVINE PROPORTION: A STUDY IN MATHEMATICAL BEAUTY, H.E. Huntley. "Divine proportion" or "golden ratio" in poetry, Pascal's triangle, philosophy, psychology, music, mathematical figures, etc. Excellent bridge between science and art. 58 figures. 185pp. 5⅜ × 8½. 22254-3 Pa. $3.95

THE DOVER NEW YORK WALKING GUIDE: From the Battery to Wall Street, Mary J. Shapiro. Superb inexpensive guide to historic buildings and locales in lower Manhattan: Trinity Church, Bowling Green, more. Complete Text; maps. 36 illustrations. 48pp. 3⅞ × 9¼. 24225-0 Pa. $2.50

NEW YORK THEN AND NOW, Edward B. Watson, Edmund V. Gillon, Jr. 83 important Manhattan sites: on facing pages early photographs (1875-1925) and 1976 photos by Gillon. 172 illustrations. 171pp. 9¼ × 10. 23361-8 Pa. $7.95

HISTORIC COSTUME IN PICTURES, Braun & Schneider. Over 1450 costumed figures from dawn of civilization to end of 19th century. English captions. 125 plates. 256pp. 8⅜ × 11¼. 23150-X Pa. $7.50

VICTORIAN AND EDWARDIAN FASHION: A Photographic Survey, Alison Gernsheim. First fashion history completely illustrated by contemporary photographs. Full text plus 235 photos, 1840-1914, in which many celebrities appear. 240pp. 6½ × 9¼. 24205-6 Pa. $6.00

CHARTED CHRISTMAS DESIGNS FOR COUNTED CROSS-STITCH AND OTHER NEEDLECRAFTS, Lindberg Press. Charted designs for 45 beautiful needlecraft projects with many yuletide and wintertime motifs. 48pp. 8¼ × 11. 24356-7 Pa. $1.95

101 FOLK DESIGNS FOR COUNTED CROSS-STITCH AND OTHER NEEDLE-CRAFTS, Carter Houck. 101 authentic charted folk designs in a wide array of lovely representations with many suggestions for effective use. 48pp. 8¼ × 11. 24369-9 Pa. $2.25

FIVE ACRES AND INDEPENDENCE, Maurice G. Kains. Great back-to-the-land classic explains basics of self-sufficient farming. The one book to get. 95 illustrations. 397pp. 5⅜ × 8½. 20974-1 Pa. $4.95

A MODERN HERBAL, Margaret Grieve. Much the fullest, most exact, most useful compilation of herbal material. Gigantic alphabetical encyclopedia, from aconite to zedoary, gives botanical information, medical properties, folklore, economic uses, and much else. Indispensable to serious reader. 161 illustrations. 888pp. 6½ × 9¼. (Available in U.S. only) 22798-7, 22799-5 Pa., Two-vol. set $16.45

DECORATIVE NAPKIN FOLDING FOR BEGINNERS, Lillian Oppenheimer and Natalie Epstein. 22 different napkin folds in the shape of a heart, clown's hat, love knot, etc. 63 drawings. 48pp. 8¼ × 11. 23797-4 Pa. $1.95

DECORATIVE LABELS FOR HOME CANNING, PRESERVING, AND OTHER HOUSEHOLD AND GIFT USES, Theodore Menten. 128 gummed, perforated labels, beautifully printed in 2 colors. 12 versions. Adhere to metal, glass, wood, ceramics. 24pp. 8¼ × 11. 23219-0 Pa. $2.95

EARLY AMERICAN STENCILS ON WALLS AND FURNITURE, Janet Waring. Thorough coverage of 19th-century folk art: techniques, artifacts, surviving specimens. 166 illustrations, 7 in color. 147pp. of text. 7⅞ × 10¾. 21906-2 Pa. $9.95

AMERICAN ANTIQUE WEATHERVANES, A.B. & W.T. Westervelt. Extensively illustrated 1883 catalog exhibiting over 550 copper weathervanes and finials. Excellent primary source by one of the principal manufacturers. 104pp. 6⅛ × 9¼. 24396-6 Pa. $3.95

ART STUDENTS' ANATOMY, Edmond J. Farris. Long favorite in art schools. Basic elements, common positions, actions. Full text, 158 illustrations. 159pp. 5⅜ × 8½. 20744-7 Pa. $3.95

BRIDGMAN'S LIFE DRAWING, George B. Bridgman. More than 500 drawings and text teach you to abstract the body into its major masses. Also specific areas of anatomy. 192pp. 6½ × 9¼. (EA) 22710-3 Pa. $4.50

COMPLETE PRELUDES AND ETUDES FOR SOLO PIANO, Frederic Chopin. All 26 Preludes, all 27 Etudes by greatest composer of piano music. Authoritative Paderewski edition. 224pp. 9 × 12. (Available in U.S. only) 24052-5 Pa. $7.50

PIANO MUSIC 1888-1905, Claude Debussy. Deux Arabesques, Suite Bergamesque, Masques, 1st series of Images, etc. 9 others, in corrected editions. 175pp. 9⅜ × 12¼. (ECE) 22771-5 Pa. $5.95

TEDDY BEAR IRON-ON TRANSFER PATTERNS, Ted Menten. 80 iron-on transfer patterns of male and female Teddys in a wide variety of activities, poses, sizes. 48pp. 8¼ × 11. 24596-9 Pa. $2.25

A PICTURE HISTORY OF THE BROOKLYN BRIDGE, M.J. Shapiro. Profusely illustrated account of greatest engineering achievement of 19th century. 167 rare photos & engravings recall construction, human drama. Extensive, detailed text. 122pp. 8¼ × 11. 24403-2 Pa. $7.95

NEW YORK IN THE THIRTIES, Berenice Abbott. Noted photographer's fascinating study shows new buildings that have become famous and old sights that have disappeared forever. 97 photographs. 97pp. 11⅜ × 10. 22967-X Pa. $6.50

MATHEMATICAL TABLES AND FORMULAS, Robert D. Carmichael and Edwin R. Smith. Logarithms, sines, tangents, trig functions, powers, roots, reciprocals, exponential and hyperbolic functions, formulas and theorems. 269pp. 5⅜ × 8½. 60111-0 Pa. $3.75

HANDBOOK OF MATHEMATICAL FUNCTIONS WITH FORMULAS, GRAPHS, AND MATHEMATICAL TABLES, edited by Milton Abramowitz and Irene A. Stegun. Vast compendium: 29 sets of tables, some to as high as 20 places. 1,046pp. 8 × 10½. 61272-4 Pa. $19.95

REASON IN ART, George Santayana. Renowned philosopher's provocative, seminal treatment of basis of art in instinct and experience. Volume Four of *The Life of Reason*. 230pp. 5⅜ × 8. 24358-3 Pa. $4.50

LANGUAGE, TRUTH AND LOGIC, Alfred J. Ayer. Famous, clear introduction to Vienna, Cambridge schools of Logical Positivism. Role of philosophy, elimination of metaphysics, nature of analysis, etc. 160pp. 5⅜ × 8½. (USCO) 20010-8 Pa. $2.75

BASIC ELECTRONICS, U.S. Bureau of Naval Personnel. Electron tubes, circuits, antennas, AM, FM, and CW transmission and receiving, etc. 560 illustrations. 567pp. 6½ × 9¼. 21076-6 Pa. $8.95

THE ART DECO STYLE, edited by Theodore Menten. Furniture, jewelry, metalwork, ceramics, fabrics, lighting fixtures, interior decors, exteriors, graphics from pure French sources. Over 400 photographs. 183pp. 8⅜ × 11¼. 22824-X Pa. $6.95

THE FOUR BOOKS OF ARCHITECTURE, Andrea Palladio. 16th-century classic covers classical architectural remains, Renaissance revivals, classical orders, etc. 1738 Ware English edition. 216 plates. 110pp. of text. 9½ × 12¾. 21308-0 Pa. $11.50

THE WIT AND HUMOR OF OSCAR WILDE, edited by Alvin Redman. More than 1000 ripostes, paradoxes, wisecracks: Work is the curse of the drinking classes, I can resist everything except temptations, etc. 258pp. 5⅜ × 8½. (USCO) 20602-5 Pa. $3.50

THE DEVIL'S DICTIONARY, Ambrose Bierce. Barbed, bitter, brilliant witticisms in the form of a dictionary. Best, most ferocious satire America has produced. 145pp. 5⅜ × 8½. 20487-1 Pa. $2.50

ERTÉ'S FASHION DESIGNS, Erté. 210 black-and-white inventions from *Harper's Bazar*, 1918-32, plus 8pp. full-color covers. Captions. 88pp. 9 × 12. 24203-X Pa. $6.50

ERTÉ GRAPHICS, Erté. Collection of striking color graphics: *Seasons, Alphabet, Numerals, Aces* and *Precious Stones*. 50 plates, including 4 on covers. 48pp. 9⅜ × 12¼. 23580-7 Pa. $6.95

PAPER FOLDING FOR BEGINNERS, William D. Murray and Francis J. Rigney. Clearest book for making origami sail boats, roosters, frogs that move legs, etc. 40 projects. More than 275 illustrations. 94pp. 5⅜ × 8½. 20713-7 Pa. $2.25

ORIGAMI FOR THE ENTHUSIAST, John Montroll. Fish, ostrich, peacock, squirrel, rhinoceros, Pegasus, 19 other intricate subjects. Instructions. Diagrams. 128pp. 9 × 12. 23799-0 Pa. $4.95

CROCHETING NOVELTY POT HOLDERS, edited by Linda Macho. 64 useful, whimsical pot holders feature kitchen themes, animals, flowers, other novelties. Surprisingly easy to crochet. Complete instructions. 48pp. 8¼ × 11. 24296-X Pa. $1.95

CROCHETING DOILIES, edited by Rita Weiss. Irish Crochet, Jewel, Star Wheel, Vanity Fair and more. Also luncheon and console sets, runners and centerpieces. 51 illustrations. 48pp. 8¼ × 11. 23424-X Pa. $2.00

YUCATAN BEFORE AND AFTER THE CONQUEST, Diego de Landa. Only significant account of Yucatan written in the early post-Conquest era. Translated by William Gates. Over 120 illustrations. 162pp. 5⅜ × 8½. 23622-6 Pa. $3.50

ORNATE PICTORIAL CALLIGRAPHY, E.A. Lupfer. Complete instructions, over 150 examples help you create magnificent "flourishes" from which beautiful animals and objects gracefully emerge. 8⅛ × 11. 21957-7 Pa. $2.95

DOLLY DINGLE PAPER DOLLS, Grace Drayton. Cute chubby children by same artist who did Campbell Kids. Rare plates from 1910s. 30 paper dolls and over 100 outfits reproduced in full color. 32pp. 9¼ × 12¼. 23711-7 Pa. $3.50

CURIOUS GEORGE PAPER DOLLS IN FULL COLOR, H. A. Rey, Kathy Allert. Naughty little monkey-hero of children's books in two doll figures, plus 48 full-color costumes: pirate, Indian chief, fireman, more. 32pp. 9¼ × 12¼.
24386-9 Pa. $3.50

GERMAN: HOW TO SPEAK AND WRITE IT, Joseph Rosenberg. Like *French, How to Speak and Write It.* Very rich modern course, with a wealth of pictorial material. 330 illustrations. 384pp. 5⅜ × 8½. (USUKO) 20271-2 Pa. $4.75

CATS AND KITTENS: 24 Ready-to-Mail Color Photo Postcards, D. Holby. Handsome collection; feline in a variety of adorable poses. Identifications. 12pp. on postcard stock. 8¼ × 11. 24469-5 Pa. $2.95

MARILYN MONROE PAPER DOLLS, Tom Tierney. 31 full-color designs on heavy stock, from *The Asphalt Jungle,Gentlemen Prefer Blondes*, 22 others.1 doll. 16 plates. 32pp. 9⅜ × 12¼. 23769-9 Pa. $3.50

FUNDAMENTALS OF LAYOUT, F.H. Wills. All phases of layout design discussed and illustrated in 121 illustrations. Indispensable as student's text or handbook for professional. 124pp. 8⅛.× 11. 21279-3 Pa. $4.50

FANTASTIC SUPER STICKERS, Ed Sibbett, Jr. 75 colorful pressure-sensitive stickers. Peel off and place for a touch of pizzazz: clowns, penguins, teddy bears, etc. Full color. 16pp. 8¼ × 11. 24471-7 Pa. $2.95

LABELS FOR ALL OCCASIONS, Ed Sibbett, Jr. 6 labels each of 16 different designs—baroque, art nouveau, art deco, Pennsylvania Dutch, etc.—in full color. 24pp. 8¼ × 11. 23688-9 Pa. $2.95

HOW TO CALCULATE QUICKLY: RAPID METHODS IN BASIC MATHE-MATICS, Henry Sticker. Addition, subtraction, multiplication, division, checks, etc. More than 8000 problems, solutions. 185pp. 5 × 7¼. 20295-X Pa. $2.95

THE CAT COLORING BOOK, Karen Baldauski. Handsome, realistic renderings of 40 splendid felines, from American shorthair to exotic types. 44 plates. Captions. 48pp. 8¼ × 11. 24011-8 Pa. $2.25

THE TALE OF PETER RABBIT, Beatrix Potter. The inimitable Peter's terrifying adventure in Mr. McGregor's garden, with all 27 wonderful, full-color Potter illustrations. 55pp. 4¼ × 5½. (Available in U.S. only) 22827-4 Pa. $1.60

BASIC ELECTRICITY, U.S. Bureau of Naval Personnel. Batteries, circuits, conductors, AC and DC, inductance and capacitance, generators, motors, trans-formers, amplifiers, etc. 349 illustrations. 448pp. 6½ × 9¼. 20973-3 Pa. $7.95

SOURCE BOOK OF MEDICAL HISTORY, edited by Logan Clendening, M.D. Original accounts ranging from Ancient Egypt and Greece to discovery of X-rays: Galen, Pasteur, Lavoisier, Harvey, Parkinson, others. 685pp. 5⅜ × 8½.
20621-1 Pa. $10.95

THE ROSE AND THE KEY, J.S. Lefanu. Superb mystery novel from Irish master. Dark doings among an ancient and aristocratic English family. Well-drawn characters; capital suspense. Introduction by N. Donaldson. 448pp. 5⅜ × 8½.
24377-X Pa. $6.95

SOUTH WIND, Norman Douglas. Witty, elegant novel of ideas set on languorous Meditterranean island of Nepenthe. Elegant prose, glittering epigrams, mordant satire. 1917 masterpiece. 416pp. 5⅜ × 8½. (Available in U.S. only)
24361-3 Pa. $5.95

RUSSELL'S CIVIL WAR PHOTOGRAPHS, Capt. A.J. Russell. 116 rare Civil War Photos: Bull Run, Virginia campaigns, bridges, railroads, Richmond, Lincoln's funeral car. Many never seen before. Captions. 128pp. 9⅜ × 12¼.
24283-8 Pa. $6.95

PHOTOGRAPHS BY MAN RAY: 105 Works, 1920-1934. Nudes, still lifes, landscapes, women's faces, celebrity portraits (Dali, Matisse, Picasso, others), rayographs. Reprinted from rare gravure edition. 128pp. 9⅜ × 12¼. (Available in U.S. only)
23842-3 Pa. $6.95

STAR NAMES: THEIR LORE AND MEANING, Richard H. Allen. Star names, the zodiac, constellations: folklore and literature associated with heavens. The basic book of its field, fascinating reading. 563pp. 5⅜ × 8½.   21079-0 Pa. $7.95

BURNHAM'S CELESTIAL HANDBOOK, Robert Burnham, Jr. Thorough guide to the stars beyond our solar system. Exhaustive treatment. Alphabetical by constellation: Andromeda to Cetus in Vol. 1; Chamaeleon to Orion in Vol. 2; and Pavo to Vulpecula in Vol. 3. Hundreds of illustrations. Index in Vol. 3. 2000pp. 6⅛× 9¼.   23567-X, 23568-8, 23673-0 Pa. Three-vol. set $36.85

THE ART NOUVEAU STYLE BOOK OF ALPHONSE MUCHA, Alphonse Mucha. All 72 plates from *Documents Decoratifs* in original color. Stunning, essential work of Art Nouveau. 80pp. 9⅜ × 12¼.   24044-4 Pa. $7.95

DESIGNS BY ERTE; FASHION DRAWINGS AND ILLUSTRATIONS FROM "HARPER'S BAZAR," Erte. 310 fabulous line drawings and 14 *Harper's Bazar* covers, 8 in full color. Erte's exotic temptresses with tassels, fur muffs, long trains, coifs, more. 129pp. 9⅜ × 12¼.   23397-9 Pa. $6.95

HISTORY OF STRENGTH OF MATERIALS, Stephen P. Timoshenko. Excellent historical survey of the strength of materials with many references to the theories of elasticity and structure. 245 figures. 452pp. 5⅜ × 8½.   61187-6 Pa. $8.95